FORTUITY

FORTUITY

by Jewel E. Ann

This book is a work of fiction. Any resemblances to actual persons, living or dead, events, or locales are purely coincidental.

ISBN: 978-1-7345182-5-2
Print Edition

Cover Designer: Sarah Hansen, Okay Creations
Formatting: BB eBooks

Author's Note

Dear Reader,

This is the third book in the Transcend Series. However, it has been written as a standalone, contemporary romance novel. There are some spoilers to the Transcend and Epoch Duet, but only necessary elements for character development.

Dedication

To all the heroes "essential workers" who could not stay home during the pandemic because we needed you. Your commitment and sacrifice will never be forgotten.

CHAPTER ONE

WHY DO THE wrong people die?

The attorney offers a rehearsed smile, as if the cruise ship didn't go up in flames. "Do you have any questions?"

My brother and his wife died, and they left me with their ten-year-old son, Gabriel.

Questions? Yes. I have so many questions.

Why didn't they purchase more life insurance? Why couldn't they have waited eight more years to die? I'm not implying I ever wanted them to die, but there's something to be said for timing, especially in death.

"Kyle and Emily wanted you to live with Gabriel in their house. Keep him in the same school. Do as much as possible to not disrupt his life."

"My nephew lost both of his parents. I think it's a little late to *not disrupt his life.*"

"Of course." Her smile slips from her face.

Pausing my temple-rubbing motions, I ease my gaze upward to meet that of the thirty-something brunette. I don't know what to say.

Her face resembles a wadded up piece of paper. The cringe isn't a good look on her. "I'm sorry. You don't have to stay in their house. You don't have to move to San Diego. Gabriel is ten. I have a ten-year-old son. They're resilient. I'm sure he will adapt to Boise, a new school, and new friends."

This doesn't feel real. Please let her be nothing more than a bobblehead in one of my crazy, early morning dreams—that I wouldn't have if I'd just get my ass out of bed instead of giving the middle finger to my Pilates class.

My brother and his wife took a cruise. How does one die in a fire surrounded by hundreds of miles of water? Just … jump in the water!

"Or … you don't have to do this at all. There is nothing that legally requires you to take custody of Gabriel."

Just wake the hell up and go to Pilates!

Kyle called to say goodbye and to let me know I would be responsible for Gabe if their plane went down on their way to Spain. It was an afterthought. A tiny footnote at the end of a long book. That was the first time Brother Dearest mentioned my *huge* responsibility. I brushed it off with "Wow! You must be desperate to choose me."

He brushed it off with a laugh and "Mom and Dad are too old to do it. But don't worry … we'll make it back in one piece."

Liar.

"Miss Glock—"

"Gracelyn," I correct her.

Her lips curl into a tiny smile. "Gracelyn, I realize no amount of money can make up for your family's loss. However, I anticipate the cruise line will pay a sizable sum to settle multiple wrongful death suits. I'm not suggesting your family settle. I just don't want you to feel like the life insurance is all you'll have to cover the expenses of raising Gabriel."

It's not the money.

Okay … that's not entirely true. I've made it forty-one years without an actual career, a husband, children, or a 401(k). Money *will* be a concern.

"*Of course* I'm taking him. I'll figure it out." I stand on shaky legs and slip my handbag over my shoulder. It weighs a hundred pounds—or maybe that's the weight of the world. My chin juts upward; believing and an air of confidence is ninety percent. Right?

"Okay. We'll be in touch. In the meantime, call me if you have any concerns or questions." She hands me her business card and escorts me to the door.

"Thanks."

After a quick stop in the ladies' room to contemplate vomiting before splashing cold water on my face, I climb into Kyle's and Emily's green Land Rover and drive to their house. We buried their remains last week. Emily was an only child. Her father died of cancer five years ago, and her mom, Sharon, has early-onset dementia. Sharon's caregiver (a cousin) took her back to the assisted living facility right after the funeral.

"Hey, how did it go?" Mom asks, rummaging through the fridge because …

So.

Much.

FOOD!

"Fine."

She shuts the door and leans against it as I plop my ass into the chair, transfixed by the table covered in food—enough baked goods to give an entire village diabetes.

"Doesn't sound fine." She wipes a tear from her cheek.

I don't know what it feels like to lose a child—or even have one for that matter. My tears fell quickly after the news of their deaths. More tears made a proper appearance at their funeral. Today, the reality of my new role replaced the tears.

I'm … a mom? No. That's not right. I'm still a fun aunt. Gabe won't think of me as his mom.

Fun aunt.

Maybe his friend.

An eight year babysitter.

"I know they thought we were too old to take care of Gabe, but that's not true. He can come to Great Falls with us. I think he'd like living in Montana." Mom wears a fairly believable smile on her weary face, but I notice her new wrinkles. Craters of pain that can never be erased.

I shake my head, snatching a stale chocolate chip cookie from one of the plastic containers. Years ago, I kicked my emotional eating habit, introduced my body to Pilates, dropped twenty pounds, and took a vow of celibacy as a last attempt at self-preservation.

Maybe I slip up and eat a few too many cookies. No big deal. I've inherited a ten-year-old.

A TEN-YEAR-OLD!

Really, Kyle, leave me your Land Rover and Emily's Pilates reformer. But Gabe? I love him … more than the world. I'm just not equipped for parenthood. What if I mess him up? I've messed up so much in my life.

The early stages of menopause tap on my shoulder every day. My unused uterus put in its request for early retirement. After I finish this stale cookie, there's a fifty percent chance my face flushes and I sweat through my clothes.

Hot flashes.

Mood swings.

Seven p.m. mandatory bra removal.

No kid, especially not a young boy, needs to witness such a hot mess.

"Kyle and Emily want him to stay in San Diego. Same school. Close to friends. While I have no desire to live here, I agree with them. The less we have to disrupt his life, the better his chances are of making it through this grieving process and returning to some semblance of normalcy."

With his aunt Gracelyn—Queen Hot Mess.

"I don't want you to be overwhelmed." Mom pulls out a chair and sits next to me, frowning at the baked goods. She's had her fair share. The emotional eating apple (or cookie) doesn't fall far from the tree.

"He's a great kid. I love him to pieces. We'll be fine."

"You need a job here." Mom goes for some sort of chocolate drizzled popcorn. It has to be staler than my cookie.

Yep. She spits it back into the bowl.

I grin. "I'll make sure he talks to someone, if he doesn't want to talk to me. I'll get a job." Glancing around at the fancy surroundings, I twist my lips. "I doubt we'll be able to stay here very long."

"Oh … no." Mom shakes her head. "The taxes and upkeep on this place must be insane."

Kyle and Emily splurged on a house they could barely afford when they should have splurged on better life insurance.

"Sell the house. Use the money to raise Gabe and put some back for his college."

I nod several times.

"Are you sure about all of this?" Mom rests her hand on my

leg.

"Absolutely."

No. Not even close.

CHAPTER TWO

Nathaniel

Two months later …

"I THINK THIS is a good thing." Morgan drops her backpack inside the four-bedroom rental on the beach.

"You say that about every place we stay." I lug our two suitcases into the narrow tile entry.

"Yes. But San Diego feels extra good."

"You're ten. I think the definition of being ten is *extra good.*"

"Three months?" She spins in a circle, her long, wavy, blond hair twirling like a kite in the wind.

My world.

This girl is my world.

"Yes." I haul the luggage up the stairs as she shadows me.

"Then I get to go *home!* Public school. And I will meet the boy I'm going to marry. Right?"

Ten is the new fourteen. My daughter is too smart.

"Three months until we settle into a place that's ours. Three months until you join the herd, eat lunch out of a bag, and find out how truly *mean* boys can be at your age. You'll meet the boy you're going to marry when you're thirty."

"Daaad!" Morgan giggles when I stop at the first bedroom.

"Unpack your stuff."

She jumps onto the queen bed adorned in white and seafoam green blankets and pillows. "Tell me how you met Mom."

"Unpack and then you can tell *me* how I met your mom since I've told you that story *so* many times." I give her a wink and find another bedroom, hoping I didn't just give her the bigger bed. She's strict with things like *first come, first served* and *finders keepers*.

Eight years ago, we left Wisconsin in search of … the world. Morgan learned to speak, read, and write—in multiple languages—by immersion. Her only school has been life. And …

Books.

Books.

Books.

I have a phone, but I've given her limited access to technology other than computers at libraries or ticket machines for subways. She has no firsthand experience with social media, apps, texting, email, or what it means to binge something on Netflix.

However, her feet have touched five continents and countless countries. She has a bag filled with stationary and pens she uses to write to all the friends she's made during her time traveling the world.

"Oh, thank god," I whisper, seeing a king bed, a balcony, and an en suite bathroom.

Three months of sleeping on a twin bed in Budapest wasn't memorable in a good way. Princess Morgan slept in a king bed with three stuffed animals because … finders keepers, no take-backs, and a deal is a deal.

"A kid!" Morgan squeals.

I smirk. It's always a bonus when we rent a place with kids

in the neighborhood—well, maybe not *always*. She's met plenty of bad influences over the years. I've had to brush it off as opportunities for character building.

My exuberant daughter spins away from her bedroom window as I lean against the doorframe with my arms crossed over my chest. "It's a boyeee! And he looks close to my age!" Fisting both of her hands at her mouth, she attempts to contain her excitement, but she fails.

"Boys are trouble."

Her blue eyes make a full swoop with her dramatic eye roll. "You were a boy. Were you trouble?"

"Yes." I pivot and head down the stairs. "The worst kind of trouble," I mumble to myself.

I met a girl. Her name was Morgan. I called her Daisy because it was her middle name and she didn't like it. She ruined me for eternity and every life beyond that. She still haunts my dreams. And I gave my daughter her name.

Nothing fucked-up about that.

When I get to the main room, I peek out the window to inspect the young lad that will stay far away from my little girl. With his nose shoved into the screen of his phone, he blindly follows a woman to our landlord's, Mr. Hans's, front door. We haven't met Hugh yet. When he emailed me the lockbox code, he mentioned he lives in the house directly north of this one.

The woman with chin-length zebra hair (black with thick streaks of blond) stops midway to the front door and squints at the *For Rent* sign in his yard. Mr. Hans gave me the impression he lived there. What's he renting?

Gracelyn

"THE BEACH. DO you like the beach?"

Gabe shrugs without glancing up at me. I study the *For Rent* sign, the houses lining the long stretch of beach, and the solid dose of *life* that feels as deep and vast as the water reaching the horizon.

"If you don't like it, we'll keep looking." The three wooden deck steps creak, announcing our arrival, as I approach the screen door. He told us to come around back. All of these beachfront homes have covered decks with lovely patio furniture and some with swings like this one. A wide and weathered boardwalk separates the decks from the sand.

After two knocks and ten seconds, the door opens.

"Hello! You must be Elvis." The old man with white Einstein hair, who resembles Christopher Lloyd (particularly his role as Doc Brown in *Back to the Future*) smiles clear to the corners of his expressive, slightly psychotic eyes. If he weren't a little hunchbacked, he'd stand at least six feet tall.

"I'm Gracelyn, not Elvis."

"Ha! Yes, dear, but when you said your name on the phone, I imagined it's a slight nod to Elvis."

"That's Graceland."

"Potato potahto. Come in." He steps aside.

I take a few extra seconds to consider my gut feeling.

The wide psychotic eyes.

His white, half-buttoned shirt with the bottom of it sticking out of his partially zipped fly.

Brown Birkenstocks.

Gray socks with his right big toe sticking out of a hole.

"My wife died five years ago." He wiggles his naked toe.

My gaze shoots to meet his.

"Haven't bought any new clothes since she died. She did all the shopping. I fixed stuff around the house. I can fix leaks and hang pictures, but I haven't figured out how to sew holes in my socks … or maybe you patch socks? I'm not sure."

"Uh, I think you just get new socks." Gabe joins the conversation.

"Is that so?" He cocks his head at Gabe. "Hugh Hans. What's your name, young man?" Hugh offers his hand to my nephew, my new and very unexpected responsibility.

These two months have not been easy. I pretend that Kyle and Emily are still on vacation and I'm simply watching Gabe. I feel confident as a babysitter. When I dwell on the tiny fact that I'm the sole person responsible for raising him … everything in my chest starts to constrict.

"Gabriel." He shakes Hugh's hand.

"Ah … Gabriel. Such a great name. It means 'God is my strength.' Bravo to your parents for giving you such a great name." Hugh's raspy, yet enthusiastic, voice seems to keep Gabe's attention, eliciting a rare smile from him as he slides his phone into his pocket.

Incredible. He's engaged, ready to give this stranger his attention. I need Mr. Hans's secret spell. I'm not sure I've seen Gabe smile more than once or twice since the tragedy.

Gabe didn't want to stay in the house any more than I did. That surprised me. I thought he'd feel comforted and close to his parents there. I thought wrong. The house sold yesterday. We have thirty days to find a place.

"My parents died." Gabe follows me into the house.

"I'm very sorry." Hugh shuts the door as Gabe and I slip off our shoes.

"It's not your fault," Gabe mumbles.

Hugh shoots me a tiny smile and a wink. "Thank goodness."

I ruffle Gabe's dark hair, and he shoos away my hand as we follow Hugh's snail's pace up the stairs.

"The second floor would be yours. The kitchen on the main floor is communal, but I've added a fridge in the garage where you can keep your perishables if you're worried I'll eat them." He stops at the top of the stairs, plucking a hanky from his back pocket to wipe his forehead. "It was four bedrooms and two baths. As you can see, I've turned two of the bedrooms into a living space with a washer and dryer behind those folding doors. There's a balcony just off the master bedroom. In another day or so, I'll be done with the stairs so you'll have a direct entrance to the second floor if you don't want to risk seeing me every time you come and go."

Gabe peeks his head into one bedroom and then the other, showing no reaction.

He shuffles his feet to the window of the smaller bedroom. "Who's that?"

Hugh and I follow him and glance out the window.

"Oh … yes. That must be the renters next door. They were supposed to arrive today. I haven't met them yet. Father and daughter. They're only here for the summer."

Gabe's gaze remains on the young girl tossing her flip-flops over her shoulder and running toward the water. She stops abruptly and glances back, maybe talking to someone, but I can't tell for sure. After a few seconds, she continues toward the water, halting where the waves crash into the beach, covering just her feet.

"She looks about your age." I nudge Gabe's arm.

"I feel a summer romance happening," Hugh adds in a singsong.

Gabe pivots toward Hugh and shoots him a wrinkled-nose look. "What do you mean?"

"He means you might get a crush on the girl next door." I rest my hands on Gabe's shoulders.

"Nah-uh." Gabe shakes his head several times.

Hugh chuckles. "Well, I'll give you two some time to look around. If you have any questions, I'll be downstairs."

"Where do you sleep? Is there a bedroom on the main level?" I ask.

"Fancy recliner. I don't sleep well. Apparently some sleep apnea thing. If I'm flat when I sleep, I stop breathing. I've been told that's not good. Tried some high-tech machine, but not my cup of tea. My clothes are in the small office." He disappears around the corner.

"So … what do you think? It won't be forever. Just until we find something more permanent and see how my new job goes."

Gabe shrugs. I assume it's what ten-year-old boys do—shrug all their answers. I've received a lot of shrugs over the past two months.

"Is that a yes shrug? An I-don't-care shrug? Or an I-need-to-think-about-it shrug?"

"It's not close to Tyler's house."

"I know, but I don't think we should spend your college savings just to stay close to Tyler. What if I make sure you get to see Tyler as much as possible this summer? His mom said they'd be gone for three weeks on vacation. Maybe when they get home Tyler can come stay here for a few days. You guys can play on the beach … make friends with the cute girl next door …"

Gabe sighs. "My friends at school are boys. Girls are …"

"Girls are what?"

He turns and rolls his eyes. "Well, they squeal about stupid stuff and say 'oh my god' about everything."

I chuckle. "Fair enough. No pressure to make friends with the girl next door. But … do you think I should tell Mr. Hans we'll take this place?"

Another shrug.

"Okay. I'm going to tell him yes, unless you tell me no with more than a shrug in the next five seconds."

No words.

No more shrugs.

Five seconds pass.

On a sigh, I deflate, easing onto my butt with my back against the wall.

"Throw me a bone, Gabe." Hugging my knees to my chest, I shoot him a pleading look. How can he not see the desperation pouring out of me?

"Like a dog?" He frowns.

"Yes. Like a dog. And I'll chase it. I'll bring it back to you. I'll sit. Heel. Roll over. I'll do anything you want, if you'll just let me into that head of yours. Tell me what you're thinking. I can only imagine what you're feeling. I've never experienced it. So guessing is all I have if you don't talk to me."

He picks at his fingernails, giving them twice the attention that he gives me. "What do you want me to say?"

I restrain from spewing off a mile long list of questions I have for him. "Yes or no. Do you want to live here for now? It's just temporary. The answer can be no. I won't ask why, and I won't ask you anymore questions today. We'll just keep looking tomorrow."

"I don't care."

"No!" I lurch forward, crawling toward him.

His eyes widen with my approach.

Lifting onto my knees, I fold my hands in front of my chest. "Please, please, pretty pretty please … a yes or no. I *need* a yes or no."

His lips twitch, and after a few seconds he can't hide his smile. It's like salvation—a needed reminder that I haven't broken him. It's still early. I have eight more years to royally mess up this kid.

"Yes." He laughs.

"YES!" I throw my arms in the air.

"You're so weird."

I climb to my feet. "It's in the Glock family. There's nothing you can do to stop it. One day … you'll be weird too." I wink and get out of here before he changes his mind or calls me something more extreme than weird—like menopausal.

Taking one last stroll through the main room, I peek into the master bedroom and en suite bathroom before descending the stairs. "We'll take it, if you'll have us."

Hugh mutes the TV from his *fancy* recliner. "You got it, Elvis."

I grin. Elvis I am not. However, Mr. Hans is quirky and endearing, so I'll let the Elvis thing slide. This place isn't ideal, or where I imagined myself just a few months ago, but I'm doing something important—maybe for the first time in my life.

Gabe will be okay. I'll figure things out for us. For now, this beach house with sand-colored tiled floors, beige walls, and white and brown speckled carpet is just fine—beachfront property I could never afford on my own. And it's fifteen minutes from Gabe's school and thirty minutes from my new job.

"Rental agreement is on the kitchen counter. You can leave a check or pay cash and move in as early as Friday. I'll get those stairs to the master bedroom's balcony finished by then."

"Sounds perfect. Thank you." As I sign the rental agreement and fill out a check, Gabe makes his way downstairs.

"Go explore the beach, Mr. Gabriel." Hugh coughs on his words a few times before clearing his throat.

"Yeah, let's check it out." I fold my copy of the rental agreement and follow Gabe to the front door. "Thank you, Hugh. We'll be back Friday afternoon with some boxes and hopefully get some movers to bring the big stuff."

"If the good Lord don't taketh me by then, I'll be here."

I'm not sure how to respond to that, so I opt for a wordless smile. Sometimes the good Lord indiscriminately takes whomever he chooses, or so I've learned. As soon as I close the door behind us, Gabe plucks his phone from his pocket and follows several feet behind me to the beach.

"I'd take off your shoes again if you don't want sand in them." I toe off my white canvas sneakers when we reach the sand.

Gabe keeps walking, nose into his phone, sand surely filling his shoes.

"Or … leave them on," I murmur. "Don't you want to dip your toes in the water?"

He shakes his head, stopping halfway to the water. "No, thank you. Not exactly my first time at the beach." He drops to his knees in the sand, hovering over his phone to shade the screen as he squints at it.

I continue toward the water, stopping just before reaching the wet sand to roll up the legs to my jeans.

"Hello!" The young, wavy-haired blond girl trudges through the sand toward me.

"Hi." I plant my hand at my forehead to block the sun from my eyes.

"What's he doing?" She nods toward Gabe. "Are you living in that house? My dad and I just got here. We're staying for three months. Then we're moving to Madison … that's in Wisconsin, where I was born. I'll start real school, well—public school—this fall. I'll be in fifth grade for now, but my Dad says I might be too smart for the fifth grade. I don't know how he knows that, since I've never been in any grade."

Wow! Okay … she's quite talkative. Good with words, not like my nephew who tends to mumble all his words, stutter occasionally, and speaks in grunts and shrugs. It's possible she's a little advanced for ten, but I know one other ten-year-old, so the comparison isn't the best.

"That's my nephew, Gabriel … Gabe. And yes, we're renting the top floor of Mr. Hans's house. Gabe will be in fifth grade this fall too."

"But what's he doing?" She wrinkles her nose and stares at him through squinted eyes.

"He's playing a game on his phone."

"Oh …" Her head jerks back, and she widens her blue eyes at me. "Do *not* let my dad see him on that. He abhors technology."

Abhors …

Definitely not a ten-year-old word.

"I don't abhor it."

My gaze snaps to the deep voice and …

Jamie!

Not really James Alexander Malcolm MacKenzie Fraser "Jamie" from my obsession *Outlander*, but his doppelgänger.

WHY?

I'm retired from men. A series of unfortunate events forced me into early retirement.

Death.

Cheating.

Houdini at the altar.

I'm lucky like that.

Now, I window-shop but never purchase. I don't even try stuff on anymore.

Neighbor Jamie's wavy, dark ginger-blond hair—that's the color of sand at sunset—ruffles in the wind, and his bronzed skin nearly blinds me because … He's. Not. Wearing. A. Shirt.

Full lips pull into a tiny welcome.

"Hello, Sassenach …" he whispers.

Okay. Not really, but I'd love to hear him say it.

"Hi, I'm Nathaniel Hunt, Morgan's dad." His American accent tramples my Scottish fantasies as he holds out his hand.

If I lick his hand, will it be weird? Too desperate? Too personal for a first encounter? Too immature for forty-one?

Probably.

"Gracelyn." I shake his hand like I'm mad at it. And I am. I'm so pissed off that he's my neighbor for the next three months. Where was he when I needed him during my active, sexual prime—before my ban on all men?

Really, I demand an answer.

He narrows his eyes a bit just before I release him. Then he quickly recovers with a smile.

"Morgan." I clear the anger from my throat. "Well, Morgan and Nathaniel, it's nice to meet you. Gabe is my nephew, but …"

And here it is—the awkward moment. Please tell me this will get easier. I don't want to spend forever explaining our relationship to everyone we meet. Yet, it requires some explanation. "His parents died, so he's with me now."

I guess the answer is yes. Yes like someone in a wheelchair explaining a million times how they ended up in a wheelchair.

It sucks explaining it.

It sucks that it happened.

"Oh my god!" Morgan's hand flies to her mouth. "My mom died while giving birth to me. I never knew her, so it's hard to miss her. He must be completely heartbroken. I can't imagine what I would feel like if my dad died."

I force a smile. "It is sad, but he's hanging in there. You should go introduce yourself. I bet he'd like that."

"Oh …" Her hand falls from her mouth and covers her chest. "Of course." She hikes up the beach toward Gabe.

Nathaniel bites his lip in a slight cringe. "She's very talkative."

"I can see that. It's refreshing. I have to drag words out of Gabe." I can't find a great place to put my hands, so I try to shove them into my front pockets, but I'm a bit bloated with my impending menstrual cycle, so it's a tight squeeze.

We stare at Gabe and Morgan making introductions, a good distraction. If I concentrate on Nathaniel Hunt too long, I will melt—most likely a PMS symptom. It doesn't have anything to do with his ripped jeans, bare feet, and sculpted torso.

Nope. That does nothing for me.

My fingers have *no* desire to make a slow trip through his

hair.

Fun fact … PMS for women in their forties is quite the head game. Some days I hate all men I see, and some days I imagine making out with all men who cross my path.

Another fun fact … It's Wednesday—hump day.

"Did I hear you say you're renting from Mr. Hans?"

"Yes. Just the top floor and a shared kitchen. How about you? Summer vacation?"

Nate slides his fingers into the front pockets of his jeans—with ease. He must not be bloated like me. "Yes, I suppose you could say that."

I nod, contemplating asking more questions to get him to elaborate. It's possible he has a story about his wife dying that he's told a million times, so I don't pry. "Is it true that you abhor technology?"

He smirks, keeping a close eye on his daughter. "I've just been raising Morgan to experience life a little more hands-on. Organically."

I glance over at the kids—Morgan's lips moving nonstop and Gabe ignoring her like a pesky bug flying around his head. "Well, that's probably a good thing. Gabe is on electronics *all* the time."

"That's …" He shrugs. "Probably pretty typical."

Typical? I suppose. I'm not sure. Yet, I feel judged. It's likely an irrational response, but my step-in-parent self feels like Nathaniel, Mr. Abhors Technology, is silently judging me for letting Gabe be on a cellphone playing games.

"He lost both parents. If electronics keep him from feeling sad or depressed, then I'm fine with it."

He chuckles. "I'm not sure that phone will keep him from feeling sad and depressed. But hey … you gotta do what you gotta do."

It's the shirt. I know it. If he'd put on a shirt, I wouldn't feel so angry.

Angry that Kyle and Emily died.

Angry that I've retired from men.

Angry that I'm probably screwing up my new role in life.

I start to defend Gabe's pastime when Morgan runs toward us, dragging Gabe by the arm behind her and thwarting my words before I bring them to life.

"Dad, you should invite them to dinner tonight."

"No," Nathaniel and I say at the same time.

My eyebrows slide together. I know. I said it too, but only because I don't want him to feel pressured. What's his excuse for such a knee-jerk reaction?

He scratches his scruffy jaw and twists his lips. "We don't have any food, Morgan. Not a slice of bread or a grain of salt. Tonight we'll get groceries, and you can have Gabe over for dinner another night."

Gabe.

I see how this is going to play out. Fine … I'm fine with it. Men are on my banned list, along with cheese puffs and caramels. Besides, I have a new season of *Outlander* to watch.

"*And* Gracelyn, so you have a friend. Really, Dad, you could use a friend." The awkwardness meter maxes out with her comment.

Nate glares at Morgan, but she's too focused on her toes, curling them in the sand. When he glances at me, I bite my lips together and avert my gaze to the water. My hands won't fit into my pockets in any sort of casual way, so I let them hang at my sides.

So awkward.

"I'm sure Gracelyn has lots of friends," he replies on a soft chuckle.

"She doesn't know anyone because she's from Ohio," Gabe mumbles, chin tipped toward his phone.

It's funny—only not really—how much attention he pays to what's going on when I'd rather he not say anything.

"Idaho." I correct him, giving Nathaniel a tight smile.

His gaze is too preoccupied with my hair to notice my facial expression. Blue eyes flit in tiny increments, and when he finally meets my eyes, he clears his throat and does this weird head shake thing like he's snapping out of a dream.

Judging my hair?

It's hair. It used to be long and all dark auburn like the flowing mane of Black Beauty … if Black Beauty had auburn hair. I cut it off at my chin, colored it black, and added some blond highlights because … well, it's hair. Okay, it's not that simple. There was a wedding and someone leaving someone else at the altar. Whatever …

Things changed, so I changed.

"We should go. Gabe and I have some packing to do."

"Can you come to dinner tomorrow night?" Morgan asks, head cocked at Gabe like this is their decision.

Nathaniel rests his hand on her shoulder. Before he can state another objection, I interject.

"We're moving in Friday afternoon, so tomorrow won't work."

"Yes! Friday night is pizza night. My dad will order pizza, and we'll help you unpack your stuff."

"Morgan …" Nathaniel moves his other hand to her other shoulder and gives her a tight squeeze. "Let them get settled. They don't need our help unpacking. There will be plenty of time for you and Gabe to have pizza another night."

Morgan and Gabe.

He's definitely excluding me. Again … that's fine. Hello! *Man ban,* I remind myself.

"*And* Gracelyn." Morgan rolls her eyes. "Geesh, Dad, stop being so rude."

"We really have to go." I grab Gabe's wrist, giving it a tug, while Nathaniel's face contorts into a slight cringe.

"Very nice meeting *both* of you," he says in spite of the embarrassment on his face.

"You too." I pivot in the sand to make a quick exit, but my left foot doesn't cooperate. The sand holds my foot in place as the weight of my body falls to the side, rolling my ankle.

"Shit—shoot." I reach for my ankle. "Sorry. I meant—"

Ouch! Ouch! Ouch!

"Whoa! Are you okay?" Gabe slides his phone into his pocket and kneels beside me with his hand on my arm.

"My dad's a doctor!" Morgan kneels beside Gabe.

"I'm not a doctor." Nathaniel squats next to my foot.

"You are. You have a PhD. And you said that makes you Doctor Hunt."

I hiss while sitting up.

Nate eases my leg into a better position, bracing my ankle with his large, calloused hand. "It's swelling. I fear you may have sprained it."

"It's fine. If I can get out of the sand, I can just walk it off."

His other hand rests on my calf as he grins. "I don't think walking off a sprain is a good idea. But *ice* is a great idea. Here. Let's see if you can put weight on it."

"Come on, Gabe, we'll get her other side." Morgan jumps right in to help me as her dad guides my arm around his neck and his arm around my waist.

"Let's get you out of the sand." He bears most of my weight as Morgan and Gabe fail to do much because I don't want to hurt them with my bloated self.

"Sorry. It's hard to hop on one foot in the sand."

"Just carry her, Dad."

"No! I'm heavy. Just … let me crawl out of the sand."

"Dad! Carry her." Morgan's incessant "helpfulness" makes my cheeks flame ten shades of embarrassment.

"You'll hurt your back. I'm heavier than I—No! Your back!" I protest when he scoops me up.

"My back is old, but not that old." He laughs, taking confident strides toward Mr. Hans's house.

"This could not be more embarrassing," I mumble, refusing to look at him even with his face so close to mine. Citrus and ocean cling to his skin, a nice combination—not that I'm trying to smell him. He's just unavoidably close.

And firm.

Firm and *bare* chested.

Very capable, *firm* arms.

I suck in my bloated stomach as if this simple act will make me ten pounds lighter.

"Careful." He eases me to my feet next to Kyle's Land Rover.

My Land Rover? I don't know whose life this is at the moment.

"Thank you." I try to bear weight on my left foot and cringe. "It's …" I hobble a few steps. "Tender but not awful. I'll be fine. Thank you. Gabe, will you please grab my shoes?"

Nathaniel crosses his very capable arms over his chest and nods once. "Ice it as soon as you get home."

but we just met you a few days ago. I guess I'm not sure what the vetting process is for this situation. First-time mom … guardian or whatever." I wrinkle my nose.

"You can never be too protective," he says.

I'm not sure I'd go that far. I think not taking a ten-year-old girl to Disney, if you have the means to do it, is a little overprotective.

"I can make him a sandwich to go, or you can vet me right now." He crosses his arms over his chest.

I don't know how to vet a babysitter.

"What kind of professor are you?"

"Anatomy."

"Have you ever been arrested?"

"No."

"Have you ever killed anyone?"

He hesitates. Holy shit he hesitates for a split second before shaking his head.

"Maybe we get the sandwich to go." My lips curl into a tight smile.

I bet an anatomy professor would know all the ways to kill someone. And what better front for a serial killer than the widower with a young daughter. I watched a documentary on serial killers. They're alarmingly charming and charismatic.

"I didn't pass the vetting process?" He chuckles.

"No. Yes. I'm not sure. I mean … would you leave Morgan with me?"

He eyes me for a few seconds before a slight smirk quirks his full lips. "Of course not."

I hobble down the stairs after him. "Seriously?"

Mr. Hans gives us a slight nod as he waters the ferns by the window. I chase—chase might be an exaggeration—I limp behind Nathaniel to the other house.

"You have to elaborate."

He glances over his shoulder when he reaches the top step to his deck, opening his mailbox to find it empty. "Elaborate on what?" He pivots to face me.

"Why you wouldn't leave Morgan with me."

"I don't know enough about you. It's that simple."

My head jerks backward as I stand idle at the bottom of the stairs while Mr. Abhors Electronics looks down on me—literally and figuratively as I imagine Morgan might say. "I'm just a woman with my life tipped upside down because my brother and his wife died and left me with their son. I don't have children of my own. I have no clue how to be a good parent. I'm just trying to keep my head above water and not screw anything up beyond repair."

Nathaniel doesn't react with more than perfectly timed blinks.

When the words I just spewed at his feet catch up to the five-second delay in my head, I close my eyes. "Okay. I just gave you all the reasons why you should feel uncomfortable leaving your daughter with me." Peeking open one eye, I squint up at him. "I might suck at this … but I'll get better."

After a few seconds he turns, takes two steps toward the door, and stops with his back to me. "After my wife died, I had no clue what to do with this newborn baby. I didn't know how to hold her properly, change her diapers, or feed her. I was a mess. A guy with a PhD but completely clueless how to take care of a baby. You'll figure it out." He opens the screen door and disappears.

CHAPTER FIVE

Nathaniel

"UH … DAD?" Morgan calls from my bedroom window while I finger through my wet hair.

We spent the first half of the day biking and building sandcastles on the beach. She wanted to get showered and changed into nice clothes before Gabe arrived home.

It's been two weeks of spying on Gabe. Obsessing over why he's not home "on time." Wondering what he's doing. Begging me for an iPad so they can play some game together. He tells her over and over that he goes to a friend's house while Gracelyn is at work. That does little to tame her anxiousness.

"What's up?" I shut off the light in the bathroom and meet her at the window that faces Gracelyn's room. "Oh. Whoa!" I cover Morgan's eyes.

"Dad …" She shoves my hand away. "I'm a girl."

There's no sign of Gabe, but Gracelyn's under her bedroom balcony, partially hidden behind ornamental grass, stripping out of her clothes—right down to her bra and panties. She shoves them into a plastic bag, pokes her head out of the grass to sweep her gaze left and right, emerges from the grass cover, and dashes up to her balcony—clearly moving better on her ankle. After she closes the French door, she yanks the shades shut behind her.

"Huh …" That's it. That's my best reaction.

"Why did she take off her clothes outside?"

"I don't know."

"Well, when they got home, she pointed for Gabe to go in through the deck door. So I'm going to go see him. If I see Gracelyn, I'll ask her why she stripped." She skips toward the stairs.

"Morgan!" I chase after her. "Don't ask her about it. If she knows we saw her, it might be really embarrassing. We don't want to embarrass her. Okay?"

"Fine. Whatevs. I won't say anything."

I haven't had any in-depth conversations with Gracelyn since they moved in two weeks ago. We sit on the deck stairs to her place or mine and watch the kids play on the beach, usually talking about them. I don't know what she does, but I can't lie … the stripping thing a few seconds ago piqued my curiosity.

Twenty minutes later, two kids streak past the front window toward the beach. They plant one of the umbrellas in the sand, drop into the beach chairs, and cover themselves with beach towels. This is new.

Gracelyn appears a few seconds later, taking a seat on the bottom step to my deck with her phone in her hand. I watch the situation for a few minutes before opening the door.

She glances back at me. "Hey. I can keep an eye on them if you have things to do."

"What exactly are they doing?" I take a seat next to her, reminding myself to keep my gaze from lingering on her hair. It's hard. I do it a lot, and I can tell that she notices it because she smooths her hands over her hair when I let my gaze linger too long.

Gracelyn's face contorts, little wrinkles forming by her eyes.

CHAPTER SIX

Gracelyn

I COULD BE off my game if I had one—which I don't—so I can't say for sure, but I'm pretty sure Nate was flirting with me last week when Gabe stayed for dinner. However, if that were true, then he would have invited me to stay for dinner too … Right?

It doesn't matter. That's all I need to remember. Man ban. Who cares if he's flirting? I have no desire to reciprocate. Well, that's not true. I walked away swinging my ass like a pendulum. The accurate phrase is: I have no desire to be in a relationship ever again.

Three strikes.

I'm out of the game.

Death.

Cheating.

Chicken.

Sounds like a farmer going vegan. Nope. It's the short story of my love life, which is a *long* story that's stretched more than twenty years.

"Mind if I ask why you're not married?" Mr. Hans pops a breakfast burrito into the microwave while I brew coffee and making scrambled eggs for Gabe.

"Unlucky at love." I grin, stirring the eggs in the frying pan.

"Does that mean you've never been in love?"

"No. I've been in love three times."

"And you've had your heart broken three times?" He takes his burrito out of the microwave and sits at the kitchen table by the window.

"You'd think so, but in hindsight, I've only truly had my heart broken once. Gabe!" I call up the stairs.

He runs downstairs, grabs his plate of eggs and toast, and runs back upstairs.

"Good morning to you too," I murmur.

Mr. Hans chuckles at Gabe as I sit at the table with my coffee and buttered toast.

"Are you good at keeping secrets?"

"I think so." He pauses his cutting motion and glances up at me.

"I hear dead people—well, just one. I hear a dead person. Or I used to. He's been quiet lately, but it was hell on my love life."

"If it's Elvis Presley, you will have made my whole day."

I grin. "Sorry to disappoint. Brandon Alan, my first and truest love. He died of a congenital heart condition when he was twenty-two. He spent his last year on the transplant list. No luck. I met him when he was eleven and I was ten."

Mr. Hans grins and so do I.

"Yes. Gabe's and Morgan's age. Crazy, right?"

"I met my wife when we were not even old enough to crawl. Our mothers were best friends. It took me seventeen years to convince her I was her soul mate. Stubborn thing thought she had to date every guy *but* me just to make sure she wasn't missing out on anything better. Can you believe that?"

I grin, knowing he has at least two toes sticking out of holes in his socks as we speak. "Unimaginable."

"So this Brandon guy, you hear him?"

"Yes. Well, I haven't in years, but I think it's because I haven't dated anyone in years. He only speaks to me when I'm in a relationship. And before you report me to social services as an unfit guardian for Gabe, let me just say that I *know* it's not really his voice. It's this leftover part of his spirit inside of me. It's my conscience disguised as him."

He finishes chewing and wipes his mouth with a hanky. I've noticed he uses a hanky for everything. "I like the scenario where his ghost is talking to you much better than you pretending that it's not really his voice."

A wry grin slides up my face as I tear my toast into small pieces, plucking them into my mouth with the same caution as my confession. "I like it too. It's like he's with me."

"Margie doesn't talk to me, but she said very few words even before she died. Looks … she gave me looks. Mostly death glares, but occasionally she smiled with pink cheeks, fluttering her eyelashes at me like she did when we were younger. How many people can say they've known the love of their life for their entire life? We were born one day apart, almost to the exact minute."

I like this story. "Who's older?"

"Well, I am of course. She died."

I shake my head and grin. "You know what I mean."

"She was one day older, and I never let the old bat forget it either."

My face hurts from the size of my grin. "I love that. Brandon and I were crazy, and he was so ornery. Always playing jokes on me. Embarrassing me so much, but it was just us. He made me up my game, always finding a better revenge." I sigh, letting my smile fade. "Just before he died, he said, 'You win, Grace. Now go find another worthy opponent.' Such a jerk. He just had to be awesome until his last breath, clearly making *him* the winner. And I think he damn well knew it. That was twenty years ago, and I still hear those words like an eternal echo."

"There's a fine man staying next door that might be a good match for you. A widower. Good looking. Age appropriate."

"No." I stand, dumping my toast crust into the trash and topping off my coffee mug. "I'm done. No more men for me. No more dating. No more catastrophes. I'm forty-one and just … done."

"Oh, Elvis, you have more than half a life left. You're really going to spend it alone?"

Leaning against the counter, I sip my coffee. "No. I have at least eight years left with Gabe. Beyond that, I can't imagine needing anything more than a library card and two or three cats. As long as my parents are still alive, I'll have them. I make friends pretty easily … I might even move back to Idaho where most of said friends live."

"Oh lord … you cannot be serious. Books, cats, and Idaho?"

"Mmm …" I rub my lips together. "Sounds amazing, right?"

Three knocks on the door make me jump, tightening the sash to my robe. "Company?" I cringe, thinking I might need to get my ass upstairs.

"Delivery. I imagine." He slowly unfolds from the chair and shuffles to the door. "Good morning."

I empty the rest of my coffee in the sink and rinse out my mug.

"Come in. Can I get you some coffee?"

Wait? I freeze. Who is he inviting into the house? I can't get to the stairs from the kitchen without passing the front door.

"Sure." Nate's voice.

My body hurls into panic mode. I'm trapped—in a short terry cloth bathrobe with bunnies on it and a hood. Yes, I have a hood with bunny ears on it. Don't even get me started on my hair that surely has a party happening in the back.

"Where's Miss Morgan?" Mr. Hans asks.

"Taking a shower."

Mere seconds before the two men enter the kitchen, I lick my hands and wipe down the back of my hair.

"Elvis, look who's joining us for coffee."

Before Nate traipses into the kitchen, I get a full second to shoot Mr. Hans a scowl.

"G-good morning." Nate trips on his words as his eyebrows stand at attention, gaze assessing my robe.

Bunnies. So what? My shoulders slide back, chin simultaneously inching upward to prove I'm confident in my own skin—and a bunny robe. "Good morning. I was just going upstairs to shower."

Mr. Hans grabs Nate a coffee mug while my confidence wavers under Nate's swelling smile.

"Do you not work today?" Nate asks.

I clear my throat. "This afternoon."

"What's the salon called? I need a trim."

"It's only for women."

He squints. "Never heard of that. Can they do that?"

"Uh … yeah. There have been men-only barber shops for years."

"Well, that's a bummer. I was hoping you could trim my hair."

"Sorry." I shrug.

"I have scissors and clippers. Margie used to cut my hair. Elvis can cut your hair at your house or right here in my kitchen. I even have a cape."

"Great!"

"No!" I protest Nate's "great."

He chuckles. "I'll pay you."

"Come on, Elvis, cut the guy's hair. He helped you move in. It's the least you can do."

I don't like Mr. Hans anymore. Not at all.

"Just a little trim around the ears and in front." Nate runs his hands through his hair.

God … he's sexy.

"I figured you were growing it out to put it in a ponytail." I smile as if I meant to say that aloud.

Nate sips his coffee and sits at the table with Mr. Hans. "Why would I do that?"

Because that's how Jamie Fraser wears his hair, except when he's in bed, doing very sexy things to—I shake my head, trying to erase the ridiculous thoughts popping into it.

"No reason. I'm going to shower. I didn't know you were coming for coffee."

"I came over to borrow a few tools," Nate says.

"Coffee first." Mr. Hans holds up his mug and Nate taps it, like two guys at a bar.

I shuffle my bare feet out of the kitchen, not feeling like toasting to anything in my short bunny robe.

"Don't worry about my hair. If you're not comfortable doing it, I'll find someone else."

My body jerks to a stop in spite of my brain telling me to politely say "okay" and keep moving. Nope. Not me. I'm offended that he's implying I can't cut his hair.

A hair stylist cuts hair.

He thinks I'm a hair stylist.

I should be able to cut his hair.

"Tomorrow morning. Your place. I like my coffee black." I continue up the stairs, beaming with pride for a full ten seconds. It's not until I'm behind my closed bedroom door that I freak out. What did I just do?

Oh my god.

Oh my god.

OH MY GOD!

I spend the rest of the morning glued to my phone screen, much like Gabe, watching videos on cutting men's hair.

CHAPTER SEVEN

Nathaniel

MORGAN AND I spend the overcast day writing letters to friends we've met around the world—real letters with paper and pens. Then she reads on the sofa while I work on my book—the book that's handwritten throughout six different spiral notebooks. It's hard to spend hours writing on a laptop while preaching to my daughter the evils of the almighty screen.

"There she goes again," Morgan, from her nest of blankets on the sofa, stares out the window—the one below my bedroom window. It's become a regular event.

Gracelyn and Gabe arrive home.

Gabe goes in through the deck door.

Gracelyn strips to her panties and bra behind the grass plants, shoves her clothes into a bag, and dashes up the stairs to her bedroom.

I won't lie … I don't exactly hate her routine. However, my curiosity grows with each episode.

"You haven't said anything to Gabe or her, have you?"

Morgan shakes her head. "You said we didn't want to make her feel embarrassed." She tosses her book aside. "I'm going over to see Gabe."

"I figured." I stay focused on the window as if Gracelyn's still undressing. As if I haven't had sex in a long time. As if—

"Do you think it would be cool if Gabe were my boyfriend and Gracelyn were your girlfriend … just for the summer?"

"What?" My head jerks in her direction as she slips on her shoes. "N-no." I shake my head like the torso of a wet dog. Where did she come up with that ridiculous idea?

She shrugs. "I've never had a boyfriend. And you haven't had a girlfriend since Mom. It would be nice to practice a little before I start school this fall."

"Practice?" I tilt my head to the side.

"Yes. If I get a boyfriend in school, I don't want him to think I don't know what I'm doing."

Kill. Me. Now.

"And …" I clear my throat. "What do you mean by *doing*?"

Eye roll. Shocking.

"That's just it! I don't know. Gabe can show me."

"Show you what?" I sit up, dropping my notebook and pencil onto the cushion beside me, my blood pressure in the unhealthy range.

"Daaad! I. Don't. Know. It's like when you try to get me to try something new to eat and I say I don't like it. You say I can't know that until I taste it. Well … I need a taste of a boyfriend."

"No! You don't."

She opens the door and tosses me a sour face over her shoulder before leaving. "Figuratively."

The door shuts.

I lose five more years off my life.

And now we have a boyfriend situation.

THE NEXT MORNING, Gracelyn arrives on time with a plastic bag and an odd smile. It's more of a cringe, scraping her teeth over the corner of her bottom lip as Gabe plops down in one of the porch chairs with his tablet to wait for Morgan. The girl who used to get ready for the day in less than five minutes now takes fifty minutes.

"Come in," I say to Gracelyn, eyeing Gabe. It's not that I don't like him. He seems nice enough. I just don't know about him being the object of Morgan's affection—her obsession. "Coffee. Black." I nod to the mug on the counter as she sets the bag on the kitchen table.

"Thank you." Her hand shakes as she lifts it to her lips.

"Is something wrong?" I stare at her shaking hand for a few more seconds before meeting her wide-eyed gaze.

"No. Why?"

"Your hand is shaking."

She steadies the mug by lifting her other hand to help set it on the counter. "I was just a little nervous. I didn't know how hot it was. Didn't want to burn my tongue."

I return a slow nod. "So, do you want my hair wet or dry?"

"It's best dry while I use the clippers."

"I only want it trimmed. No need for clippers unless you think the back of my neck is too hairy."

Her lips part, but no words come out.

"Just trim it up a bit with scissors so I don't have hair hanging in my eyes."

"The order is clippers and then scissors."

I chuckle. "I don't want it buzzed."

"The clippers have different guard lengths." She seems … upset? On edge. It's weird.

"O … kay. You're the expert." I pull out a chair and sit

down while she dumps the contents of the bag onto the table. After plugging in the clippers, she inspects the guards and a small smile jumps onto her face when she catches me watching her.

"Let's do this." She shoves one of the guards onto the clippers and flips the switch. "Oh!" She startles when it hums. "That tickles my hand."

"Maybe I should remove my shirt or grab a towel."

"What? Oh … shoot. No." She shuts off the clippers and grabs the folded cape by the bag. "Sorry, I spaced on the cape. I'm just … out of my element."

"But you do this for a living."

"Not in people's kitchens." She wraps the cape around me.

I tug on the neck a bit.

"Too tight?" She narrows her eyes.

"It's fine." Breathing is overrated.

The clippers come to life again.

"Just a trim," I remind her.

"Yes, *Nate.*" She guides my head forward so my chin tips toward my chest as she brings the clippers to my nape and swipes up. "Shit!"

"What?"

She shuts off the clippers. "Um … nothing. You know … I think I'll just use the scissors. Clearly it's what you've wanted me to do. And you know what they say?"

"What's that?"

Gracelyn unplugs the clippers, shoving all the pieces back into the bag before grabbing the scissors and comb. "The customer is always right."

I nod. "I suppose you do get a lot of requests for styles and colors that you fear the customer won't end up liking."

"You guessed it."

"I filled a spray bottle if you want to wet my hair. It's over by the sink along with a towel."

"Whatever the customer wants." She grabs the bottle and wets my hair … a lot.

"Wow … you used the whole bottle of water."

"Too much?" She wrinkles her nose while furiously wiping my face, neck, the cape, and even the floor.

"Nah … I like it wet." I chuckle.

She stops, staring at me with lifted eyebrows and pink filling her cheeks.

"My hair. I like my hair wet. Get your head out of the gutter, Elvis."

Her eyes narrow. "It's not in the gutter. I was just … just looking at your hair." Shifting her gaze to my hair, she steps forward and runs her fingers through it, putting her chest inches from my face.

I shouldn't like her chest in my face, but I do. Just like I like watching her undress and run up her balcony stairs. And the damn short bunny robe … I like it too.

"You're right. I don't need to cut that much." She's not cutting *anything*. She's just combing my hair with her fingers.

I close my eyes because it—she—feels good. Of course, I've had women cut my hair before, but they've never done it with one leg between mine and their breasts so close. It's unclear at the moment if she's trying to give me a trim or seduce me.

She grabs the scissors and makes her first cut.

Snip.

Snip.

Snip.

I keep my eyes closed. Everything she does is slow and gentle. After every few cuts, she combs her fingers through my hair some more. If this haircut lasts all day, I'm good with that. I don't need a girlfriend, in spite of Morgan's not-so-brilliant idea.

A good haircut works plenty of magic. I might opt for more frequent trims while we're here this summer.

"Why the grin?" She rips me away from my thoughts.

I straighten my lips and peek open one eye. "Nothing."

"I think I should just call it." She steps back, cocking her head to inspect my hair.

"Call it?" I chuckle. "Sounds like you're giving up or someone died? Is that what you tell all of your clients when you finish?"

"Oh my gosh, Dad! You're getting a Mohawk?" Morgan skips into the kitchen.

I glance over my shoulder at my daughter with her hair dried straight and her lips fully glossed. In an instant, I regret letting her get tinted lip balm.

"No Mohawk. Sorry to disappoint you. Just a trim."

"Then why did Gracelyn shave part of your hair in the back."

I reach for the back of my head at the same time I face Gracelyn again. She grimaces as my fingertips feel the one-by-two-inch strip of buzzed hair.

"What did you—"

"Listen ... the guard came loose on the clippers. I think because they are so old. It will grow back in no time. Really. If you wear a hat out in public, it will be no big deal. And honestly the rest of your hair is long enough and wavy enough that you might be able to style it to cover up the bulk of it. OR ..." Her cringe flips into something resembling excitement. "You can wear it in a ponytail. It's totally in right now."

Morgan cups her hand at her mouth and shuffles out of the kitchen with wide eyes. "Gabe! Gracelyn ruined my dad's—" The slam of the door cuts off her voice.

As I wordlessly blink at Gracelyn, she bites her lips together, wringing her hands in front of her.

"*So* sorry. This has never happened before. Just tell me what you want me to do."

"Well ... *fix it.*"

"I can take you someplace, but I won't touch those clippers again. I don't trust them."

My lips part, and I try to keep my jaw from reaching the floor. "The clippers. You don't trust the clippers?"

"I feel terrible."

"Mmm ... I can see that." I tear off the cape.

Her frantic apologies and anguish-ridden face lead me to believe she has no intention of fixing my hair. I'm not sure I want her to attempt it at this point. Gracelyn is a lot of things at the moment, but confident is not one of them.

"What are you doing?" She takes a few steps backward.

"Going to get a haircut." I toss the cape onto the table and brush off my jeans before exiting the kitchen to find a hat in my bedroom.

"I ... well ..." She follows me upstairs. "I'll stay here and watch the kids."

"No. You won't." I sort through a half dozen hats in the dresser drawer.

"Please don't let this ruin your summer here. I don't want Gabe and Morgan to be affected by an equipment malfunction."

I grunt a laugh, pulling on my baseball cap backward to get

more coverage for the back of my head. Damn … I wish this woman didn't look like my Jenna. She even argues like her—the perfect amount of stubbornness to balance her fear. When we first met, Jenna feared every little fight would end us.

"You're staring at my hair again. Is it your wife? Or are you contemplating shaving my head in my sleep?" Gracelyn hugs her arms to her chest.

I eliminate the space between us, peering down at her until she swallows hard under my scrutiny. She botched up my hair. I deserve a few seconds of making her squirm. "Yes."

Her full, rosy lips part. "Uh … yes what? Yes, you're staring at my hair and thinking about your wife, or yes you're contemplating shaving my head in my sleep?"

The smattering of freckles along her nose and cheeks reminds me that she's not Jenna—that and her bigger breasts and slightly curvier hips.

"I have a strict man-ban," she says in a breathy voice.

She's beautiful. My ability to stand this close to her and think that without feeling guilty means I'm not a broken man. I'm just out of my element, out of practice, and maybe a little out of my mind.

"What's a man-ban?"

Another hard swallow. "It means I've retired from dating and men in general."

"And you're telling me this because?"

After wetting her lips, she rubs them together. "Because you're standing so close to me."

I smirk and take a long step backward. "Better?"

Her shoulders relax. "Better."

"I haven't dated anyone since my wife died. So don't read into anything I do as a threat to your *man ban*. And if I'm being honest, a bad haircut doesn't do it for me."

She scratches her throat, twisting her lips to the side. "You seemed to enjoy it until Morgan pointed out the tiny flaw. I heard several contented sighs and even a short hum."

Rubbing my mouth, I hide my grin. "Fine. It was good until it wasn't. Now, I have to go get it fixed, which will probably involve losing most of my hair. *Hmm* … that doesn't sound amazing." I sigh after my hum to let her know not all sighs and hums are good signs.

But … I did enjoy her fingers in my hair. Was it worth it? That's yet to be determined. I'll make that decision when I look in the mirror tonight before I go to bed.

"Did I mention I'm really sorry?" She curls her hair behind her ear and wrinkles her freckled nose.

I sidestep her and head toward the stairs. "Yes. You've been very generous with apologies and gratitude. You're eternally welcome, and most likely I will always forgive you. How much more could you possibly screw up in the next eight weeks?"

"Please don't say it like that." She follows me to the kitchen. "That's a lot of pressure to put on me to be perfect. So much could happen in eight weeks."

I chuckle while sweeping up the hair mess. Although … it's not much more than that initial strip of hair from the back of my head. What did she cut with the scissors?

As if she can read my mind, Gracelyn snatches the bagful of hair supplies from the table and shoots me a nervous smile. "I promised Gabe I'd take him to see his friend today." She retreats a few steps. "So … I'm…" her thumb makes a jabbing gesture over her shoulder "…just going to go."

"Okay." I empty the dustpan into the trash can under the sink.

"You don't have to thank me for my time."

With my back to her, I freeze, eyes narrowed. She really just said that?

"But I'll still thank you for the coffee. So … thanks for the coffee."

I slowly turn toward her. She slides her hands into the back pockets of her frayed denim shorts. I keep my lips neutral, but inside I have the biggest damn grin clawing its way to the surface. Happiness comes in small packages. It's not so much a state of mind, but a moment.

In this moment, I want to wipe that grin off her face. She ruined my hair. At the same time, I want to stare at her, try to figure out the little things—like stripping outside and stuffing lingerie into pockets. It's been a long time since I had any sort of desire to figure out a woman.

"You're welcome." The smile breaks out along my face like the sun burning through the clouds. I can't stop it. Usually, I *can* stop it. All I have to do is think of Jenna and how much I miss her—or Daisy, my best friend who died when we were kids.

Not today. Gracelyn earns this smile from me, and she has no clue what a huge breakthrough this is in my life.

"Well, you're welcome too." She narrows her eyes a bit.

Yes, Elvis … I know you're fishing for a thank-you from me, but I'm not feeling the haircut gratitude at the moment.

While I adjust my hat as a reminder of what transpired this morning, her gaze flits from my hand making the adjustment to my unblinking eyes.

She clears her throat. "Well … I'll see you around." Turning on her heel, she scurries out of the house, leaving me with this ridiculous grin.

I can't wait to see her around. If I can make a specific request, I'd like to see more of her after-work routine and less of her with clippers in her hand.

CHAPTER EIGHT

Gracelyn

"I'VE NEVER SEEN him like this. I don't even recognize him," Morgan's voice wafts through the paper walls.

I grab my phone from the nightstand to check the time. It's a few minutes before eight on a Saturday morning. Don't kids sleep in anymore? I used to sleep in on the weekends when I was their age. The three plus decades I have on them doesn't change my desire to sleep in on the weekend.

"He looks like someone in the military. I mean … he has hair, it's just really short," Morgan continues without using her library voice.

I bolt to sitting, running my hands through my hair. The haircut fiasco yesterday.

Shit! They had to buzz Nate's hair … because of me. That's what she's talking about; it has to be what she's talking about.

Throwing on shorts and a tee in record time, I open the bedroom door.

"Hi, Gracelyn." Morgan smiles from her usual spot on the brown leather sofa next to Gabe. She likes to watch him play video games and talk his ear off. I think deep down he likes her, but he's playing it cool.

Gabe? He ignores me. His usual behavior in the morning when he's in the zone. I can't wait for school to start so I don't feel like such a failure letting him play games all day long.

"Good morning, Morgan." I return a smile.

"I tried to tell him he's going to rot his brain, and he should take a break and let me play for a bit." Morgan rolls her eyes.

Gabe doesn't react.

I ease into the recliner next to the sofa, tucking my legs beneath me. "I don't think your dad wants you having a turn at rotting your brain."

"Dude ..." Gabe sighs without taking his eyes off the TV. "I can hear you. I'm not rotting my brain."

I wink at Morgan and she giggles.

"What's your dad doing?" I have to ask.

"He just got home from jogging, so he's probably on the porch doing push-ups and stuff like that. Wait until you see his hair. It's gone! All gone."

I cringe.

"Well..." she twists her mouth "...it's not *all* gone as in literally. It's just so short. The guy who fixed it said he had no choice but to go that short after you messed up the back. He said ... wait—" She covers her mouth with her hand. "Never mind."

"He said what?" I cant my head, hugging my arms to my chest.

"I'm not supposed to tell you. It's just hard to keep so many secrets from you."

I release an easy laugh. "So many secrets? How many secrets are you keeping from me?"

With wide eyes, Morgan bites her lips together and shrugs.

"If you share one or two of these secrets with me, Gabe will let you play that for fifteen minutes."

"No. I won't." Gabe disputes my promise.

"*Yes.* He will. If he wants me to take him to the park later to play Fishy with his friends, he'll let you have a turn."

"Fishy?" Morgan turns her attention to Gabe. "What's Fishy? You could invite me. I love games."

"What did your dad say that you're not supposed to tell me?" I don't really care about Fishy. I want to know Nate's secrets.

"Just stuff to not make you feel bad. He said it's okay to keep secrets if it's to protect someone's feelings."

"You don't have to protect my feelings. I can take it."

"Fine." She sighs. "But don't tell him I told you."

I make an X over my chest.

"He said he feels sorry for your clients if you ever have to use the clippers. The guy cutting his hair laughed. When Dad noticed I heard him, he said not to repeat it. He said he shouldn't have said it, but I think that's code for he thinks he shouldn't have said it in front of me. Like when he uses a swear word."

Of course, he and some other *guy* enjoyed a laugh on my behalf. So typical.

"That's it? That's what he was worried you'd tell me?"

Her nose wrinkles. "Well, maybe one other thing. He thinks it would make you feel bad if you knew that we see you undressing when you get home from work."

"What?" Gabe grimaces without looking away from the screen.

Bad? No. I don't feel bad. Embarrassed? Definitely. It's pretty embarrassing. I always glance around before doing it. And I do it as quickly as possible. The side of the house isn't visible to that many people—except for Morgan and Nate with the two windows facing my balcony. I always check to make sure they're not looking out the window.

"I saw you first, and I told my dad. He covered my eyes, but I said, 'Dad! I'm a girl too!'" She rolls her eyes.

Rubbing my lips together, I nod slowly. "Did he cover his eyes?"

She shakes her head. "I'll tell him to close his eyes if it happens again."

Gabe tosses the game controller onto Morgan's lap and stands. "I'm going to get breakfast."

As I follow him down the stairs, he glances back at me. "Why don't you shut the blinds? My mom forgot to shut the blinds once to their bathroom, and my dad saw her undressing to get in the shower as he pulled into the driveway. He was *not* happy."

I can see that. Kyle was a little possessive of Emily. The good news for me at the moment—if there can be any good news after Morgan's confession—is that Gabe thinks I undress in my bedroom with the blinds open, not outside under the balcony.

"Morning. Morgan wake you two up?" Mr. Hans asks. "Woke me up." He pours a cup of coffee.

I grin. "This generation doesn't sleep in."

"This works." Gabe grabs a bag of chips from the counter and heads back toward the stairs.

"No way, buster. You're not having chips for breakfast."

I snatch the bag from his hand when he sulks back into the kitchen.

"Fine. Eggs with cheese."

"We're out of eggs." I have to disappoint him again.

"Fine. Then I'll eat the chips."

I shove the bag behind me when he goes to reach for it

again.

"I've got some cooked eggs in the fridge. Boiled and pickled. Help yourself."

"Um … no thanks." Gabe's face scrunches into disgust.

"Go ask my dad for eggs! We got some last night!" Morgan hears everyone and everything. It's a little creepy.

I nod toward the door. "Go ask nicely to borrow two eggs and tell him I'll replace them this afternoon."

"Can you do it, please? If I don't get back upstairs, she's going to mess something up on my game because she has no clue what she's doing."

"I heard that!" Morgan calls.

I return the exasperated expression he usually gives me. It does nothing. Gabe turns and runs back up the stairs.

"Ask him if he's done with my stud finder," Mr. Hans adds.

"Fine. I'll go comb my hair and brush my teeth."

He chuckles. "Why? Are you going to kiss him?"

"What?" I narrow my eyes at him.

"Your hair is fine. And unless you get in his face, he won't smell your breath."

"I'm not kissing him."

In real life.

I can't control what happens in my sleep. It's possible Nate has a Scottish accent in my dreams.

"My shoes are upstairs. I have to go up there anyway."

"Sure." He grins before sipping his coffee.

"I told you, I'm not interested in any man."

"Sure thing, Elvis."

I give up on the fight and quickly brush my teeth, wash my face, pull my hair back into a small ponytail, roll on deodorant, lotion my legs, and change my shirt to something less wrinkled.

It's not like I changed into sexy lingerie. Besides … he's already seen that.

Instead of confronting snoopy Mr. Hans again, I exit through my bedroom and down the stairs he built for me. I knock on the frame to Nate's screen deck door.

"Come in!" he calls.

The door squeaks when I open it. After I slip off my canvas shoes, I tiptoe my bare feet toward the kitchen, at least I think that's where Nate's voice just came from.

"Good—whoa!" I jerk my head back.

Nate gives me a strained smile as he finishes pull-ups on a bar secured in the doorway between the kitchen and the living room.

Shirtless.

Sweaty.

Tan.

Low riding shorts.

Muscles for days.

And … dreadfully short hair.

"Your hair," I whisper.

He finishes five more pull-ups and drops to the floor. Wiping his face with a white towel, he chuckles. "Hank said the ponytail suggestion would make me look like an actor on some Scottish time-travel series. He assured me I wouldn't want that in spite of women going crazy over him. So the only alternative was to take it really short in the back and on the sides." He ruffles the top of his hair which is a little bit longer, but not much. "He left me a little wave on the top."

"Jamie?"

Nate flings the towel over his shoulder. "What?"

"He implied you'd look like Jamie from *Outlander*?"

He lifts his shoulders slowly. "Um, maybe. I don't watch the show, and he didn't remember the name of it."

"What's wrong with Jamie?" I cross my arms over my chest.

Nate's gaze follows my arms, and he grins. "You're one of those women, aren't you?" A grin tugs at the corners of his mouth.

"I don't know what you're implying by *those* women. Yes, I've watched *Outlander.* And I've read the books. It's really a brilliant storyline with rich historical references. The show has stunning scenery and some quite impressive battle scenes."

"But you're not attracted to this Jamie character?"

"Listen, James Fraser is a fantastic character. I enjoy watching him because he's a superb actor."

"Hank said his girlfriend watches the show, and it's filled with graphic sex scenes."

"Pfft … filled is a bit of an exaggeration."

"I see. So … what's up?"

I rip my gaze from his chest and narrow my eyes. "What do you mean?"

"You're here. Is there a reason? Or did you want to have coffee with me? I'm hot at the moment, so I'll probably have some water, but I'll make you some coffee."

"Well …" I jerk my head in the direction of my place. "The kids are over there."

"That's fine. They don't drink coffee. Let me go put on a shirt."

Yes. *Please* put on a shirt.

He runs up the stairs, and I … okay, I won't lie. I watch him run up the stairs. Then I sigh, closing my eyes and replaying those last five pull-ups.

"How's Gabe doing? I've been meaning to ask." Nate jogs down the stairs a few seconds later.

"Oh. He's good. I think. I'm not entirely sure. He sees a therapist every other week, but I have no idea what they discuss because he doesn't want to talk about it with me."

"It's hard to deal with losing someone—or in his case—the *two* most important people in his life. Maybe your role isn't to be his therapist. Leave that role to the actual therapist. You should let yourself be his friend. His break from thinking about them or talking about them." He hands me a cup of coffee and sits at the table across from me with his glass of water, an apple, and a knife.

It's hard to imagine that cutting an apple could feel like a slow seduction, yet … Nathaniel Hunt with his muscular, veiny hands cutting an apple kinda does it for me.

Apple porn.

What's next? Will my legs start to shake when he sips his water?

"Honey Crisp?" He offers me a wedge of the apple.

I close my hanging jaw and swallow the pooling saliva from his apple porn while relinquishing a small nod and a weak "thank you."

"I'm sorry about your hair." I nibble the edge of the apple slice.

Nate smirks. "Why? Does it look bad?"

"No. You look good—fine, I mean … it—your hair—is okay."

Nice, Gracelyn. Super smooth.

He pauses his glass of water an inch before his lips and inspects me through intense eyes. "Have you ever been married?"

Okay. We're going there. I did not see that coming so

quickly. Does he know I'm fantasizing about him?

Is this a date? Are we having a coffee and apple date?

"Almost." I absentmindedly run the apple along my lips.

After a few seconds, I notice his gaze is affixed to the apple—or my lips.

It drops from my hand because he does weird stuff to me with a single look. This draws a tiny chuckle from him as I snatch it from the table and shove as much of it into my mouth as possible, which happens to be the whole apple slice.

It's more apple than I can handle, but now I've demonstrated just how much I can shove into my mouth. Is he thinking what I'm thinking? God … I hope not. Men don't go through weird hormonal kidnappings in their forties like women do. Or do they?

"Broken engagement?" he asks.

I chew.

And chew.

Swallow. Swallow. Swallow.

My level of awesomeness is off the charts this morning. I shake my head a few times. Then I nod an equal number of times. "Good question," I mumble with my hand in front of my mouth while I clear the last of the apple from it.

Smooth like the grittiest sandpaper.

"He left me at the altar. So technically it was before we were married." I twist my lips. "I suppose that's a broken engagement."

"Damn." He winces.

"Yeah, I think the minister whispered the same word right after Michael closed his eyes for a few seconds, opened them, leaned forward, kissed my cheek, and whispered in my ear, 'Sorry. I just can't,' before taking long strides out of the church."

"Wow … that's …" He eats the last piece of the apple and shakes his head slowly.

"Third strike." I blow out a slow breath. "It was the third strike. Three men have crushed me. I've officially retired from dating. I call it a man ban."

If he has any illusions that this is a coffee and apple date, I think I just crushed those.

"No explanation? Just a *sorry, I can't?*"

It's a complicated question that's impossible to answer without explaining everything. Nate doesn't want to hear *everything.*

"Just those three words." I shrug. It's true. That's all Michael said. It's what he did just seconds before saying those words that said *everything.*

Nate shakes his head and leans back in the chair, lacing his hands behind his head. It does nice things to his arms and chest. "Morgan wants me to find someone. I think she's worried I'll be lonely when she goes to college. It's not that simple. And I think I can keep myself busy without finding someone to keep me company. When my wife died, I knew Morgan would be the last woman I would ever love. Then …" His gaze falls to the table as his brow furrows.

"Then what?"

With a tiny head shake, he murmurs, "Nothing."

"I think it's a misconception that every human needs to have a significant other to be happy."

His blue eyes lift to meet my gaze. After a few seconds, he nods. "Absolutely."

"It's a big world. Lots to do."

Nothing. I have nothing to do except raise Gabe and die

with a houseful of cats.

"How old are you? Can I ask that?" He grins.

"Yes." I chuckle. "You can ask. I'm forty-one. Can I ask your age?"

"How old do you think I am?"

"What?" My head rears back. "No. You can't ask my age and then make me guess your age."

"You could have asked me to guess your age." That smirk of his is … dangerous.

"And what would you have guessed?"

"Forty-one."

"Liar." I squint at him.

Something delightful dances in his eyes. It's been a long time since a man has looked at me the way Nate's looking at me. My body reacts in ways it *knows* it shouldn't react to any man—warm and tingly in regions far south, and even the hillier areas of my body have decided to perk up a bit. I tug on my tight T-shirt because my thin bra feels insufficient at handling those blue eyes on me.

"Fifty." I grin.

Nate's eyebrows shoot up his forehead. "Fifty?" After a few slow blinks, he strokes his scruffy jaw and chin. "Is it the gray in my beard?"

"It's the expression on your face. I don't think you're fifty, but after putting me on the spot to guess your age, fifty is me being nice."

He laughs. It vibrates down into the bottom of my belly, settling like a warm piece of pie with vanilla ice cream.

"Forty-six."

"Morgan's right. You need someone."

"Oh, but you don't? You can quit the game, declare three

strikes, and ban men from your life, but I should keep playing?"

"How many strikes do you have?" I drum my fingers on the table.

His lips corkscrew for a few seconds. "Two."

"See." I point a finger at him. "You have one more chance. Don't let it go to waste."

"Mmm ... if that's the case, I think I'll save my third chance for the nursing home."

I giggle. "Really? The nursing home?"

He lifts one shoulder and drops it just as quickly. "Why not? A younger woman of course. Some hottie in her late eighties with her own teeth and who still wears red lipstick."

My smile threatens to crack my face. "Not me. If I had my last chance to use in the nursing home, I'd seduce a male nurse. We'd be the topic of all the gossip, and the other old biddies would hate me, always scowling at me from behind their pussies."

"What?" Nate coughs on a laugh, eyes wide, lips parted.

I giggle to the point of tears, hiding my face behind my hands as I shake with laughter and memories. "My ..." I try to catch my breath while wiping the tears from the corners of my eyes. "God ... it's been so long since I've thought about that. My grandma had a walker, the kind with the tennis balls on the back legs. After Christmas dinner, she asked my brother Kyle to be a dear and grab her pussy." I snort, falling into a fit of laughter again as Nate's expression deepens with shock.

"Kyle was fifteen at the time. Sh-she got so frustrated with him because he just sat there with his mouth agape, eyeing our mom and dad. Grandma just kept yelling at Kyle. 'Kyle! Shake a leg. Grab my pussy. I need to use the restroom.' Finally, my aunt Jean translated for Grandma. Apparently, Grandma called her walker her pushy, but she also lacked good word enunciation, so pushy sounded exactly like pussy."

Nate barks out a laugh and presses his fisted hand to his mouth as his face turns red from laughter.

"So now I can't see one of those walkers without thinking about Grandma yelling at Kyle to grab her pussy."

"He must have been scarred for life."

"Yeah." I sigh. "We never forgot it. Kyle broke his leg in his early twenties before he met Emily. When I first saw him hobbling around on crutches, we made eye contact and he frowned. Then he said, 'You know what I could use right now?' I squinted at him for a few seconds, but as soon as he grinned, I knew what he was going to say. We said, 'a pussy,' at the same time. I miss those days of laughing at the craziest things. I miss …"

Nate's gaze falls to my chest and the heel of my hand rubbing circles over it. "Him. You miss your brother."

More tears burn my eyes, but they're no longer tears of laughter. "Yeah," I whisper.

"It gets easier, but it never disappears. I still think of so many funny moments I shared with my wife. I just don't think of them quite as often. And when I do, they don't make me as sad. After I brought Morgan home, I found myself saying Jenna's name aloud when Morgan would do something cute. I wanted to share it with her."

"Exactly …" I curl my hair behind my ears. "A week before we moved here, I couldn't find the spare key fob to Kyle's Land Rover, so I called him. I. Called. My. Dead. Brother's. Phone. How crazy is that? And I can't tell you how many nights I sit next to Gabe on the sofa, watching a movie, and for a split second my mind actually thinks, 'I wonder if they'll be home soon.' Because when I used to visit them, I'd babysit Gabe so they could have a night out alone."

He nods several times, the smile on his face fading a fraction as is mine. I guess there's no easy way to talk about lost wives and brothers without it stealing something from the moment.

That's okay. Right? Death should steal a tiny piece of happiness from the living for approximately eternity. It means that person's life meant something to someone. I wonder if I will steal a piece of anyone's happiness when I die?

"I should get back. How much do we really know about Mr. Hans? We're here and he's alone with our children."

Nate's eyes flare. "Shit. You're right."

We stand at the same time and make a beeline for the door. I slip on my canvas shoes, but Nate doesn't bother to put shoes on at all.

"You're such a bad influence," he mumbles, following me out the door.

I whip around before we make it to the porch stairs. "Me? No way, buddy!" I poke my finger into his chest.

He grins, grabbing my hand and just … holding it at his chest while we mirror the most contagious smile. The warm feeling in my belly blooms to life again. I don't even remind myself of my man ban because after thinking about Kyle and Emily—after missing them yet again—I need this feeling. A temporary Band-Aid on my heart.

Nate's thumb feathers over my wrist, arresting my breath as a wave of goose bumps shoots up my arms. For one insane I-will-never-ever-think-about-it-again second, I wonder what it would feel like to kiss him.

One.

Okay … I'm done thinking about it.

I slide my hand from his and offer a shaky smile just before turning back around and skipping down the porch steps. "Bad influence my ass," I say just loud enough for him to hear me.

"Elvis, your ass is a lot of things, but a bad influence is not one of them."

Holy shit. Shit. Shit. Shit!

I stop.

He stops.

We stand in silence, a small line of two.

Sweat pours out from my armpits, so I hold my arms close to my body.

"Shit. I just made things awkward. I … I'm sorry I said that. It just came out. And nothing like that has left my mouth in many years. Not since … well … *many* years," he talks to my back.

I talk to my nipples and nether region, telling them to cool the hell off.

Tick. Tick. Tick.

I need to respond. What do I say? He feels bad. I feel like a volcano. It was inappropriate.

Yet, I secretly want to fist-pump the air, run to my bedroom, and do some weird dance only a giddy young girl would do.

Clearing my throat, I force my legs to take me to the house. "It's not your fault I have such a great ass."

Biggest lie I've *ever* told. I do not think I have a great ass. Not even good. It's adequate at best. However, I have nothing to lose when I'm on a man ban, so I just own it like I've never owned anything before this moment. And I add some extra sway for good measure.

"'Bout time." Mr. Hans shuts off the television and sits up in his chair. "Sorry, Elvis, I couldn't stop Gabe from eating chips for breakfast because you took too long."

Dammit!

Hugh's gaze drops to my hands and then to Nate standing behind me. "No eggs? Did you bring back my stud finder?"

Whipping around to face Nate, I cringe. "Oh my gosh! I … I totally spaced my whole reason for going over to your house. You were exercising…" *with your shirt off, but never mind that* "…and you offered me coffee. And we started talking, and I completely forgot."

In a nutshell, I forgot more than the stud finder because of shirtless Nate. I also forgot to discuss my stripping incidents.

"So … I'll go get the eggs—"

"Two, please." I shoot him a toothy grin. "I'll pay you back after I go to the store later."

"*Two* eggs and the stud finder."

I return a sharp nod.

"And you'll go check on the kids."

"Yes, I'll go check on the kids."

"I checked on them ten minutes ago," Mr. Hans says.

I glance over my shoulder. "Thanks, but I'll check on them again anyway."

"You're worried I did something to them. Smart girl. You can never be too careful."

I bite my lower lip, eyes wide. "Okay then. I'm…" I point to the stairs "…going now."

Nate makes his way to the front door as I head up the stairs. Three steps in, I peek over my shoulder. He's still at the door, watching me.

"What?" I ask.

He shakes his head, that grin taunting me with everything he's not saying. "Nothing. Nothing at all."

CHAPTER NINE

Nathaniel

"DO YOU LIKE Gracelyn?" Morgan asks as we build a sand castle a few days after coffee, old lady pussy conversation, and the out-of-character ass comment on my part.

I peer at her over the top of my sunglasses that have slid partway down my nose. Random conversations with my daughter are my favorite moments of every day. I've loved our time traveling together over the past eight years. No topic has ever been unwelcomed.

Jenna's death.

Religion.

Sex.

Why two men were kissing on the subway in London.

Every gathering of protesters.

Every homeless person we've encountered.

We talk about everything.

I help her make sense of her world.

She helps me make sense of mine.

"I like Gracelyn just fine. Why?"

"Because you get a weird smile on your face when you're with her."

"I smile when I'm with *you*."

She dumps the bucket upside down, but the sand crumbles

meet them at the hospital with wine running through your veins," I say just as she takes another sip of wine.

She spits it back into the glass and coughs. "Oh my god! You're right! What was I thinking?"

"I'm kidding." I laugh. "He'll be fine."

"Kidding?" She glares at me. "You mean you're trying to make me feel inadequate and bad about myself. That's what you're doing. Not. Cool. Buddy!" She shoots out of the chair and dumps the contents of her glass into beach grass on the other side of the railing with her back to me.

"Gracelyn. I'm sorry. I really was just kidding—"

Her body shakes.

Shit.

I made her cry.

"Please don't …" I rest a hand on her shoulder, guiding her to turn toward to me.

She's … not crying. She's laughing.

"I'm *kidding*. Kidding is fun. Right?" The smile on her face stretches to her eyes. "But …" She points at me. "The look on your face is priceless."

I try to act like I knew she was joking, but I didn't. "You're pure evil." My head inches side to side in total disbelief. She reminds me of Jenna in so many ways it renders me speechless. "I want to kiss you," I think I say those words aloud, but I'm not sure.

I definitely *think* them. Did I mean to say them? I'm not sure about that either.

All amusement vanishes from Gracelyn's face. I'm out of practice and not just at kissing. I'm out of practice at everything related to anything beyond friendship. We can't be more than friends because of geographical challenges and … she's done with men.

"I'm *not* going to kiss you." I clear the frog from my throat and take a step back. "And since I'm not going to do it, I probably should have kept that thought to myself."

"You're leaving," she whispers.

I nod.

"And I'm …" Her brows draw together.

"Done with men." I finish for her.

"Yeah."

Sliding my hands into the back pockets of my faded gray shorts, I twist my lips to the side, feeling as high, as awkward, as alive as I did the night I asked Jenna out on our first date. "Then it's settled. I won't kiss you."

Gracelyn rubs her lips together, making me want to kiss her even more. "I should go."

Taking her cue, I move back one more step to give her space to grab her wine bottle. She retrieves the bottle and shuffles her bare feet to the porch steps.

"You don't have to go." I feel like my uncontrolled kiss confession just drove a wedge between us. With a little less than two more months here, and Morgan and Gabe finding a close friendship, I don't want it to be weird.

Gracelyn rests her hand on the railing, dropping her gaze to the ground. "I do. Or else …"

I wait. She doesn't finish. She doesn't move.

"Or else?"

There's something incredibly sexy about the way she looks at me over her shoulder. She's done it several times, and each time I think my heart trips over its next beat.

A tiny smile, that appears to hold a secret, curls her lips. "If

I stay, I might forget I'm not supposed to want you to kiss me."

Not just one beat. My heart trips over the next five beats, making it hard to breathe and impossible to speak.

CHAPTER TEN

Gracelyn

I'M NOT DRUNK, yet I stumble home, up the stairs, and into my bedroom. Collapsing onto the bed, I hug my left arm to my chest, letting my right thumb and forefinger massage the clasp to the white gold bracelet that's easily hidden by my watch.

"Say something," I whisper, closing my eyes. "You should have something to say about Nate. So just ... say it."

Brandon doesn't say a word. I know he's thinking all kinds of things like how I have no business having any sort of intimate thoughts about a man who is leaving in two months. I've managed to ruin all of my relationships since Brandon died. I *know* he's thinking shit about that. He told me to find a worthy opponent, but I've failed. *He* was my worthy opponent. I have to believe he's waiting for me in my next life.

However, right now, in this life, it's hard to not feel this pull to Nathaniel Hunt—especially when he looks at me like Brandon used to look at me and when he says he wants to kiss me.

Gah!

I want to be kissed by him. Just once. Would it count if it were one kiss? Would it have to mean something more than just a kiss? A grin takes over my face, thinking about his smile when he said it. The way his shoulders hugged his ears, giving off a boyish vibe even with some gray peppered along his scruffy jaw.

"Elvis, we're back. And we have dessert," Mr. Hans yells from downstairs.

I expected privacy—the upstairs being an apartment. Instead, my landlord yells like my dad, and the neighbor girl practically lives here. And for some reason I love it. They feel like family, and I think both Gabe and I need that right now. It won't last. Morgan and Nate will go home to Wisconsin, and eventually I will need to find a place to raise Gabe that doesn't involve a shared kitchen.

I miss Gabe when he's not here. While I've always loved him, I don't remember feeling like I missed him when I lived in Idaho. It didn't take long to feel like he's mine—maybe not my son, but my responsibility and mine to love in a way that feels deeper than I loved him before. The kind of love that makes me miss him when he's not here.

"Did you hear Mr. Hans?" Morgan pokes her head into my bedroom. Yep, no privacy.

I grin, not moving an inch from my spot on the bed. "Yes. I heard him. Thanks."

"What are you doing?" She plops her butt onto the edge of the bed and lies back next to me.

What am I doing? Great question. I'm missing Gabe and his parents for that matter. I'm listening for my dead boyfriend's voice. And I'm thinking about your dad kissing me. I'm sure she'd love for me to say all of this aloud, but I don't.

Instead, I roll toward her and she rolls toward me.

"What was it like traveling the world for so many years instead of being in school like your peers?"

Her lips twist as her eyes roll to the side for a few seconds.

"Hmmm … I don't know. I've never been in public school. We left Wisconsin when I was two. Traveling the world is all I've ever known. I'm excited to just be normal for once, but Dad thinks I'll feel trapped. I think I'm going to find a boyfriend and lots of girlfriends to talk to about my boyfriend. I want to fall in love."

I grin. "You're ten."

She lifts a shoulder. "My dad was younger than me when he met Daisy."

"Daisy?"

"Yes. The first girl he loved. She died. And he named me after her—Morgan Daisy."

I let that play in my mind a few moments. Nate lost his wife and he named their child after his first love. Interesting.

"Your dad said you'd like him to find someone so he's not lonely when you go to college. Did he …" I bite my bottom lip while searching for the right way to ask this. "Did he ever have a friend—a female friend—while you were traveling?"

"Like a girlfriend?"

I grin. "Yeah."

"No."

I nod slowly.

"Do you like my dad? I think he likes you. Or at least he likes looking at you and giving you a special smile. We're not staying here and you're not moving to Wisconsin, so I think he thinks you're a bad choice to be his girlfriend."

Her words and brutal honesty bring a smile to my face. "I'm done having boyfriends. I've had bad luck with them. I'm sure you'll have much better luck."

Morgan frowns. "I'm not sure. When I asked Gabe if he wanted to kiss me, his nose scrunched up like this." She wrinkles her nose. "I don't think that's a good sign."

Whoa … okay. She likes Gabe a lot. Or she wants to know what it's like to kiss a boy. He never mentioned this to me. I'm way over my head right now with this young girl waiting for me to say something.

"You're young."

"Ugh!" She rolls onto her back and drapes an arm over her face. "Now you sound like my dad. I know everyone thinks ten is young, but I don't feel young. Why is ten too young to kiss a boy? How old were you the first time you kissed a boy?"

I chuckle, rolling onto my back too. "Well, I probably shouldn't tell you this, but I was nine. A *ten*-year-old neighbor boy kissed me in the back hallway of our church right before he got baptized. I was shocked. It was just a quick peck on my lips when nobody was looking, but I was in shock. He gave me this devilish grin and said, 'My last sin before they're all washed away.' And we never spoke of it again. And for the record…" I roll back toward her, and her head flops to the side to look at me "…I was fourteen before another boy kissed me."

Morgan's eyes widen. "I can't wait until I'm fourteen. I just can't. I want to know what it feels like. I want to know if it will feel like Romeo and Juliet."

"You've read Shakespeare?" I quirk an eyebrow.

"Oh yes. I've read *Romeo and Juliet* more than once. And Jane Austen's *Pride and Prejudice.* However, I like modern stories even better, like *The Fault in Our Stars*, even though it's sad. And I love *Twilight* and *The Hunger Games.*"

She's ten! I think I was reading Judy Blume at ten. Definitely not Shakespeare and vampire romances.

"My dad's writing a book. It's a memoir. He says it's a love story about me and him."

I smile. "You have a great dad. I hope you know it."

"I know. He's the best. So … are you coming downstairs for dessert? It's red velvet cake. Mr. Hans picked it up from a bakery. It's Hunter's favorite."

"Cake sounds perfect."

Morgan jumps out of bed and holds out her hand. I take it. I'd hoped I'd find friends here; I just never imagined it would be a ten-year-old girl and a seventy-year-old man.

"What took you two so long? Don't worry, we saved you some cake." Mr. Hans smiles from his recliner with Hunter on the sofa, her thumbs dancing along her phone screen. Gabe will get along well with her.

"Cake, Morgan?"

My steps falter when I hear Nate's voice from the kitchen.

Mr. Hans winks at me. "I invited Nate for cake too."

I nod slowly. "I see. Whose birthday is it?"

"Life is a celebration. Cake needs no excuse."

So much for having some time to digest what Nate said to me and my flirty reaction to his kiss comment. I put on a neutral face and drag my timid ass into the kitchen.

"Cake, Gracelyn?" Nate glances up from the counter, a knife in one hand and a plate in his other hand.

"Mmm … yes, Gracelyn. You want cake." Morgan rolls her eyes back in her head as she slowly chews a bite, standing next to Nate.

How am I supposed to look at him when I saw him barely an hour ago and he said he wanted to kiss me, and I returned the desire without the actual kiss? I guess we're going to be two people who want to kiss but know that it will never happen.

"Thank you." I take the cake, giving Nate a two-second glance. It's all I can give him without completely selfcombusting into a pile of ashes.

"Mr. Hans … this is so good." Morgan traipses out of the kitchen.

"It is good. I haven't had cake in a long time." I slowly lick the frosting from the fork.

Nate glances at the floor, eyes narrowed, and hunches down. After a few seconds, I move around to his side of the island.

"Did you drop something?"

Hunched like a baseball catcher, gaze still to the floor, he crooks a finger at me.

I set my plate on the counter. "Did you lose a contact lens?" I squat next to him behind the counter.

He lifts his gaze to meet my squinted eyes. The corner of his mouth bends just as his hand slides behind my head and his lips press to mine.

What the hell?

My lungs freeze while my heart pauses and my mind explodes. There's no tongue to this kiss, just hungry lips. It knocks me off balance, and I fall to my knees, resting my hands on his shoulders.

Nate pulls back half an inch, letting his lips hover next to mine, the warmth of his breath covering my stunned mouth. "I'm not even sorry." He shrugs.

My mouth opens as if it wants to speak, but I have *no idea* what to say.

"Dad …"

Nate bolts up, leaving me on my knees. "Yes?"

"Can Hunter use—" Morgan's eyes narrow at me, my head barely peeking over the counter. "Gracelyn, what are you doing?"

"I'm …" I give her a tight smile.

Nate says, "Picking up a few crumbs."

At the same time, I say, "Tying your dad's shoe."

His explanation is much better.

Morgan laughs. "Um … okay. You're both acting weird."

I climb to my feet.

"Can Hunter use what?" Nate asks.

"Your bike so we can go for a bike ride."

"Are you going to stay around here?"

Morgan nods. "Pinky swear. We won't go too far."

"I'll need to put the seat down for her."

"Yes! Thanks, Dad. I'll go tell her." Morgan runs out of the kitchen.

Nate covers the cake with plastic wrap and nods to my plate with the half-eaten piece of cake. "Are you going to finish that?"

Cake. He wants to talk about the cake?

My head inches side to side.

"Too good to let it go to waste." He picks up the plate and finishes my cake.

YOU KISSED ME!

"By the way …" His gaze remains on the plate as he scoops up the last bite. "Morgan knows I know how to tie my own shoes."

"You kissed me!" I whisper yell.

"I did." He sets the plate in the sink and turns to look at me. "Still don't regret it, but I won't do it again if you didn't like it."

"That's … that's …" I shake my head. "Not the point at all."

"No?" He cocks his head.

I'm in trouble. Nearly two more months with this guy—cliff-diver, Jamie doppelgänger, kiss stealer.

"It can never be more than a kiss." I tip my chin up.

"Not even a second one?"

"Dad? Coming?" Morgan calls from the other room.

He pushes off the counter and brushes past me, leaning next to my ear for a split second and whispering three words, "Think about it."

CHAPTER ELEVEN

Nathaniel

"BED, SQUIRT."

Morgan slips her bookmark into her book from her beanbag chair as I fold a load of laundry on the sofa. "You don't have to tuck me in if you don't want to." She hugs her book to her chest.

"What would make you think I don't want to tuck you in?"

Twisting her lips, she shrugs. "I just don't want you to think I *need* you to do it … that you *have* to do it."

It's official. She's breaking my heart. I try not to let it show on my face.

"Do you feel like you're too old for me to tuck you into bed?"

She won't even look at me. Her gaze sticks to her bare feet as she rocks back and forth on them.

I don't want to make her feel bad. My heart wants to give her wings, not clip them. But damn … it's hard. "So are you thinking a hug right here?"

Her head lifts an inch at a time. Big blue eyes meet mine, and she smiles even with her bottom lip trapped between her teeth. "Definitely." She shifts her book to her right hand and wraps her arms around my neck.

I hug her a little tighter—a little longer. "Goodnight. I love you."

"Love you too, Daddy."

Daddy.

I'll take it. Most of the time she calls me *Dad* in front of other people, but I still get *Daddy* when she hugs me.

She heads up the stairs, and I put away the towels, start the dishwasher, and lock the doors. After brushing my teeth, I shrug off my shirt and start to close the shades over the door to my balcony. Just before they're completely shut, I stop. Flipping off the light so I can get a better view, I cup my hands at my face against the glass.

There's a body on its back on Gracelyn's balcony. I hope it's her, and I hope she's alive. Stepping out onto my balcony, I rest my forearms on the railing. "You okay?"

"Yep." She doesn't move. Her gaze remains aimed at the sky, hands folded on her stomach.

My head falls back, and I take in the starry night. "Are you sleeping outside?"

"Nope."

"Have you forgiven me yet?"

"It's hard to forgive someone who regrets nothing."

I grin even though she can't see it.

"It's your wife, isn't it? I look like her. Do I kiss like she did?"

Dropping my head, I run my hands through my hair—or lack thereof.

"It's okay," she says. "It's hard to let go of someone when it feels …" She sighs. "When it feels like you didn't *let go.* Like you had this hold on them and they just disappeared without you letting go. And they … they took a piece of you with them. Everyone else is just a piece of a different puzzle."

Her words play in my head for a few seconds. "I suppose,

but for me, it's been ten years. I don't feel like I'm looking for a piece to a puzzle."

"Can you honestly say when you kissed me, you weren't thinking about your wife? Because I was … I was comparing you to every man I've kissed before you."

"Yeah? Well, how did I compare?"

I can't see her face, but I want to believe she's grinning as much as I am. "I'm not sure. It was too unexpected."

"Sounds like a solid reason to try it again."

Gracelyn laughs. "So two? We kiss once more, and then we're done kissing? This is so … weird. I have never discussed kissing with any guy before you."

"No?"

"No." More chuckling. "It's not something you discuss. You just … do it."

"Noted."

She sits up, turning to face the railing, crossing her legs in front of her. "Noted, huh? So now you're taking notes about me? Will I make it into one of your future books? Maybe a novella about your summer in San Diego. Will you use my real name? Will you mention my great ass?"

"Great Ass will be the chapter right after Clipper Disaster."

"Real funny."

I take a seat on the balcony, resting my back against the door and sliding my knees toward my chest. "What are you thinking about … out here, alone, staring at the stars?"

She releases a heavy sigh. "Just … my life. How I got to this point. How I'm supposed to navigate the future with a young boy. Kyle and Emily left me with this responsibility that goes beyond feeding him three meals a day and driving him to school. I have to consider the friends he has and their influence. I have to think about his life after high school. Will I have what it takes to make sure he's armed with everything he needs to be successful in life? Look at me. I'm not exactly the picture of success."

"You'll be fine."

"You don't know that."

She's right. I don't.

Easing my head back against the door, I look for my own answers in the stars. "Jenna and I agreed that we would travel the world with Morgan while she was young. We'd school her by letting her learn from life and different cultures. We wanted her to be so much greater—have so much more knowledge and awareness than she would have ever received inside four walls with a massive herd of her peers. So I did it … I honored our dream for Morgan even after Jenna died. Now, I have this young girl who is too smart for her own good, too mature in some ways, and cultured beyond anything ninety-nine percent of her peers could ever imagine. I'm faced with the very real possibility that she won't fit in when she goes to school. And as much as I can get defensive and make excuses, like any kids who don't like her are just stupid and not worth her time, the truth is she wants to fit in. Morgan doesn't want to be different, smarter, more cultured. She wants girlfriends who will paint her nails and boyfriends who will make her smile."

"Nate … she will thank you for what you did. Maybe not on day one of public school, but someday she will thank you for giving her the world in the first ten years of her life. Morgan's future is going to be so bright. I can't even imagine how profoundly different my life would be had my parents been able to give me what you've given Morgan."

I smile even though she can't see me. "Are you just saying

that to make me feel better?"

"Absolutely. Hard truth? She's going to get a computer, cellphone, and boyfriend, and you'll be an afterthought."

Barking out a laugh, I shake my head. "Remind me not to come to you when I need my next pep talk."

"I'll remind you not to come to me for anything. All my good advice and worthy pep talks are saved for Gabe. Everyone else gets the sludge from my brain, the insight from the morals of my tragic stories."

"The only thing tragic about you, Elvis, is that you've given up on men."

She grabs the railing and pulls herself to standing, drumming her fingers on the rail a few times. "I didn't give up on them … they gave up on me. Night, Nate." Gracelyn disappears into her bedroom. The door lock clicks behind her two seconds before she closes her blinds.

"Night, Gracelyn," I whisper, enjoying the slight cool breeze under a blanket of clear night sky.

CHAPTER TWELVE

Gracelyn

"MISS ME?" I ask Gabe when he hops in the vehicle with his overnight bag.

"It was one night." He shuts the door and fastens his seat-belt.

"Well, I missed you."

"Now you sound like my mom."

"Sorry." I back out of the driveway and head toward home. After a few minutes of thinking about it, I can't keep my mouth shut. "Actually, I'm not sorry I sounded like your mom. I've been so worried that I'm doing everything wrong. Maybe missing you when you're gone overnight is actually doing something right."

"Um … whatever."

I bet he said those same two words to Emily and Kyle a lot. That makes me feel good. So far, I haven't damaged him beyond repair.

Eight more years, Gracelyn. You've got this.

"What do you want to do today? I have the day off."

"I don't care. I'm sure Morgan will decide what I do to-day."

I grin. "You don't like Morgan?"

He shrugs. "She's … okay. Different."

"Okay is good, right?"

Another shrug. "It's fine. She just … I don't know. Asks a lot of questions."

"Like what?"

"I don't know …"

I'm not sure why he starts every sentence with "I don't know" and then follows it up with an answer that proves he does in fact know.

"She always wants to know what I do with my other friends. And when I tell her, she asks why. She's always hovering over my shoulder when I'm playing games. And she asked me a few days ago if I had a girlfriend."

"Well … maybe she likes you."

"I don't think so."

"Why do you say that?"

"I don't know."

"Do you like her?"

"She's … fine. Whatever."

"Do you like girls?"

He whips his head in my direction. "You think I'm gay?"

Holy shit …

"No. I'm …" Okay. Call me naive, but I didn't see that coming. Wow! I just showed my age and lack of knowledge about his generation. I guess ten-year-olds are more informed about sexuality than I was at his age. I'm not sure I knew what the word gay meant at ten. I'm so … out of touch.

"I wasn't implying that I thought you were gay. I … it's fine if you are. And that's just a side note. But I was meaning are you interested in girls or boys or whatever at this point? I don't fully remember what my life was like at ten. I just remember girls were interested in boys or having boyfriends before the boys I knew even looked at girls as anything more than a forced pick on a dodgeball team in PE."

"I've had a girlfriend."

"Okay. Good. Great. I … I'll just shut up now."

As soon as we arrive home, Morgan bolts out of her house and meets Gabe at the front door.

"How was your slumber party?"

"Sleepover. Not slumber party." He rolls his eyes at her before opening the deck door.

"What did you do? Did you stay up all night? Did you sleep in sleeping bags?"

Gabe tosses his bag on the bottom step before heading to the kitchen. I glance around for Mr. Hans and Hunter, but they're not here. I think he mentioned taking her shopping today.

"Want me to make you a sandwich?" I ask Gabe.

"I'll make him one. What do you want?" Morgan asks.

Gabe grabs a sports drink from the fridge. "Turkey, but I can make it."

My brow furrows as I watch the two of them mill around the kitchen, foraging for food. Since when did Gabe learn to make his own sandwich?

"I'll make lunch for both of us." She reaches for the plates on the second floating shelf by the stove. "Gabe, grab us plates." He sets his drink on the counter and stretches his arm toward the plates.

I grin. He can't reach them either. "Maybe in another year you'll be tall enough." I stretch my arm over them and retrieve two plates. "Go play. I'll make your sandwiches."

Morgan sighs. "Fine. Let's go, Guac." She grabs his arm and tugs on it.

He shoots me a look, and I wink at him. He rolls his eyes

but not before cracking a tiny grin. Yeah … he likes her.

I assemble two turkey sandwiches and cut up an apple for them to split.

"Want to hear a secret?" Morgan asks Gabe as I climb the stairs with their plates in my hand.

"I guess," Gabe answers with no enthusiasm.

"This morning my dad and I stopped by the store to pick up a few things. He let me get this huge chocolate chip muffin and it was so good, but anyway … we were in the line to pay for our groceries, and he let me hold his phone. He told me to scan through the pictures and find some I'd like to have printed in an album."

"That's the secret?"

I stop at the top of the stairs, but the floor creaks and two heads whip in my direction. "Here you go." After handing them the plates, I ease into the recliner. Morgan's gaze flits between her plate and me, but she doesn't continue her story. Taking the awkward cue, I grab an empty glass from the end table and make my exit—partial exit. Descending three steps, just out of sight, I take a seat and wait for Morgan to continue her story.

She doesn't disappoint. "While I was scrolling through the photos on my dad's phone, I looked up just as he was putting a box of something … oh my gosh … you're never going to believe what … onto the counter. I was like *what the?* And I asked him about it as soon as we got in the car, but he said he was picking them up for Mr. Hans and that I shouldn't say anything. So whatever you do … *don't* you dare tell anyone I told you. Okay?"

"Whatever."

"Guac! You have to pinky swear."

I hold in my giggle because she's being so dramatic and secretive, but Gabe shows zero curiosity about her secret.

"Fine. I swear."

It's probably a laxative or hemorrhoid cream. I'm not sure he knows what either of those things are, but I have no doubt Ms. Smarty Pants will fully inform him. It makes me think of all the talks I need to have with him. I have no idea what Kyle and Emily taught him or what he's learned in school or through friends. On one hand, I don't want to overshare too early, but I also don't want him running into too many Morgans in the world and feeling stupid when he doesn't know about something.

"Condoms!"

Thump.

Clunk.

Thump.

Clump.

Crash.

The dropped glass from my hand survives the carpeted stairs but suffers an ill fate at the bottom with the tiled floor. I drown my gasp with a hand over my mouth and fly down the stairs.

"What was that?" Gabe calls.

"Um … nothing. Just dropped a cup. Keep eating. No big deal." I pick up the pieces while the word *condoms* echoes in my head.

Nate bought condoms. There's no way he bought them for Mr. Hans. No. Way.

My head is ready to explode with clashing thoughts.

We kissed.

He bought condoms.

Morgan saw them.

She told Gabe.

Does Gabe know what condoms are?

Why did he buy condoms?

Maybe they're not for me. How many women is he kissing?

"Whoa, what happened?" Mr. Condoms comes through the screen door.

"Glass slipped. My fault."

Your fault!

I take the larger pieces to the kitchen and toss them in the trash before retrieving the broom and dustpan from the garage.

"Let me hold it." Nate takes the dustpan from me.

I do not make eye contact as I relinquish it when I sweep the mess into it or when I take it from him and head back to the kitchen.

"Where's Hugh?" he asks after I return the broom and dustpan to the garage.

"Not sure. I think he agreed to take Hunter to the mall." I wash my hands without looking at Nate and his sexy smile, his slightly fitted gray tee, or his muscly calves.

"I see. Well, I'm taking Morgan to the ice rink. Does Gabe like to ice-skate?"

My head snaps up, my gaze laser focused on him now. "Ice-skate?"

"Yeah."

"You ice-skate?"

He chuckles, crossing his veiny arms over his expansive chest. "I played hockey for years. I like finding adult leagues that let me jump in and substitute when they need someone. There's open skating today, and Morgan loves to skate. She's more of a figure skater. No interest in hockey."

"I played hockey too."

"You?" His thick brows lurch up his forehead.

"Um … yeah. Why the look? Girls can play hockey too."

"No." He shakes his head. "I mean … I know. I'm from Wisconsin. I know a lot of girls who played hockey or just ice-skated a lot in general. I just …" His head continues to shake. "I'm not sure why I'm surprised by this."

I turn around and lift the back of my hair so he can see the nape of my neck.

"Damn … you have a tattoo." He moves closer, inspecting the crisscrossed hockey sticks tattooed where no one sees them unless my hair is pulled up.

I used to wear it in a ponytail or a messy bun a lot … when it was longer like Black Beauty's. I turn back toward him. "For your information, I have more than one tattoo." I smirk.

He wets his lips and gives me the sexiest smirk. I feel it tickle deep in my belly and a little lower as well.

"Is that so?"

Returning a shaky chuckle, I step back. It's too hot to be so close. "Yeah. It's so."

Dragging his teeth along his bottom lip and his gaze down my body, he releases a deep hum. "Can't wait to see them."

Condoms. Condoms. CONDOMS!

"They're not visible when I'm clothed."

His gaze makes a lazy retreat to mine. "What about in your bra and panties?"

Biting back my smile, I shake my head slowly.

"Well … fuck …" he whispers.

I feel those whispered words like his tongue dragging along the most intimate parts of my body.

When I make an effort to take yet another step backward,

my backside hits the counter. My hands rest on either side, and I clear my throat. "Gabe! Come down here, please."

Nate smirks. He knows I'm desperate to end this moment. There's just no need for me to let my hormonal body suffer another second under his gaze—the one who likes to stare at my hair and other parts of my body.

"Yeah?" Gabe and Morgan head directly toward the fridge to get two bottles of juice.

"Gabe. Did your dad ever teach you to ice-skate?"

"Yeah, but I'm not great at it."

"Oh, Dad! Let's take Gabe and Gracelyn with us." Morgan's plea to Nate is filled with her usual enthusiasm.

"Too late, Squirt. I already came up with that idea."

"Yes! Gabe, wait until you see my dad. He could have played in the NHL. He's so good."

A cocky grin settles onto Nate's face. I don't exactly hate it.

Gabe shrugs. "Gracelyn has hockey sticks tattooed on the back of her neck. She and my dad played too, but she's probably as good as your dad."

I frown at Gabe. "You've never seen me play. How can you jump to that horrible conclusion?"

Gabe smirks behind his bottle of juice.

"Oh! Let me see your tattoo? I want a tattoo so badly, but Dad says I have to wait until he's dead. I know that's just code for eighteen."

I turn and push my hair up again. The shorter length just barely covers it.

"That is *so* cool. See, *Dad*, not all people who get tattoos are crazy."

Nate finds his own frown, giving Morgan a firm scowl. "Go get ready."

"Go change your clothes, Guac. I'm going to change mine."

They run off, leaving me to deal with a guy who abhors technology and possibly tattoos.

"Crazy, huh?" I push off the counter and plant myself right in front of him.

Peering down at me, his lips twitch. "If you didn't think they're a little crazy, then yours wouldn't be hidden."

I got them in my early twenties. And their placement has a lot to do with my mom not seeing them. I didn't think they were crazy at the time; I just didn't want *her* to go crazy. They're intimate. Very few people have seen all three of them. Brandon saw them a week after I got the last one. The unveiling was very seductive and led to a long night where he showed no signs of a weak heart.

"Hmm..." my focus locks on his lips "...maybe you're right. Maybe you're wrong."

"What are they? A puck? Hearts? An infinity symbol with the name of your first love?"

"You'll never know. I'm going to change my clothes ... maybe stare at my secret tattoos for a while." I brush past him.

"Fine," he says, following me toward the stairs. "While I wait for everyone to get ready, I might go stare at my naked self in the mirror too." He pushes open the door.

At the last second, halfway up the stairs, I glance over my shoulder.

"There it is." He grins as if he was waiting for me to turn around.

"Go before your head doesn't fit through the doorway." I continue up the stairs.

CHAPTER THIRTEEN

"COME ON, GUAC. I'll hold your hand." Morgan grabs his hand. I'm not sure he needs her help, but he doesn't pull away. Maybe he likes her more than he cares to admit.

I finish lacing up my skates and stand while Nate follows right behind me. "Show me your moves, Elvis." He stops at the threshold to the ice and waits for me to go first.

"In all fairness, it's been several years since I've been on the ice." I tug my pink sweatshirt down, feeling a little self-conscious in my black leggings.

Nate seems to like them. Whenever I look at him, he's checking out my legs.

"Stop with the excuses." He nods for me to go.

I roll my eyes and take off. There are only four other people here besides us. A man and a woman with their two girls who look a few years younger than Gabe and Morgan. They're racing along the ice and spinning in circles like they came out of the womb doing toe jumps and salchows. The mom hangs out by the wall like she's not too steady on skates while the dad glides with confidence, holding up his phone to record the girls.

Thankfully, I feel confident even with the time lapse. Gabe has escaped Morgan's hold on him, staying a few feet behind her as she skates forward and backward, talking his ear off.

"How's the ankle?" Nate catches up to me.

I give him the side-eye and shrug. "It's fine."

"Race you, Dad." Morgan zooms up beside Nate.

"One … two … go!" he yells before sprinting to the other side of the rink.

"You didn't say three! Cheater!" She chases after him. He slows up at the last minute to let her win.

I turn and wait for Gabe. "So your dad did teach you to skate."

"Some. I like Rollerblading better."

"I like it too. We should do it together sometime."

Another shrug. "Okay."

"Lift me, Dad!" Morgan skates toward Nate, and he grabs her waist, lifting her above his head while skating backward. She stretches her arms and legs out in a long line.

"That's pretty cool," Gabe mumbles.

"Can you lift me up?" I ask.

He snorts and shakes his head. "If you want to kill both of us."

"Did you see me, Guac?" Morgan rushes over toward us after Nate puts her down.

"Yeah. I saw." He totally downplays his reaction to her.

"He gasped and said it was pretty cool." I wink at Morgan.

Her face lights up. Gabe shakes his head. "I did not." He gives me a death glare before they skate off in the other direction.

"I've been asked to get them soft pretzels," Nate says as he rests his hand on the small of my back. "Come with me?"

"Only if you're buying me one too."

"That's it … isn't it?"

As we step off the ice and sit to take off our skates, I give him a quick glance. "What's it?"

"It's not an infinity tattoo you have on your right butt cheek. It's a pretzel."

I laugh. "Yes. With extra salt."

"I knew it." He shoves his feet into his loosely laced sneakers and holds out his hand.

I take it and let him pull me to my feet—way too close to his chest. A slight pause turns into a good ten seconds of just staring at each other. I make the responsible choice to nod my head toward the refreshment stand. "Pretzels."

Nate has a way of grinning at me like he knows exactly what I'm thinking. God … I hope not.

"Four pretzels with salt," Nate orders and pays.

While we wait for the teenaged boy to get the pretzels for us, we stroll around by the cases filled with skates and other equipment to purchase.

"I saved forever to buy my first pair of new skates." Nate shakes his head. "My parents didn't have a lot of money, so I burned through so many pairs of hand-me-downs from friends who seemed to get a new pair of skates every six months. I still remember how incredible it felt to stick my feet into a brand-new pair of skates."

I smile. "I bet you also remember how it felt to endure blisters while breaking in those new skates."

"That might be true too." He chuckles as his hand brushes mine. His index finger clasps mine, and we just stand side by side peering at skates.

"Here you go," the kid from the counter calls.

He curls his finger tighter around mine like he doesn't want me to pull away as he leads me back to the counter.

I'm on a man ban, yet I feel oddly disappointed when he

does release my finger so we can each carry two pretzels toward an empty table—they are all empty since the couple and their two girls left.

"Morgan!" Nate holds up a pretzel.

I glance at my watch. "Do you realize they close in fifteen minutes?"

"I do." His lips contort like he's fighting a grin, but his gaze stays on Morgan and Gabe heading our way. "Eat up," he says to the kids and winks at me before disappearing around the corner toward the entrance.

"Where's he going?" Morgan asks with her mouth full.

I shrug, taking a slow bite of the warm pretzel.

A few minutes later, Nate returns. "Let's do this, Elvis." He's carrying two sticks and a stack of pucks.

"Do what?" I furrow my brow.

"See who has the best shot." He nods toward the rink and the guy placing a goal at one end and several cones in a line.

"Yes! I bet my dad will win."

I frown at Morgan. She giggles, picking salt off her pretzel.

Nate continues past me. "Chop, chop, Elvis."

I roll my eyes and take one last bite of pretzel before following Nate. We put our skates back on and step onto the ice.

"Three shots each. You have to weave between those six cones and make your shot before the line."

"What does the winner get?" I stop a few yards before the first cone.

"If you win, I'll send you to the spa for a day."

A spa day perks me up a bit. "And if you win?"

He smirks, shifting his gaze for a brief second to the kids eating pretzels. "I get to see your other tattoos."

I release a nervous laugh. "Um …"

"What's wrong? Are you worried I'm the better hockey player?"

I shouldn't have agreed to cut his hair. Just like I shouldn't agree to this little competition, but I'm terrible at not doing what I shouldn't do.

"Deal."

Nate's grin reaches his ears. "Fantastic. Ladies first." He drops three pucks near my feet.

I roll my neck a few times and hold my stick out, twisting my torso side to side a few times. "I could use a spa day. It better include a mani-pedi too."

"Anything your heart desires." He winks.

I glide the puck in and out of the cones and land my first shot in the net by an inch at best.

Nate says nothing when I return to the start of the cones wearing a cocky grin.

My speed picks up along with my confidence as I take the second puck through the cones and shoot my second shot right in the middle. "I want a hot stone massage … at least ninety minutes." I toss him a wink as I skate in circles around him twice.

"Watch it … I feel a choke coming on."

"Never." I go full speed with the last puck, and it bounces off the crossbar.

"So close." Nate greets me with a devilish smirk.

"It's not over." I feign confidence.

"Oh … it's over, Elvis." Nate putzes his way around the cones and uses one hand to take his shot.

Goal.

"Luck," I say, holding my head high.

"Luck, huh?" He stickhandles the puck like a drunk guy

before making another one-handed shot.

Goal.

"Do you want me to rub up against you … maybe my *luck* will rub off on you for next time."

"What happens if there's a tie?" I tap my stick on the ice.

"Tie goes to you."

"No. I don't like that." I twist my lips. "It's a wash. No spa day. No tattoos."

"Sounds boring …" He skates backward, expertly maneuvering the puck through the cones without breaking eye contact with me. Then … because I've been a bit down on my luck anyway … he keeps his back to the goal and shoots.

Son of a bitch.

Nate doesn't turn. Not one single glance back. He skates toward me knowing damn well he made the shot. "Time to go, kids." He breezes by me, nabbing my stick.

MY TWO UNSEEN tattoos create this wedge between us. On the way home, we don't speak to each other, just the kids. I feel his occasional sideways glance on me during the drive, but I close my eyes and ignore it, opting to focus on the breeze washing over me in his very cool convertible.

"Can Gabe come over for dinner?" Morgan asks the second we climb out of the car.

"Sure. I have fish we can grill. You guys good with fish?" Nate asks, his attention split equally between me and Gabe.

"I like fish." Gabe follows Morgan to the door.

"What about you?" Nate smiles, letting his eyes make their usual slow inspection of my hair before his gaze inches down my body.

I glance at my watch. "I actually have something I need to do. Rain check?"

He glances at the sky. "Rain's not predicted, but I'll take one."

"Great. So … thanks for feeding Gabe." I dig the key fob to the Land Rover out of my purse.

"I take it I've been thoroughly vetted? You're good with leaving Gabe with me."

"I don't trust you, but I trust Morgan." I give him a tight smile before turning and walking through the grass toward the SUV. "Send him home after dinner. I have a feeling he was up most of the night at his sleepover."

"Good mothering."

I glance at him as I climb in the Land Rover. Nate's smile is genuine, and I think his compliment might be too.

"Thanks." I start to shut the door then stop. "Nate?"

He stops his retreat to the house and turns.

"I'm not prying. And I hope it's not crossing a line to ask you this, but what color was your wife's hair when she was pregnant with Morgan?"

He squints, saying nothing for several seconds. "Uh … brunette. Why?"

"No reason. Night."

CHAPTER FOURTEEN

Nathaniel

THE FOLLOWING AFTERNOON, I work on my book from my bed while Morgan knits in her room. She's an expert knitter. Little do Gabe, Mr. Hans, and Gracelyn know … they're getting knitted gifts before we head home in August, and Hunter's getting something too.

I angle myself away from plain sight when I see Gabe head toward the deck. A few seconds later, um … okay. I assumed the person sneaking under the deck would be Gracelyn, but it's not. I move closer to the window but stay off to the side. The woman strips and shoves her clothes into a plastic bag before surveying the area to see if the coast is clear. Who is this …?

"Whoa …" I whisper. It's Gracelyn after all, but with red hair. Like Ed Sheeran red hair, which is actually more orange looking. She curls it behind her ear on one side and dashes up the stairs.

"I'm going to Gabe's!" Clearly I'm not the only one focused on their arrival.

"Why don't you play outside for a while? It's nice."

"Ugh … fine. I'll tell him we have to be outside … but only for an hour. I was outside most of the morning with Hunter and you know it."

"When did you start making the rules?" I yell downstairs, knowing she's already halfway out the door.

Click.

I pretend she didn't hear me, but I have a feeling she ignored me. She really needs to go back to nine and stay there forever. After capping my pen, I make my way downstairs. If I'm honest, I want them to play outside because I know it will bring my new redheaded neighbor out as well.

The screen door creaks as I ease it open and peek around the corner. On cue ... the three kids run onto the beach with a Frisbee and a volleyball. Gracelyn takes a seat on the porch swing, wearing a short blue sundress that looks incredible with her new hair color.

As I approach the porch, she smiles. It's a little more reserved than the smile I'm used to getting from her. "Love the new color."

"Yeah. I'm sure you do." She averts her gaze to the kids as I take a seat on the swing next to her.

"I take it you don't like it."

She shrugs. "It's fine."

"Is everything okay?"

Angling her body to face me, she gives me that same tight smile. It's weird, like she's waiting for me to answer the very question I just asked.

"I take it everything is *not* okay?" I say slowly.

"Wow ... look at you spending less time looking at my hair right now ... my newly colored hair ... in favor of meeting my gaze." She points her index and middle fingers at her eyes.

"I just said I like your hair."

"Mmm ... yes." She turns away from me again, shifting her attention to the kids playing Frisbee.

"Gracelyn, I'm not good at guessing games. Just say it. I don't know what I did."

"Listen, this has nowhere to go anyway. You're leaving in under two months, and I'm done with men. So while the kiss was nice—well, maybe more than nice—and the flirting and goofy wager over seeing my tattoos was fun, it's time for a reality check."

"O—kay. And what reality check is that?"

"I'm not your wife."

My head jolts back. "What are you talking about? What does Jenna have to do with this?"

"This attraction started because my hair reminded you of her when you two first met. You *always* stare at my hair before you look at my eyes or anything else, but just now ... you looked at my face and my dress, *then* you looked at my hair for less than a second. And the disappointment on your face was so obvious. I'm no longer her. Which..." she runs her hands through her orangey hair "...is the reason I changed the color. I deal with enough ghosts in my life. The last thing I need is to be the ghost of your dead wife."

I open my mouth to speak but nothing comes out. There are no words. Should I be apologetic? Angry? I honestly don't know because I didn't see this coming. It's impossible to make sense of everything she just said. "I ... I fear you misunderstood—"

"It's fine, Nathaniel."

Now it's Nathaniel. She's definitely upset.

"It's okay to hold on to her. It's okay if you never really move on. It's okay if you never find that kind of love again because she was *the one,* and no one else will ever come close. Take some sage advice from someone who knows ... threesomes don't work. If your heart can't let go, then you will take her with you into every new relationship. And even though she's dead and no one can see her … they will *feel* her."

It's clear now. The man who left her at the altar must have lost someone. And he couldn't let that someone go. That's the look she saw in his eyes before he skipped out on her.

"I'm sorry," I say with complete sincerity. "I think I read into all of this wrong. After years of moving from one place to another, making friends, leaving friends, but living in the moment with Morgan, I assumed *we*—you and I—could have this moment. A fun moment that felt emotionally safe *because* we both knew there would be no expectations at the end of summer."

I sigh, redirecting my focus to the kids on the beach since Gracelyn won't look at me. "I don't have huge cliffs to dive off of in Madison, but I seized the moment when I had the opportunity. I wanted to make the memory. Morgan and I have experienced so much that we will likely never experience again. And as much as we miss some of those experiences and people we've met along the way, there's no regret." I stand, stepping away from the swing, keeping my back to her. "I kissed *you*, Gracelyn Glock. And I did it without regret. I did it without thinking of Jenna."

Descending the few steps, I return to my deck and take a seat to watch the kids. I had no idea Gracelyn was so emotionally trapped in her past.

THE NEXT MORNING, I wake with some clarity. If I'm completely honest, the resemblance to Jenna was almost spooky when I first met Gracelyn. I've seen other women with traits that reminded me of Jenna. It doesn't change the fact that I kissed Gracelyn, not a ghost of my wife.

It also doesn't change the current situation. We're leaving in less than two months, and Gracelyn has her plate full with Gabe, the loss of his parents, her new role in life, and a past that includes misfortune with love.

"Daaad!" My favorite alarm sounds just as I finish putting on my jogging shorts and tee.

"Mooorgan!" I call from the bathroom as I apply deodorant.

"Oh my gosh! Oh my gosh! Oh my gosh!" She bounces into the room ready to explode with excitement. "Hunter and Mr. Hans are downstairs. She wasn't supposed to tell me this because Mr. Hans wants to discuss it with you first, but she did. And now you have to promise to say yes. You *have* to say yes, or I will never forgive you."

Narrowing my eyes at her complete insanity, I nod my head toward the door. "They're downstairs right now?"

"Yes."

I move toward the door.

"No. Stop! Just let me tell you first."

I frown. "Make it quick."

She blows out a slow breath, her hands gripping both of my arms as she peers up at me. "Mr. Hans and Hunter are meeting her parents at Disneyland. They're renting a place for four days and doing *all* the fun stuff at the parks! And Mr. Hans said Gabe and I are invited too! Oh my gosh! PLEASE say yes! You HAVE to say yes!"

"Morgan—"

"Daaad! PLEASE!" She drops to her knees and folds her hands in front of her. I have seen many sides to my daughter, but this level of begging and complete desperation is new.

In ten years, I've been away from her overnight just once. I left her with her nanny while I went to a conference, but I trusted her nanny completely. And they were confined to the house. Disneyland with Mr. Hans and Hunter's parents, whom I have not met, is a much different scenario.

"While you pick up the pieces of your crumbled self, I'm going downstairs to talk to Mr. Hans." I take a step toward the door, and she dives for my leg, wrapping her arms around it.

Who is this girl?

I keep moving with her attached to my leg. She releases me when we get to the stairs, hot on my heels as I descend them to a smiling Hunter and Mr. Hans waiting in the entry.

"Good morning." I return a smile. "So I hear there's been a grand invitation to Disneyland?"

Mr. Hans chuckles. "Yes. My hearing isn't the best, but I heard Morgan giving you the details."

I nod slowly, shooting Morgan a quick glance. Her face is red, her nose scrunched, like this is torture.

"We're leaving this afternoon. I know it's short notice, but when Hunter's parents decided to rent a place that houses six, she was quick to do the math and ask me if Morgan and Gabe could come too since Morgan has apparently never been?" He furrows his brow as if he can't believe that's true.

"No. She hasn't seen Disney." I refrain from mentioning all the wonders of the world that she has seen that are a million times better than Disney.

"Well, we'd love for her to come, but only if you're comfortable with it. I'm not trying to pressure you."

"Is Gabe going?"

"Gracelyn said if Morgan goes, he can go," Hunter says, tightening her long, blond ponytail.

Great. Now Gabe's fun fate is all on me too. How kind of Gracelyn to drop this decision in my lap.

"Well, I need to take a jog and clear my head before making this decision."

"Gracelyn leaves for work at noon, so you have to make your decision before she leaves." Hunter grimaces as she sets the countdown clock.

I glance at my watch. "It's eight. I'll be back by nine and make my decision by ten. Does that work for everyone?"

Mr. Hans chuckles, resting his hand on Hunter's shoulder. "That's fine. And it's okay if you're not comfortable with it. We'll find plenty of other fun stuff to do later if Hunter comes back to visit."

"It's not okay," Morgan mumbles beside me.

"Enjoy your jog. Let's go, Hunter. How do pancakes sound today?"

"With blueberries like Grandma used to make?"

"I'll see what I can come up with." He leads her out the door.

As soon as they're at the bottom of the deck stairs, I reach for my running shoes.

"It's going to be no, isn't it? It's always no. You never want me to do anything without you. You're always worried that something will happen to me."

"You mean, I love you," I mumble back to her as I finish tying my shoes.

"Why don't you put me in a fish tank or a bird cage? Why don't you just lock me in my room? Then you don't have to worry about me making friends or scraping my knee or kissing a boy. You don't have to worry about me falling in love, getting married, and dying like Mom did."

"Morgan …" I turn just as she runs up the stairs and slams her bedroom door shut.

Perched at the screen door with my hands on each side, I watch the array of seabirds flock to the shore, squawking and pecking at each other and the scraps of food and trash that have littered parts of the shoreline. I think of how hard I worked to make it through school, to become a professor … how hard I worked to convince Jenna that she should date me. I think of how long we waited to have Morgan because we wanted to be ready. We waited for the "perfect" moment.

Then I think of Jenna dying. I think of my best friend dying tragically before I ever reached the age of reason. I think of everything I've tried to control in my life and where it's gotten me. If I wanted to keep Morgan in a glass box, I wouldn't have packed our bags and set out to conquer the world.

Nothing can be given without letting go.

I knock on her door several times before slowly opening it. Morgan quickly wipes her face and hangs her legs off the opposite side of her bed, giving me her back and two cold shoulders.

They could get in a fatal car accident on their way to Disneyland. Someone could take her if she gets too curious and wanders off on her own. A ride could break and kill her. She could get food poisoning, homesick, a flesh-eating fungus from a swimming pool … or a million other things that terrify me.

Or … she could feel the rush of a roller coaster. She could be dazzled by princesses and incredible fireworks displays. She could get her face painted and eat Mickey Mouse-shaped pancakes with her new friends. She could gain a sense of confidence away from me. She could spread her beautiful wings.

"I don't know if the place they're renting will have a washer and dryer, so pack enough underwear."

Morgan whips around, mouth in the shape of an O on a huge gasp. "I can go?"

I nod once. Before I can take a breath, she's in my arms, hugging me so hard it nearly squeezes tears from my eyes. "Daddy … thank you. Thank you. Thank you. I love you sooo much. You are the best dad ever!"

"Can I get that in writing?"

She pulls away.

I wipe her residual tears. "I'm going to give you a mile-long list of warnings and precautions I want you to take. You've heard them all before, but you have to let me say them again anyway."

"Absolutely. I'll pack and you do your dad thing." She retrieves her bag from under her bed.

I love this girl. She's my world. My hands will release her … set her free. But my heart can't let go, which means she will rip it from my chest and carry it with her forever. And I will wait for her to return … for my heart to return.

She packs. I preach.

Then she runs next door to tell Gabe to pack his bag too.

I. Am. A. Wreck.

CHAPTER FIFTEEN

Gracelyn

HE LET HER go.

I never expected Nate to let Morgan go. His shocking decision meant I had to let Gabe go too. I have no idea if Kyle and Emily would have said yes. Brother Dearest is probably looking down on me, tsking me at this very moment.

I set my microwave dinner on the table and pour a glass of wine. If I'm going to be irresponsible, I might as well go all out. Silence haunts me. I forgot what it's like to eat alone … to be alone.

Even when Gabe goes to a friend's house, Mr. Hans is here. I should embrace this moment, but it's oddly depressing. However, it's not a foreign feeling. I'm no stranger to loneliness. After my wedding debacle, I embraced it.

Surely I can handle four days of my old life.

After dinner, I take a walk along the beach, curling my toes in the damp sand while the harmonious waves of the tide crawl into the shore. Turning around, a mile or so down the coastline, I make my way back before the sun extinguishes for the night. I step onto the boardwalk and brush the sand from my feet, the creak of a board brings my gaze up.

Nate tips back a bottle of beer, eyeing me from the chair on his deck. I brush my hands together and make my way to the bottom of his stairs.

"You let her go."

Resting the bottle on the arm of the chair, he nods. "I let her go." He sounds … different. Monotone. Depressed.

While I, too, fretted over the decision, hence the reason I passed it off onto him, I think—I hope—it was the right one. I messaged my parents about it, of course, after he already left. They agreed it was the right thing to do.

I consider sharing this somewhat comforting information with Nate, but I'm not sure he's ready to hear it. "Night." I offer a tiny smile and head home to finish my bottle of wine and binge on Jamie—I mean—*Outlander.*

Popcorn.

Wine.

Bra off.

Jamie on.

By the end of the second episode, my wine is gone, my cheeks are flushed, and I'm feeling super relaxed.

Knock.

Knock.

Knock.

Knock …

The knocking continues at a slow but steady pace, like a drunk woodpecker.

"What … is … it?" I say to no one as I take the stairs slowly, like *I'm* drunk, but I'm not. I'm just … super relaxed.

No shits left to give.

I giggle at my squirrel brain. Then I giggle at my brain calling itself squirrel brain. Finally, I open the door with one hand while I hold what is now just the bottle of wine in my other hand.

"Nathaniel." I smile. It feels like a good smile. At least I think I can still feel my smile.

He doesn't look at my hair. Nope. He starts at my bare feet and works his way up my body—naked legs, fringed-edged denim booty shorts, and a black tank top. *Then* he fixes his gaze on my hair. Figures.

"Nope. Sorry. I'm still a redhead. Not your dead wife." I bite my lips together. Did I just say dead wife? Surely not. I continue, "Is that all you wanted?"

He narrows his eyes and cocks his head.

Enough with my hair already!

"What is that?" He reaches for the top of my head but stumbles over the threshold.

I grab his torso to steady him, but it makes me wobble a bit. Is he drunk? How irresponsible of him.

"What is what?"

Nate makes a second attempt to reach for the top of my head.

"Ouch!" My hand tries to stop him, but it's too late.

He chuckles, dangling my bra between us with several of my hairs stuck to the hook. "Your bra was hanging from your hair." He laughs a little more.

Yeah, he's intoxicated.

I snatch it from his hand and hide it behind my back … like he didn't just see it. I wrangled the murderous thing off during the first episode of *Outlander* and tossed it over my shoulder. It must have snagged on my hair.

"Are you drunk?"

He shakes his head. "No. Not drunk. Not sober enough to drive, but not drunk. You?" He grabs my wrist and lifts my hand, the one holding the bottle of wine.

"I'm not drunk. I'm just relaxed."

"I miss Morgan already." He frowns. It's an adorable frown. The really relaxed version of me wants to kiss it right off his face.

"And I can't check in with her because she doesn't have a phone because I'm a paranoid asshole dad who dreamed too big for reality."

"Want me to text Gabe to get an update?" I lift the bottle to my mouth and lean clear back. Shit ... it's empty. I glance over at the chair, just inside the living room, and make the terrible decision to toss the bottle onto the chair.

Crash!

It doesn't make it. Instead, it shatters on the tiled floor.

"Smooth ..." Nate lifts his eyebrows, studying the mess on the floor. "I think you cracked the tile."

"Oops. Shit." I cringe. "Welp," I sigh. "Good thing I know where the broom and dustpan are." I make a wide turn to avoid the broken glass with my bare feet and grab the broom and dustpan from the garage.

"I feel like I just helped you clean up a mess on this floor."

"You did." I sweep up the mess and squat next to Nate, who's holding the dustpan *again* to collect it.

He lifts his head, putting our faces a breath apart. "I don't think you're Jenna," he whispers. "I didn't kiss her that day in the kitchen."

My lips rub together, remembering that kiss.

"I don't have the emotional capacity to fall in love with you," I say, staring at his mouth for a second before dragging my already sluggish gaze to his eyes. "And I just don't want to. Love hurts too much."

"Then don't." He closes the tiny space and kisses me.

I drop the broom. He drops the dustpan.

Nate's hands frame my face, guiding me to standing while deepening the kiss. Afraid of the mess gathered at our feet, I break the kiss and glance down. He hooks his arm around my waist and lifts me up, taking a big step into the living room with its beige carpet and a blanket covered sofa.

He sits on it, positioning me to straddle his lap. I grin a second before kissing him. His hands settle on my hips for a long kiss. When I hum into it, he moves his hands to my ass, scooting me closer to him. Squirrel brain makes an attempt to focus on not dry humping my neighbor. It's just a kiss. We knew there would be a second kiss.

It's a really great second kiss. Technically, it's a third kiss, but since the glass disrupted the second kiss, I'm declaring this Kiss 2.1.

Kiss 2.1 is better than the original second kiss. Maybe it's his exploring tongue or his hands gripping my ass. Maybe it's my braless nipples hard and rubbing against his chest. But most likely, it's his erection pressed between my legs.

Do. Not. Dry. Hump. Him!

Squirrel brain knows what she's talking about.

I lift on to my knees to get a better angle—just at his mouth.

"Ouch!" I pull back.

Nate eases his grip on me. "What? I'm sorry. Did I do something?"

Leaning to the right, I pull my left leg up to look at my knee. Something sharp cut into it.

"What is—"

"Oh my god … get it off!" I flinch as if I can disconnect the rest of my body from my leg and the huge, thick, yellow toenail partially embedded into my skin. "Yuck! Get. It. Off!" I flick at it, but it doesn't move.

Nate laughs. "Hold still." He pinches the end of it and pulls it away. A drop of blood pools on my knee.

"Eww!" I fly off his lap and bolt into the kitchen, hopping up on the counter by the sink and turning the water on hot while I douse my leg with soap and scrub it with a sponge.

Nate saunters into the kitchen, still holding the weapon between his fingers. I nearly vomit. He drops it in the trash.

"Wash your hands! That's so disgusting. Who leaves their gnarly, razor sharp, fungus toenails on the sofa?"

He pumps the soap into his hand. I cease my scrubbing for a second to pump the foam soap three more times.

"Are we good? Will this suffice to remove the toenail fungus germs?" He smirks, scrubbing his hands in the other side of the sink.

"It punctured my skin. I should probably get a tetanus shot or something."

He bites his lips together and narrows his eyes at my frantic scrubbing motions while he dries his hands with a paper towel. "I think you've got it covered. It just nicked the skin."

"It was like a dagger in my kneecap!" I run my leg under the hot water. It burns, but I need to kill the bacteria, fungus, Ebola … whatever might have been living on that toenail.

Tearing off several more paper towels, Nate shuts off the water and guides my leg over the edge of the counter. His eyes find mine as he presses the towels to my knee—where the injury is undetectable. I try to keep a straight face after my meltdown over a toenail, but a minuscule grin pulls at my lips. Nate doesn't even try to hold back.

"I'm not sure he'll refund your deposit when he sees the cracked tile, but you might be able to make a case for calling things even if you tell him about the toenail and show him the extensive damage to your kneecap."

"Shut up." I roll my eyes.

He shifts to the side and nestles himself between my spread legs, keeping one hand pressed to the towel on my knee while his other hand moves a few strands of hair away from my eyes.

"I'm …" I glance away. "Sobering up a bit. Now I'm a little …" My teeth dig into my bottom lip and my nose wrinkles.

"You're a little what …" He brushes his lips over my cheek, letting his hand slide to the back of my head.

I draw in a shaky breath and whisper, "Nervous."

"Have *you* gone a decade without having sex?"

I pull back an inch, eyes narrowed. "No. Have you?"

He nods slowly. It makes my chest hurt.

"Why?"

He lifts one shoulder in a shrug. "Morgan. When she turned two, we left. And we haven't been back to Madison in eight years. Traveling with a young daughter doesn't bestow that many opportunities to be intimate. And never staying in one place very long makes it even harder."

"So … not once? Not a quick hookup after she was in bed? Nothing?"

He chuckles. "Nothing."

"Do you even …" I can't say it. I'm not sure why I even started to ask the question. Of course, he does. Right? Surely all men do.

His face turns a vulnerable shade of pink as he scratches his forehead and tips his chin down. "Uh … yeah. I've done *that*." He sets the wad of paper towels aside and fiddles with the clasp of my white gold bracelet that Brandon gave me.

Surely my dead boyfriend has something to say now. I wait

for his voice in my head—although it never sounds like it's in my head. The clarity and volume always sound like he's in the same room where anyone else in the room could easily hear him.

"How's your book coming along?"

Nate's lips corkscrew as he continues to fiddle with the bracelet, head bowed. "I'm trying to figure out how to end it. I thought the ending might be our arrival back in Madison at the end of summer. Sometimes I wonder if the book ends when Morgan goes off to college, but I'd have to cut a lot from the book if that were the case, and only include major events and highlights."

"Will Gabe, Mr. Hans, and I be in it? Will we make the cut?"

With a grin sliding up his face, he lifts his head. "I'm not sure about making the cut, but all three of you have made an appearance."

"What's my name?"

He gives me a funny *duh* look. I recognize it as Gabe's resting face. "Gracelyn."

"What happened to changing the names to protect the identities of the innocent?"

"That would require you to be innocent."

"Jerk." I narrow my eyes.

He smiles a second before kissing me again. It's not an upgraded version of our second kiss. It's a third kiss. A standalone. And it's slow, like the slide of his hands up my bare legs.

Slow like the brush of his thumbs along my inner thighs.

Slow like the need building between my legs.

Maybe he's gone a decade without having sex, but these full

lips of his sure do know how to kiss. I should be better at this … less nervous. Yet, I'm not. He shows no lack of confidence.

I'm a hot mess.

Insecurities make a single file line at the door to my conscience, each with a case to plead. The last time I had sex, my body was better, my confidence less wavering, my direction clearer. Even without opening the door, I can hear the chattering insecurities.

More cellulite.

Less perky breasts.

Emerging red dots along my chest—cherry angiomas according to the internet.

My ass isn't as firm.

I have pubic hair that's fairly maintained, but I'm not sure it's groomed into the right configuration. Maybe Nate prefers no pubic hair. Well, he's in for a surprise.

Does he have pubic hair? Michael always shaved his area.

Did he bring over a condom?

Does he assume I'm on the pill? I'm not.

Do I worry about STDs with a man who hasn't had sex in over a decade?

Will we have sex right here?

I didn't make my bed this morning.

Surely he won't think we can resume on the toenail-infested sofa.

Maybe we'll lose our pants right here and just go to town. That's what Jamie and Claire do on *Outlander*.

It's pretty hot.

Anal … oh god … what if he's into anal. I read that it's quite common. I don't have lube. I assume I would need to douche, but I have not douched that hole. Actually, I haven't douched the other hole either. My doctor recommends against it.

I pull away, breathless and burning up. It's not my typical, premenopausal hot flash. It's a Nate-induced one. "My brain is ready to explode."

His eyebrows knit together. "Are you overthinking this?"

"No." I rub my lips together. "Yes." I drop my chin and shake my head. "Five minutes ago, I overthought it. Now, I'm just in crazy town."

"We can talk about it."

"No … god no." I laugh as more heat pools in my cheeks.

"There's nothing to worry about. You promised to not fall in love with me. I'm going to return the favor. If we become good friends, we can be pen pals when I leave. Morgan and I have lots of pen pals around the world."

He bought condoms … and now he's suggesting we be pen pals?

I'm thinking about the hairstyle of my muff, and he's thinking about stationary and stamps. This gap might be too wide to bridge.

"Wow …" I trace the logo on his T-shirt with my finger. "If that kiss didn't make us friends, I fear making it on your pen pal list might be an impossible feat."

He wraps his hand around mine, bringing my tracing finger to his lips and giving it a soft kiss. "I fear the haircut fiasco momentarily derailed our friendship."

God … he's so sexy. Not Jamie sexy. Nathaniel Hunt brings his own brand of sexy, and I'm completely bewitched.

Six weeks.

I can do six weeks.

Bewitched doesn't have to lead to love. Kissing my neighbor doesn't break my man ban if we're not technically even friends.

Letting him keep my left hand next to his lips, I comb my right hand through his tragically short hair. "Would showing you my other tattoos put me back in the friendship zone?"

He perks an eyebrow. "I'm inclined to say yes."

"Okay."

He releases my hand and takes a step backward. I slide up my shirt, keeping my braless breasts covered while showing him the tattoo two inches beneath my armpit (usually covered by a bra).

"It's a stemmed cherry." He chuckles. "Is your third tattoo a halved avocado on your ass? Or is it a salted pretzel?"

"No." I grin, pushing my tank top down.

He crosses his arms over his chest. Nate in a fitted tee with gray cargo shorts that hang perfectly from his narrow hips does it for me. *He* does it for me.

"Why a stemmed cherry?"

"I like them."

He rolls his lips together. "I see. You're going to need to elaborate."

"I was twenty when I got them. When you're twenty, liking cherries is a solid reason to get a tattoo of one."

"Fine. I'll buy it. Looks like we're one tattoo away from the friend zone."

"I fear you're going to be disappointed. I had to balance things out." I lift my shirt on the other side—same area below my armpit.

Nate's smile does funny things to my stomach and makes my heart race in my chest. When he laughs, I want to kiss his lips again, call it our first kiss, and promise a million more before he leaves in six weeks.

"Let me guess ... you like elephants."

"Very much. Maybe even more than cherries."

He runs his finger over my three simple elephants. Small. Medium. Large. Even the large one isn't very big. They're interlocked—tail to trunk. And they hide nicely under my bra when I'm wearing one.

"Hockey. Cherries. Elephants. Got it." Instead of withdrawing his finger from my tattoo, he feathers it down my side.

My heart instructs my lungs to stop breathing. I think they know on their own. It's impossible to breathe with him touching me.

"No tattoos for you?" I manage to squeak four words without using oxygen. I release my shirt, but his hand stays on my side, holding my breath hostage.

"Nah. I've thought about it, but I think I've waited too long. You have to get started at a younger age, when choosing what to get permanently inked into your skin is as easy as a favorite fruit or animal." He ghosts his fingers back up my shirt to my three elephants—and arrestingly close to my bare breast.

It's a subtle show of intimacy—a patient seduction. Maybe he hasn't had sex in more than a decade, but Nathaniel Hunt knows how to turn a woman on, and it's effortless.

"Unmarred skin." I swallow hard. "That's intimidating. Or boring." I relinquish a grin that wavers between smirky and nervous.

Hand close to my boob!

His confident smile takes over his face. "I have a birthmark."

"Where?"

He leans into me, teasing his lips along my ear as he whispers, "You'll have to look for it."

I fist his shirt, pushing him away just enough to put us face-to-face. "You're a tease. I think you're hiding your insecurities under this false confidence." Giving him another shove, I hop off the counter and head back to the broken wine bottle mess.

"What are my insecurities?" He follows me.

Retrieving the dustpan full of glass and the broom, I pad back into the kitchen, giving him a tightlipped smile as I pass him. "Hmm … let's see. I think you're feigning confidence." I empty the glass and return the broom and dustpan to the garage.

"Feigning? What makes you think that?" he asks as soon as I close the garage door.

I lean back against it and cross my arms over my chest, mirroring his stance against the island. "Because you don't have a slice of pizza tattooed on your bicep or a hockey puck on your calf. Because you said it yourself: things matter more now than they did twenty years ago. So you steal kisses. You look at me like I'm the girl in science class that caught your attention, but when you touch me, I feel your insecurities. Erectile dysfunction is nothing to be ashamed of. You're not the young, virile man you once were. I'm not the limber seductress I used to be." I shrug.

"Wow …" He rears his head back and presses a hand to his chest like clutching his grandmother's pearls. "I feel a little violated. When did this go from a kiss to ED? You're skipping a lot of bases. You're assuming I'm planning on having sex with you. We've known each other a month. I …" He leaves his jaw hanging open while shaking his head slowly. "I don't know what to say." He pops his lips several times, eyes wide and rolled to the side. "I think I'd better go. I've tempted you too much. You need to cool off a bit."

It's official.

I'm in trouble.

"First, you know damn well I'm cool like a cucumber or your sex drive that's been frozen in time. Second, I do have to work in the morning because I'm a real adult with a real job. Third, I have to finish my *Outlander* episode. So … yeah, you'd better get home and slip into your old man flannel PJs, grab your Sports Illustrated Swimsuit Edition and bottle of lube." I flash a toothy grin, feeling pride swelling in my awakened ego.

Nate's grin shows commendable restraint. Then he rubs his lips together, wetting them. The full smile breaks out seconds later, one increment at a time, like a flower blooming or the sun waking up on a clear morning. "I sleep in the nude."

"Me too."

I don't. Nope. I wear boy-shorts, ratty tees, and fluffy socks. In the winter, I sleep in a full sweat suit, hood up.

Nate's gaze takes a leisurely stroll along my body before he pushes off the counter. "It's been fun. Night, Elvis."

Keeping a safe distance, I follow him to the door. "Night, neighbor."

CHAPTER SIXTEEN

Nathaniel

MORGAN CALLS ME using Mr. Hans's cellphone the following afternoon. I try to play it cool, but again, she breaks my heart with how grown-up she is way too early.

"We spent the whole day on rides. I went on the Tower of Terror, and this ride that makes you feel like you're flying. I got my picture taken with all the princesses and Goofy too. Dad! It's amazing here. You were so wrong. How could you not know that I'd love it here? Gabe rides with Mr. Hans on most of the rides, and I sit with Hunter. Dad, she's so cool. She has a boyfriend. A boyfriend! So I've been asking her lots of questions so you don't have to pretend you don't know the answers when I ask you."

Kill. Me. Now.

"I'm glad you're having a good time. I miss you." I cringe. Is it okay to say that? Or am I smothering her? I don't know anymore.

"I miss you too. I wish you could have come too. You'd love it. Have you been on a roller coaster before? They're amazing!"

I laugh. "Yeah, I've been on a roller coaster. Some people are scared of them."

"Hunter is. So I ride with Gabe. You have to be forty-eight inches. I'm good. Tall like you, Dad."

I lean back on the sofa and set my notebooks off to the side as a grin forms along my face. Of course, my daughter loves roller coasters. I love them too and so did Jenna. She's the product of two very adventurous people. I imagine Jenna giving me an approving nod for letting our little girl spread her wings and soar on a new adventure—even if it's without me.

"Your mom loved roller coasters too."

"She did? I knew it. I've always known she was awesome."

"Yeah ..." I whisper as her words drive into my heart like a freight train.

"I have to go. We're going to dinner and then to watch a parade and fireworks. I'm *so* excited!"

"I'm excited for you. Love you."

"Love you too, Daddy."

Daddy ...

I melt. "Bye."

After she disconnects, I toss my phone aside, right as Gracelyn arrives home, taking her usual stripping position under the balcony and behind the bushes. A better man would turn a blind eye and let her do her thing in privacy.

I'm a lot of things, but after last night, I'm not sure I'm a better man. Confirming my lack of chivalry, I make my way to the side of the house, finding my best smile for when she glances up after shoving her clothes in the plastic bag.

"Elvis." I lean against the side of my house, crossing one leg over the other while slipping my hands into the pockets of my shorts—refusing to look like I'm doing anything else but watching her.

She frowns, hugging the plastic bag to her chest. "Pervert."

"Bird-watching."

"There are no birds in these bushes."

"Not yet, but bird-watching involves patience."

There it is … the grin she doesn't want to give me. I'll steal everything I can—grins … kisses.

"Turn around."

"Why? It's no different than wearing a bikini. That's what you said. Right?"

Huffing out a quick breath, she rolls her eyes, almost as expertly as Morgan. She steps out with more confidence than I sense she's really feeling. Basic white bra and orange boy-short-style underwear the same orange color as her hair. She looks like Halloween a few months early.

"Total perv …" She stomps up the stairs.

"I'm not even sorry."

When she reaches the top, she pauses. "Here's your bird." She flips me the middle finger without looking back.

I laugh as she shuts the door and slings the curtains shut. Retracing my steps, I grab the mail out of the mailbox and take a seat on the porch rocking chair. There are several letters for Morgan from pen pals and a postcard to both of us from Swayze, the nanny I hired shortly after Morgan was born. The only girl, besides Morgan, I've kissed since Jenna died. Well … and now Gracelyn is on that short list. My relationship with Swayze was complicated—life-changing.

I've always wanted only the very best for her. And as I see her two little girls, both with her blond hair and blue eyes, playing on the beach in Mexico, I'm reminded just how fragile life really is, how some loves never die. It gives me hope that this life of mine has more to give than I probably realize.

Morgan and Nate,

Hope you're finding magic.

~Swayze, Griff, Eloise, & Harley

Always a simple postcard.

Always with the same four-word greeting. *Hope you're finding magic.*

I usually return the sentiment, without words, just a postcard with a picture of Morgan. I think she knows why I have nothing more to say. She knows I lost too much. She knows her happiness is my happiness. Every postcard from her is a reminder that I did the right thing.

I let go.

"My pen pal competition?"

I glance up. Gracelyn in a white sundress with yellow straps and yellow stitching along the bodice brings me out of the past and all that I lost.

"Maybe." I set the mail on the round table by my chair. "Nice to see you dressed."

"Said no man ever." She ascends the steps in her yellow flip-flops.

"How was your Scottish porn last night?"

She smirks. "Jamie never disappoints."

"Do you think your obsession with this Jamie guy is the real reason for your man ban? Unrealistic expectations."

She twists her lips to the side and tucks her hair behind her ears. "Obsession is your word, not mine. And my man ban was born of bad luck, not a hot guy in a kilt."

When she turns around to sit in the other rocker, I wrap my hand around her wrist and pull her to me, justifying it with nothing more than a look. Guiding her onto my lap with her back against my chest, I slide my hands around her waist and rest my chin on her shoulder.

"This feels *friendly*," she whispers.

"Well, I know about the cherry and elephants. And you

know I wear flannels to bed—only I don't. So I guess all that's left is to decide if you'll go to dinner with a single dad who *doesn't* wear a kilt."

"What did you have in mind?" She leans her head back, giving me access to brush my lips along her neck. As I dot slow kisses from her shoulder to her ear, she covers my hands with hers, lacing our fingers together.

I don't know why this feels so easy.

So fated.

So unavoidable.

"A patio with a view, good wine, an insane amount of appetizers, and dessert even when we're stuffed."

She turns her head, smiling as my mouth finds hers. Her hand presses to my cheek. It's slow like us.

Destination unknown.

Fortuity.

When she pulls back, I take a minute to remind myself she is my here and now. An experience. A beautiful memory in the making. She's not Daisy or Jenna. I will leave. She will stay. And that's okay.

"You had me at good wine."

CHAPTER SEVENTEEN

Gracelyn

IT'S NOT AN ocean view. It's a breathtaking garden with floral covered trellises, secluded tables adorned with candles, good wine, and appetizers that look like works of art.

"You do well."

"Well?" Nate refills my wine glass.

"The menu didn't have prices. I know what that means."

A hint of sadness steals his expression. "I did fine—but not until I was much older and secured a job as an anatomy professor at the university. I told you about my hand-me-down skates. Jenna had money. Family money."

I take a sip of wine. "I almost had money."

He grins. "All but the Powerball number?"

"If only … That's still good money, though … all the numbers but the Powerball." I laugh. "No. I had two opportunities to not live paycheck to paycheck. As soon as I finished my undergrad for med school, I dropped out. Then I was seconds from saying 'I do' to Michael, president of an investment firm in Boise. I like living on the edge. Savings accounts and IRAs bore me."

"So boring." He spoons more food onto my plate. I'm stuffed and we're still on appetizers. "I grew up poor, but my mom had an affair with a rich man. My goals were to not ever be so poor that I wasn't sure if I'd have three meals a day, but not so rich that I'd sleep with another man's wife—like morals and decency didn't apply to me."

My nose wrinkles. "I'm sorry."

"It's fine. She came back. Things worked out. It's a small scar compared to other events like losing my best friend at such a young age."

"Sorry," I repeat.

"No. Please … let me change the subject. I'm not at all looking for sympathy. I'm just …" He shakes his head. "Oversharing."

"Not oversharing. I'm asking all the wrong questions. Not that I'm implying there is such a thing as too much information in a relationship, but ours is different. Maybe we save the heavy stuff for pen pal status …" I tap my fork on my lower lip. "That is … if I make pen pal status, which really should be email status. However, I kinda dig the old-fashioned handwritten letter, envelope, and stamp. The forced patience that comes with snail mail. The race to the mailbox to see if you've received a letter. I can't remember the last time I waited for something with any sort of anticipation that wasn't coming from Amazon."

"Well …" He sighs and shrugs. "I hope you make it that far."

"Me too, but I've suffered worse disappointment in my life. So don't think that you can lord this over me. I won't be asking for your address."

His eyebrows inch up his head. "There you go again … making crazy assumptions. It would be a P.O. box, not my actual address. I imagine you could cross the line into a stalker."

"Says the creepy guy who watches me out his window."

He points his knife at me for a few seconds before cutting through a candied Brussel sprout. "I can't figure out why you don't change your clothes at work."

"It's a hairy place." I divert my gaze to my plate. "Just … so much hair circulating in the air. It's just better to do it right before going inside."

"But you're riding in your vehicle."

"I cover the seat."

"But—"

"Seriously? Am I really getting the third degree over this when you clearly seem to enjoy my current stripping protocol?"

"True. It's rather titillating."

"You mean arousing." I peek up at him.

"Possibly."

Over the next two hours, we finish only a fraction of the food ordered, get a sack full of leftovers to go, and take the long way home because it's an enjoyable night and the breeze feels so intoxicating.

"Don't fuck up my streak."

I whip my head toward him just before getting out of the car after we pull into the driveway.

"Okay, Mr. Vulgar. What exactly does that mean?"

"Let me get your door. You may have forgotten how to act on a date, but I haven't."

I rest my hands on the sack of leftovers and bite my lips together, patiently waiting for his chivalrous self to open my door.

He opens it, takes the sack, and locks the car after shutting my door. Before I have a chance to hug my arms to my body, he clasps my hand and leads me to his door. I think going inside is a bad idea. It's been too … everything, but mostly too perfect. I don't want to mess it up with a stray toenail or my nerves getting the best of me again. My ability to refuse his silent offer dies along with all other words. Again, I can't think or breathe when we're touching.

"So …" I fold my hands in front of me as he sticks the leftovers in the fridge. "I had a nice night. Thank you so much for dinner."

He shuts the fridge door and retraces his steps toward me.

"It was good." Here it comes—my nervous mumbling continues. "The company was good too."

Nate stops in front of me, studying me with a mysterious grin like I'm thoroughly amusing him.

I swallow hard and wait for him to say something … do something, but he's much more interested in making my nerves reach an unhealthy level by *not* saying or doing anything.

"Say something." I stare at his chest, a safe zone.

"I feel like you're getting ready to call it a night, but I'm not done with you yet."

Gulp …

"I know you bought condoms." I say those five words, but they come out as Iknowyouboughtcondoms! A brand-new word. An SOS of sorts.

"What?" He furrows his brow.

See. One word.

My nose wrinkles and I glance up at him. "Morgan told me you bought condoms. She said you said they were for Mr. Hans, but we both know that's not true. And maybe you have other potential pen pals I don't know about, and maybe you bought them for one of them. I'm just saying …" My words slow and fade into a whisper. "I know you bought condoms."

How does he remain so unaffected? So cool? When I asked—without saying the actual words—about him masturbating, he showed signs of being human by dropping his gaze and blushing ever so slightly.

With a slight nod, he nibbles his bottom lip. "Yeah … did she also mention she gave him the condoms?"

"Seriously?" I chuckle.

"Yes. I was outside talking to him on the deck, and she ran outside and gave him the box with a 'Here. My dad got you these.' He gave me a wide-eyed look."

I giggle more. "What did you do?"

He scrubs his hands over his face. "What could I do? I went along with it, and said I hoped they were the right ones."

My laughter settles deep into my belly, making it hard to breathe. "Wh-what did you s-say when he … gave them back?" I press my hand to his chest to keep from falling on my ass with my giggle fit.

"That's the thing … he's never given them back to me."

"What?" My other hand finds his chest too as I collapse into it.

"I'm glad you find this funny." He gathers my hair into a small ponytail and tugs it, forcing me to look at him and his frown.

My laughter dies from my chest compressing to his and his tugging of my hair. I feel it in places that shouldn't be connected to my hair follicles. "Stop looking at my mouth unless you're going to ki—"

It's a nip, more than an actual kiss. His teeth capture my bottom lip, just to shut me up. He sucks it into his mouth. A moan cuts through the air, and it takes me a moment to realize it's mine. The kiss turns into my hands clutching his shirt. He releases my hair, sliding his hands down my back. One hand grabs my ass, the other hand slides between us, pausing at my ribs for a few seconds before sliding up an inch.

There's that moan of mine again. This time the slide of his thumb over my nipple elicits my automatic reaction. The fabric is thin, and I'm not wearing a bra because of the cut of the dress. He squeezes my ass again … and again. The short skirt works its way up until his hand cups my ass over my panties. As his tongue slides against mine, his hand slides into the back of my panties, grabbing a handful of flesh.

It all happens so fast. I guess that's the speed two people go when it's been *so* long since having sex.

More moans.

His other hand moves to my backside.

He's lifting me up.

My legs wrap around him.

Several steps.

A wall hits my back.

His erection pushes between my legs and my bunched-up dress.

One strap of my dress falls off my shoulder, and he has my bare breast in his hand, kneading it, pinching my nipple, and driving me fucking insane!

"Condoms …" he mumbles against my neck, biting and sucking my flesh. "We … have … to … find … them."

I agree.

That will require him to stop kissing me. That will require him to put me down. And right now, we're in a good place—specifically his cock is in a good place, causing intense pressure and friction in the most perfect spot.

"O-K … in…" I shamelessly grind against him "… just…"

holy crap that feels good "… a … minute."

There's a special message system going between my vagina and my nipples. It translates into confetti, trumpets, and a high probability of fireworks.

He dips his head and flicks his tongue over my nipple before his mouth completely covers it.

"Nate …" I arch my back away from the wall as he presses me to it—pressing *there.*

Oh god … glorious THERE!

"Fuck … we've got to stop." His mouth works its way from my breast to my shoulder. He bites it playfully before resting his forehead on it.

I rock my pelvis against him.

He thrusts in response.

"Gracelyn … I…" another thrust "…need … more."

I do too, but I've never been opposed to short-term goals. They're my specialty more than long-term goals. If he lets me orgasm now, I'll be in a better frame of mind to get the condoms.

"Torture …"

Thrust …

Thrust …

Thrust …

He pleads his case while gripping my ass and moving me right where he needs me. And as luck would have it—*exactly* where I want to be.

No!

He pulls away, easing me to my feet. Our labored breaths fill the fraction of space between us as my legs decide if they're going to hold me upright.

No joke. If the slightest breeze crosses my clit, my eyes will roll back in my head with an orgasm. I'm *that* close. I attempt to play it cool, pulling up the strap to my dress before smoothing down the skirt. My panties have been thrust into no-man's-land. I'll deal with them later.

"We have to go find them."

I nod, only partially coherent. I'm so drunk on Nate right now, I'd never be able to walk a straight line.

"K." I nod again several times. "Where?"

"Your place. Maybe in his bathroom." He grabs my hand and drags me next door. "I'll check the bathroom; you check drawers in the kitchen and living room." He grabs my face and kisses me hard, stoking the fire. I wrap my leg around his leg, looking for any friction.

Seriously, anything!

"Go." He pulls away.

I look in all the side table drawers and all the kitchen drawers.

Nothing.

It would have been quicker to just drive to the closest convenience store.

I hear banging of drawers and clattering of things being riffled through in the bathroom. When I peek inside, Nate looks at my reflection in the mirror, a mix of pain and desperation.

"No luck?" I cringe.

He turns and attacks me again. His hands holding my face. His tongue frantically exploring the inside of my mouth.

There has to be something we can use. Plastic wrap. A sandwich bag. *Something!*

This … *this* is how even really smart, mature, levelheaded women get pregnant. They go way too long without sex and find something better than a Scottish, kilt-wearing hottie. They (I) dry hump a man who hasn't had sex in over ten years.

There's no way this ends well. He's going to rip off my clothes and deposit ten years' worth of sperm inside of me. Yep. Here we go ...

Nate shoves down both straps to my dress and ravages my breasts. He keeps them distracted with his mouth while his hands not so patiently pull off my panties.

It's not that I didn't go through a time in my life where I dreamed of having children. I did. That time passed. My womb is no longer taking applications. I just inherited a ten-year-old. And I have a super important but rather shitty job.

Lives depend on me being responsible. I can't die. I can't forget to get Gabe registered for fall classes. And I can't let my temporary neighbor deposit millions of half babies into my vagina.

"Oh boy ..." I push away, out of breath, *really* turned on, and freaked out of my mind. A few labored laughs escape as I continue to step back, going in reverse until I hit the threshold to the kitchen.

A safe six feet away.

I wrinkle my nose, feeling equally as frustrated, as I tuck my breasts back into my dress and pull my panties up my legs. Nate looks nothing short of tortured—an animal desperate for its first meal after months of hibernation.

"I'm not on birth control. I don't want my first letter to you to be an ultrasound picture of tonight."

He catches his breath and nods once while resting his hands on his hips and dropping his gaze to his feet. "You're right. I'm just ... It felt ..."

"Yes. And yes." I blow out a long breath and grin. "I know. Trust me … I know."

Nate threads his fingers through his hair, closing his eyes and tipping his head back. "Fucking condoms … I … I should have just told Morgan they were mine."

I take a few seconds to commit this moment to memory. My female psyche has been weakened over time from a roller coaster of ups and downs—acceptance, love, hope, rejection, disdain, abandonment. As often as I tell myself that things like wrinkles, great hair, and perfectly toned muscles don't define me, I'm often crippled by self-doubt. Just because I've lost hope … lost the desire to find lasting love, doesn't mean I'm immune to the sheer elation of someone desperately wanting my touch … my kisses … my body. So I'm doing my best to pause time and *feel* this moment, to imprint the need and anguish he's feeling because he can't have me the way he *needs* me.

Tomorrow and a million tomorrows after that, Nate won't need me, but *now* he does. It's hard to explain how feeling needed means more than feeling loved. I realized this after Brandon died. It wasn't just love; it was more. I needed him. Humans don't function well when their needs are not met. I have not been okay. For nearly two decades, I have *not* been okay.

"Thank you," I whisper.

Nate pulls his hands out of his hair, letting them flop to his sides. "What can you possibly be thanking me for?"

Hugging my arms to my chest. I roll my lips together and shrug. "It's hard to explain, but it's big. It's sincere. And I won't ever forget it."

He grunts the hint of a laugh before blowing out a slow breath. "I'm going home to take a cold shower."

"Dinner was phenomenal, but the company was indescribable."

The residual disappointment and anguish melts from his face. "Agreed."

"Night, Nate."

"Goodnight." He turns and sulks out the door.

I lean my back against the wall, close my eyes, and smile. It feels … Well, I'm not sure what word to use. It's just incredible to *feel.*

After slipping into my not-so-sexy tee and boy-shorts, I brush my teeth and wash my face. Then I contemplate reading a book or watching a show.

The book wins.

I look for my Kindle in my purse, but it's not there. I check a few other places before opening my nightstand drawer.

"You've got to be kidding me." In my drawer is the box of condoms and a sticky note with Mr. Hans's chicken scratches on it:

I think you'll need these before I will. Dare I say have fun?

I'm not sure why he gave them to me instead of returning them to Nate, probably to mess with both of us.

It's ten-thirty. I'm ready for bed. Makeup is off. And Nate's probably had a cold shower or done other things to remedy his situation.

"Just go to sleep," I tell myself.

Ugh … I never listen, and that's what brings me to Nate's door at a quarter to eleven. It's dark. There's no sign that he's still awake. I should go. I turn, heading back to the stairs. Then I turn back around.

After doing this so much that I'm dizzy, I ring the doorbell.

I can't. Go!

I run down the stairs with my bare feet and scantily clad body—total chicken. I hear his door creek open, and I freeze. It's really dark. If I hold stone still, maybe he won't see me and go back inside assuming it was some young kid playing a prank.

"At least leave a plate of cookies if you're going to ring my doorbell and run, Elvis."

"Shit …" I whisper, turning around slowly.

He walks down the stairs, bare chest, bare feet, and low-hanging jogging shorts.

"I was uh …" I hold up the box of condoms. "Just dropping this off. Mr. Hans put them in my nightstand drawer. I had no idea. I was looking for my Kindle, not condoms."

He stops in front of me.

"So … here." I shove them into his chest. "That's all. Night." When I let go, they drop to the ground.

He studies me like the condoms don't exist. "How do you feel about late-night dips?"

I glance out at the water. "Not too good."

"I agree. It's a terrible idea. We should definitely do it."

"Wha—Nate!"

He bends down, tosses me over his shoulder, and races to the water.

"No! Nate! This is a terrible id—" Cold water fills my ears in a whoosh as he submerges us.

"C-cold …" I say when he drags me to the surface with

him. Nate warms me with his mouth on mine. I might drown, but it will be in this kiss, not the eternity of water embracing us.

"Jerk ..." I try to push away when he releases me to catch a breath.

His response is to pull me back to him for another kiss. My fight washes away with the tide, leaving me with my arms and legs wrapped around him. At some point, I forget where we are, losing all sense of direction and time. He becomes the only north I need.

Goose bumps scatter along my skin from the night's soft breath. Capable arms carry me up the beach as he kisses my lips, along my jaw, and down my neck.

"Don't hate me," he whispers, releasing me to my feet.

"What are you doin—NATE!"

He sprays me with the hose, and the water is colder than the ocean. I shudder, hugging myself as he quickly rinses himself off.

"T-t-towel ..."

"No towel. Sorry." He chuckles, grabbing my hand and pulling me behind him, making a slight detour to grab the dropped box of condoms. "I didn't exactly plan this, but we need to get rid of our wet clothes." Stopping at his door, he traps the condoms under his arm and grabs the hem of my tee.

I stiffen my arms to stop him from peeling off my shirt. "Sorry." I release a nervous laugh. "Instinct. I suppose you saw them earlier."

He dips his head and brushes his lips over mine. "I did."

I relax my arms, letting him work my soaked shirt up my torso. It lands on the deck with a slap.

He kisses me.

I remind myself he's not mine.

His patient hands work my shorts down my legs, leaving me naked and incredibly vulnerable.

He kisses me.

I remind myself he's not mine.

My shaky hands pull off his shorts and briefs.

He kisses me.

I remind myself he's not mine.

With the box of condoms in one hand and mine in his other hand, he guides me into the house, up the stairs, and to his bedroom.

Maybe my own insecurities obscure my ability to see him as anything short of perfect, but he touches me with steady hands, confident lips, and a strength that tips my world on its side.

A breathless anticipation settles into my chest when he pulls away, leaving me naked in the center of his bed as he rolls on a condom. How is he not shaking? I'm certain the only sound in the room is my body quivering right down to my bones.

"You're so sexy …" He grins, pressing his hands to my knees.

I smile.

"And beautiful."

He's not mine. He's not mine. He's not mine.

I pretend he's a foster puppy—cute, playful, irresistible, but temporary. The cuteness will wear off. The playfulness will turn into destruction, and the irresistible part will turn into responsibility. I don't want to be responsible for anyone's happiness, not even Gabe's. I'm just trying to keep him safe, fed, and educated for the next eight years. He can go find his own happiness after that.

"What if you don't remember?" I smirk as he parts my bent knees and glides his hands along my thighs.

"What if I don't remember how to have sex?" It's too dark to clearly see the expression on his face. He's nothing more than a silhouette, but I imagine the bend of his lips conveys complete confidence.

"Well ..." I can't hide the break in my voice, my nerves cracking my words. "I'm sure you can remember where things go, but there's an art to this."

He settles between my legs, propped up on his arms, hovering above me like an animal trapping its prey. With every dip of his head to kiss along my hip bone, my stomach, my breasts, he taunts me. My breaths quicken, and my hips lift from the bed, searching for him.

"I'll let you decide later," he whispers along my neck as a finger slides between my legs.

My breath catches, and I release it with a soft moan just before his mouth captures mine. It's slow like my fingers threading through his hair, like his body lowering to mine, like the way he fills me.

I don't expect such patience. He wasn't patient earlier when we couldn't find the condoms. It's been a decade. I expect things to move along rather quickly.

They don't.

Now that we're here in the moment, he takes his time. Two tangled bodies. The glow of the moon and the stars filtering through the thin curtains just enough that I can see the glint in his eyes when he rolls us over, me straddling him. His hands slide to my breasts. I cover them with mine, closing my eyes as we move slowly together.

CHAPTER EIGHTEEN

"CAN I ASK you a question?"

"Hmm?" He hums in my ear with his chest to my back, our legs scissored, and his arms enveloping me.

Reality remains shrouded in darkness. I'm not sure what time it is, but he seems fine with me staying here, so I don't think about my wet clothes on the porch or anyone holding me accountable in the morning.

"Are you still mad that she's gone … Jenna? I mean … grief is automatic. It's the normal emotion that fades over time, but the anger lasts. At least … it does for me."

"Well, it hasn't been that long since your brother and his wife died. I've had a lot longer to deal with the loss of my wife."

I should drop it. It's pretty weird that I brought up his dead wife after having sex with him for the first time. Does she talk to him like Brandon talks to me? Well, he hasn't in a while, but I know it's only a matter of time before he weighs in on this bad idea.

"What do you think happens after we die? I mean … no one knows for sure, so it's okay to have an opinion, a guess."

Nate doesn't say anything, doesn't move. Maybe he's asleep. I twist my neck to glance back at him. He's not asleep.

"Is this conversation too heavy?" My nose scrunches.

His head inches side to side, eyes slightly narrowed. "No.

It's … interesting."

I maneuver to face him, resting my head on the pillow. "I think so too. Most people don't want to talk about death, Heaven, Hell, ghosts …" I throw that out there. Why not? It doesn't have to mean that I believe in them, that I hear my dead boyfriend's voice, that I sometimes wonder if he's watching me—shaking his head and rolling his eyes that I'm forty-one and single.

"Or reincarnation …" He feathers his fingers down my arm, following it with his gaze.

I smile. "I like the idea of reincarnation. I like when I see someone I *know* I've never met, but something just feels familiar. I like déjà vu—moments that have no explanation in your brain, but something … your heart … your soul … just knows."

"My …" Nate presses his lips together.

"Your?" I press my palm to his cheek, tracing his bottom lip with my thumb.

He kisses it, bringing his gaze back up to meet mine. "Nothing."

The words "don't hold back" and "just tell me" die on the tip of my tongue. I'm holding back. I'm not telling him things. If we were in a different place in our lives, at a different time, with a million miles of open road in front of us, I would tell him. I would want him—need him—to know everything.

"I should go." I share a sad smile.

He slides his hands over my hip, resting it on my bare ass. "Why?"

Curling my lips together, I shrug. "I don't know. It just seemed like the right thing to say." I chuckle.

He leans in and presses his lips to my forehead. "You *should* go," he whispers. "I have to be up early in the morning."

"Oh." I stiffen, suddenly feeling like I've overstayed my welcome. "You do? Sorry." I start to pull away.

He tightens his grip on my ass and laughs with his lips still pressed to my forehead. "No. I don't. It just seemed like the right thing to say."

"Jerk …" I shove his chest.

He chuckles, grabbing my arms and pinning them above my head as he rolls on top of me, ravaging my mouth until I surrender the fight. As I relax, he eases his hold on me and works his lips down my body, kissing, biting, laving every inch of skin.

I keep my arms outstretched above my head, close my eyes, and bite my bottom lip as he drapes my legs over his shoulders and proves he's an expert who needs no practice.

"God … Nate …" I grab his hair and keep him *there* for roughly eternity.

A HALF-EMPTY BED greets me in the morning.

No note.

No fresh picked flowers.

No coffee and toast.

I'm glad. Really … I am. Notes, flowers, and food fall under the realm of courting and wooing. We're neighbors having sex. No need to wrap the situation in Christmas lights and adorn it with a glittery star.

A grin slides up my face as I climb out of bed and stretch. I pad into the bathroom.

"Oh my god …" I cringe. Is that salt on my face or just

excessive eye crusties? And my hair!

Note to self: a dip in the ocean followed by lots of sex equals a hair catastrophe. I *wish* this were just a little bedhead. It's been many years since I've gone to sleep with wet hair that's not at least had a comb run through it. I wonder when it got bad. Did it look a little less hideous with my head on the pillow? Gah! I doubt it.

Nate saw this. Even if we *were* able to be more than neighbors having sex, there's no way he'd leave flowers, breakfast, or a love note to *this* situation.

I try to comb my fingers through it, but it's way too tangled and matted. I'll probably have to shave it down like Nate's. As panic sets in, my mind goes in many directions.

Where is he? Probably downstairs.

What do I have to wear? Nothing.

Can I fix my hair here? Unlikely.

Am I willing to let him see me like this—on purpose? I'd rather not.

Preservation mode takes over. I tug open dresser drawers until I find a shirt. Any shirt. I slip it on. Luckily it hangs below my ass. It doesn't fix the hair situation. I could tip my chin up and face him or I could sneak out.

The balcony.

I'm not sure why Mr. Hans didn't build steps down from Nate's balcony. Thankfully, the air-conditioning unit is right below. I climb over the railing and inch my hands down the spindles. Then I let one leg start to hang down before dropping my other leg. "Shit!" The weight of my body jerks my arms, but I keep a firm grip—dangling from the balcony.

Not gonna lie … I thought my feet would touch the air-conditioning unit. I thought this would be easy. No big deal.

They don't. Worse than that, with my arms above my head, the shirt has ridden up my body, exposing my bare ass and somewhat neatly trimmed muff. If I let go, I could collide with the unit instead of landing on it. My bare feet could get torn up if I land in the patch of rocks. Or I could just die.

Death might be preferable if I don't get this figured out before someone sees me. My hands start to slip.

"No no no ..." All the muscles and tendons in my wrists and arms start to burn.

"Good morning."

I whip my head around, trying to see over my shoulder, but my outstretched arm obscures my view.

Nate.

"I take it you're not a fan of stairs?"

"Help. I'm slipping!"

He chuckles. "Oh, Elvis, I'm going to help you. Then you're going to explain this."

Kill. Me. Now.

"Let go." He slides his hands almost to my waist.

"I'm heavy. You might not—" My hold gives out. "HELP!" My body *literally* slides down his. His arms wrap around me, bringing me to a stop a few inches before my feet touch the ground.

"Why aren't you wearing a shirt?" I ask. Maybe I can shift the focus.

He gives me a grin that makes me angry and kind of turned on at the same time. "Well, I'd say because you're wearing it, but truthfully, I just got back from a jog. I think it's interesting that, given the current situation, the question that's being asked is why I'm not wearing a shirt."

I don't care about my ass that's still hanging out in the

breeze, or the fact that he caught *me* hanging from his balcony. It's my hair.

Vain? Probably.

If we were an old married couple, committed and legally bound for better or worse, I wouldn't be so vain. We're not that couple.

We're neighbors having sex. That requires a certain level of attraction and a certain level of hygienic effort.

I … am a fucking mess.

He's not even looking at my hair. No shits given. Why the hell did I panic?

"You have some sleepy bugs on your face."

Rolling my lips together, I nod slowly. "Thanks for noticing. Could you just put me down?" I wriggle out of his hold as he sniggers. After shoving the shirt down to cover myself, I take quick strides toward my balcony stairs, leaving a handful of my dignity in the wind.

"You're really not going to tell me why you were hanging from the balcony?"

"Shit!" I rattle the stupid handle that won't open because the door is locked. I slowly walk down the stairs, chin tipped toward my chest, desperate to find the nearest rock to crawl under.

He's tailing me, but I don't care at this point as I skulk to the deck door.

"Are you kidding me?" I whisper to myself, encountering yet another locked door. I didn't lock it when I left. I know I didn't. The handle must have been locked from when I went to bed, and I didn't check it when I decided to deliver the condoms. Still holding the handle, I press my forehead against the door and roll it back and forth.

"I have some cut up fruit. Toast. Eggs. Coffee. Want to join me for breakfast?"

Keeping my head glued to the door, I mumble, "I want a shower, shampoo, and conditioner. Lots of conditioner. My own clothes. And to rethink the decisions I've made in the past ten minutes."

"Did you … try to escape because of your hair?"

I don't answer.

"There's a huge bottle of conditioner in Morgan's shower."

No response. If I keep my eyes closed long enough, this moment will disappear. Right?

"Well, you know where to find me."

After a few minutes of wallowing in self-pity, I hear voices down the way. The moment has *not* disappeared. I guess erasing time is not my superpower after all.

I'm still wearing a tee.

Disastrous hair.

Crusty face.

It's time to take shelter. Easing to the edge of the deck, I glance in both directions. There's a group of kids headed this way. I have to go now.

My desperation lands me at Nate's door in under five seconds. I don't knock. I sulk inside and straight up the stairs to Morgan's bathroom and the big bottle of conditioner.

After a long shower of working my fingers through each tangle and matted area, I dry off and use one of Morgan's elastics to pull it back into a small ponytail. Still … I have nothing to wear except Nate's tee.

The aroma of coffee and something sweet leads me downstairs into the kitchen.

Nate glances up from his phone, cup of coffee, and cinnamon roll. "Feel better?" He grins.

"I'm locked out. No. I don't feel better."

"Have a seat." He nods to the chair bedside him, where he's poured me a cup of coffee too and set a cinnamon roll and fruit on a small plate.

I glance past him into the living room and fetch a throw blanket from the sofa to wrap around my waist before sitting next to him. He smirks from behind his mug of coffee.

"You bake, huh?" I eye the roll as I bring the coffee to my lips.

"Technically, yes. I baked these. Now, if you ask if I mix ingredients, roll out dough, and whatever else is involved in making cinnamon rolls … then no. These came from one of those tubes where all you have to do is bake and frost them."

"That works." I shrug.

"Do you bake?"

I pull apart the roll and pinch off a bite. "I don't, but I can. My family was pretty old-fashioned. Mom has always stayed at home. She still wears aprons that belonged to my grandma. You know … the ones with white shoulder straps and deep pockets?"

Nate's grin mirrors mine as he nods several times.

"She'd putter around the house in a dress and one of her many white eyelet aprons or linen pinafores doing shit all day—laundry, baking, sewing, ironing, cleaning. You name it. If we scraped a knee, she had ointments and Band-Aids in one of her apron pockets. Lose a button? No problem. She had a mini sewing kit in her apron. Stain sticks, tissues, pacifiers, aspirin, and antibiotic ointment for the dogs ears … all in her apron. It was like her tool belt for the day. My dad says she's an old soul born a generation too late. When Kyle and I would bring friends home for the first time, they all assumed she was our grandma, not our mom. Of course, not because she looked old, it was the apron. And … she didn't work outside of the home."

"That's awesome." Delight overtakes Nate's face. "So she taught you to bake?"

"Sorry … that long story went nowhere. Yes, she taught me to bake, iron, fold fitted sheets, sew, and kiss booboos. Dad taught Kyle how to mow the lawn, change a tire, fix a leaky faucet, and hang a picture. Ironically, I never married or had kids, so all those domestic skills were lost on me. And Kyle went into a very white-collar profession where he chose to hire everything out, including simple things like mowing the lawn and fixing a leaky faucet. I'm sure our parents' motto for years has been *where did we go wrong?*"

"Conventionalism isn't reality," Nate says while staring at me rubbing my hands. "Did you hurt yourself … hanging from the balcony?"

I pause my movements and reach for my coffee. "No."

"You have to tell me why? It's flat-out cruel to keep it a secret at this point."

I roll my eyes. "My hair. Are you happy now? I didn't want you to see my hair. I'm not sure my hair has ever looked so hideous. *I* couldn't look at it without cringing and feeling the need to look away. And we're not *together*. What we have is based on physical attraction. Or … it was." My nose wrinkles. "That's no doubt over now."

"First…" he wipes his mouth with a napkin after taking the last bite of cinnamon roll "…I'm not that shallow. And if I were, we could still enjoy each other's company for the rest of the summer. A paper sack over your head works just fine."

It's not funny. Not even a little. Okay … my lips betraying me by sneaking out a smile might mean it's a tiny bit funny. "So you just want me for everything below my neck?"

"No. I think we'd cut a hole where your mouth is."

I shake my head and laugh. How did we go from aprons to paper sacks? "So I can breathe?"

"Um … sure … that too."

"That *too*? Okay, so the main reason for the hole is so that you can kiss me. I see where your priorities are."

His lips curl together, and he rubs his fingers over them, hiding a look.

"Not to kiss me …" Realization settles into my cheeks in the form of a huge blush. Could I be any more naive? The hole is for something else, for something that didn't happen last night. Nate is a lot of things, but at his core, he's still a guy with normal guy desires.

Once my mind accepts his original meaning, my thoughts conjure the craziest images of what it might look like. Giving a guy a blow job with a bag over my head and a hole cut out at my mouth is not sexy. It's so weird. Really weird. And now I can't get the image out of my head.

"You're imagining it, aren't you?" He chuckles.

I cover my face with my hands. "Yes! And it's awful. Why did you have to say that?" I giggle because it is awful, but it's oddly funny in my messed-up mind. "Oh my gosh …" I drop my hands from my face. "I need to get into my house. I need clothes, and I want to brush my teeth. Surely Mr. Hans has a key hidden somewhere. Can I use your phone to call him?"

Nate wets his lips and rubs them together, his brow wrinkling a little. "He asked me to keep an eye on things, so he gave me a key. I can let you in if you need in."

Slowly, I push back in my chair and stand, leaning forward to plant my hands on the table. "You … have … a key?" My teeth gnash. "I live there, yet he asked you to look after things? Look after what? Me?" My voice escalates with each word.

Nate gives me a tightlipped expression, eyes wide. "I think he's like your parents, a little old-fashioned."

"That doesn't explain why you're just *now* telling me you have a key!"

His lips twist to the side as he lifts one shoulder in a half shrug. "I wanted …"

"You wanted?" I lean in more, getting in his face.

"You …" His gaze slides down my body. "In my shirt. In my house. I wanted more … you." He grins like that's the golden answer, like I'm going to fall for his charm.

"I want to fuck you on my kitchen table before real life returns in two days."

What the … what!?

That … that came out of his mouth.

Nice guy Nate.

Widower Nate.

Single dad Nate.

There's no way I heard him correctly—even if my nipples have jumped to attention, volunteering for duty.

The number of rational comebacks is endless. My brain doesn't do rational well. "I need to brush my teeth." Clearly the obvious answer to someone wanting to fuck me on a kitchen table.

Nate grins. "I need to take a shower."

Like the ultimate sign, the blanket around my waist loosens and falls to the floor.

Nate scoots his chair back. "Come here," he demands with

an eerie calmness as he spreads his legs.

Shirtless Nate.

I'm like a fly willingly tangling myself in his web, knowing I won't be able to escape before he completely consumes me.

I step into his space. His hands slide up the back of my legs, and he grins when I visibly shiver from his touch.

Yeah, you do things to me, Nathaniel Hunt.

I like Nate's hands. They're large, calloused, and some of his knuckles are knobby like he's suffered jammed fingers over the years. Capable … they are very capable hands that don't remind me of anyone—not Brandon, not Andy who cheated on me, and not Michael. Maybe that's the thing I like most about Nate. He's physically nothing like my three previous strikes. I don't spend time comparing him to anyone else. Well, except I'm doing it now because my mind spins out of control when he touches me.

"Gracelyn … what?" he whispers.

"May." I roll my eyes. "I was born in May. So … Gracelyn May Glock."

"Gracelyn May …" He slides his hand along my cheek and pulls me down to his lips.

He just jogged. Where is his appalling odor? Am I immune to it? Am I oddly attracted to his dried sweat? I think so because I find my mouth following a trail down his chest behind my hands, over his sternum, and down his abs. Nate pulls out my ponytail holder—Morgan's—as I kneel on the floor. His fingers ease into my hair, and his stomach muscles flex beneath my lips.

I grin. Pulling away, I trace a heart-shaped birthmark to the left of his navel. It's really just an absence of pigment. "Found it."

When I glance up, he drags his teeth along his lower lip, eyes darker and filled with something that makes me feel very powerful at the moment. He draws in a slow breath when I pull down the front of his jogging shorts and briefs.

"Jesus …" he whispers as I take him into my mouth.

I'm certain he's no longer thinking about my matted hair or my crazy ass hanging from the balcony.

My hands and mouth take turns. He leans back in the chair, his grip on my hair tightening. My gaze lifts to meet his, but his head is back, neck stretched taut.

"Surprise! Oh! What the—"

When we hear Morgan's voice, Nate jumps, seriously gagging me before yanking his shorts up to cover things. I bolt up with my back to her and wipe the gag tears from my eyes.

"Uh … Dad …"

Pushing the shirt down as far as it will go, I turn slowly.

"You're back." He clears his throat and races to give her a hug as she drops her bag on the floor. "Early … why are you back early?"

She pulls away, eyeing me with … well, I'm not sure what that look is on her face. Confusion and something else. Please tell me she didn't see her dad's penis in my mouth … me stroking and licking it. Please … please … please …

"You're wearing my dad's shirt."

I glance down as if it's news to me. "Yeah. I … uh … I got locked out of my house and fell into the water, so your dad loaned me a shirt." That about covers it.

"Mr. Hans gave my dad a key to your house."

Smart little shit.

"Oh!" Nate dramatically slaps his palm against his forehead. "He did. I totally forgot. My mind was all over the place with you leaving so quickly." He glances back at me. "Sorry … I had a key all this time."

Biting my lips together, my eyes flare as I nod. "Mmm-hmm. Well, I'm just going to run home."

Morgan's untrusting gaze shifts back to Nate.

Thank god.

"Hunter got sick. Food poisoning in the middle of the night. Her parents took her home, so Mr. Hans decided we should head home too."

"Well, I'm glad you're home safely."

I sneak past her as she narrows her eyes at him. She knows … she's ten, but she knows. She's not blind. And that image will *never* leave her brain. Me and my stupid need to bring him condoms last night. Not only am I on course to destroy Gabe's childhood, I'm set to ruin Morgan's as well.

When I slip in the deck door, I hear Mr. Hans whistling from the office, probably unpacking, so I sprint upstairs. My luck has taken a tiny upswing. Gabe's in his room, unpacking his bag with his back to me, so I make it to my room and ease the door shut without making a sound. When I'm safe in the bathroom and plopped onto the toilet to pee (because Morgan nearly scared it out of me), I can't hide my grin. Closing my eyes, I brush my fingers over my lips. Nate is still on my skin, stuck to my lips, and lingering on my tongue. And the image of him stretching his head back and the moan that vibrated from his chest is etched into my brain forever.

Sadly, Gabe will never be able to hang out with Morgan again. If she saw and understood what was happening in the kitchen, she will tell him. Secrets are not her strong suit.

CHAPTER NINETEEN

Nathaniel

I WAS QUICK. I'm fairly certain I covered my junk before Morgan saw it, but she's been quiet all day, knitting from the recliner while I work on my book. It's the looks. When I glance up, I catch her glaring at me. Maybe I should say something, but if she didn't see anything, if she's not sure what was happening when she got home, do I dare spell it out for her?

B L O W J O B

I think not.

"I'm going over to see Gabe." She shoves her yarn and needles into her canvas bag.

"Why?"

"Um …" She stands. "Because we're friends."

I play it cool, keeping my eyes on my notebook. "You spent two days with him. Maybe he needs a break."

"No. He doesn't."

"Maybe you should tell me more about your time at Disney. You were really excited on the phone, but since you've been home, you haven't said anything." I risk a glance up at her.

She frowns and sighs.

It's coming. I know it. Eight years of being on my very best behavior won't matter. I kissed the nanny in the hallway when

Morgan was a baby sleeping in her crib. That's been my biggest indiscretion up until now.

"I need to ask you something." She turns her back to me and crosses her arms over her chest.

This is new.

I close my notebook and lean forward, resting my arms on my knees, hands folded. "I'm listening."

"Can we go to the store?"

I wait a few seconds to answer because I'm not sure I heard her correctly. "Sure."

"Ugh!" She covers her face with her hands. "I started my period on the way home. I'm using a wad of toilet paper right now, but I need other stuff."

Well, shit … I didn't see that coming. No third degree over what she did or didn't see in the kitchen. She got her first period.

"That's great."

"It's not great!" She whips around. "I need a mom!"

My head jerks backward. I don't want to make Jenna's nonexistent role in Morgan's life seem insignificant, but we've made it this far. I think I can handle a box of sanitary napkins.

"Listen, Squirt—"

"Stop calling me that! I'm a woman now. I could have babies!" She turns and runs up the stairs.

"Holy shit …" I try to keep from laughing, but it's hard. My baby went to Disneyland and came home a little woman with all the raging hormones. In my delusional mind, we had a few more years. I'm in trouble.

After I let her news settle, I head next door via Gracelyn's private entrance. Something tells me she's hiding in her room … possibly for eternity.

Knock, knock, knock.

She peeks through her curtains before unlocking the door.

"Hey." I close the door behind me.

Big eyes stare me down.

"I need a favor."

This elicits a few blinks from her. "A favor? Your daughter caught us doing really inappropriate things and you need a favor? I need an update! What did she say? What did you say? Do you think she's going to say anything to Gabe? Should I say something to him first and get ahead of the situation?"

I shake my head. "N-no … It's not about that. She hasn't said anything about that. I don't think she saw anything, or if she did, it wasn't clear enough to pique her curiosity and ask me about it."

Blowing out a slow breath of relief, Gracelyn nods several times. "That's good. Thank god." She slips her hands into the pockets of her capris. "So what's the favor?"

"Morgan got her first period."

"Oh … that's …"

"Early." I shrug. "At least it feels early."

"She needs pads?"

I nod.

"Got it." Gracelyn disappears into her bathroom and returns with a box of pads. "They're bigger … well, more absorbent than she'll need." Her nose wrinkles. "You know what I mean. Just get her something that's regular absorbency."

"Actually, I was hoping you could help her out. It's not about the pads. I can get her pads, but she had a little breakdown and needs, in her words, a mom. I think what she needs is a female. Can you be a female?"

Gracelyn chuckles. "I think I can manage something close

to female."

"I'd be forever indebted to you."

Her eyebrows slide up her face. "Forever indebted? I like the sound of that."

"Okay, not forever. For the next…" I glance at my watch "… five weeks."

Her smile fades, and she nibbles her lip while staring at her feet. "I'm sorry I did what I did in the kitchen."

"No. *Please* don't be sorry for that." I lift her chin with my finger. "I really, really need you to not be sorry for that. It was …"

Dark hazel eyes wait for me to finish.

"Just …" I duck my head and brush my lips over hers. "It was too damn good to ever regret."

I nip at her lips and take a step backward before she makes things fuzzy in my head again.

"You're only saying that because she didn't question anything other than your shirt on me. She didn't give you the third degree. Had she royally embarrassed you and demanded answers to what we were doing when she came into the kitchen, I think you would not have this no-regrets attitude."

"I think we can both agree there are regrets. I made the huge mistake of going for a jog instead of making breakfast before you had a chance to escape. The timing was off."

Her lips pause, nose wrinkled. "You just explained every tragedy that has ever happened in the world. The timing was off."

"Nope. Sorry …" I shake my head. "Your mouth doing what it was doing to me could never be tragic. The only thing tragic about it was the ending. Do you have any idea how difficult it is to move on with your day after getting half a blow job?"

She giggles. "Sorry. No. I don't really know that feeling because I'm female … which is why I'm going to go talk to Morgan about her menstrual cycle. Do you have any idea how difficult it is to devote seven days of every month to bleeding from one of your orifices?"

When I realize she's not feeling that sympathetic to my partial blow job, I open the door and step aside. "Thank you for your service."

Gracelyn pauses as she walks past me. "You're welcome." Her finger traces the length of my cock over my shorts.

"Not cool. Not cool at all." I frown.

She smirks and steps outside, leaving me with a growing problem.

CHAPTER TWENTY
Gracelyn

MY FIRST PERIOD arrived at the tender age of thirteen. All of my friends got theirs around eleven. I didn't want to be the first to get it. What young girl wants to pioneer that situation alone? However, being the last to get it also meant I was the last to get boobs, the last to look like a budding woman instead of a boy with long Black Beauty hair … that was actually auburn.

Yes, my hair has always been my most attractive trait. That's why it was the first to go when I declared my man ban. No need to deal with a swarm of men chasing my mane. I'm only eighty percent exaggerating.

By the time I got my first period, nobody cared. My friends and their big boobs had moved on to grown-up things, like tampons and letting boys in school feel their big boobs. Nobody cared about Gracelyn Glock's official debut into womanhood. No parties were thrown for me. My mom simply curled my long hair behind my ear, smiled, then retrieved a sanitary napkin from one of her apron pockets. *"Sticky side down, Gracelyn. There's more under the sink. And change it every time you go to the bathroom so you don't smell."*

I was a straight A student. Can we talk about how insulting it was that she felt the need to tell me *sticky side down*?

"Morgan?" I knock on her bedroom door. "Can I come in?

It's just me."

The door creaks open an inch. A big blue eye peers at me. "I don't want to talk to *him* right now."

I contain my smile. "It's just me."

She opens the door. I step inside and close it as she plops onto her bed.

"I brought you some pads." I hold up the bag.

She rolls her eyes. "He told you. Has he told everyone? Does Gabe know?"

"No. Just me. He thought I might have some pads to get you by until you go to the store. How are you feeling?"

She hugs her stomach. "Prostaglandins are definitely causing my uterus muscles to contract. I'm achy."

I stare at her unblinking.

She shrugs. "I have a book about girls. My dad thinks it's about making friendship bracelets and stuff like that. It's not. It's about our changing bodies."

I grin and nod. "Sounds like a good book. If you're not feeling well, you could try a warm compress on your belly. Pain relievers are an option too, but you'd have to discuss that with your dad." I set the pads on the bed beside her. "These are really absorbent pads. You shouldn't need more than just regular pads. So when your dad takes you shopping, look for regular ones. It's up to you if you want wings. They can protect your underwear. I personally don't love them because they stick to … everything." My lips pull into a tight grin.

"Like your pubic hair?"

"Yes." I chuckle. "Like that."

She folds her hands in her lap, legs dangling from the side of the bed.

"Listen … I've never been a mom, so I'm not an expert on

all mom things, but I'm a girl. So if you ever need a girl to talk to about…" I shrug "…anything, you can talk to me. Okay?"

Morgan's gaze lifts from her hands to meet the sincerity in my eyes. I feel we're having a moment. It's not maternal; it's friendship. I think she views me as her friend, and I really like that.

"Anything?"

I nod. "Yes. We are friends. Nothing is off the table."

"Thanks."

"You're welcome. You know where to find me if you need anything else." I turn to open the door.

"What does a penis taste like?"

I freeze. She didn't say penis. No way. I heard her wrong. "Wh-what's that?" I ask without looking back at her.

"A penis. Does it taste like any other part of the body?"

Fuuuck!

"Um …"

Now would be a good time for an earthquake or a meteor to take out the West Coast.

A stroke.

A heart attack.

A sinkhole to engulf this house.

"It's no secret my dad likes you. If you want to have sex with him, that's okay too. I'm not stupid. I know people have sex even when they're not making babies. And I know a little about oral sex from my book—the one my dad thinks is about friendship bracelets—but it only explains what it is, not why people do it. I guess I'm just wondering if you like the taste of penises. I can't imagine they taste good, but my dad also says you have to try something fifteen times before you know if you really like it or not. He also said some things are …" She snaps her fingers several times. "What's the word he used ..." More finger snapping. "Oh! An acquired taste."

This isn't my normal time of the month to get hot flashes, but every sweat gland in my body just emptied onto my skin, drowning me in embarrassment. It takes me a few seconds to remember I'm forty-one and Morgan is ten.

Time to act like the grown-up.

Turning, I bite my lips together so hard I'm certain I'll have permanent indentations.

Her nose wrinkles when she sees my unavoidable reaction. "I think I saw something in the kitchen I wasn't supposed to see."

I nod slowly, taking a seat beside her so we can stare at the door instead of each other. "I think you're quite advanced for ten, but I'm still not sure what is or isn't appropriate to discuss with you. Still ..." I scratch my forehead. "I think you know more than I want to imagine and *definitely* more than your dad wants to imagine. So let me just say that I am so very sorry that you saw what you did."

"I'm not mad."

I chuckle. "Well, that's good. Really. However, you deserve to be ten. Even if you know things that kids older than you don't know, it doesn't mean you should be any other age but ten. You shouldn't see what you saw. And again, I'm incredibly sorry about that. I'm glad you have books that explain things to you, but please don't forget your job is to play Frisbee and comb beaches for shells. It's okay to think about what it will feel like the first time a boy kisses you, but no more than you should think about driving a car. It's out there ... you'll get there, but it shouldn't be rushed."

Morgan draws in a slow breath and blows it out all at once,

her body deflating. "You're not going to tell me what a penis tastes like, are you?"

I rub my hands over my face and shake my head. "No," I mumble before dropping my hands back to my lap.

"Do you think you'll marry my dad? Hunter said her mom isn't her real mom, but her stepmom. She said her real mom met another man, and her dad got married to a different woman last year. Hunter got to be one of the bridesmaids and wear a really pretty dress. I guess I'm just wondering if I'll get to be a bridesmaid if you marry my dad."

Ugh …

I scoot to face her, resting my hand on her leg. "You said you know people don't always have sex just to have babies?"

She nods.

"Well, sometimes when adults like each other, they kiss and do … other things. It doesn't always mean they will get married. I like your dad. He's handsome and fun and a great dad to you, but you have a home and family waiting for you in Wisconsin. That's where you belong. And I have Gabe now. His home is here. His friends are here, so this is where I now belong. I am just one of many friends you and your dad have met over your time traveling the world. We are friends. You and I. Your dad and I."

I squeeze her hand and she grins.

"And I hope we will be friends forever. Pen pals." I wink at her.

"I'd like that. Maybe I can *email* you." She smirks.

It's funny how she thinks emailing me would be such a coup. "The possibilities are endless."

"Maybe you and Gabe could come visit us in Madison."

"Maybe. Now …" I pat her leg and stand again. "I'm going

to see what Gabe's up to. If you need any help with your period, don't feel embarrassed to ask your dad. He's a doctor, you know."

"No way. I'm not talking to him about this. He'll make it weird," says the girl who just asked me what a penis tastes like.

"Okay. Then I'm your person."

"Thanks, Gracelyn. I bet my mom was cool like you."

I don't know why this brings tears to my eyes, but it does. "Thank you, Morgan," I whisper before leaving her room.

CHAPTER TWENTY-ONE

Nathaniel

"EVERYTHING OKAY?" I ask as soon as Gracelyn comes down the stairs after being up there for a long time.

She gives me nothing but a look. Maybe a weird look. It's definitely a hard stare, like I'm supposed to read her mind or something. I'm not sure. She brushes past me and out the door to the deck. I follow her.

She turns, hands clasped behind her back. "Shut the door," she whispers.

Narrowing my eyes for a brief moment, I shut the exterior door and the screen door. "What happened?"

"First, I just want to say that whatever you thought you *owed* me before … take it times ten now." Her lips curl inward as she gives me a toothy—kind of scary—grin.

"Okay. Can you elaborate?"

"Where to begin …" Her lips twist and she rubs her chin, eyes rolled to the side. "Do I start with the fact that she *did* see what we were doing in the kitchen? Or do I tell you how I know this which is …" Her gaze returns to mine, eyes slightly narrowed. "She said … and I quote, 'What does a penis taste like?'"

"Oh god …"

Her lips part. "Uh … yeah. Oh God. Jesus. Lord. And Mother Mary. I wanted to die. Legit *die*."

I cringe. "I'm sorry. I can't believe she …" Closing my eyes, I pinch the bridge of my nose. "I shouldn't be surprised." Dropping my hand, I sigh. "I've taught her … encouraged her to be curious, to always ask lots of questions. I've never sheltered her from the truth."

"Good job, Dad of the Year. Now bend down, lick your dick, and go tell your daughter how it tastes." She turns and heads for the steps.

"Stop!" I grab her arm and turn her back toward me. "I'm serious. What did you say?"

Gracelyn rolls her eyes, a clear sign that she spent too much time with my eye-rolling daughter. "The truth. I said it tastes briny with a hint of copper and rust like an oyster. I told her it's the most succulent, mouthwatering thing she will ever experience."

I release her arm and have a mini stroke right here on the deck.

"Don't collapse, Daddy-O." She gently slaps my cheek several times. "I didn't answer her question. I stressed the importance of letting herself be ten and innocent. I apologized more than once for letting her see what she saw. And that's about it."

Still in shock from the briny and succulent remarks, I blink several times. "H-how … w-what did she say?"

"She said you're an overprotective, neurotic, freak of a dad and begged me to show her the ropes of being a true woman before you guys go home in August."

I frown, not finding her humor too funny in light of my recent mini stroke. "I live next door to Satan."

She grins. "Don't be so hard on Mr. Hans. He's not evil all the time." She pivots and saunters home.

I tell myself it's not the appropriate time to watch the sway of her ass ... then I do it anyway.

"I'm ready." Morgan opens the door.

I turn. "Ready ... yes. Um ... let's go to the store. Maybe we can go out to dinner. How does that sound?"

"Whatevs ..." She breezes past me. "I just have to watch my salt intake because it's my bloated time."

Gone. My little girl is gone.

Stifling my chuckle, I close the door and follow her to the car.

"Hey, wanna go Rollerblading with me and Gracelyn?" Gabe asks, sitting in their driveway and shoving his feet into skates.

"Sorry ..." Morgan flips her hair over her shoulder before opening the car door. "I have some personal and grown-up things to do. Maybe in three to five days."

"Uh ..." Gabe squints against the sun and shrugs. "Whatever."

I cough to hide my amusement while sliding into the vehicle. On the way to the store, I contemplate discussing the blow job intrusion with her. Of course, I'd find a better way to phrase it. Her lack of conversation—which is odd for her—keeps me silent as well. Maybe the best thing is time.

"This aisle." I nod to the aisle with personal hygiene products.

"Um ..." Morgan turns and presses her palm to my stomach. "I've got this. Please wait here."

I hold up my hands. "Fine. I'll wait here."

Thankfully, there is no one else in the aisle as my little-girl-turned-woman-overnight scuffs her flip-flop clad feet down the aisle. She stops and faces right, leaning forward a bit to study the products. After a minute or so, she grabs a package and walks toward me with her chin held high.

"Got it. Let's go."

I pluck the package from her hands.

"Dad!" she whisper yells like I've embarrassed her.

"These are underwear for urinary incontinence." I hand them back to her with a smirk glued to my face. "Want to try again? Or would you like my help?"

She scowls. "I've *got* it."

Again, I hold up my hands in surrender. She stomps her feet back down the aisle and takes a good five minutes to locate the right products, pick one out, and return to me with them hugged to her chest.

"Think I should take a look and make sure you got the right product?"

Another evil look gets slung in my direction. "No. It's the right thing this time."

"Okay … let's go."

We stop for pizza. Morgan asks me how much salt is in everything we order. I assure her it's all low sodium. Some lies are okay. Right now, I want to have a fun dinner with my daughter and talk about her trip to Disneyland instead of feeding her concerns of menstrual cycles and water retention.

AS IT APPROACHES bedtime, I get the nerve to broach the subject I've been dreading all day. Shutting off the TV after back-to-back documentaries, I angle my body on the sofa to face Morgan. "About earlier … when you got home—"

"I talked with Gracelyn. She already apologized."

I nod slowly. "Okay. But *I* didn't apologize because I honestly didn't know what you did or didn't see. So I'm sorry. I know you're very smart, and you know more than most kids your age, but reading about something and seeing it are two different things. I just ..."

"I've seen your penis before. It's no big deal."

I cringe. Yes, my daughter, who has never prioritized privacy until the past six months, has walked into many bathrooms to brush her teeth while I've showered. She's seen me. I've seen her. We're family. It's just anatomy. However, seeing someone suck said penis is not the kind of openness I've ever wanted to display to her. I fear that she's not making a big deal of it now, but years from now she will think back and her mind will scream, "Gross! I saw the neighbor lady giving my dad head!"

"Still, I'm sorry. I felt like a terrible dad. And I learned an embarrassing and hard lesson. You know I think it's important to never act like I don't make mistakes. It's important to acknowledge when I mess up. I messed up."

"I forgive you."

She's amazing, but I'm not stupid. That will haunt her someday. I'd better put some money away for future therapy.

"Thank you. Now ... it's time for the tuck, young lady."

"Daaad ... we're done with that. Remember?"

Why must she keep reminding me of her premature independence?

"Fine." I grab her and sling her onto my lap, tickling her. "Then just a kiss and tickle goodnight."

"Stop! Stop!" She giggles while trying to wriggle out of my hold.

After I shower her with kisses all over her face and neck, I let her go.

She steps back, out of breath while peeling hair from her face and cringing. "You made my pad get all wrinkled and shoved up into my area." She tugs at the crotch of her shorts. "You can't do that to me when I'm having my period."

My eyes grow wide, and I nod once. "Very sorry."

She frowns. "You're forgiven this time. Just don't do it again, please."

Again, I find myself holding my hands up in surrender. Letting go … I'm constantly having to remind myself to let go … let her be her. The butterfly emerging from its chrysalis.

She blows me one more kiss. "Night, Daddy. I love you."

"I love you too. Sweet dreams."

After picking up our popcorn mess and movie blanket fort, I grab a beer and escape to the porch.

"Nice night."

I squint to see Mr. Hans, but it's only an outline on his porch swing.

"It is. Sorry to hear Hunter is sick, but I want to thank you again for taking Morgan. She had the best time, even if it was only two days. I fear I'm now destined to make a return trip with her."

"Oh, gosh … it was my pleasure. She's such a great kid, and Gabe is too. Hunter was thrilled to have them there. However, I see my other tenant had a mishap with my tile and a bottle of wine."

"Send me the bill. Don't tell her I'm paying for it, but send me the bill."

"I think I can just take out that one piece of tile and replace it, as long as I still have one or two of those tiles left over. Otherwise, I'll have to replace the whole entry. I'm not sure you want to pay for that. Honestly, I'm tempted to just toss a rug there and not worry about it. She felt really terrible about it."

"Send me the bill. Really. Either for your time if you do have a tile to replace it or for all new tile."

"You rich or something?" He chuckles.

"Or something ..." I take a swig of my beer.

"If I didn't know better, I'd say you like her."

Rolling the mouth of the bottle along my bottom lip, I inwardly grin. "Oh yeah? What makes you think that?"

"I've seen you two together. I may be old, but I know how a man looks at a woman who he's smitten with. Boy ... you've got that look."

I chuckle. "Smitten ... haven't heard that word in a while." My dad used to tell everyone how smitten I was with Daisy Gallagher, my childhood friend. He wasn't wrong.

"Morgan said her mom died while giving birth to her. You and Elvis have that lost love in common. I'm in that group too."

"Gracelyn's fiancé left her at the altar; he didn't die. Did he?" I ask.

"Nah ... another guy ... in her early twenties. Some kind of heart condition took him. He didn't get a transplant in time."

"Huh ... I didn't know that."

"If you ask me, I'd say it's the reason she's single. She's a hard worker. Loves that boy to death. However, I don't miss the fear in her eyes. Pretty damn sure she never saw this life coming. I imagine you felt that way when you lost your wife. With my wife, I knew it was coming. I had time to prepare. Doesn't make it hurt less. Just means you don't spend as long in denial that you're alone and you're never going to see them again."

I blow out a slow breath. "Yeah …"

CHAPTER TWENTY-TWO

Gracelyn

"CAN I STAY with Mr. Hans today? Tyler has a dental appointment today, and I don't want to go, but his mom won't let me stay at their house alone."

I sip my coffee at the table, scrolling through my email on my phone. "Mr. Hans isn't here. And I'm not asking our landlord to be your …" I search for something besides babysitter. Gabe hates that. "Well, I'm not asking him to keep an eye on you. I think that's crossing a line, especially given the fact that he already went above and beyond and took you to Disney."

And I feel terrible about the broken tile.

Gabe puts his cereal bowl in the dishwasher, a skill I showed him very quickly after he became my responsibility. I'd like to say it's because I'm naturally an awesome parental figure, but it's not. He's not a toddler. I shouldn't have to pick up after him. I have enough issues picking up after myself some days. Emily may have coddled him. I'm not a natural coddler. If I'm completely honest, I'm harder on him because he's a boy. I've been with too many unskilled men. Gabe won't be one of them, if I have anything to say about it.

"Ask Morgan's dad," he says.

Hmm … I'm not sure how I feel about that. It's been five days since I sucked him off in his kitchen—not true, he didn't get off. I just sucked him; licking and stroking was involved too.

Shit … my face feels hot just thinking about it.

Morgan has refused to hang out with Gabe, which I suspect is because of her period. I remember being her age and thinking that somehow everyone knew when I was having my period. I worried they could see the outline of my pad or smell the blood like vampires. It's such an awkward and confusing age.

No Morgan time has meant no Nate time either—unless I count him unabashedly watching me strip each day. Perv …

Perv that I really like.

"Maybe. I need to get dressed. I'll see if they're home when I'm ready to leave. If so, I'll ask. If not, just make sure you're ready to go."

"Fine," he mumbles, heading upstairs.

I don't usually wear makeup to work, but knowing I might see Nate this morning makes me want to look my best. He's clearly seen my worst. I feel the need to remind him that I don't always resemble a rag doll that's been mauled by a dog.

"Ready?" I knock on Gabe's door as I head downstairs in my rolled-up skinny jeans, white canvas shoes, and black fitted tee—makeup on and my hair still down. I'll put it up when I get to work.

Without waiting for Gabe, I walk next door, surprised to see Nate and Morgan on the deck with the two rockers facing each other and a table in between them, playing chess.

"Who's winning?" I ask.

"Me," Morgan says, studying the board.

Nate glances over his shoulder at me, his smile touching every inch of my body. "Morning. Off to work?"

"In a few minutes." I climb the steps and stand next to Nate's chair, gazing at their chessboard.

"Does Morgan always win? I can see her being the better player."

She giggles, taking Nate's bishop with her queen. "Yes. I usually win."

"She's lying." Nate's hand falls to the side of the chair.

I stiffen when his fingers ghost along my calf.

"I'm not lying. You say you let me win, but I think you just don't want to admit I'm better."

"Can I get you a cup of coffee?" Nate asks.

"No. I've got to get going. I don't know what you guys have planned for today, but Gabe is not wanting to go to his friend's house because Tyler has a dental appointment. And I hate to ask Mr. Hans, so—"

"Oh! He can hang out with us today! I'm better now." She winks at me.

Yep. She was on period lockdown.

Morgan continues, "We're going to lunch and then a museum because it's supposed to rain later. Right, Dad?"

"That's right. We'd love to have Gabe join us," Nate says without hesitation.

"Hey, Gabe!" Morgan glances past me. "You get to hang out with us today."

I turn toward Gabe as he walks up to the deck. "Looks like you get your wish today." I slide my handbag from my shoulder. "I'll leave you with some money, in case you end up at a museum or out for lunch."

"I've got it," Nate says, standing.

"No. Here." I hand Gabe thirty dollars.

"Let's get you a to-go cup of coffee. Gabe can take over for me. You know how to play chess, buddy?"

Gabe shakes his head.

"I'll show you. I'm an expert." Morgan smirks as Gabe sits in Nate's chair.

"I had coffee," I say.

"I'm sure you did." Nate gives me a look and jerks his head toward the door. "But it could be a two-cup day. Better play it safe."

I glance at my watch. Since I don't have to drop Gabe off at Tyler's, I have a few spare minutes.

"Thanks for letting him stay with you and Morgan today." I follow Nate to the kitchen, but he doesn't stop in the kitchen.

He turns right to the hallway with the laundry room and half bath.

"Where are you—" As soon as I turn the corner, he grabs me, pinning me to the wall and pausing a breath away from my lips.

"Good morning," he whispers with a wicked grin forming along his sexy mouth.

I rub my lips together. "Morning."

After a dizzying kiss, he releases me and swats my ass. "Have a good day."

"What about my coffee?" I follow him around the corner into the kitchen.

"I'm actually out of coffee." He grabs an insulated, stainless steel cup from a floating shelf.

"Then what are you doing?"

He fills it with water and puts a lid on it. "It's like you haven't met my daughter. She will notice if you're not carrying a drink out of the house." He cranes his neck to look out the deck window before handing me the cup and kissing my cheek.

"Don't scalp anyone today."

The cup.

The kiss on the cheek.

It's all too familiar.

"What?" He narrows his eyes when I freeze, speechless for a few seconds.

I shake my head. "Um … nothing. Th-thanks for the water." I can't look at him because I suck at lying.

Brandon.

He used to make coffee for me before my first class my sophomore year of college. He'd put it in a travel mug, hand it to me, tell me to have a good day, and kiss my cheek.

"And thanks again for letting Gabe crash your day." A nervous smile forces itself onto my face just before I turn and convince my legs to take me to the door without tripping over anymore old memories. "Have fun, you two. I'll see you later."

Gabe and Morgan mumble a goodbye. When I get in the Land Rover, my shaky hand slides the mug of water into the drink holder.

"You used to shake around me too."

Grunting a laugh, I fiddle with the clasp to the bracelet he gave me and close my eyes for a few seconds. "Nice of you to finally show up."

Brandon chuckles. *"I've always been here. I just didn't have anything to say."*

Opening my eyes, I start the engine. His voice is clear. It's not a whisper or an echo of memories from the past. I can't see him, but he's here. And maybe I tell people like Mr. Hans that I know it's just in my head, but I'm not sure it is.

"I had sex with a man who's leaving in five weeks, jumped half naked from his balcony, and his daughter caught us in a very compromising position. Yet, you have nothing to say until now?" I back out of the driveway. If anyone saw my lips moving, they'd assume I'm hands-free on a phone call.

"I'd say he's a worthy opponent. My job here is done."

Tears fill my eyes. "Shut up. You don't mean that. There's nothing worthy about him. He's just stumbling through life like me. A wounded animal. How does that make him a worthy opponent? Oh … and did I mention he's moving?"

"You never sucked me off like that. He must be special."

I roll my eyes. "Jeez … how did your perversion live when everything else died?"

"You have a child."

I frown, focusing on the traffic. "He's not mine."

"Oh, Grace … don't say that. Gabe needs to belong to something real and tangible. You don't have to lie to the world and say he developed in your womb, but let him be yours. Let him belong. If you adopted a puppy, you wouldn't say this is a *dog. You'd say this is* my *dog. Your responsibility. Yours to love."*

I bat a few tears away from my cheeks and grip the steering wheel. "Why are you here? Why today?"

"To give you my approval. My blessing to move on. Which is ridiculous because I gave it to you before I died. You're so stubborn, Grace."

"I did move on. It's not my fault Andy cheated on me and Michael left me at the altar. That was me … moving on. I can't force anyone to love me." I take a sip of the water Nate sent with me because arguing with my dead boyfriend makes my throat dry and scratchy.

"You could try to be more lovable."

"Wow! That's a bit harsh, don't you think?"

Brandon laughs. Should dead people be allowed to haunt

the living with laughter? He's dead. His good times are over.

"Harsh is calling my name while another guy makes you orgasm."

"It slipped. I apologized. That didn't make it right for Andy to *slip* his dick into some other girl. Saying your name wasn't cheating."

"But were you thinking of me? Hmm … if I recall, I believe you were. Not gonna lie … I was fine with it at the time. If I'm being honest, Andy wasn't the one for you. Twenty-seven-year-olds who still live at home and have their mom do their laundry should be banned from the dating world."

I roll my eyes. He's not entirely wrong, but Andy was trying to open a restaurant. His mom was almost as June Cleaver as my mom—only she didn't have an apron.

"I'm not sure if you stalk him the way you stalk me, but Andy now has three restaurants. He married a politician. And they have twin boys who are both phenomenal basketball players. Maybe I saw Andy's potential before anyone else did."

"Yes. The potential to fuck another man's name out of your mouth. That's talent."

I pull into the parking lot and shut off the engine. "I'd love to stay and chat, but one of us is still alive with a job and responsibilities."

"Bummer. We didn't get a chance to discuss you getting left at the altar. That was classic. I saw that coming. I'm not sure how you didn't."

"Go away," I grumble, exiting the vehicle.

CHAPTER TWENTY-THREE

Nathaniel

MORGAN SPENDS THE morning teaching Gabe how to play chess. Once he beats her, she declares it's time to do something else. She might have inherited my competitive gene.

We grab burgers for lunch and ice cream for dessert, and make it to the museum before it starts to rain. After only an hour, Gabe expresses his level of boredom. I'm not sure if it's because he's not as obsessed with miscellaneous knowledge like Morgan, or if it's because he's been to all the museums in San Diego. My persuasive daughter doesn't think twice about him wanting to leave after only an hour. Now, had I been the one suggesting we leave that early, she would have had a meltdown.

I'm losing ground with this girl. I used to walk on water. Now she rolls her eyes and gives me this look like, on my best day, I merely stomp in a muddy puddle.

"You and Gracelyn should move to Madison with me and my dad," Morgan declares, sitting next to Gabe in the backseat while I chauffeur them home.

I glance in the rearview mirror at Gabe.

He keeps his gaze focused on his phone. "I'm not moving."

"Why?"

My instinct is to save Gabe from the impending onslaught of Morgan questions and possibly even some begging, but my curiosity keeps me quiet.

"Because I like it here. My friends are here. My soccer team is here. I don't want to move. My grandparents said I could move to Montana with them, but I wanted to stay here. That's why Gracelyn moved here instead of taking me back to Ohio with her."

"Idaho."

I smirk at Morgan correcting him.

"Whatever. You get my point."

"You'd make friends in Madison, just like me. We could make friends together."

"I already have friends."

"Yeah, but don't you ever want to make new friends? Different friends? I've made lots of friends while traveling with my dad. We write letters to each other and sometimes even send pictures or postcards. It's really fun. You could send your friends here pictures from Madison."

"Or I could stay here."

"Guac ... you're no fun. Besides ..." She doesn't finish, so I make another glance in the mirror. Her head is bent, her hands cupped at his ear as she whispers something.

"My aunt is not marrying your dad."

"Shh! Could you be any louder?"

"We should talk later. Don't you think, Morgan?"

"No, Dad. We don't need to talk. I know what you're going to say. You're not marrying Gracelyn. She already told me that, but you can't *really* know that. Things change. Feelings change."

"Not for everyone," Gabe mumbles. "My dad said Gracelyn is cursed. She will die with an apartment full of cats, which is weird because she doesn't own a cat."

Morgan laughs. "That's crazy."

I don't laugh, but I do wonder why his dad said that. Gracelyn is a lot of things, but she's not a cat lady. The old lady at a nursing home seducing a male nurse is a much more fitting role.

As soon as we get home, Morgan and Gabe go to Mr. Hans's house—I'm sure to play video games. I settle on the sofa and call my parents. We try to connect every few weeks.

"When you bringing our granddaughter home?" Dad answers without a hello.

I grin. "Soon." After eight years away, a little over five weeks more should feel like nothing. "Have you found a place for us to live?"

"Didn't know it was my job."

I chuckle. "It's not, but you're usually poking your nose into stuff, so I figured you'd have a list of possibilities. Christina is sending me a list tomorrow." When I decided to pack up my two-year-old daughter and travel the world indefinitely, I also chose to sell our house. Not out of financial necessity, more because I knew she would never remember it. It's the house I bought with Jenna. It's where we lived when we created Morgan, but it was also the house where I brought home my newborn baby … without her mom.

We need a clean slate.

"I miss her face. Your camera broken?"

I shake my head. We usually video chat so he can see Morgan. He's watched her grow all through the lens of a camera. "Morgan's not here. She's at the neighbor's house. Didn't figure you cared to see my old, graying mug."

"Talk to Jenna's family recently?"

I grin because my sexy as fuck neighbor just arrived home,

and she's stripping for me. "Uh ... we video chatted last week with her sister Rachael. She's getting married this October and wants Morgan to be her junior bridesmaid."

"I bet she'll love that. Your mom has been stockpiling so much shit for her. Stuffed animals, dolls, play dresses ..."

Gracelyn makes it hard for me to focus on his words, especially now that I know how good she tastes, smells, and feels beneath me. I know the rhythm of her breaths as they increase from my touch. I know the pitch of her moans when she orgasms.

"You still there?" Dad asks.

I adjust myself because my brain does its own damn thing and my body responds without my control. "Yeah, what were you saying?"

"I said your mom has been stockpiling things for Morgan."

"Tell her to not overdo it. Your granddaughter has made a lot of transitions over the last six or so months. Who knows what she'll still like by the time we get home in August."

"Too late. She passed the overdoing it part five years ago. I fear we'll need a storage shed before long."

I laugh, moving to the window so I can get a better look at Gracelyn's dash up her stairs. Just as she sneaks out of the bushes, her gaze locks with mine. Her eyes narrow and she flips me the bird before making her dash. My usual, or according to Morgan, "special" smile for Gracelyn steals my face.

"How are you feeling about coming home? That book of yours ready to be published?"

I turn away from the window. Show's over. "It's getting there. I'm not sure where to end it. I've been adding more content about our time here since this is technically still part of our epic-eight year journey."

"Is there much to write about San Diego? I assumed all your life lessons, reflections, and soul-searching had been achieved by now. Lord knows if I spent eight years circling the globe, I'd have all my shit worked out."

I chuckle. "You do realize I did this for Morgan, to open her mind and shape her early on to be more aware of the world, its vastness, and its diversity. This hasn't been the Nathaniel Hunt Soul-searching Tour."

"Then the book you're writing is all about Morgan?"

My father never stops making valid points, never stops reminding me that, although I have way more years of formal education than he has, he will always have more life experience and earned wisdom. Therefore, he will always make me feel like a child with something to learn from him.

"There might be a few self-reflective, soul-discovering moments in the book."

He releases a soft laugh that sounds more like a cough. "Anything interesting there?"

Yes. My quirky, sexy, endearing, and rather addictive neighbor. "Our landlord is a great guy. And he's renting the upstairs of his place to a woman who just got custody of her ten-year-old nephew after his parents died. So Morgan has a friend. That's where she's at right now. Downside? He's addicted to screens, and Morgan is not immune to it anymore."

"Well, you've got five weeks. I don't think five more weeks will erase the impact of the previous eight years."

"I'm not so sure. The internet is a powerful drug."

"Well, tell Miss Morgan we want to see her precious face."

I nod. "I'll have her FaceTime you later. Give mom a hug for me."

"Will do. Talk to you later."

"Bye, Dad." I slide my phone onto the kitchen counter and start unloading the dishwasher.

The screen door creaks open.

"Hey, what do you think of flying Grandma and Grandpa Hunt out here for the Fourth of July?" I ask Morgan.

"I think holiday travel is pricey and not in my budget."

I grin, setting a pile of clean plates on the shelf before turning toward Gracelyn. "Thought you were Morgan."

She holds up the mug I gave her this morning and sets it on the counter. "No. She and Gabe just left to run to the hardware store with Mr. Hans."

I narrow my eyes. "Without asking me?"

Gracelyn leans her hip against the counter and slides her fingers into the pockets of her denim capris. "She said she's allowed to make certain decisions by herself now."

"Bullshit," I say on instinct. "Her body might be doing some more mature things, but she's still ten and needs permission."

"I figured you'd think that. I also figured you'd say yes if she did ask, so I didn't push her to come ask you because I like being her friend." Gracelyn's freckled nose wrinkles. "I don't want her to think I'm parenting her too."

I nod slowly.

"Why are you looking at me like that?" she asks.

"Like what?"

She swallows hard when I take several steps toward her. "Like you're thinking ..." Doe eyes shoot up to meet my gaze.

"Thinking what?" My tongue glides along my lower lip, stealing her attention.

"Inappropriate thoughts," she whispers.

"Because I am."

"Um …" She presses her hands to my chest and trips on a nervous laugh. "We are never doing anything in this kitchen again. So don't get any ideas."

I grin, reveling in the way she can't maintain eye contact and her fingers curling into my shirt like she doesn't want me to come closer nor does she want me to step away. "There are other rooms in the house. Doors with locks on them. And I anticipate they will be a while. Morgan likes new things, and she hasn't been to too many hardware stores."

Another nervous laugh before she rubs her lips together, taunting me. "It's weird. One minute you're this responsible, doting father, and the next minute—"

I lean down and brush my lips up her neck to her ear. "The next minute I'm wanting to fuck my neighbor six ways from Sunday?" My teeth graze her ear.

"Yeah …" she says in a breathy voice. "Th-that …"

"What can I say …" I kiss along her jaw as my hands grip her ass. "You've awoken the beast." I kiss the corner of her mouth. "Offered him sex." My lips move to the other side of her mouth. "And left me hanging for five days."

When our mouths meet, her nervous demeanor vanishes. Her hands tug harder at my shirt, our tongues explore, and soft moans mesh between us while I carry her up the stairs to my bedroom.

So many important things to remember …

I'm leaving.

She's staying.

Sex sobriety is a thing. After a long dry spell, one taste can make a person go insane with need for it. All. The. Time.

I made it ten years, yet five days felt like an eternity.

Oh and the really important thing …

I'm leaving.

She's staying.

Sex not love.

Sex not commitment.

"Lower …" she moans.

I grin, working my way down her naked body. When I stop too long in one spot, like her perfect breasts, her head rolls to the side, back bowed from the bed. Her seductive voice tells me to go *lower*.

"God … I like you … right … there."

It's hard not to grin every time she expresses her pleasure. It's hard not to grin when she reaches for the condoms in the drawer before I get a chance to do it. It's hard not to grin when she wants to be on top, controlling everything when … she knows I'm going to take that control away from her very quickly.

Before I flip her over and take back that control, I enjoy the view.

"What?" She opens her lust laden eyes, hands cupping her breasts. I don't blame her. They're fucking spectacular. Her cheeks flush even more when I grin, my hands sliding up her thighs straddling me, my thumb rubbing her clit.

"You're sexy as fuck."

"Shut up …" She giggles and bites her lower lip to hide her smile as those whisky eyes flutter shut again.

She's giving me something. What? I don't know for sure. It feels equally selfish yet completely necessary. This makes me feel like a man in a way that nothing else does.

It's carnal.

It's instinctual.

It's human on the most basic level.

After I flip her over, it's only a matter of seconds before she grabs a pillow and covers her loud chants of gratitude to God. No offense to God, but I'm certain the praise is meant for me.

Satiated and nothing more than a pile of breathless bodies, we remain unmoving for a few seconds. And … she's up.

We have a strict, unspoken, no-cuddle arrangement. It's called sneaking around to have sex. It's called a sex only relationship.

"You should get up." She glances at me while hooking her bra.

I prop my arm behind my head. "I will."

"Like … now. That took longer than I thought it would. They could be back any minute."

"Sorry." I chuckle. "Maybe next time you shouldn't hold out for that second orgasm. Pretty damn greedy if you asked me."

"I don't know what you're talking about." She steps back into her capris without making eye contact.

"Well, God does. You interrupted his busy day several times just to brag." I stand and saunter to the bathroom. "And don't even get me started on how damn bossy you are."

"I'm not bossy."

Depositing the condom in the trash, I wash my hands and return to the bedroom to retrieve my clothes.

Her gaze snaps from my junk to my eyes.

"You are *so* bossy." I get dressed at a slightly less worried pace. "*Harder. Faster. Lower. Don't stop.* You're such a conductor. I should get you a maestro's baton, or maybe you'd like something more dominating." Before buttoning my shorts or putting on my shirt, I step in front of her with a wry grin. "A riding crop?"

With a sexy smirk, she sucks on her finger then presses it to my lips for a second before drawing a line to the waistband of my briefs, her gaze following her finger.

My dick starts to stand up again, volunteering for another round.

"I think I ride you just fine without a riding crop."

Together we watch her finger teasing my waistband … teasing the head of my erection strained against it. I whisper, "Lower."

On a breathless laugh, she withdraws her finger and retreats a step. "Nothing good can come from that."

I tug on my shirt and suffocate my dick behind my zipper. "I beg to differ."

"Thank you."

When our eyes lock again, something more serious, more sincere, ghosts across her face.

"For sex?" I cock my head a fraction.

A tiny smile curls her lips. "No. Well … yes. Kind of." She shrugs. "After Kyle and Emily died, I struggled to feel much of anything. It was oddly familiar. I've been there before."

I don't say it because she hasn't told me, but Mr. Hans did. She's referring to the boyfriend she lost. I want to ask, even though I *shouldn't* want to ask. We can't make this personal. The freckles all by themselves will make it hard to say goodbye.

"And then I had this huge responsibility. A ten-year-old. Panic … the first real and visceral feeling I had after they died was panic, but you …" Her lips submit to a full smile. "You've made me feel something besides panic. So, thank you."

After thinking of the correct, kind, yet not-too-sentimental response, I nod once. "You're welcome. For the sex. It's the least I can do."

She curls her hair behind her ears. "How long has it been since your parents have seen you and Morgan?"

"Eight years."

Her eyes double in size. "Seriously?"

I nod. "I offered several times to fly them to different locations like Paris and Tel Aviv, but my mom has bad arthritis, so they don't go to many places."

"And you never went home? In eight years, you never dropped by home to do a few loads of laundry or spend the holidays with your family?"

"Nope. This is the first time we've been back in the United States since we left. I figure once I put her in school, we can travel the states over breaks and summers. Road trips."

Gracelyn nods before her face wrinkles into a confused expression. "Gosh, I wonder if Gabe is expecting me to take him on vacations. I mean … places besides Montana to visit my parents."

"Did Kyle and Emily travel with him?"

"Yeah. I mean, some. Not every spring break, but I feel like they always took a summer trip. All of his friends have been going places. I was grateful to Mr. Hans for taking him to Disney, even if it was only for two days."

I nod. "I was grateful for that too."

She rolls her eyes. "I'm sure you were."

"I'm grateful he invited Morgan and Gabe to the hardware store today—even if I'm not happy she went without asking my permission."

Gracelyn possesses the unrestrained giggle of a young girl with a gleam in her eye that no amount of tragedy has managed to steal. While I first noticed a shadow of familiarity in her hair, a whisper from my past, it's all the tiny things unique to her that make it hard to look away and hard to hide this grin. I fear being her pen pal will feel like a crushing consolation prize in five weeks.

"You should bring your parents here for the Fourth of July, but don't ask for Morgan's thoughts on it. Just do it and surprise her. My parents are coming for the holiday."

I sit on the edge of the bed and frown. "Sounds like a busy, sexless gathering for the Fourth."

The corner of her mouth twitches. "That's not entirely true. My parents have sex every night—still—with few exceptions. It's always been one of my mother's June Cleaver, Suzy Homemaker roles." She fights the full-on grin. "When she explained the birds and the bees—yes, that's exactly what she called it too—she put it in the context of a goodnight kiss between married people. Something married couples do after they brush their teeth and turn off all the lights. She *still* says to my dad, 'Bill, time to turn in and get things done.'" More giggles. "Get. Things. Done. Who says that? I'll tell ya who … my mom."

I chuckle, shaking my head. "How does your dad react?"

"Oh god …" Running her fingers through her hair, she blows out a long breath. "That's the best part. He swats her ass and says, 'I'm ready anytime you are.' And in case you think I made false assumptions about this, I didn't. The walls in their house are thin; the bed creaks like an old swing, and my dad grunts like an animal in the desert using his last few breaths to make it to a water hole."

Snorting, I fist my hand at my mouth and shake with silent laughter.

"Don't laugh." She waggles a finger at me. "I've been assured it's the secret to a long and happy marriage. Not that I'll ever know." Her brow furrows.

I grab her wrist and pull her to me. She straddles my lap, resting her hands on my shoulders.

"I feel sorry for the dumb ass who left you at the altar. I guarantee he didn't find anyone who put out every single night."

"No …" She rolls her eyes. "Don't say *put out.*"

"Well, I can't wait to meet your parents."

"And yours?"

I nod. "Yes. I think you're right. Surprising Morgan is a great idea."

"Are you going to tell your parents that …" Her lips press together, eyes wide.

"Tell them what?" I inch forward, burying my face in her neck, nipping her skin until her shoulder and head jerk together. "That I *get things done* with my neighbor."

"Yeah." A few giggles. "That."

My hands slide up the back of her shirt and my lips brush along hers. "Are you going to leave your balcony door unlocked at night?" I nip at her bottom lip.

She pulls it from my teeth with a grin. "Sure. But my mom's a light sleeper, so don't be surprised if you wake her since they'll be in my bed and I'll be on the sofa."

"I'm not liking this setup."

"It could be fun. Just keep a condom in your pocket at all times so we can seize the moment."

Fuck me … this woman.

I grin. "Get-R-Done."

"No." She covers my mouth with her hand. "Don't ever say that again. You're my real-life Scottish soldier—minus the accent and kilt. Don't ruin it by sounding like a redneck. Understood?"

I nod once.

"Guac, let's get the Frisbee!"

Our eyes widen as we hear Morgan's voice on the side of the house by the balcony. Gracelyn flies off my lap and down the stairs. I follow, just not as quickly.

"Dad, where's the Frisbee?" Morgan sails through the door as I make my way down the stairs. She eyes Gracelyn standing at the bottom of the stairs, failing miserably at not looking guilty of murder or lewd sex acts. "What are you guys doing?" My daughter eyes us suspiciously.

"Newsflash, young lady … emphasis on the young. You still need to run your plans by me even if you think you don't need permission. That includes riding with the neighbor to the hardware store. Got it?" I cup her face and make her look at me.

"Fine." She frowns. "Where's the Frisbee?"

And just like that, she no longer cares what we were doing.

CHAPTER TWENTY-FOUR

Gracelyn

OVER THE NEXT week, a whisper of self-preservation tells me to focus on work, spend time with Gabe, make sure he gets to his last therapy session until after the holiday, soccer camp, laundry, and prep for my parents' arrival. Basically, avoid Nathaniel Hunt—giver of orgasms, stealer of sanity, man-ban obliterator.

"I hear something. I think they're here." Gabe runs down the stairs, and I follow him, feeling just as excited to see my mom and dad.

"They're here." Gabe tries to slide past Mr. Hans, who's sliding his socked feet into his Birkenstocks at the door.

"Sorry to disappoint, buddy, but it's not your grandparents. It's my exam van."

"Exam van?" Gabe asks, deflating from the news of it not being his grandparents.

"It's a mobile screening program. PSA. DRE. And a testicular exam."

"A what?" Gabe cringes.

"Oh … wow. They come to your house for that?" I ask.

Mr. Hans opens the door. "Just the driveway. It's like a mobile dog groomer, only for my prostate. And I'm not having them groom anything. Although, I could probably use some tidying up down there."

Gabe's face continues to wrinkle in disgust as I press my lips together and snort a laugh.

"PSA? Public Service Announcement?" Gabe asks.

Mr. Hans starts to step outside. "Prostate Specific Antigen … it's a blood test."

"What's the D-thing?" Gabe's curiosity just won't let this subject die.

"Digital Rectal Exam," he calls just before the screen door shuts behind him.

"What's that?"

"Nothing you need to know for about forty more years." I smile, brushing past him to sit out on the deck swing.

"Oh … that's not good." Gabe pushes through the screen door, staring at his phone.

"What's not good?" I ask, looking up my parents' location on my phone. They're still at the airport, probably waiting for a rental car. I told them I'd pick them up, but Dad likes to have his own car, and he hates letting anyone else drive.

"I looked up rectal exam. It's gross."

"Gabe …" I give him a sour look. "Don't look up anything with the word rectal involved. Please preserve your innocence a little."

He makes his way to the side of the house.

"Where are you going?" I pop to my feet from the swing and follow him.

"I just want to see the van."

"Just … stay back. Mr. Hans doesn't need you gawking at him when he comes out."

Gabe keeps inching his way toward the driveway. "I don't hear him."

I stop at the stairs to my balcony and take a seat, laughing.

"What do you expect to hear?"

"If someone stuck something up my butt, I'd be screaming."

"Shh … just get back here." I giggle.

"Hey, Gabe!" Morgan calls as she and Nate pull into their driveway on their bikes. "You moving?" she asks.

He shakes his head. "It's not a moving van. It's an exam van. They're doing something to Mr. Hans's butt."

Oh. My. God …

Nate unhooks his helmet and grins at me as I roll my eyes. "Please tell me he misheard what's actually happening," he says, sauntering toward me as Morgan and Gabe circle the van like it's a spaceship and they can't wait to see the aliens.

"I wish." I give myself one really quick look at Nate in his biking shorts, black fitted biking shirt, fancy biking shoes, and messy hair that's starting to grow back. Then I force my eyes to stay on his face, squinting against the sun. "My nephew now knows that PSA is not just a Public Service Announcement, but also a prostate specific antigen test, DRE stands for digital rectal exam, and when you're old, someone will drive a van to your house to give your testicles an exam as well. Oh!" I hold up my finger. "Mustn't forget to mention that Mr. H also compared it to a dog grooming truck, which segued into full disclosure that he could, in fact, use a *tidy up down there.* So how was your bike ride?"

He laughs, sitting next to me on the narrow steps which puts us close together as we watch the kids wait for the aliens to emerge. "It was a good ride, not nearly as informative as living with an old man who freely shares medical knowledge, but still good."

I shake my head, but it doesn't stop my cheesy grin. It's

funny and not at the same time ... but mostly funny.

Nate nudges my shoulder with his. "If I didn't know better, I'd say you've been avoiding me."

"Just been busy. My parents are at the airport, I assume waiting for their rental car. When do your parents arrive? Have you managed to keep it a secret? Surely you have, otherwise I'm certain Morgan would have been screaming it from the rooftop."

"Oh, she would definitely be in hyper-Morgan mode. They arrive late tonight. I'll make up a fun dad excuse like late-night ice cream and we'll get them from the airport. I'm not making them rent a car."

"Hey!" I pinch his side, and he jumps. "I'm not making my parents get a rental car. My dad is just too controlling to let anyone drive him. I've learned to let him do his thing because I'll never win the argument anyway."

I turn my head toward him, feeling his gaze on me.

"I could kiss you right now," he whispers, eyeing my lips.

"But you won't because young eyes could be on us."

"You might be right." He grins. "You might be wrong."

I shrug. "Then do it. Kiss me."

Nate's gaze flits over my shoulder toward the driveway then returns to me. "We'll see. In the meantime, I'll count your freckles."

"Eighty-two," I reply. "I counted them this morning. Eight-five yesterday. I'm losing them in spite of all the sun."

"You didn't count your freckles."

I didn't, but I like the way his eyes dance with amusement at the tiny prospect that I might not be lying. "Don't pretend you know m—"

He kisses me. Holy shit! He's kissing me!

It ends as abruptly as it began. I'm afraid to look behind me.

"Please tell me they didn't see that."

He smirks. "Tell me you care."

I open my mouth to tell him how much I care. Why he should care. And … some other great responses. Nothing comes out.

"When's the last time you had your PSA checked? Testicles examined? Finger up your rectum? I bet while they're in the neighborhood they could squeeze you in."

He wets his lips, making another quick glance over my shoulder. "I'm good on the PSA until I'm fifty. You examined my testicles quite thoroughly last week. As for the finger up my ass—"

I cover his mouth. "Stop! Don't go there."

He turns his face to break free from my muzzle, vibrating with laughter.

"When are you leaving? When will I be rid of you?" I narrow my eyes at him.

His laughter fades as his smile simmers into something bittersweet. His gaze stays connected to mine for a few seconds before he redirects it over my shoulder again, but I don't think he's tracking the kids, planning his next kiss. It's different.

A different I feel in my chest.

I'm not supposed to feel Nathaniel Hunt in my chest.

He's not supposed to take root in my mind.

His touch isn't allowed to linger on my skin.

Yet, here he is … making a mark that I fear will be difficult, if not impossible, to erase.

"I'll be gone before you know it. Nothing lasts."

"Memories last."

Nate returns his attention to me, a hint of tension in his brow as he gives me several tiny nods. "True. Memories last."

"We've made some …" How do I be sincere without cracking my chest open and handing him my heart like a fool? "Well, we've made some fun memories. Unexpected memories. You must feel that a lot. Traveling the world for eight years has to have filled your mind with lasting memories. I'm sure you've made so many friends all over the world."

He nods again. "I have. Some more *friendly* than others."

I blush, curling my hair behind my ears. "Why San Diego? I mean, if you're only exploring one stop in the U.S., how did you decide on San Diego?"

"That was all Morgan. She wrote down three major cities from each state on pieces of paper, put all one hundred and fifty in a hat, and had me draw one. I drew San Diego. So … it's as simple as fortuity."

I grin. "Wow. That's crazy. I'm officially a fan of fortuity."

His knee nudges mine. "Me too."

"Can we go inside?" Morgan's voice, like always, carries a long way as she starts giving Mr. Hans the third degree. "What did they do? Did it hurt? How do things stay in place when the van is moving? Where did they take the blood from?"

Nate stands. "I'd better rescue the poor old guy."

"Probably." I squint, shading my eyes with my hand as the three of them walk in this direction.

"Dad! Gabe's grandma and grandpa are coming tonight. They're from Montana. I've never been to Montana. We should go sometime."

Nate tugs on her ponytail. "You poor thing. I never take you anywhere."

She rolls her eyes.

"Fit as a fiddle?" Nate asks Mr. Hans.

His words trip over his half chuckle, half cough. "Good … to go for another twenty thousand miles. How's your prostate?"

Nate grins at me just before I turn and follow Gabe and Morgan. "Still the size of a walnut, but thanks for asking."

I snigger without glancing over my shoulder.

"Where are your grandma and grandpa going to sleep? We have two extra bedrooms. They could sleep at our house? Or you could sleep at our house? Dad … can Gabe sleep at our house?"

I jump in and save us all from the madness. "Thanks, Morgan, but they're sleeping in my bed and I'm sleeping on the sofa."

Mr. Hans heads into the house while the rest of us hash out sleeping arrangements on the boardwalk between the two houses, the wind whipping my hair in my face.

"Well, you could stay with us. You could sleep with my dad." She shoots Nate an ornery look, and I die. This girl is too damn smart. Ten going on thirty.

"Uh … that's weird." Gabe laughs, kicking at some dried bird poop. "She'd sleep with you because you're a girl, not your dad."

Morgan cups her hands at her mouth and leans toward Gabe. He does the typical boy thing and backs away from her advance.

"They like each other," she whispers loud enough for everyone to hear.

"Okay … let's go inside, Gabe, and track Grandma and Grandpa on my phone." I ruffle his hair.

Gabe ignores me and wrinkles his nose at Morgan. "You're being weird."

She rolls her eyes before squealing from Nate tossing her over his shoulder. “You are definitely being weird, Squirt! Let’s go get showers. You stink.”

“Stop!” She giggles. “I don’t stink.”

Just before I go in the house, I glance over at Nate opening his screen door and giving me one last glance.

It’s a good glance, the kind that happens in slow motion, or at least that’s how I’ll always remember it.

Fortuity …

CHAPTER TWENTY-FIVE

Nathaniel

"WHY WON'T YOU let me go over there?" Morgan pesters me as we eat macaroni and cheese with peas and carrots on the deck in our favorite rockers. I had to bear-hug her to keep her from running outside when they arrived.

Narrowing my eyes, I point my fork at her. "You know why."

"Ugh …" She throws her head back in true Morgan dramatic fashion. "You said we are just people, all connected. You said we make villages … make family wherever we go."

Valid point.

I did say that many times.

"That *is* how it is with the rest of the world, but in the United States, family is defined by blood, law, and loyalty."

"I'm loyal."

I shake my head. "We haven't been here long enough to prove loyalty. Therefore you are the snoopy neighbor girl, who has suddenly found her father to be the most boring person in the world, looking for any excuse to be with anyone else but me."

"You're so needy."

"Ouch!" I fake jabbing my fork into my chest. "That was fatal."

"Whatevs … I'm going to my room."

"You've been spending a lot of time in your room. What do you do up there?"

"Read. Knit. Plan my wedding." She flings open the door.

"Can't get married without my blessing."

"That's not true," her voice echoes before the door clicks shut.

My needy self finishes my gourmet meal—not out of a box. Nope. I make macaroni and cheese from scratch. It's a skill I picked up when we stayed in a tiny German town that didn't have it in a box. Yes … parts of the world have not experienced the miracle of macaroni and powdered cheese from a box.

When I hear voices next door, I stop my gentle, creaky rocking. Gabe runs down the deck stairs followed by Gracelyn and her parents. Her mom smiles at something Gracelyn says as they both slide their purses over their shoulders in the same casual manner.

She's a slightly more filled-out version of Gracelyn with a tousled gray and auburn pixie cut, dangling earrings, and red lipstick. The man resting his hand on Gabe's shoulder looks like a giant in dark trousers and a white button-down. His gray comb-over reveals his hidden dome when the breeze grabs it. Really … he must be at least six-seven. A broad-shouldered man who could be cast for the role of a basketball coach.

Gracelyn does a double take as if she wasn't expecting me to be sitting so still watching her.

"Off to dinner?" I ask, feeling the need to say something since she's spotted me.

My question stops everyone. Her mom lifts an eyebrow at her daughter, who can't keep from smiling at me. Yep, I'm the neighbor who has a thing for your daughter. She's pretty fucking perfect. I'm not sure her mom reads all of that in my grin, but it's there. It's always there.

"Yes. Gabe wants pizza. Um …" Her words falter as her parents eye her.

Of course, they want to know who I am. As the father of a girl, I already know I'd sure as hell want to know why some guy I'd never met was eyeing my daughter like his favorite snack.

I save her because I try to imagine what a guy could do to win me over if Morgan liked him. The answer is nothing, but she's ten. "Hi. I'm Nathaniel Hunt. My daughter and Gabe have become good friends." I stand at the edge of the deck and lean on the railing. No need to shake hands and hold them up too long. That's what Morgan would do. She'd talk them into starvation. Of course, I mean that in the most loving way.

"Yes, uh …" Gracelyn plasters on a cool smile, but her pink cheeks tell the real truth, and her mom's brow-lifted gaze at her says she knows there's more to this story too. "Nate, these are my parents, Sharon and Forest."

"Nice to meet you," they say in unison.

Sharon clears her throat and eyes me with her daughter's smile. "Married?"

"Mom!" Gracelyn grits through her teeth.

"Widowed. It's just me and my daughter."

"I'm so sorry." Her smile fades.

I shake my head. "It's been ten years. But condolences to you for your loss too."

A small smile reappears along her red lips, but it's not the same one. It's sad. It's … life. "Thank you."

"I'm hungry," Gabe sighs.

Forest grips his shoulders. "Then let's get you fed."

"Enjoy your dinner." I smile.

Gracelyn's parents follow Gabe to the front of the house, and she drags behind them, holding my gaze for a few extra seconds.

I wink and she grins a little more before looking forward. That woman … she makes every day a little better. I can't really explain it. Jenna had that same magic, so did Daisy. And of course … no one has it quite like Morgan.

Instead of thinking how it will feel to leave Gracelyn, I sit down in my rocker and give thanks to whatever power has granted me the gift of sharing parts of my life with so many great women.

"SLIP ON YOUR shoes." I slide my wallet into my front pocket and retrieve the key fob from the counter.

Morgan glances up from her beanbag and her knitting. "It's almost my bedtime. Where are we going?"

"It's a holiday week. I feel like ice cream."

Her eyes widen, jaw unhinging. "Are you serious?"

"I could tell you were a little envious of Gabe's grandparents coming for the Fourth, so I thought ice cream might make things better."

She caps her needles and jumps up. "Ice cream makes everything better."

"Oh!" I grunt when she hugs me so hard I take a few steps back.

"Thank you for being the best dad ever."

I hug her. "You're wrong. My little girl … who is trying way too hard to become a woman … *she* makes everything okay."

We get ice cream. We make a mess of it. We laugh.

I take all that she'll give me. The future holds plenty of regimen, unbendable schedules, and homework. Right now, ice cream makes sense.

"What is this? Where are we?" Morgan asks, sitting up straighter.

"It's the airport. I have to grab something."

"What do you grab from an airport?"

I shoot her a quick sideways glance. "You'll see."

"Just tell me."

"Just wait." I laugh.

"I can't wait."

"You can."

"Daaad!"

"Mooorgan!"

She crosses her arms over her chest and grumbles something I can't understand.

We park and go inside. "Have a seat." I nod beside me as I sit on a bench by the arrivals.

"What are we doing? Is this another treasure hunt?"

I'm kind of awesome at setting up treasure hunts for her. "Not tonight."

"Then what?"

"Then patience."

She leans her head on my arm. Ten minutes later, just as she starts to nod off, I nudge her. "Who's that? They look familiar."

Sitting up and yawning, she rubs her eyes. "Who?"

I point.

"Oh my god ..." she whispers.

I try to remain calm, but it's been eight years since I've seen my parents in person.

"That's … that's my grandma and grandpa."

Mom cries as soon as she spies us on the bench. I swear my dad has tears in his eyes too. Me? Yeah, I'm fighting it too.

"My babies …" Mom drops the handle to her suitcase and holds out her arms.

"Grandma!" Morgan runs to her.

I follow, quickly finding my dad's embrace. We've talked and video chatted. It's not the same.

"Grandpa!" Morgan pulls away from my mom and we swap.

"My boy," she whispers past the emotion in her throat.

"Missed you guys." I let her hug me a little longer before pulling back. "I'm so glad you agreed to come."

"I can't believe you did this!" Morgan is fully awake now.

I'm not sure we'll get her settled down to sleep for days.

"You guys are better than ice cream." She presses her hands to her face like she still can't believe it.

They laugh as I grab mom's suitcase and lead everyone to the exit.

"I can't wait to show you our house. And you're going to love Gabe. He's the neighbor I told you about. And Mr. Hans is our landlord. He took me to Disneyland, which is the happiest place on Earth. And …" She doesn't stop talking until we make it home. Even then, she takes a breath and keeps going.

Eventually, I get her to bed and my parents settled into a guest room. They're on a different time zone, so I don't keep them up any later talking.

The next morning, I get up early for my jog. When I return, *everyone* is up and gathered in my kitchen. *Everyone.*

"Morning. Morgan invited us all for breakfast. Hope that's okay?" Mr. Hans gives me a wink from the kitchen table where he's drinking coffee with my dad and Gracelyn's dad. My mom, Gracelyn, and her mom are making eggs, sausages, and pancakes. The culprit and her sidekick are in the living room watching television.

"Wow … so … everyone's met, I assume."

Gracelyn glances over her shoulder after flipping a few pancakes on a griddle I didn't know we had and smirks. "It's all your daughter. She said something about a village, but I didn't catch all of it."

Feeling too sweaty and probably too smelly to join the fun, I jab my thumb toward the stairs. "Well, I'm going to grab a quick shower."

I don't linger in the shower with a house full of guests downstairs. When I get out, I tie the towel around my waist, brush my teeth, and roll on some deodorant.

"I'm going to miss that body."

I glance up, a little startled by the voice and smirk from my favorite neighbor sitting on my bed, looking pretty fucking spectacular in her yellow sundress, glossed lips, and bare feet dangling off the side.

"This body is going to miss you looking at it."

"Just came up here to let you know breakfast is done, and if you don't hurry up, Gabe will eat all the pancakes."

"Then I'd better hurry up."

Her gaze makes a slow trip up my chest, her tongue wetting her lips as she nods. "Yeah … better."

I chuckle. "You leaving, or are you staying to watch me get dressed?"

When her eyes meet mine, she grins. "I might stay." She

shrugs. "After all, you watch me strip all the time."

"Sometimes." I correct her, retrieving briefs and shorts from my dresser. When I drop my towel, her eyes bulge into saucers.

Yes. I have an erection.

"Whoa …" she says slowly.

I smirk, stepping into my briefs. "What can I say? I really like your dress."

She coughs a laugh as her smile grows. "Yeah you do."

After buttoning and zipping my shorts, I snag a tee from the closet and slip it on. "Did you enjoy the show?" I hold out my hand to her to pull her off the bed.

She places her hand in mine. "More than you can imagine."

I pull her toward the stairs. "Does your mom know you like to stare at naked men after they shower?"

She snorts a laugh. "No. She raised me better than that."

I turn toward her after taking one step down. "What happened?"

She presses her hands to my cheeks. "Professor Nathaniel Hunt, American Jamie, hockey showoff, endearing single dad …" Her thumb brushes along my bottom lip. She does it a lot.

I like it … a lot.

"He said he wanted to kiss me." She shrugs, trapping her lower lip between her teeth, giving me that sexy smile. "And it shook me like a snow globe or maybe more like a martini because after he said it to me, I felt drunk …" Her voice lowers to barely even a whisper. "You're so…" she shakes her head slightly, like she's trying to figure it out as she goes "…intoxicating."

Encircling her wrist to keep her thumb at my lips, I nibble it. "This … selfish … un-fatherly part of me wants to die right now."

Her brows knit together. "Why?"

"So I can come back in another body and be the young nurse you have an affair with in the nursing home."

Her head inches side to side as her mouth inches closer to mine. "So intoxicating …"

"Dad?" Morgan calls from the living room.

We smile. I release her hand, and we descend the stairs.

Neighbors.

Friends.

Pen pals.

CHAPTER TWENTY-SIX

Gracelyn

"NATHANIEL IS QUITE handsome," Mom says as we swing on the deck, watching Nate swim with the kids while Dad and Mr. Hans get groceries for our holiday celebration tonight.

"He's fine."

"Fine or *fine*?"

I grin. "Your point?"

"I see him look at you."

"We're neighbors. Gabe and Morgan are friends. It's hard to not occasionally *look* at each other."

Nate's mom pushes through the screen door, carrying a glass of lemonade. She takes a seat in the rocker opposite us.

"I was just telling Gracelyn how handsome your son is."

Thanks, Mom …

She smiles. "Just like his father. Nathaniel has been through so much. I'm glad he took Morgan away and lived the dream he and Jenna had always hoped to share with their little girl. We didn't think he'd do it. So much happened after Jenna died. Nate's past. His nanny. Trying to figure out how to be a single dad."

The nanny. I need more information on this nanny. Why mention her unless there was something to it beyond just hired help? It's odd.

"We're glad it's about over, though. Eight years is a long time to go without being able to hug your child and your granddaughter." She frowns. "I'm sorry, Sharon. That was insensitive. Nathaniel told us you lost a child. It's unimaginable."

Mom keeps her gaze on the water as we swing our legs in unison. "No apologies. You weren't insensitive. I'm sure eight years felt like a lifetime. Honestly, I still keep thinking I'm going to see Kyle or that he's going to call me. It might take me eight years or more before reality really hits. It's easier to think that he's traveling." She rests her hand on my leg, and I rest my hand on hers.

"Our little granddaughter sure thinks the world of Gabe."

"I HATE YOU, GABE! I HATE YOU! I HATE YOU! I HATE YOU!"

Our three heads whip toward the beach, the commotion, and Morgan marching up the sandy hill in her red bikini, hands fisted and wet hair plastered to her face.

"I may … have spoken too soon," Nate's mom murmurs.

Nate follows Morgan, shooting us a confused expression while Gabe grabs a towel and dries off, not seeming the least bit phased by the recent outburst.

It's so very … male-female, yin-yang, Mars-Venus.

"You're up," Mom says, nudging my arm as Nate's mom sets her drink on the little round table and heads to their house.

"I'm up." I nod. "Yeah, I'll just … talk to him."

"You let him know you're on his side, no matter what."

After standing, I glance over my shoulder. "What if he's in the wrong?"

"He needs a team. He'll need you the most when he's wrong."

"You know I'm terrible at this, right?"

She smirks. "Doesn't matter. I'm always on your side. I'm *your* team."

Tears burn my eyes as I smile. "Thank you," I whisper over the lump in my throat.

If I don't mess this up, if Gabe turns out okay, it's because I've had the very best mom setting the very best example. There are so many things I remember about her raising me, but the underlying emotion has always … *always* been love.

After Brandon died and his family left his bedside, she stood in the doorway to his room and refused to let anyone take him away until my last tear fell, until my hand released his. She insisted I stay with her for two weeks after Andy cheated on me so she could protect me from anyone telling me to just "get over it and move on."

When Michael left me at the altar, she had the DJ play my favorite songs as my family and friends stayed to eat all the food, drink all the alcohol, and cake … Mom insisted I cut the cake. I'm pretty sure I ate most of it too. She never asked me why Michael walked away because she knew.

She knew it was my fault. Yet … she was on Team Gracelyn.

When Gabe makes his way to the porch with messy hair and a towel wrapped around him, Mom goes inside. I nod to the steps, and we sit next to each other, staring out at the water.

"So …" I sigh. "What just went down?"

"I can't tell you."

"Well, I guarantee you Morgan is over there telling her dad everything. It—"

"No." He shakes his head. "Trust me. She's not."

"Why do you say that?"

"Because she doesn't want to get in trouble."

I chuckle. "I'm not following. It seemed like you did something to upset her, but *she's* the one worried about getting in trouble?"

He nods.

"Did you threaten to tell on her? Is that why she's upset?"

Gabe shakes his head.

I don't speak pre-teen. It's a complicated language that's a mix of vague words, crooked facial expressions, shrugs, nods, and head shakes. A translator would come in handy right now.

"What if I keep it a secret?"

Another head shake. "You won't."

"Why do you say that?"

"Because grown-ups share everything."

"Is she taking drugs, drinking, or smoking something she shouldn't be?"

"No."

"Did she steal something or kill someone?"

He smirks and shares an eye roll. "No."

"Then you can safely tell me, and I won't tell Nate."

He blows out a long breath. "She has a phone."

"A cellphone?"

Gabe shoots me a look. I'd say a "duh" look. "Is there any other kind?"

"Actually, yes, but we can go over that later. How did she get a cellphone?"

"When we went to Disneyland with Hunter, she got a new phone, but they didn't have to give back her old phone because of how old it was. So she gave her old phone to Morgan so they could message and do stuff on social media. She can only use it with Wi-Fi. She can't actually call anyone. Hunter set up an email account for her too."

"Wow … okay. Sounds like a real coup."

"What's a coup?"

"Sorry … it's … I just meant it was quite the plan to get her a phone without her dad knowing."

"You can't tell him."

"I'm not, but now can you explain why she hates you?"

He picks at a string hanging from the towel. "I won't follow her on TikTok."

"Oh … well, I'm not that familiar with TikTok. That's why she hates you?"

His nose wrinkles.

"Gabe …"

He frowns. "I don't follow any girls on there because they do the most annoying stuff. My friends don't follow girls either. And she just kept bugging me to follow her and asking why I wouldn't. So I told her."

I wait.

Nothing.

"I'm going to need to know exactly what you told her."

"You said you wouldn't say anything."

"I'm not, but I still need to know what I'm working with here so I can find some way to deal with the damage."

Rolling his eyes to the sky, he shakes his head. "I said I don't follow girls because they are annoying. She asked if I thought she was annoying."

"Annnd?"

"I said sometimes. And she just lost it."

"Wow … okay. Well, I think she likes you … a lot. So I'm sure when you said that, it hurt her more than it would if she didn't like you so much."

"I know … it's just that she's always talking, always asking me things that I don't know, saying weird stuff, bragging about places she's been. And she's leaving next month, so I don't know why she thinks we need to be best friends. I have other friends. It's not my fault that she doesn't."

Ouch …

How do you teach a child to reason when they are not mentally capable of doing it very well?

It sucks to like someone when they don't like you back the same way. I was Gabe. I was the one who just couldn't reciprocate equally. Maybe the heart is like a child—impulsive and unable to reason.

I tried to love Andy and Michael the way I loved Brandon. My brain pushed my heart to feel something it didn't—it tried to make it see reason and reality. We can't turn off the sun, run from the wind, or push back the tide. Some forces are just too strong.

Love isn't an emotion. It's a force.

"Well…" I wrap my arm around him, hugging him to me while kissing his wet head "…I won't make you apologize for your feelings, but when things cool down, you should consider apologizing for hurting hers."

We glance left at Nate walking our way.

"I'm out of here." Gabe stands and runs inside.

Nate's gaze narrows as it follows Gabe's retreat. "Where's he going?" He stops at the bottom of the steps, crossing his arms over his chest.

"Inside to change his clothes."

"Well, we need to talk. Morgan refuses to let me into her room. She won't talk to my mom either. I need to know what happened."

My nose wrinkles. "I think you need to wait for Morgan to tell you."

"Do *you* know?"

Biting my lips shut, I nod.

"Then tell me."

"I can't. I promised Gabe I wouldn't."

Nate's eyebrows slide into peaks. "Are you serious? That's not how this works. We're the parents. We stick together to get these issues solved. You can't not tell me because you pinky swore."

"It wasn't a pinky swear. Just a regular promise." I smirk.

Nate doesn't show signs of finding this humorous at all.

"Look …" I stand, brushing off the back of my shorts, my one step putting me closer to eye level with him. "I don't know how to navigate all the drama that comes with raising a child, but I do know I want Gabe to feel comfortable confiding in me. We need that kind of trust. So while I won't tell you details, I can say it's nothing awful, just something that ended up being a little hurtful on his part. I fully expect him to eventually apologize to Morgan."

He stares at me without blinking for several seconds. "Wow … okay. I thought we had developed some sort of team effort to deal with them. Apparently not."

When he turns back toward his house, I grab his arm. "Whoa … whoa … wait. Where are you going? Are you seriously mad at me? It's not a big deal. Can't you just trust me and be patient? Wait for Morgan to tell you in her own time?"

"You're letting them pit us against each other. You're protecting him when he just needs to be honest with everyone. You're acting like an accomplice not a parent."

I release his arm. "You're just pissed off that Gabe's not

afraid to tell me the truth. Maybe if you stopped trying to control her so much, she might not lock you out of her room … out of her life."

He opens his mouth to reply but closes it just as quickly and walks away. I fight the urge to stop him again, to try again to reason with him. I'm no better than Gabe at explaining my feelings without offending anyone.

"We're loaded up."

I turn toward my dad's voice as he, Nate's dad, and Mr. Hans head my way with bags of groceries. "Hey. Great." Fake smiles have never been easy for me, but I do my best. Our parents are here. Mr. Hans is excited about our grilling plans tonight, and it's a holiday. I'm not going to let two ten-year-olds ruin this.

"Which place?" Dad asks when they reach the boardwalk.

"Mine …" I grin at Mr. Hans. "Yours." I wink.

He chuckles as I lead them up the stairs. "Technically, they're both mine."

The men deposit the groceries on the island, and my mom and I start unpacking everything.

"Beer?" Mr. Hans opens the fridge.

David and my dad perk up and take cans from him as he hands them out.

"We're good. We have food to prepare." I wink when he holds up two more cans for us.

He shrugs. "Okay, we'll just get out of your way then."

The guys disappear to the deck.

"How did things go with Nathaniel?" Mom asks as I wash vegetables.

"Not good. I don't think he adheres to the same team motto. He thinks I'm supposed to be on his team, not Gabe's. He's upset that Gabe told me what happened, but I wouldn't tell him because I don't want to break my promise to Gabe. If it were something major, something life threatening, I'd say something."

"Maybe you should say something to Morgan. Woman to woman."

"But I'm Team Gabe."

She grins while taking the scrubbed potatoes and peppers from me to cut up. "You don't have to talk to her about Gabe. Talk to her about Nathaniel. Maybe get her to open up to him."

"You want me to be Team Nate?"

"Oh, baby ..." She eyes me with an ornery grin. My grin. We share the same smile. "I'm quite certain you were Team Nate before we arrived."

I frown, returning my attention to the running water and veggies. "He's mad at me."

"Lovers' quarrel."

"We're not lovers." I laugh.

"Have you kissed him?"

I scrub the last few layers really hard. "Can you believe Morgan had never been to Disneyland? Nate doesn't like stuff like that. I guess he thinks it's too commercialized. He's in for a rude awakening when she goes to public school this fall."

Mom nods slowly while cutting potatoes. "So he's a really good kisser?"

I grin. "Yeah ... he's a phenomenal kisser."

"Go." She turns, pointing the knife at me. "I've got this. Go make things right. Go be Team Nate."

I narrow my eyes, not wanting her to be right *all* the time, even if she is. "Fine."

CHAPTER TWENTY-SEVEN

Nathaniel

AS I DRINK a much-needed beer on the deck with the rest of the guys, Gracelyn shuffles her flip-flop clad feet in our direction.

"Mom need help?" her dad asks.

She shakes her head, climbing the stairs. "No. We thought it would be best if I came over here to check on Morgan."

"What's wrong with Morgan?" Dad asks me.

"Nothing. She's fine." I take a swig of my beer, eyeing Gracelyn, letting her know with a look that my daughter is fine and doesn't need her to do anything.

"Just girl stuff." Her lips pull into a smirk as she opens the door.

I don't like anyone undermining my authority with my child, so I set my beer aside and follow her into the house where Morgan is helping my mom make deviled eggs for the party. She's also doing all the laundry and dishes from now until she fesses up, but I doubt she'll disclose that.

"Hey, Morgan, can I talk with you alone for a few seconds?"

Morgan looks up from the table and the partially peeled egg in her hand and gives my mom a look as I hang back just inside the door.

My mom smiles and nods. "I'll head over and help your

mom as soon as I'm done here."

Gracelyn waves her off. "She's good. I'm heading back over just as soon as I'm done talking to Morgan." She turns to follow Morgan upstairs. They give me an evil glare but don't say anything. I hold my own. This isn't my fault they're keeping secrets from me. I'm the only functioning adult in this situation.

When I hear the bedroom door click shut, I inch up the stairs and hover next to the door with my ear almost touching it.

"Gabe told me about your secret."

"Gah! He's such a snitch."

Gracelyn laughs a little. "I'm not defending what he said to you, even though I do believe he wasn't intentionally trying to be mean or hurt you. And the only reason he told me everything was because you put him in an impossible situation because you don't want to tell your dad."

"I can't tell him. He won't understand. I'm already sentenced to laundry and dishes for something he knows nothing about. He would kill me … literally kill me if he found out."

I stand corrected. She has no issue telling Gracelyn about her punishment. And for the record … I would never *literally* kill her for anything. I roll my eyes before closing them and shaking my head.

"Listen, I don't have a sob story to give you about my terrible childhood. Honestly, I have great parents. It's not that I never got in trouble. I did. But I never questioned their love for me, the way you should never question your dad's love for you."

"He doesn't want me to grow up. He doesn't want me to be like other kids. He worries about everything. And … and I feel like I'm his whole world, which I know should be a really great feeling. But it's not. Why can't he be happy even if I do something that he doesn't like? Why can't he love me if I'm normal and like other kids?"

Ouch!

I flinch. That hurts.

"First, normal doesn't mean you're not unique. No two people are exactly alike. Your dad wants ..."

I lean closer to the door, but I can't hear anything. What does Gracelyn think I want? She's been a parent for two seconds. How can she know what I want for this young girl who has owned every inch of my being for over ten years?

"Your dad wants the best for you. The problem with wanting the best for someone is that it changes. What was best for you yesterday might not be the same today. It's hard to see changes that are sometimes so subtle. It's why adults feel like kids grow up in a blink. Trust me, you will always be a tiny, swaddled baby in your dad's eyes."

"But I'm not a baby."

"I know. And he knows it too. Moms and dads don't like to think that their babies are getting bigger. So we're always a few steps behind in seeing it. You need to just give your dad that little extra time to see it."

"What if he never sees it?"

"He will."

Another thirty seconds of silence follows. I hate this door. I hate feeling so completely shut out of her life when I feel like she needs me the most.

"Now ... I want to give you a little advice about boys. Ignore them until they chase you, until they write you a million love letters, until they steal flowers from their mom's rose garden to give you, until they steal that first kiss and give you the best grin before they tell you they regret nothing."

Morgan giggles.

This woman … she's slowly killing me.

"I like that," Morgan says. "Stolen kisses. I want to plan on stolen kisses."

"No. Stolen kisses are never planned. And here's another thing you need to know right now … ten-year-old boys don't write love letters or steal more than candy at the bank. Gabe's still trying to figure out how to be Gabe. He's desperate to hold onto the familiar since his world disappeared a few months ago. And he, too, is trying to figure out where he fits in. Give him a chance to apologize."

"Will you talk to my dad? I know if I tell him, he'll take it away."

"Then you have a weak case. You're the smartest young girl I have ever met, and I was a pretty smart cookie when I was young, but you're smarter. So if you think you deserve this chance, then *you* have to show him with your words, not mine."

Morgan's sigh is audible. "Fine."

That's my cue to leave before they open the door. I hightail it downstairs into the kitchen.

"Eavesdropping?" Mom asks, filling the halved eggs.

"No." I grab a drink of water. "Yes." I grin just before taking a sip.

"I like Gracelyn."

I nod.

She grins. "Morgan does too."

"Yeah." I set the empty glass onto the counter.

"Wrong place, right time."

I'm inclined to play dumb and make her spell it out for me, but I'm not dumb. "We both know that."

Mom shrugs, returning her attention to the deviled eggs spread out on several plates on the table. "Knowing won't stop anything. And it won't make it any easier to leave."

Before I can respond, Morgan and Gracelyn come down the stairs, giggling about something. When they see me, their smiles vanish. It's not the effect I want to have on either one of them. It sucks.

"Well…" Gracelyn nods toward the screen door. "I'm just going to see if my mom needs help finishing up. We can probably have Mr. Hans start the grill soon."

As she goes to turn, Morgan throws her arms around Gracelyn's waist.

"Oh …" Gracelyn says on a startle.

"Thank you," Morgan whispers.

"You are in trouble …" my mom whispers in a singsong voice so only I can hear her.

"You're welcome." She hugs Morgan back and kisses the top of her head.

CHAPTER TWENTY-EIGHT
Gracelyn

"HOW DID IT go?" Mom asks when I walk into the kitchen.

I answer her with an unexpected hug from behind like the one Morgan gave me.

She pauses her stirring of the brownie batter. "Whoa … what is this all about?"

"I wanted to be a mom," I whisper in her ear, resting my chin on her shoulder. "Brandon and I were going to have two kids, a dog, and goldfish. I wanted the chance to be awesome like you. Maybe not with the apron, but still pretty awesome."

She laughs on a tiny sob, resting the spoon in the bowl and covering my hands with hers.

"I *hate* that Brandon is gone. I *hate* that Kyle and Emily died. I *hate* that Gabe lost the two most important people in his life. But…" I draw in a shaky breath "…I'm going to love him like a mom would love her son. I'm going to give him everything I would have given my own children. This is the most heartbreaking way to come into motherhood, but I'm going to embrace what I've been given. I'm going to make you proud."

She squeezes my hands. "Oh, Gracelyn … there hasn't been a single day of your life that I haven't been proud of you. And I've *always* known you'd be a wonderful mom. Don't ever doubt that … and don't ever doubt yourself."

"We're here for the meat," Nate and his dad stop at the entrance to the kitchen, eyes wide.

I release my mom, and we wipe our tears and put on our best smiles.

"Is … everything okay?" Nate asks.

"Just girls crying over girl things. You two boys wouldn't understand." Mom winks at them before returning her attention to the brownies.

I pull the tray of prepared hamburgers from the fridge, finding it hard in my emotional state to meet Nate's gaze. "Are the other two guys starting the grill?" I sniffle, in bad need of a tissue.

Nate takes the tray from me and hands it to his dad. "Yes. It's ready to go."

I stare at the floor, knowing my eyes are red. If I glance up, I'll start crying again. Where did all of these emotions come from?

My breath catches when his hand cups my face, lifting my chin, forcing me to look at him. His dad and my mom are in plain sight. They're seeing this. Nate doesn't look at them. I don't look at them.

His thumb brushes along my wet cheek, and he smiles.

Fuck you, Brandon.

Why doesn't he say something? I'm falling in love with another man—not like I fell in love with Andy, not like I fell in love with Michael. I'm falling in love with Nate the way I fell in love with Brandon.

Heart first.

Slowly.

Completely.

Brandon never cared what anyone thought. He never hid his feelings for me, his affection, his love. Brandon wrote me love letters. He stole flowers from his mom's garden to give to me.

Nate's going to write me letters too. With his hand on my face, there's no doubt they will be love letters. He steals kisses. He doesn't hide moments like this, even though we have every reason to hide it.

If I think for one second that Nathaniel Hunt isn't going to unintentionally break my heart when he leaves just as much as that young man in the hospital bed did years ago when he took his last breath, then I'm fucking delusional.

This is going to hurt.

"Gabe and Morgan are outside talking. You did good, Elvis." He releases my face and turns toward his dad, who eyes us with a slack jaw and unblinking gaze.

"I'll get the door," he says to his dad.

David closes his mouth, swallows hard, and nods once before following his son out the door.

I glance up at my mom.

She shakes her head while walking the pan of brownies to the oven.

"What?" I ask.

"You know what."

"He's leaving. I'm staying. I know."

"That's not it." She shuts the oven and sets the timer.

"Then what?"

Her gaze falls to my wrist as she nods once.

My other hand crosses my body to cover my watch and, more specifically, the bracelet she's eyeing.

"You're not ready."

I fiddle with the clasp. "It's been nearly twenty years."

"Tell that to the bracelet that you refuse to take off."

"I take it off."

"Have you gone a whole day without wearing it?"

I shrug. "I don't know."

"Well …" She opens the fridge and pulls out pitchers of iced tea and lemonade. "When you go twenty-four hours without wearing it or thinking about it … then you're ready."

"Ready for what?"

"That man who had his hand on your face like he thinks you're the most precious thing in the world, second only to his daughter … and maybe his mother. I'm not sure yet."

"Let me go back to my original statement—he's leaving and I'm staying."

"Is that why you're still wearing the bracelet? Would you take it off if he were staying or if you thought you could pack up Gabe and follow them to Wisconsin?"

I start to say something but clamp my jaw shut and deflate a little because I'm not sure how to respond. My heart and brain aren't in sync on this yet.

"It's okay, Gracelyn. It's not simple. Your decisions are no longer just about you. Nate's decisions are not just about him. I can't even begin to imagine how hard it would be to develop and navigate a new relationship at your age, with Gabe new in your life and a new love interest living halfway across the country." She starts washing the dishes, and I grab a towel to dry.

"Maybe he's practice. Maybe he's been brought into your life to help you let go a little more. I don't really believe in your three-strike theory, your man ban." She glances over at me and grins. "I think your heart will one day be ready to love another man the way you loved Brandon. Hearts are meant to beat and keep us alive. They're also there to love, not sit on a shelf in timeout, or in your case, a strikeout. When the time is right, get back in the game and let that heart of yours fall in love again. Okay?"

It already has …

CHAPTER TWENTY-NINE

GABE AND MORGAN laugh and play like nothing happened earlier today. Kids don't know the art of holding grudges quite as well as grown-ups.

They wait for the fireworks to start while eating brownies and ice cream. Mr. Hans and our dads sit on Nate's deck and drink more beer. Mom and Shauna hang out inside, making a couple cups of decaf to have with their brownies.

I stand at the water's edge in my bare feet, feeling mesmerized by the ebb and flow of the soft tide over my red painted toes.

"Walk with me?"

I turn toward Nate, pinning my blowing hair behind my ears while glancing past him. Nobody's paying any attention to us. Mr. Hans and our dads are watching Gabe and Morgan.

"Yeah." I smile and start walking down the beach.

Nate's hand finds mine as the horizon morphs into beautiful shades of orange, red, and purple. "The secret … it's the phone isn't it?"

My head whips up, eyes wide.

He doesn't look at me. His gaze tracks the miles of coastline before us. "I was walking past her room late one night, and something was glowing from under her sheet. She fell asleep with it in her bed, and the screen was lighting up with a notification from Hunter asking if I'd found out about the cellphone yet."

"And you didn't say anything …" I shake my head. "She's a wreck. Scared to death to tell you. Why not put her out of her misery?"

"Just like you said, she needs to find the words to just be honest with me."

"Oh my gosh!" I shove him. "You were listening to our conversation."

He chuckles, his bare feet splashing into the water before correcting himself and taking my hand again. "Of course, I was listening. Knowledge is power."

"And trust?"

He shakes his head. "Trust is fragile. You have to be careful with it. It's easy to break someone's trust, even if you love them. I'm not saying it's not an important component of a relationship, but it can't be everything. I was an ornery child, who occasionally got into fights and told many white lies. My parents didn't always trust me, but they always loved me. They forgave my mistakes and my lies. You have to treat trust like modeling clay that can be broken and repaired a million times, not like a priceless vase that belonged to your dead grandmother."

"So … Andy, the guy who cheated on me, should I have forgiven him and let him earn my trust back?"

Nate's lips twist. "That's not my question to answer. Trust is a leap of faith. I think if you wanted to trust him, if you wanted to believe the words from his mouth, then you would have given him a second chance. Here's the thing … you have to love the person more than you hate the lie. There's not a lie Morgan could tell me that I would hate more than I love her."

"What will you say to her when she tells you about the

phone? Will you tell her you've known?"

"I don't know yet. I'll just have to see what feels right in the moment. Now, are you going to tell me why they had a falling out?"

"Are you going to say anything to her if I do tell you?"

"No. All is well with them now. No need to say anything."

"Okay then. She asked him to follow her on TikTok, and he wouldn't because he only follows other boys. When she asked why, he expressed his displeasure with girls his age. He said they were annoying. She asked him if he thought she was annoying. He answered like a typical ten-year-old boy... basically picking the wrong time to blurt out his true feelings. And that's when she loudly declared her hatred for him."

"Ahh, that explains her request to go home early."

I slow my pace. "Go home early?"

"Yes. She wouldn't tell me why she had the outburst. She wouldn't let me in her room. And she said she wouldn't come out of her room until I agreed to take her back to Madison earlier."

"W-well... what did you say?"

"She's out of her room. What do you think I said?"

I want to vomit. I knew this was coming, just not so soon. It's like being told you have a year to live and having that reduced to one month without any warning. My heart and my brain have a lot of shit to sort through in preparation for saying goodbye.

"What's the new departure date?"

"Two weeks."

Forcing my feet to keep moving, when my knees want to buckle under the news, I nod slowly. "Two weeks," I whisper because I can barely breathe.

"I thought it was just because of her argument with Gabe—a knee-jerk reaction. Once she started to make her case, and I realized it had very little to do with him, I couldn't argue with her reasoning."

Swallowing past the suffocating swelling of emotion in my throat, the blistering ache in my chest, and the nausea swirling in my stomach, I act my age. I act like the mom I now am. "Good for her for articulating her feelings and making a case for what she wants."

"Yeah …" He sighs with as much believability to his words as I infused into mine. Maybe the most important part of being an adult with a child is the ability to say what needs to be said, the strength to do what needs to be done, and the bravery to smile like it's not secretly killing you.

"She wants to help choose the house we're going to buy and have plenty of time to shop for school clothes and supplies. She wants to paint her new room and visit Jenna's grave. Did I mention my wife was cremated? When Morgan expressed her desire to visit her mom's grave … as if it will be the most important moment of her life … I didn't have the heart to tell her. So I bought a plot and headstone. Her dad arranged it several years ago. I haven't even seen it yet.

"And she wants to spend time with Jenna's family—her dad and Jenna's sister and brother. My daughter can't wait to grow roots in the garden that gave her life. During our eight years abroad, it's all I wanted—to one day go *home* and have her embrace the life she can't remember leaving behind. But …"

I let go of his hand and hug my arms to my body, gaze following my sandy feet. "No buts. It's a beautiful plan. The perfect end to an incredible, once in a *million* lifetimes' journey."

"You're the but."

I grunt a laugh. "I'm not the but. We talked about this." Here it goes … the responsible adult in me is sucking in a big breath of bravery to say the right thing … to do the right thing.

"We did. And you said you didn't have the emotional capacity to fall in love with me."

"Yes. That's what I said."

"How has that worked out for you?"

"Fine."

"Fine? Really?" He steps in front of me, halting my steps. His finger lifts my chin. "Because I'm not *fine*."

Don't cry. Don't cry. Don't cry.

Say the right thing.

Do the right thing.

And paste on that fucking unbearable smile.

Gabe is mine. He is my new world. I had forty-one years to get my shit together, find love, and have two kids, a dog, and goldfish. I couldn't make it happen. This is my new life, and while I never would have asked for it, or wished for it, I am going to embrace it.

"Twenty-one," I whisper.

Nate's eyebrows draw together.

"Brandon took my heart when I was fourteen. He ruined it for every other man when I was twenty-one and in my third year of college. Premed. I wanted to be a cardiologist *because* Brandon had a heart condition that had no cure. I told him to just hold on, and I would find a way to fix him." I lift a shoulder and drop it along with my gaze. "He didn't wait. At the end of the following year, I dropped out of school … I mean, what was the fucking purpose at that point?"

"I'm sorry," Nate whispers.

"It was young love. That never lasts, right?" My tears join the shallow water at our feet. "And maybe it wouldn't have lasted, but his death … it lives inside of my heart like an incurable disease." I laugh. "Life dies in a blink, but death … it lives for eternity. It's infected every relationship since him."

I wipe my tears and glance up at him. "So here's the whole truth, because I like to share the part that lets me look like a victim instead of the villain that I am. Andy cheated on me because when we were having sex, I called him Brandon. He felt like that was cheating as much as him actually screwing someone else. And this …" I hold up my wrist and tug on the bracelet. "Brandon sold his baseball card collection several months before he died so he could buy this for me. And twenty years after his death, I'm still wearing it. This…" I tug it again "…is the reason Michael left me at the altar. He knew about Brandon. He knew Brandon gave it to me. And he never asked me to take it off during the two years we dated and our six-month engagement. Not once. Until … the night before our wedding, he asked me to not wear it anymore once I became his wife. He didn't want to share me with my past."

Nate wipes my tears as I keep my gaze averted to the sliver of light still lining the horizon.

"I agreed. I mean … it's just a bracelet. Why wouldn't I take it off and hide it with a pile of photos or at the bottom of a cedar chest along with other sentimental things from my life? The next morning, I woke up and started the fun of hair and makeup, getting ready for my wedding day. My. Wedding. Day."

I close my eyes briefly and shake my head. "My mom helped me into my dress at the church. She made a few last-minute fixes to my hair. And then she handed me a box—a gift from Michael. A stunning diamond pendant necklace. It looked amazing with my strapless dress. I cried. Mom wiped my tears and fixed my makeup. Then she gave me a few minutes alone before joining my dad and bridesmaids waiting for me at the entrance to the sanctuary filled with our family and friends. I tried to take off the bracelet. At first, I thought I couldn't do it because my hands were too shaky, so I poked my head out the door and my maid of honor rushed to help me. The second she removed it … I just couldn't breathe.

"She kept asking me what was wrong. I couldn't answer. I just knew that the moment she took it off, it felt like she was taking away my ability to find oxygen, and my heart pounded in my chest as panic set in. So I held out my wrist and whispered through labored breaths for her to put it back on. If Michael loved me, he wouldn't let something as insignificant as a bracelet stop us from getting married. It made perfect sense in my head, so I walked down the aisle. His sister read a bible verse, someone else sang a song, the minister spoke words of love and commitment.

"It. Was. My. Wedding. Day. A perfect September day in the mid-seventies with sunshine and no wind. My dream dress. My best friends in navy blue with bouquets of soft yellows and pinks. Flower girl. Ring bearer. It was perfect … except the man taking my hands to exchange vows wasn't Brandon. And he didn't like the shiny bracelet on my wrist. I knew … I knew the exact moment the wedding was off. It was the way his whole body deflated when his gaze landed on my wrist. It was the raw emotions in his eyes when he met my gaze. He knew I would never take it off. And I knew he would never be my husband."

I rest my hands on his chest and draw in a shaky breath. "Take your daughter home. Buy her the clothes she wants, not the ones you think she should wear." I slide my hand up to his cheek and brush my thumb over his slight grin. "No buts. No regrets. Okay?"

He wrings out more tears just by encircling my wrist and kissing my palm before brushing his lips to my bracelet and pressing a kiss over it. "Okay," he whispers.

CHAPTER THIRTY

Nathaniel

I FIND A brave face. Gracelyn's hurting. I know that emotion all too well. It's not like I have a solution. My daughter wants to go *home* more than anything. Gabe wants to be here where he can cling to what normalcy and routine he has left after so recently losing his parents.

I want to pack my freckled-faced friend in my suitcase and steal her away from … from what?

Reality?

Tragedy?

Some days I'm certain the two are one and the same.

She wraps her arms around my neck as I slide mine around her waist and bury my face in her neck.

"Ten years of embracing celibacy. Ten years of settling into a new normal. Ten years and you had to derail me at the finish line."

She laughs, but I feel her body shake with uncontrolled sobs. "You jerk … you just had to steal that kiss."

I want to steal so much more than a kiss. As fate would have it, with the exception of my mother and daughter, the women I've chosen to love have either died or have already given their hearts to someone else.

"We should head back. The fireworks will start soon."

"Yes." She wipes her face and gives me a sad smile.

"Pen pals." I take her hand. "It's not sexy, but it's intellectually stimulating."

"Not sexy, huh? Clearly you've never been pen pals with me. I demand sexy. I demand the occasional poem. Unless you can't keep up."

"Oh … I can keep up."

She releases my hand. "I doubt it!" Her feet dig into the sand, and she swerves up the beach a few feet to the water-packed sand, running as fast as she can.

I grin, just watching her hair blow. Her legs propel her away from me, and when she finally makes a quick glance over her shoulder—that damn flirty over-the-shoulder smirk—I take off after her. She pumps her arms as I keep a steady distance between us. As we near the houses, I close that distance, hook her waist, and throw her into the water.

"Naaate!"

I turn and walk up the beach like it never happened.

"Daaad!" Morgan hops out of her chair on my deck where everyone has gathered to watch the fireworks.

"What?" I respond as I near the boardwalk.

"Watch out!" Gabe yells.

"Oopf!"

Too late.

Soaked Gracelyn jumps on my back, tackling me to the sand. "Not. Cool!" She maneuvers herself on top of me and starts shoveling sand onto me with her hands, like a dog burying a bone. She's wet and sandy. I'm wet and sandy.

"Look!" Morgan yells as the fireworks start in the distance, about ten houses down from us.

Gracelyn hops off me and tries to brush herself off.

"Here." Mr. Hans tosses her one of the kids' towels from

the railing.

She holds it pinched from her fingers, away from her body, while tiptoeing to the water spigot on the side of the house.

"You'd better just head in for a shower." Her mom laughs.

My parents could not have bigger grins on their faces as I follow Gracelyn. I smirk because I can't not feel their tiny moment of happiness. They never thought I'd recover after losing Daisy and Jenna. This feels like a recovery, but it's temporary.

"Jerk," Gracelyn mumbles as she rinses the sand off.

I take the hose from her and hold it over her head. She shivers while running her fingers through her hair, her nipples hard against her thin top. She steps out of the stream and catches me staring at her. I wait for her to make another jerk or pervert remark, but she doesn't, and she doesn't pull her shirt away from her chest. My gaze works its way back down her body as I turn the hose onto my sand-covered body. A boom of fireworks illuminates her for a few seconds. My gaze stops on her fingers rubbing the clasp of her bracelet. After a few more seconds, she turns and takes her balcony stairs to her bedroom.

I finish rinsing off and wind up the hose. After I shrug off my shirt and wring it out, I take several steps toward the back deck and our families celebrating the ending of the day under the kaleidoscope in the sky. Stopping before anyone can see me, I turn and follow my instinct … I follow *her.* Even if I can't have her, it doesn't stop me from being the guy who chases her.

She jumps and turns toward me with her wet, discarded shirt wadded and hugged to her chest as her eyes widen in surprise.

I shut the door, letting the curtains fall shut behind me. "If you take that off..." I nod to the bracelet "...a day from now, a month from now, ten years from now ... if it's not until your next life ... I want to be the first to know."

Her lips part, but her eyes remain unblinking and red with emotion.

"Okay?" I take two steps, putting us toe to toe.

A shaky breath rattles her body.

"Say it."

She rubs her quivering lips together and blinks, sending a new stream of tears down her cheeks while keeping her gaze locked to my chest.

"Say it."

She shakes her head slowly. "Y-you can't ask that ... y-you c-can't just call ... *dibs* on me in the next life."

"Yes!" I can't hide my emotions any longer. My fingers dive into my hair as I tug at it, feeling overwhelmed with frustration. They go from my hair to her face, framing it as I back her into the bathroom until her backside hits the vanity. I bend down forcing her to look at me. "I've traveled for eight years and countless miles to get here. Right. Here. It's my turn to get the girl. I've *earned* it. So ... yeah ... I call dibs. Dibs. Dibs. Dibs! I will fucking level anyone in this life or the next that tries to steal you from me. So just ..." I blow out a breath and close my eyes. "Say it."

She grins. "I'm still having an affair with the young male nurse at the nursing home."

My desperation slides into a smile as I close the distance to claim her lips. "The fuck you are."

She giggles into the kiss. "Don't think you can be alpha with me," she mumbles as I kiss my way down her neck while ripping away the wadded-up shirt from her grasp.

"Nate!" She grips my hair as my teeth tug at her cold, stiff nipple.

"Nate ..." Her voice softens as her body surrenders.

"Dibs ..." I whisper along her stomach as my fingers curl around her panties.

Her breaths fly out of her mouth like violent gusts of wind as she leans back and lifts her hips to let me slide her wet panties down her legs, dropping to my knees.

"Dibs ..." I whisper again, spreading her legs and kissing my way up the inside of her thigh.

"Dibs ..." she moans, closing her eyes when my tongue claims her.

She falls apart on the counter, calling my name. Poor Andy must not have known what the fuck he was doing.

"You are so mean." She grins, staring at me with a drunken gaze as I stand and unfasten my shorts. "Kiss stealer. A bully claiming dibs on me *forever*. And then taking me to the edge and making me beg."

I smirk. "Guess that makes me the alpha, no matter how many fistfuls of hair you try to yank out of my scalp."

Her gaze falls to my hand tugging down my zipper.

"No condom. No sex." She crosses her legs and gives me a challenging look like she's won something.

My other hand slides into my pocket, retrieving a condom. "Condom. Sex." I toss it onto the counter. "But let's shower first. I don't want you to get sand in your mouth." I throw open the shower curtain and turn on the water.

"How would I get sand in my mouth?" She eases off the vanity.

I step out of my shorts and briefs, knowing her shameless gaze will go right to my erection, and her tongue will instinctively swipe along her lower lip.

Her gaze shoots to mine, filled with realization.

I smile, tapping my teeth together. "Gritty."

She flips her hip out, crossing her arms over her chest. "What makes you think I'm going to do that?"

I stroke myself several times, *gently*, really fucking gently because … sand. "Just a hunch."

"Dream on. You threw me in the water."

"Get in the shower."

She narrows her eyes. "You get in."

She's her own little firecracker. Anything less wouldn't be half the fun.

"Fine by me." I get in and slide the curtain shut, wasting no time squirting soap into my hand and sudsing up. I'm entirely clean by the time she peeks inside. "Come on in." I shrug. "But only if you want to."

She rolls her eyes, stepping inside. "It's *my* shower."

"Then you should have called dibs."

Before she can work another word out of her smart mouth, I kiss her. We kiss until her fingers curl into my chest. We kiss until they slide down my abs like she's counting them. We kiss until she grabs my cock and strokes it. That's when she lets go of my mouth and kisses her way down my body.

When whisky eyes find mine, a breath before she takes me into her mouth, I don't smile. I'm not stupid. Nope. I close my eyes and wonder if the day will ever come that I can really have her. Words mean nothing if another man forever holds her heart. I close my eyes and *dream on* …

Like forty-somethings pretending we're still in our twenties, we use that condom within minutes of getting out of the shower—again against the vanity since her parents sleep in her bed. I guess that proves we're not in our twenties. A couple of twenty-somethings wouldn't think twice about having sex on someone else's bedsheets.

God … I miss my twenties.

For lack of another choice, I have to slip back into my wet, sand-covered briefs and shorts as Gracelyn slides on clean, white panties then pulls on a black cotton T-shirt dress. She won't look me in the eye, and her teeth work her lower lip overtime. I brace for what she's working up the courage to say to me.

She clears her throat, sitting on the end of the bed as I run my fingers through my wet hair. "What you said earlier …"

"It was desperate … hopeful … but mostly desperate. If you're never ready, then you're never ready. I just had to say it so I could leave without any regrets." I try to put her mind at ease before she chews a hole in that sexy lip of hers.

Gracelyn plays with her bracelet and nods. "Before … everything." She laughs a little. "Before Brandon. Before I had the chance to fall in love. I dreamed of you. You didn't have a face or a name. Your voice was simply a medley of my favorite love songs, the whisper in my head when reading my favorite poems about love. You were the reason I woke up two hours before school to do my hair and makeup in hopes that some boy would give me a second glance. It was you … the idea of you. The dream of you. The promise from my adoring mother that someday I would find my Romeo. When my brain managed to think about something other than hockey or boys … my *heart* was still thinking of you."

She curls her hair behind her ear and risks a quick, almost shy, glance up at me. "It's hard to believe that Brandon was nothing more than something … *someone* I had to experience to find my way to you. And now it's hard to understand how you're here. Yet, you're leaving. And six months ago, I would have loaded up my car and followed you anywhere and just ... figured out how to deal with my past one day at a time, but I can't follow you. And you can't stay. And that's okay. It means we have people who need us ... need us to do the right thing more than we need each other right now. So ..."

She blots the corners of her eyes. Her bravery is just as beautiful as she is. "I'm going to focus on doing right by Gabe. And in my free time, I'm going to work on these memories that still haunt me. And if some unforeseen path brings us together, I will feel blessed beyond words." Her red eyes meet mine. "And if it doesn't, I want you to know ... you've been everything the ten-year-old version of me dreamed you would be. And more. So much more."

I don't know what to say. I had no idea we were coming to San Diego so this woman could stitch up every single one of my wounds, kiss every scar, and remind my heart that it has an infinite capacity to love. Swallowing past the boulder in my throat, I run my hand across her dresser to a stack of photos.

"Don't look at those!" Gracelyn jumps up and reaches for them, but I hold them up out of her reach.

"What do we have here?"

"Ugh!" She steps back and covers her face. "Kyle used to take photos. Candid ones and never anything flattering. My mom brought them from home. She's been going through some old boxes of his that they still have, looking for things that Gabe might want. For whatever crazy reason, she thought I'd want those. I don't. They will get burned."

I grin, flipping through them. A young, long-haired Gracelyn with ten times as many freckles. Several with her tongue out, but not at the camera. He caught her sticking her tongue out at someone else. There's one of her with her fingers in her ears. One of her sleeping on a blanket in the sun, drool all down her cheek.

"Stop!" She shakes her head. "They are terrible. It was my first summer home from college. All of my freckles had converged into one big freckle face. So embarrassing." She covers her face.

"This one." I set the other ones down. "I'm taking this one."

"You're doing no such thing." She reaches for the picture, but I turn away from her. "Fine … at least show me which one so I can accurately plan my level of embarrassment if you show it to anyone else."

"It's this one." I hold it with both hands up in the air so she can see it, but not actually reach it.

"My eyes are closed." She rolls her eyes.

"You're giggling. I can almost hear it. And you're wearing a bikini. The sun is on your beautiful face. It's … perfect."

Her smile fades a little as she takes a second look at it. "I was trying to get some sun, and Kyle kept standing in the way, making this huge shadow over me. I was getting pissed off. He tried to apologize. I wanted nothing to do with it—stuck my lip out in a permanent frown. He bet me ten bucks he could make me laugh. I said no because I knew it meant he'd tickle me. He said he could do it without laying a finger on me. So I agreed." She continues to study the photo, her smile slowly recovering.

"Clearly he won the bet. What did he do to make you laugh?"

"He said, 'Kyle! Hurry up and grab my pussy!'" She giggles.

Her hair isn't as long now. Her earrings are usually hoops instead of diamond studs like in the picture, and her freckles aren't as widespread, but the smile is the same, and her eyes nearly close when she can't control her laughter.

Knock. Knock. Knock.

Her hand flies to her mouth, eyes wide. "Um … sweetie? Are you two … uh … done?"

Gracelyn grabs her watch off the dresser. "Oh my god … it's almost midnight."

"We were thinking about turning in. Gabe is asleep."

"Go!" she whisper yells, pointing to the door.

I silently chuckle and hold up the photo and mouth, "Dibs."

She rolls her eyes and pushes me to the balcony door. I step out, but before she can close the door, I reach back inside, grabbing the back of her head and pulling her to me for one last kiss.

"You and your stolen kisses."

"Night." I turn and make it down two steps.

"Nate?"

I turn.

Her smile is gone. Time for more bad news, a heavy dose of Gracelyn reality check. "Tonight was …" Her forehead wrinkles as she fights for the words. "It's just going to get harder …" She dances around the actual words.

I nod. "Tonight was the last time."

She ghosts her fingertips over her lips and nods.

CHAPTER THIRTY-ONE

Gracelyn

I OPEN THE bedroom door with a deep cringe resting on my face. "I am *so* sorry."

"He didn't have to leave out the balcony door."

I grin, turning to retrieve a nightshirt from my dresser. "Yes. He did. I feel so bad for missing the fireworks. Are his parents mad? Morgan? Mr. Hans? Gah! We just ditched the party. We just had a lot to talk about."

"Talk huh?"

My cheeks bloom crimson. "Yes. We talked."

Mom glances in the bathroom with towels on the floor and probably some sand too. "Is he a good *talker*?"

"Night, Mom. Maybe get Dad off the sofa so I can turn in too." I slip into Gabe's bathroom and shut the door after grinning at my dad conked out on the sofa, snoring.

After brushing my teeth, I sneak into Gabe's room, slide his blankets up a few inches, and press my lips to his head. "Love you," I whisper without waking him. Then I make up my temporary bed on the sofa and fall asleep with a smile on my face and an aching heart in my chest. It's a healthy balance.

The next few days fly by with me working and my parents spoiling Gabe with attention, new games for his PS4, and all kinds of baked goods. I don't find time alone with Nate again. Even after our parents go home, we manage to avoid each other with the exception of small talk with the kids in the same room or out on the deck sipping iced tea with Mr. Hans.

It just … hurts too much.

Days pass and I can't slow them down.

By moving week—things start to get real. Morgan doesn't spend as much time playing with Gabe because she's packing and helping Nate clean the house.

"Are you going to miss Morgan?" I ask Gabe while we eat breakfast with Mr. Hans at the kitchen table.

Gabe shrugs. "I don't know."

No means no. I'm pretty sure "I don't know" means yes, but he sure as hell won't ever admit it.

"Well, I'm going to miss them. Present company excluded, they have been my favorite renters. Kind of felt like extended family," Mr. Hans says.

After a small nod, I sip my coffee as he eyes me. He's been eyeing me for the past week. I know he's figuring out what to say. There's really nothing to say.

In just over two months, a stranger and his daughter crawled into our lives and left a permanent mark on all of us. We made each other smile, laugh, and cry. We shared good food, endless days of playing on the beach, and drinking lemonade on the deck at sunset.

"Well …" I blow out a long breath; it's insane how many times a day I have to remind myself to just breathe. I haven't had to do that since Brandon died. "I need to get to work. Are you going to Tyler's or are you old man sitting?"

Mr. Hans winks at Gabe.

Gabe grins. "Better keep an eye on the old man. And I might see if Morgan needs help."

I knew it. He's going to miss her too.

I stand and carry my plate and cup to the dishwasher. "You know what a good going away gift would be for Morgan?"

"What?" Gabe asks.

"You should follow her on TikTok."

Gabe frowns. It's not a no. It's a frown. I shrug and head upstairs, letting him mull that over for a while.

It ends up being a crazy day at work after Jennifer calls in sick. No one else is available to fill in, so I just buckle down and keep working. My last client cancels, so I take a long sigh as I seat my last one for the day. I'm hungry and a little dehydrated.

As I secure the cape around her, the door chimes. Walk-ins are rare, but occasionally someone shows up desperate to be seen. The answer today will be no. My feet are screaming. I crane my neck to see the counter.

Oh my god!

No more neck craning. If I had a shell like a turtle, I'd draw the stupid thing into it. The young girl in my chair and her mom waiting a few feet away both eye me with suspicion. It could be the frightening grimace on my face.

"Give me a few seconds. I'll be right back." I turn, coming into full view.

"Gracelyn?" Morgan narrows her eyes and cocks her head.

Nate? He's an expressionless statue open to uncomfortable interpretation.

Surprise?

Shock?

Anger?

Disappointment?

"Hey! I'm a little surprised to see you here."

"The feeling's mutual." Nate's mad. That's definitely a mad

tone of voice.

The phone rings, but it can only save me for a minute or so. I hold up my finger to them and answer it. "Lice Out, how can I help you? I can fit you in tomorrow at eleven. What's the name? And the best phone number? Okay … see you then. Bye." I hang up the phone.

"We thought you cut hair."

I smile at Morgan. "Yeah, well … I never exactly said that, but I can see how one might have inferred that."

I hate the look Nate's giving me. My heart is drowning in wreckage like the Titanic because they are leaving in two days. I was going to tell him the truth … just when they were a couple thousand miles northeast of here.

"Morgan has lice," Nate says in a stiff tone.

She scratches her head.

I cringe.

"We weren't sure where she got it, but I think it's pretty clear now."

My eyes widen. "Uh … not from me." I point to the cover on my head. "I cover my head and wear this white smock. And as you may have noticed…" I give him a tight smile "…I strip down outside and put my clothes in a bag before I go inside. And once inside, they go directly into the wash. I had lice when I was twelve. Newsflash … I don't have them anymore. So keep looking for your culprit because it's not me. However …" I return my attention to Morgan and smile. "I'll get you fixed up, but you'll have to wait an hour or more. I'm just getting started with someone else."

"That's fine." She holds up a book. "I brought something to do."

I nod, keeping my Morgan smile, but it falls from my face

when I slide my gaze to Nate. If I didn't have someone waiting for me, I'd take the time to explain … although it should be pretty self-explanatory.

"Okay. See that yellow chair …" I point to my right. "Go have a seat so I can check you. If you don't have lice, there's no need for you to wait around."

"She has lice." Nate frowns.

With a tight smile, I narrow my eyes at him. "Well, it's protocol that I take a look first before you sign the papers and before I start treating her. And this is my area of expertise, so you should just let me do my thing." Yep, I'm a lice technician, not exactly life goals here, but I do a lot to help people. And as with any unappealing job that's necessary—someone has to do it. Why *not* me?

He sighs. "Do your thing."

The words on my tongue want to be set free, but I have work to do, so I nod and head over to check Morgan. "You definitely have them. Sorry, sweetie. Just hang out and read your book. Okay?"

She nods, opening her book.

I get the forms for Nate to read and sign. "Just set them on the counter when you're done. I'll have to check you too."

"I don't have them," he grumbles.

"Well, I'll let you know if that's true." I curl my lips into a flat line before returning to my first client.

Nate sits in a chair that gives him a straight view of me. *Lovely.* So for the next ninety minutes, I feel him glaring at me, and with each quick glance I make in his direction, he confirms those feelings. I never see him blink. He has laser focus on me. What must be going through his mind? I highly doubt it's sentimental emotions over how much he's going to miss me.

Our love story will end from a bad case of lice. I can't wait to hear Brandon's thoughts on that.

After I give the young girl and her mom instructions for home and the car and they exit, I thoroughly wipe everything down, wash my hands, and don new gloves. I explain the steps: the air treatment, the inch-by-inch combing through her hair with a lice comb and dimethicone oil.

While I do my thing under the watchful gaze of the guy who seemed to love me pre-lice, Morgan talks nonstop about all the things she's excited to do when they return to Madison. At times I get tears in my eyes, but I don't let Nate see them. I'm not just going to miss him. I'm going to miss this chatty, smart girl who's filled with so much life and curiosity. Truth? We really have become friends.

"I kissed Gabe," she whispers so Nate can't hear her as I take off her cape.

My eyes fly open. It's too hard to hide my shock. "Oh … wow."

She glances at her dad, giving him a fake smile before turning her back to him. "I just had to know. And I wanted him to be my first kiss."

"What did he do?" I whisper.

Morgan frowns. "He didn't do anything. I think I'm the first girl he's kissed. He just wrinkled his nose and said, 'Thanks.' I thought I'd feel butterflies, but I didn't."

I smile. "Well, now you know. Always hold out for butterflies." I glance up at Nate. "Your turn. I need to check."

He sighs, standing and making his way to the chair I'm patting with my hand.

"It could have been Hunter. It takes weeks after exposure to realize you have them."

"I'm sure Mr. Hans will love us accusing his granddaughter of giving Morgan lice."

"You're good." I stand back and smile.

He doesn't reciprocate.

"Doesn't matter. She's good. You're good. She can wash that oil out when she gets home. I'll give you a roller for your car seats. Strip beds. Clean and vacuum bathrooms and bedrooms. That's it." I swallow the new round of pain. I hate how he's looking at me. Yes, it was a lie, but no one brags about working in a lice clinic. We just get weird looks, and friends and family don't want to get too close. Maybe I should have been honest from the start. Maybe he would have kept his distance and not wanted to steal kisses. He also might have not wanted Morgan hanging around at our house or playing with Gabe, and that would have been tragic for both of them.

"This machine is really cool." Morgan inspects the air machine. "I bet I could do what you do when I grow up."

I start to grin. "No!" Nate's hard no startles me. His shoulders sag as his mouth bends into something resembling displeasure or regret while rubbing his temples. "I didn't mean it that way. I just meant it's a little early to think about what you want to do for the rest of your life."

I press my lips together to keep from saying words that I will surely regret.

"I know … I know." Morgan grabs his arm and gives it a tug. "Let's go. I want to get my hair washed, and we need to clean and pack and do so much. Maybe I need to use the bathroom first." She wrinkles her nose at me.

I point to the restroom down the hall.

Nate has the nerve to give me this look … like he's waiting for me to make things okay. He said it. Not me.

"Take your daughter home, *Professor.*"

"I'm sorry." He lobs those two words at me like they mean something. They fall flat on the floor between us. I'll sweep them up later and throw them in the trash. I can miss him terribly *or* feel hurt by his words, but dealing with both of these emotions is more than I can handle.

I shrug. "I work in a lice clinic. Now you know. Does it matter? In two days … will any of this matter?"

Morgan runs out of the restroom. "Ready! Let's go." She tugs on his arm.

"Bye, sweetie." I smile at Morgan, turn, and start cleaning.

CHAPTER THIRTY-TWO

THE NEXT NIGHT, I try to distract myself by reading on the sofa while Gabe and Mr. Hans play chess downstairs. Morgan officially has him hooked, and I'm thrilled because it gets him off a screen.

"Hey, come on in," Mr. Hans says.

I lean toward the voices. It's Nate and Morgan.

"We leave really early, so we thought we'd say our goodbyes now," Nate says.

My entire heart catapults into my throat—pulsing, aching, suffocating. I can't hear them past my body going into pain mode. And I can't bring my legs to standing. I'm too weak and nauseous.

"Hey!" Morgan pokes her head around the corner at the top of the stairs.

I feel the burn before the tears. She plops down on the sofa and hands me a notecard and a gift wrapped in tissue paper. "It's my email address and my grandma's and grandpa's address. I'll send you my address as soon as we have one. And that's my TikTok handle and my Instagram handle. We should follow each other."

A smile pushes back my tears, for now. "Does your dad know about the phone yet?"

She pulls it out of her pocket and shows me the lock screen photo of her and Nate on the beach. "Yes. He even took a selfie with me." A long breath comes out of her little body as she grins. "You're right. He's changing too. I was so scared to tell him, but it was also killing me to not tell him. So I just … said it. I said it all really fast. And you know what he said?"

I shake my head.

"He said, 'Well, okay then. Looks like you deserve a shot at this.' Then he said he'd take it away if I wasn't responsible with it. Then he checked to see if there were any parental controls set. And there were, which is odd."

Nate set them. I already know he took her phone while she was sleeping and he set them.

"So odd." I nod.

"Want to know something else?"

"Of course."

"Gabe requested to follow me on TikTok. He said it had nothing to do with the kiss because he thinks of me like a sister, not like a girlfriend." She shrugs. "We'll see. Once my boobs come in, he might change his mind."

I laugh and the tears try to make a return. "What's this?" I tear open the tissue paper.

Her nose wrinkles. "It's just a hat. I wanted to knit everyone something. Hats are quick. I wanted to knit you a scarf, but since we're leaving early, I had to make everyone a hat."

I slip the light blue hat onto my head. "I love it. Thank you. I'm going to miss you. I'm going to be the only girl now."

"Me too, but we might get a dog, and if we do, I want it to be a girl."

"As you should."

"Well …" She lifts her shoulders then drops them on a sigh. "I'd better get going. We're getting up really early in the morning."

I pull her in for a big hug, quickly reaching up to wipe a few tears right when they fall. "Promise me you'll be *you*. Promise me you'll call me anytime you need to talk girl stuff. Promise me you'll wait for the boy who truly deserves your heart. And..." A few more tears escape "...promise me you'll take care of your dad."

"I promise."

I release her. "Here. Hand me your phone. I'll put my number into it so you have it … your dad will then too. Just in case you guys leave anything behind or … I don't know. Need something." I finish typing in my contact information and hand her phone back to her.

"Cool." She smiles. "If you're ever in Wisconsin …" She quirks her lips. "My dad says that to our friends whenever we pack up to move to our next destination. I don't think anyone will ever pop in to say hi. I think he just says that because it makes it sound like we might see them again." Her smile melts into a tiny frown. "I don't think we will. Bye forever kind of sucks. So …"

I smile, letting a few more tears fall, but this time I don't try to hide them from her because she has a few falling down her cheeks too. "If you're ever back in San Diego …" I grab her hand and squeeze it while my other hand wipes her tears.

"You have to come downstairs and say goodbye to my dad, but don't expect tears. He's not a crier."

I laugh and wipe my tears with my shirt. "Got it. No tears."

She takes my hand and leads me down the stairs.

"Ready to get to bed, Squirt?" He looks at Morgan, not at me.

She releases my hand and hugs Nate. "I'm not going to be able to sleep. I'm too excited."

He bends down and kisses her head.

"Okay …" She pulls away and gives Mr. Hans a hug. Then she forces one on Gabe, and that brings smiles all around.

My gaze goes to the red hat on Mr. Hans's head and the black hat on Gabe's head. Morgan is a beautiful, incredibly generous young lady. And I'm going to miss her so very much.

"Thanks for everything." Nate hugs Mr. Hans. "Enjoy the rest of your summer, buddy." He gives Gabe a hug. "I hope you have a great soccer season. I'm going to miss you." He squeezes him tightly. My heart feels it.

Then … things get really uncomfortable. The air in the room becomes thick and suffocating. All eyes fall to *us*. It's time for Nate to hug me goodbye.

I just need it to be done. My strength is crumbing. "Safe travels," I say.

Nice and generic.

Detached.

Unemotional.

Friendly.

I hug him, but just as his arms start to go around my waist, I step back and plaster on a smile while looking at Morgan because … I will need to be put back together from a million pieces if I look at Nate now.

Morgan and Gabe make nothing of the awkward hug or the lack of eye contact, but Mr. Hans looks pained.

Pained for me.

Pained for Nate.

Maybe even a bit of his own pain. He knows what it's like to be separated from the one you love.

As they open the door to leave, I head back up the stairs, holding my breath and every emotion causing pandemonium in my chest. At the last second, I glance over my shoulder just as Nate looks up a few seconds before the door closes.

After Gabe goes to bed, I take a long bath, pressing a cold washcloth to my swollen eyes. Then I pour a glass of wine a few minutes before midnight and sneak back up to my room without waking Mr. Hans. With my lights off, I crack open my curtains a few inches. The light of the moon hits Nate's balcony like a spotlight.

I narrow my eyes. He's sitting on the floor of the balcony with his back against the door, knees bent with an arm resting on each knee and … he brings something to his mouth. He's smoking. It can't be a cigarette. I know he doesn't smoke. So it has to be pot. A tiny laugh escapes me. Nathaniel Hunt is an incredible dad, and I'm sure a brilliant professor, but he's also so incredibly *human* with a hidden vulnerability.

Me and my full glass of red wine take a seat on my bed, legs crisscrossed, and no judgment whatsoever toward Nate and his joint. If anything, I might feel a little envy.

I thought I was bad at goodbyes. He's worse.

After our last time together, I prided myself *and* him on our level of maturity, making the right decision, knowing better than to drag it out any further. Yet, here we are … drinking and smoking. Not talking. Not saying a proper goodbye.

We sit in silent misery for two hours. I'm not even sure he's still awake until he finally climbs to his feet, stares at my window for a few more seconds, turns, and goes back inside. Without turning to lie on my pillow or crawl under my covers, I collapse onto my side next to my empty wine glass and close my eyes.

The next morning I wake when I hear something outside.

Sitting up, I rub my eyes and look out the window. The sun is just barely lighting the sky. Nate and Morgan load luggage into their rental car. Nate closes the trunk and glances up at my bedroom window. I step back behind the curtain, so he doesn't see me. Reality has settled into its usual full-body numbness. It's instinctual to protect the heart from exploding into a dust of nothingness. The pain will set in over time. I'm very experienced with pain.

I stiffen as footsteps tap the wood stairs to my balcony. Pressing my back to the wall on the other side of the door, I hold completely still.

Tap. Tap. Tap.

I hold my breath because it's loud and labored at the moment.

Tap. Tap. Tap.

"Gracelyn, please open the door."

I scrape my teeth along my bottom lip over and over again.

"Please …" his voice breaks.

Something behind my ribs starts to break too.

"That wasn't a goodbye … last night. It was awful. I don't want to get on the plane with that goodbye. But … I have to go, so *please* just open the door."

There is no *good* to this goodbye. It's a bad bye. He's right … it's awful. Opening that door will not make it better. It just won't.

"Fine …" Something *thunks* against the glass door. Sounds like his forehead. "There's not enough time left to say everything that needs to be said. And Morgan is waiting in the car. So …"

I wait.

And wait.

Then I hear footsteps retreating.

So? SO?

My heart pounds my chest like a hard, angry fist. Every breath feels insufficient. He took the oxygen and left me with a long *so …*

Pressing my hands to my chest to keep my heart from breaking out, I squeeze my eyes shut, but all I see is him …

Nate carrying me and my sprained ankle off the beach.

Nate grinning at me shoving lingerie into my pocket.

Nate playing with the kids on the beach, chasing Morgan like a monster.

Nate stealing that first kiss behind the counter.

The second kiss …

Every smile.

Every touch.

Every whisper.

"Nate …" his name rips from my throat.

In nothing but gray boy-shorts and a white and pink heart patterned tank top, I swing open the door and run down the stairs and toward his car. He stops with his back to me a few feet before the trunk of the backed-in rental car. He's wearing jeans and a black rain jacket, a good choice with the rumbling sky.

I open my mouth, but the only thing that comes out are loud breaths. I squint as the sky starts to spit drops of rain. My shaky hand finds the clasp to my bracelet, and I remove it, keeping it fisted in my right hand.

Still … he doesn't face me.

"I was embarrassed …" I find my voice. "And I don't know why, because it's a necessary job that a lot of people would never do, but I shouldn't have cut your hair. I should have told you the truth. And none of this matters because in a few hours you'll be hundreds of miles away from here. I won't tell you goodbye because I can't. Even though I know this is the right thing, it doesn't *feel good* right now. You can't leave me with a simple *so*. You have to finish what you were going to say."

My feet pad across the wet ground until I'm standing behind him. I won't make him face me, but I need to hear his words as the rain gets heavier and thunder rumbles in the not too far distance.

CHAPTER THIRTY-THREE

Nathaniel

"IF YOU'RE EVER in Wisconsin ..." I say. It's not what I was going to say ten seconds earlier. From her door to here, I let reason sink in, and it's telling me nothing good will come of telling her what I wanted to say.

"I love you too," she says.

"Fuck ..." I whisper, turning slowly.

She's soaked, arms hanging limp at her sides. As my gaze makes its way down her drenched body, it stops at her naked wrist. Her fisted hand slowly opens and the gold bracelet falls to the ground. Gracelyn doesn't flinch, doesn't look down like it was an accident.

I know there's a hundred percent chance that Morgan's turned around, watching us. I know she'll have a million questions the second I get in the car. And I know I won't have a clue how to answer half of them.

Still, my hands go straight to Gracelyn's head, my fingers threading through her wet hair as I kiss her. It's not the kind of kiss you give someone in front of your ten-year-old daughter.

It's the kind of kiss you give someone when you *love* them, and you know this might be the last time you ever kiss them.

It's the kind of kiss that makes the other person stumble backward and grab hold of your wrists to keep from falling.

It's the kind of kiss that sustains past the point of reason, to the point of your lungs burning … until the last possible second to leave before missing your flight.

"So much …" I rest my forehead against hers as the rain hits in unrelenting sheets. "I love you *so much.*"

Gracelyn pulls back an inch at a time until our bodies no longer touch. The rain begins to blur her face as she retreats …

One step.

Two steps.

Three steps.

The bracelet slides past my feet with a gush of water. It's going to end up in the storm drain. She just keeps taking steps backward. When I can't bring myself to turn and leave, she does. She turns and walks with no sense of urgency to her balcony stairs. Right when she gets to the top, she looks over her shoulder.

It's exactly what I need to turn and climb into the car.

"Dad …" Morgan says my name, eyes wide, as I start the car and pull out of the driveway. "You love Gracelyn. I saw the kiss. Dad it was … wow!"

I run a hand through my wet hair, keeping my eyes on the road. "I do. I love Gracelyn … but I love you more."

WE ARRIVE IN Madison by dinner.

We find a house in less than a week.

We pay cash for it and move in the following week.

We go school shopping.

We take flowers to Jenna's grave.

We invite all our family over for a housewarming party.

We go to Morgan's back-to-school night, and I feel completely unprepared. I have to remind myself how to get to the school and what grade she's in.

"I hope we have all the right supplies," Morgan says as I follow her through the maze of hallways. She wants to find the room on her own, open her locker on her own, ask her teacher questions on her own. I think my only job is carrying the bag of supplies.

"Right here. Room twenty-five. Mrs. Calloway." She goes into the room filled with kids while I follow her, giving the name on the door an extended glance.

"She's pretty," Morgan whispers and points to the other side of the room where the blond-haired teacher smiles and nods to the group of students and parents huddled around her.

Funny story …

I hired a nanny for Morgan shortly after she was born. Her name was Swayze Samuels. She was fifteen years younger than me. And she knew things about me that happened before she was born. Personal things. Things only my best friend, Morgan Daisy Gallagher, knew. However, my best friend died when we were kids … before Swayze Samuels was born. The most life-changing year of my life has been and always will be the year Swayze Samuels was Morgan's nanny. It was the year I discovered my nanny had a part of my best friend's soul woven into hers. She had memories she couldn't place, but I knew.

Reincarnation. Transcendence. Rebirth.

I still don't know exactly how to explain it. I just know that *I believe.*

The first half of the book I've written is about that year—the year I discovered something you have to experience to truly believe.

My point?

Well, in spite of the one kiss that happened between us, she belonged to another man. She married that man—Griffin Calloway. Morgan was the flower girl at their wedding.

Mrs. Griffin Calloway is Morgan's teacher—her first and only nanny.

"Right?" Morgan nudges me.

"Sorry. What did you say?"

She sighs. "I said my teacher is really pretty. Don't you think?"

I grin, unable to take my eyes off her. "Yes. She's beautiful."

Mrs. Calloway—Swayze—glances up. She just … stares for several seconds before the biggest grin takes over her face, and she shoulders her way through the small crowd, heading straight toward me.

Fuck …

If she cries, I'm going to—

Too late.

She blinks and several tears run down her face two seconds before she throws her arms around my neck. "I couldn't believe it," she whispers next to my ear, keeping a death grip around my neck. "When I saw the name Morgan Hunt, I just … was too afraid to hope it was true."

"Missed you," I whisper past the lump in my throat.

She pulls away and looks at Morgan, who closes her hanging jaw when realization hits her. She's seen all the post cards of Swayze and her family.

"Oh my gosh … you're her."

Swayze nods. "Can I hug you?"

Morgan smiles. "I like hugs."

And just like that … eight years vanish. Two of my favorite

girls have been reunited. Everything should feel right in the world, but it's not. It's close, though, and close might be as good as it gets for me.

Swayze shows Morgan around the classroom and her desk. She helps her unpack her supplies—something I'm not allowed to do—and she introduces her to some of her classmates. I'm sure Swayze will love every one of her students, but I know she will have a favorite, and I kind of love it. I love that my daughter's first experience in public school will be under the watchful eye of the woman who I trusted most with my tiny baby ten years ago.

Again … fate's not perfect, but at this moment it feels close.

"Let's let Sway—" I catch myself. "Mrs. Calloway spend some time with the other parents and students." I rest my hand on Morgan's shoulder and smile at Swayze.

"Okay. I'm so excited for Monday!" Morgan can barely contain her emotions.

"Me too." Swayze winks at her. Then she points at me, eyes narrowed. "Dinner tomorrow. I won't take no for an answer. We have a lot of catching up to do."

"Oh! Can I come?"

I tug on Morgan's ponytail. "Not tomorrow. Grown-up time tomorrow. Kids another time."

"Yes, absolutely. I can't wait for you to meet my girls."

"Well, you have my number. I had to fill out a million forms with my number on it."

Swayze laughs. "I do. I'll text you later after I inform my grease monkey that he's on dad duty tomorrow night."

"Sounds good. Goodnight."

Swayze gives me a tiny smile and head shake before sighing

and whispering, "Professor Hunt … in the flesh."

I take a chapter from Morgan's book and roll my eyes before turning and following Morgan out of the room.

CHAPTER THIRTY-FOUR

Gracelyn

I GET MY first letter from Morgan a week after she starts school. Gabe gets one too. His is longer. I'm envious of his long letter, and he's envious of my short one. Go figure …

Dear Gracelyn,

We have a house—an actual home. I don't have to mark off days until we move again, and Dad put a tire swing in the backyard. I said I wanted a pool, but supposedly there are too many trees. He's thinking a tree house instead. I guess he and his best friend, Daisy, had one when they were young, but it wasn't on their property. He wants it to be where he can "keep an eye on me." Some things never change.

My teacher is Mrs. Calloway. She was my nanny after I was born. My dad tried to explain that she has part of Daisy's soul inside of her that gives her some of Daisy's memories. He said she made him a believer in reincarnation. I like that. Wouldn't it be really cool if one of my friends turned out to be my mom reincarnated? I hope it's not Candace. She's not nice. It's been one week, and she's already had to go to the principal's office twice. Eleanor, goes by Elle, is my best friend right now, but it's early. Dad said to just be cool and get to know all of my classmates, except for the boys. He said I should stay away from the

boys. I have my eye on Able right now because he sits next to me at lunch since his last name is Iqbal and we sit in ABC order. How crazy is that? When I told Dad, he said, "Welcome to the herd."

That's all I've got for now. You should write me back and tell me if Gabe's been in trouble at school yet because I know he won't tell me. Also, make sure to follow me on TikTok and IG. I've been posting lots of pictures and videos with my new friends. Of course, they have actual phones that don't require Wi-Fi to work.

Hug Mr. Hans for me.

Sincerely,
Morgan Hunt

The nanny. Reincarnation. Her teacher.

My head spins to the point of making me dizzy. I didn't look up Morgan on social media right away because I needed a minute. I needed to grieve.

Now my curiosity has been thoroughly piqued, especially since I have not heard one word from Nate. Granted, I haven't reached out to him either. Grabbing my phone from my nightstand, I walk back out into the living room and sit next to Gabe again as he finishes his letter from Morgan.

"I'm going to follow her on social media."

He tosses his letter aside—I assume after finishing it. "I wouldn't. It's all just a bunch of weird girls dancing and a few of her dad putting up a swing in the backyard. Oh … and a million pictures in her stories of her teacher. That's really weird." He grabs the remote and turns on the TV.

"Did you finish your homework yet?"

"I don't have any."

"Well, did you read for twenty minutes?"

"I read Morgan's letter."

I laugh. "Doesn't count. Get your reading done and then you can play games."

He tosses the remote next to Morgan's letter and stands. "You sound like …" he doesn't finish.

"Your mom?"

He turns and blinks a few times—nothing emotional, just a blank look followed by a single nod.

I smirk. "Good. Must mean I'm doing it right."

After he shuts his bedroom door, probably to do shit on his phone instead of reading what he's supposed to be reading, I request to follow Morgan on social media. Within seconds, she approves my requests and I can see her posts.

Gabe was right. There are a lot of dancing videos with a bunch of girls I've never seen. I stop on the photos of Nate putting up the tire swing. It looks like a beautiful wooded lot they have. The polar opposite of this beach house. I like the ocean view, but after living in Idaho for so many years, I became a bit partial to lots of trees.

I scan through the people following her, curious to see if Nate has an account because I know he would be following her if he did. I don't see an account for him. Then I click on her story and a picture of her and her teacher together on the playground with the hashtag #bestteacherever.

Mrs. Calloway is beautiful and young. Maybe early thirties. I think back to Nate's mom mentioning the nanny while talking about all that Nate had been through. Reincarnation? Wow … how did that never get brought up? Maybe the same way I never mentioned I hear my dead boyfriend's voice. Which … I don't know. He might be upset about the bracelet or simply has given up on me, or maybe he really does approve of my recent choices and therefore has nothing to say.

Now that I have their new address, I use my new stationary to write Nate a letter, but it doesn't go so well. I can't find the right words to start it beyond "Dear Nate," and even that feels questionably too formal.

Dear Nate,

~~***I miss you.***~~

Too forward.

~~***How's it going?***~~

Too generic.

~~***Why haven't you contacted me?***~~

Too accusatory.

~~***Saw photos of you putting up the tire swing, you look really hot.***~~

Too horny.

~~***Am I your only female pen pal?***~~

Too desperate.

~~***How's your nanny? I hear she's your best friend reincarnated. That's cool.***~~

Too much of a stalker.

All six wadded up pieces of paper land in the trash. I start over with the easy letter.

Dear Morgan,

The excitement in your words jumps off the page. Thank you for the letter. The tree swing looks fun, and your backyard is beautiful. A tree house would be amazing! I'd love to see more pictures of your new house.

Sounds like school is going well, and you have a great teacher. I bet Mrs. Calloway is just as excited to have you in her class as you are to have her as your teacher. I just followed you on social media. It brings a big smile to my face to see you so incredibly happy with so many friends. You are such an uplifting young lady. I knew kids would be drawn to you, except Candace, she sounds like trouble.

I bought Mr. Hans new socks at Costco. He says they suffocate his toes, so he's gone back to his old socks with holes in them. I think he just misses his wife, and he knows she bought them for him.

Speaking of missing people, I miss you so much. Gabe won't let me braid his hair or paint his nails. Don't tell him I told you this, but he read your letter before anything else when he got home from soccer practice. Before a snack. Before playing video games. Whether he admits it or not (and he won't because he's a boy), he misses you too.

I'll post some pics and video of Gabe playing soccer. So far he's staying out of trouble at school, but I'll keep you updated.

Sincerely,
Gracelyn

I mail the letter the next morning after dropping Gabe off at school. And I wait …

I post pictures and videos from Gabe's soccer games. Morgan comments on all of them. She posts pictures and videos with friends and from her aunt's wedding. She was a junior bridesmaid. I show a heart reaction but rarely comment unless it's a picture in her house. Then I mention things like "Love the paint color you chose for your room!" or "New beanbag chair?"

Nate indulges her with more selfies together, and those are my favorites. I never comment, but I hit the heart button so fast I can barely keep my hand from shaking. He's growing out a beard, and it looks so damn sexy, gray and all.

I haven't brought myself to post a selfie, even though I've taken a million, used filters to soften my freckles and wrinkles, and even applied makeup, beyond just lip gloss, a few times. It feels too "see me, look at me" when the person in the world I want most to see me won't even drop me a letter.

CHAPTER THIRTY-FIVE

Nathaniel

"OH MY GOSH! It's snowing! Can we buy a sled? Can we go skiing? Where are our ice skates?" Morgan jumps on to my bed.

I pull the covers over my head, which only doubles her efforts to get a reaction out of me.

"Daaad!"

"School. You have school. And it's a dusting of snow. It will melt by noon."

She straddles my body and yanks the covers away from my head. Her lips turn downward into an exaggerated frown. "What can I do for you?" She steals my line.

I say the same thing to her when she has her period or something goes wrong at school. Navigating her new way of life, her ever changing personality, and hormones is not exactly easy. She loses it when I try to guess what's wrong and solve her problems when I don't even know them. So I've learned the best approach is a simple, "What can I do for you?"

I sit up so we're nose to nose, and I grin. "Toaster waffles, extra butter, extra syrup. Juice. I'll make the coffee."

"Daaad …" She presses her hands to my cheeks.

I don't get this kind of attention from her often. She has a phone and lots of friends now. Life changes.

"You miss her."

I gather her hair up in back and smile. "I don't know what you're talking about."

"Gracelyn. We've written like a hundred letters to each other …"

I raise an eyebrow.

She sighs. "Okay, not *literally*, but at least six. How many have you written to her?"

My lips twist.

"Zero!" She holds up her hand with her thumb and fingers together making a zero. "Why did you kiss her like you did … *in the rain* … if you're not going to write her a letter?"

I release her hair and curl it behind her ears. "And what should I say if I write to her?"

The truth? I have no fucking clue, and that's why I haven't brought myself to do it. Well, not true. I've started dozens of letters, but they've all ended up in the shredder.

She rolls her eyes to the ceiling. "Hmm … maybe: My Dearest Gracelyn, the world is a dark place without you. I can still taste your lips on mine—"

"Whoa!" I grab her sides, making her jump. "What have you been reading? Where have you heard such things?"

Morgan giggles as I continue to tickle her. "Stop!" She wriggles out of my hold and jumps out of bed. My darling little girl looks adorable in her girly jeans with sequins on the back pockets and her pink (always pink) sweater. She crosses her arms over her chest. "I'm serious. You have to send her a letter. I would be so mad if a boy kissed me like that and then ghosted me."

"Ghosted you?"

She rolls her eyes. "God … you're so old."

I climb out of bed, slowly stretching my arms above my

head. "You're right. I am old, but not too old to dig a grave and bury any boy who tries to kiss you like that ... or at all for that matter. Make yourself useful, go get those waffles put into the toaster."

"Write her!" she yells as she stomps down the hallway of our three-bedroom ranch on a wooded cul-de-sac.

It's not as big as the house I sold before traveling with Morgan, but it has plenty of room for the two of us, and it was recently completely renovated. The ceilings are tall, the exterior walls are mostly windows, and the floors are all newly refinished, light sapwood walnut.

After breakfast, I start my usual routine. Drop Morgan off at school. Work on editing my manuscript until noon. Exercise for an hour, which usually means a jog and a boot camp routine of push-ups, burpees, pull-ups, and sit-ups. Shower. Grab a sandwich. And hunker down in my office for the rest of the afternoon, working until it's time to get Morgan.

Today, however, I don't go back to my manuscript after lunch. I force myself to start *and* finish a letter to Gracelyn. One shot. I forbid myself to start over. If I mess up, I scribble through the words I don't want, and just keep going. It's a fucking mess by the time I stuff it into an envelope, seal it, stamp it, and address it to Gracelyn Glock.

Before I second-guess myself, I drop it off at the post office on my way to pick up Morgan from school. No turning back now.

Gracelyn

"MAIL'S ON THE counter," Mr. Hans says as soon as I come

down the stairs after throwing my work clothes into the washing machine. "A letter from some guy in Madison, Wisconsin."

"Guy?" I shoot him a crooked smile while passing the living room on my way to the kitchen. "You mean Morgan."

"Not this time."

I pick up the letter with Nate's name in the upper left-hand corner and hug it to my chest. Closing my eyes, I jump up and down, silently screaming inside with excitement.

"I was excited too." Mr. Hans startles me.

"Shit!" I jump out of my school-girl reaction, completely embarrassed that he saw it.

He winks, shuffling his feet to the fridge.

"I'm uh …" I clear my throat as if I'm suddenly mature again, not that it matters at this point. "Just going to go read it upstairs."

After retrieving a can of flavored sparkling water from the fridge, he pops the top and grins. "I figured."

I nod, giving him a stiff smile as I take slow steps toward the stairs, maintaining that pace until the last five stairs. Then I sprint the rest of the way to my bedroom, close the door, and jump onto my bed. I pull my phone out of my pocket and check the time. I have to leave in an hour to pick up Gabe from practice.

Taking a deep breath and blowing it out, I open the letter and unfold it. A smile hits my face so quickly; it almost brings tears to my eyes. His letter is a mess. It's a maze of words, some scribbled out, some left for me to read. Clearly, he chose to conserve on paper, unlike me and the entire forest of trees that I've tossed in the trash without sending one … not one of the many letters I've written him.

Gracelyn,

I thought writing to you would make things easier, bridge the two-thousand-mile gap between us. I thought it would make me feel less alone as Morgan fills her free time with new friends, figure skating, listening to music, and practicing the piano. She's wanted to take piano lessons for years, but I'm sure she's already told you that.

It's not easier … writing to you. Nothing is easy at the moment. We're settled. Morgan is happy. My parents and Jenna's family are thrilled to have her back in their lives. I'm a few days away from finishing the edits on my manuscript. On the weekends, I've been working on building a tree house for Morgan, but it's getting cold, so I might have to wait until spring to finish it. I have plans to surprise Morgan with a puppy for Christmas.

My life is textbook perfect at the moment. Yet, I can't bring myself to just BE happy. It's complicated.

How are your parents? Mr. Hans? Gabe? Who's renting the house next door? I guess I'm really asking who's the lucky person who gets to watch you strip every day?

Am I jealous?

Abso-fucking-lutely.

A professor in my old department at the university is retiring at the end of the school year. I'm going to apply for his position. It's probably a long shot. I miss teaching. Maybe a full-time job will infuse more normalcy into my life again.

It's funny how easily Morgan jumped into a routine. She thrives on it, which I never expected. I'm the one who can't seem to adjust. For eight years we've

lived by the motto: What adventure can we find today? Now, we live by a calendar, move about like robots on autopilot, and rush to not run late.

I never took the chance to thank you for fixing our lice situation. It was the last thing I needed just two days before leaving. Instead of showing my gratitude, I acted like a dick. I'm sorry.

Hopefully, it won't take me four months again to find the right words to write to you. If it does, I hope your holidays go well. I hope Gabe won't feel a resurgence of loss, but don't be surprised if he does. You probably already know this from experience. The holidays are hard.

Love,
Nate

I hug the letter to my chest and fall back onto the bed. *Love Nate …*

Done. That's the easy part.

He reminded me that love doesn't hold on. It lets go. That day in the rain, I let Brandon go. I let Nate go. Yet, the love is still there. I carry it in my heart and in the permanent memories that no one can ever take away.

How did I let him leave without exchanging numbers? Oh, that's right … pen pals. I need to hear his voice. I need to see his face. Morgan would give it to me.

Play it cool.

My inner voice sucks. She has way more patience than I do.

Maybe I can draw him out, make him feel as needy as I do. I rest the letter face down on my chest, with one hand over it like I'm hugging it. With my other hand, I lift my camera up as high as I can reach, close my eyes, find a soft smile, and snap the shot.

When I see it, I grin. It's perfect. Changing it to black and white like the photo Nate stole of me in my bikini, I post it to Instagram (my first posted selfie) with the simple caption: Love letter. (And a red heart emoji.)

There's a one hundred percent chance of Morgan showing it to Nate. I want him to know how much I love it, and I want him to know before snail mail will deliver a response from me. I'll play his archaic game of pen pals, but that doesn't mean I can't post all the things I want him to see—things that have no real words, like the way I feel right now.

CHAPTER THIRTY-SIX

Nathaniel

After telling Morgan the snow wouldn't last, we get a foot of snow a week later and school gets let out early. Morgan skates her feet to my charcoal gray Mercedes-Benz SUV and slides into the backseat.

"Hey! How was your day?"

"Dad ..." Her wide eyes peer at me in the rearview mirror. "You are not going to believe this."

"Okay ..." I pull ahead ten feet and stop again as I make the slow trip through the school pickup line.

"Look! LOOK!" She shoves her phone in my face. "I took a screen shot before leaving the building, since my dad is super mean and won't let me have cellular service."

I take the phone from her, glance up to move my vehicle another ten feet before returning my gaze to the Instagram photo of Gracelyn. My heart practically breaks out of its cage.

"Love letter! Dad, did you write her a love letter? Was it you? Please say it was you. I really want it to be you."

When the car behind me gives a gentle honk for me to go, I hand the phone back to Morgan. "I wrote her a letter. I'm not sure you could call it a love letter."

"Daaad ... if you love her, then it's a love letter. Do you still love her?"

So much ...

"What do you want for dinner? I have makings for tacos."

"When Gabe and I turn eighteen, will you find her? Will you take her flowers and ask her to marry you?"

I laugh, but it's not that funny. Eight years. Imagining eight years to wait is pretty fucking painful. Four months has been its own hell. "One day at a time. I don't like to wish my life away ... wish your childhood away. A lot can happen in eight years."

"I know ... she could marry someone else before then. Or you could marry someone here. If Mrs. Calloway weren't married, you could marry her. Well, maybe not. You're a lot older. Her husband brought her lunch last week, so the class got to meet him. He has tattoos and he's *so* cute. After he handed her her lunch, he kissed her cheek, and everyone said *aw.* Her face turned red."

I don't expect anything less. If I'm honest, I've wanted Swayze's happiness far more than my own. "She married a real boyfriend." I smile, knowing the joke is lost on Morgan. Daisy used to say she was using me until she found a real boyfriend. Griffin Calloway walked to the ends of the earth and slayed the Devil himself to save Swayze from the demons of her past. Daisy got her real boyfriend ... just in a different life.

"What's a *real* boyfriend?"

I glance back in the mirror to her cocked head and curious expression. "A boyfriend who loves you beyond reason, even when he's not sure you love him the same way."

"I want one of those."

"In twenty years, baby girl ... twenty years."

Two weeks later …

I STARE AT the envelope addressed to me from Gracelyn. I told my editor I'd have the manuscript to her by tomorrow. If I open the letter and read it, I know my concentration to get the last few changes made will be shit. That's why I can't open it yet.

Five minutes later, I open it.

Dear Nate,

Thank you for the letter. I follow Morgan on social media, so I get to see the occasional picture of you. The beard is perfection. I wish I could feel it. Is it soft or scratchy? How would it feel brushing along my inner thighs? Yes, I'm thinking that. A lot.

I'm not even sorry.

Unless you let Morgan read this. Please don't let her read this.

I adjust myself because she's got me hard already just from that one sentence.

Gabe had a great soccer season. He averaged two goals a game. I offered to put him in basketball, but he said it won't be a lot of fun without a hoop outside. Guess who had a hoop installed in the driveway three days later? You guessed it. Mr. Hans is the best. I know I need to think ahead about finding a place of our own, but it makes me sad to think about leaving him. I feel like he's grown to need us in an emotional way. Is that crazy?

We're going to Montana to spend Christmas with my parents. I think you're right about how hard these holidays will be on Gabe. It will help to have as much

family around him as possible. Mr. Hans is going to his daughter's for Thanksgiving, so it will just be me and Gabe. I plan on making the full dinner. Did I ever mention I have mad cooking skills? I think I did.

We might check with the hot single guy next door to see if he has plans. I bet he'll appreciate my cooking. He doesn't have the Scottish soldier look (only an elite few can pull that off), but he's in his mid-thirties, drives a Tesla, wears tailored suits, and the talk in the neighborhood is that he likes older women.

What have you been up to?

I heard Morgan's teacher was her nanny. There was also some mention of reincarnation of your childhood girlfriend. I feel like there's a story there that could have been shared when I told you my deepest secrets???

I'm humbled and so honored that Kyle and Emily chose me to take care of their son. I love Gabe to the moon and back. This is where I need to be. It's where I want to be. Yet, I can't bring myself to just BE happy. It's complicated.

I read a self-help book last week. It stressed the power of intention and thoughts. Words shape us in ways that affect us on a cellular level.

Thankfully, I'm not missing you. In fact, not missing you has consumed me. It's almost as time-consuming as not loving you. Not thinking of you. Not feeling your lingering touch. Not finding it hard to breathe at the idea of never seeing you again.

I guess I hope you're not missing me too.

Your not lovesick ex-neighbor,
Gracelyn

I lean back in my chair and run my fingers through my hair that's longer again and as scruffy looking as my beard.

Hot single guy next door? I can't even think about that right now. It makes me want to get on a plane, bang on her door, throw her over my shoulder, and steal her forever. I slide the photo of her out of my pocket. Yes, I carry her with me. I just … want her.

It's not that I wouldn't wait eight years or a lifetime for her. I would. I just don't want to. My love for her makes me antsy and completely unsettled. How do I erase the distance between us so we can stop *not* missing each other?

CHAPTER THIRTY-SEVEN

Gracelyn

"WANT TO HELP?" I glance over my shoulder at Gabe as I mix the stuffing. The house smells of fresh thyme, parsley, onions, garlic, turkey, and apples and cinnamon.

He shrugs.

I smile. "I'll take that as a yes. Wash your hands. I'm going to show you some kitchen skills that will turn you into a great husband someday."

"My dad couldn't cook."

I chuckle. "I know. Grandma tried to teach him, but he was truly unteachable."

"He could do other things," Gabe says in a somber tone that matches his partial frown.

I wipe my hands on a towel and lean against the counter as he washes his hands. "Yeah. Your dad had a lot of talent. He was good at all sports. He was a good photographer. He could do anything on a computer. And he knew his way around a car. Grandpa had him changing tires and the oil on the cars at an early age. Not much older than you."

With his focus aimed at the towel in his hands, he nods slowly. "I know. He said when I turned twelve he would show me how to do that … change a tire and the oil." He shrugs. "Guess that's not going to happen."

I press my finger under his chin, and Nate doing the same

thing to me flashes through my head.

Gentle.

Loving.

A simple gesture that says look at me. See me. I've got you.

"I'm here for you. If we need to watch some videos on YouTube someday and figure these things out together, we will. I'm not afraid to learn new things. You shouldn't be either. Nor should you be afraid to have a moment."

He moves his gaze from my chin to my eyes. "A moment?"

"A moment. Many moments. Whatever you need. When emotions hit you like this, where you realize your dad won't keep a promise he made, when your crazy aunt is the only family you have on Thanksgiving, or just for no particular reason at any given time, don't be afraid to say I'm sad. I'm mad. I'm down.

"You don't need an excuse. I lost the first man I ever loved over twenty years ago, and I still have days that I want to stay in bed and just … miss him. We can't control how we feel on any given day, just how we deal with those feelings. Promise me you won't ignore them. Promise me you'll give them the attention they deserve. If you want to hit something, I'll buy you a punching bag. If you want to cry, I'll be the first to hand you a tissue. If you want to watch your favorite movie over a tub of popcorn and a whole bag of licorice … I'm your person. Okay?"

"I want to see their graves. Morgan said she took flowers to her mom's grave. I haven't seen their graves since the funeral."

"Of course." I hug him, resting my lips on the top of his head.

He helps me finish Thanksgiving dinner. We leave the mess in the kitchen, throw on our coats, and find a grocery store that's open. The pickings for flowers are slim, but we scrounge a small bouquet that will work.

When we get to the cemetery, I let Gabe lead the way. He knows exactly where their headstones are located. Standing between them, he murmurs, "Where do I put the flowers?"

"Wherever you want. The top of the headstones, the bottom. It's up to you."

"Should I say something? Morgan said she read her mom a poem."

"Do you have a poem?"

He shakes his head.

I grin and take a seat in front of Kyle's headstone. Gabe takes my cue and sits in front of Emily's.

"Hey, Kyle … Em … happy Thanksgiving. Gabe brought you flowers, but he didn't save you any pie."

Gabe grins. A little laugh even escapes. "Aunt Gracelyn makes good pie, but not as good as yours, Mom."

I return the same grin. He's got this. My cemetery experience is pretty extensive. I used to visit Brandon on a weekly basis. I'd eat dinner with him. Sometimes I'd bring a blanket and pillow and lie beside him, reading him a few chapters of whatever book I was reading. When life got really tough, I'd bring my planner and ask for his advice on what I should do with my life. He helped me make plans that I refused to make without his help. Sometimes he'd remind me to pencil in shaving my legs.

Leaning my head back against the cool granite, I close my eyes and listen to Gabe tell his parents about his summer with Morgan, their trip to Disneyland, and all the goals he made during fall soccer. He laughs while telling them about Mr. Hans and the van that checked his private parts.

I can't help but giggle too.

When all the giggles disappear, silence takes its moment. Then he whispers, "I miss both of you."

My tears have no self-control, but when I give him a sideways glance, I see his don't either. It's his first visit since the funeral. Reaching over, I squeeze his hand. "It gets easier … the visits … they get easier."

When we get home, I send Gabe upstairs to just chill … play games, whatever, while I clean up the mess. As I'm drying the last dish, I hear his voice. It's not his usual yelling at the screen during a game. It's a conversational voice. I hang the dishtowel to dry and head up the stairs slowly.

"It was weird talking to them. Do you think they heard me?" he asks.

"Yeah. I think so." It's Morgan's voice.

I smile at him when I reach the top of the stairs.

"Here's Gracelyn." He turns his iPad toward me.

Morgan smiles and waves. "Hi. Happy Thanksgiving. Ugh … I'm so stuffed." She frowns and presses her hand to her stomach.

"Happy Thanksgiving to you too." I move a little closer and squint at the screen. "Are you home?"

"Yes. This is my room." She moves her phone in a slow circle, showing off her pink room trimmed in white and LED lights lining her ceiling.

"It's beautiful."

"Do you want to see everyone else?"

"Uh … no … um …" I back away.

"It's Gabe and Gracelyn." Her voice is a little muffled as the camera moves around from her feet walking out of her bedroom to the tall ceilings to a big room filled with people gathered around an impressive stonewall and fireplace.

"Hi, Gabe. Happy Thanksgiving," Nate's mom says.

"Happy Thanksgiving." Gabe turns the iPad toward him again.

"Hey, buddy." Nate's voice sends me into cardiac arrest. I've missed his voice. "I miss you. Are you doing okay?"

Gabe shrugs. "I guess so."

"Did you have a good Thanksgiving dinner?"

He nods. "Gracelyn made a ton of food. It was really good. I helped with the pies."

Nate chuckles and it nearly brings me to my knees. The state of *fine* is fragile. Fine is balancing a table on the end of a stick pin. The slightest movement can end in catastrophe. Hearing Nate's voice isn't a slight movement; it's an earthquake.

"I have to use the bathroom real quick. Here … you can talk to Gracelyn."

I shake my head a dozen times really fast.

Too late.

Gabe just sets the iPad on the sofa, giving Nate a nice view of the ceiling, as he makes a straight line for the bathroom. Taking a long, unstable breath, I sit on the sofa and slowly reach for the iPad. The anticipation unravels my heart.

It's been four months (or forty years) since I've seen him. My heart doesn't know because it's felt like eternity since the day he pulled away in the rain.

I pick up the iPad, and emotion burns my eyes the second they land on him—his thick, wavy hair, the shine in his blue eyes, that beard that's trimmed a little closer than the last picture I saw of him, and a fitted red sweater.

He gets my scraggly hair, my weary face with no makeup,

and the white hoodie I haven't taken off since we returned from the cemetery. Basically, I'm the opposite of sexy at the moment.

It doesn't deter him from smiling like he's always smiled at me—a slow growing grin, like tulips opening in the spring.

"Hey, you," he says.

"Hey, yourself." My smile has less control. It goes from nothing to a hundred percent in under a second, a lot like my heart rate.

He's in a room filled with family. What can we really say?

"So … Thanksgiving dinner was good?"

I nod, pressing my lips together because my grin completely lost control for a few seconds.

"Yours?"

"Yeah." He nods.

I nod more.

We're good at nodding.

"Did your neighbor join you for dinner?" he asks in a way that no one else would question because they don't know about the letter.

My mouth twists to the side for a few seconds just to make him squirm. I know he's hit his limit when he runs one hand through his hair before rubbing his jaw.

"He couldn't make it. Maybe for New Year's."

"Oh!" Morgan grabs the iPad and Nate disappears in a blur. "On New Year's, at midnight you get to kiss someone."

I grin. "I've heard that. Who do you kiss on New Year's Eve?"

She rolls her eyes. "Just my dad. It's always a sloppy kiss. Then he tickles me until I have to go pee." She lowers her voice and moves closer to the camera. "I don't really have to pee. I just say that so he'll stop tickling me."

I laugh. "I used to do that too when my dad or brother would tickle me."

Gabe comes out of the bathroom.

"Gabe's back. I'll let you two talk. So glad I got to see you."

"You too."

Gabe takes the iPad and flops back onto the sofa. As they start chattering again, I head to the bathroom to run a hot bath and *not* miss Nate.

CHAPTER THIRTY-EIGHT

TWO WEEKS BEFORE Christmas, I get a package from Nate. I tear it open and read the short note:

Now you'll know ...

Xo Nate

It's a thick stack of papers. The first page reads:

Transcend

By Nathaniel Hunt

It's his manuscript.

I press my hand to my mouth. In an hour, I have to pick Gabe up from his friend's house, but I can't resist reading just a few pages.

Nathaniel Hunt – Age 10

"Nate and Morgan sitting in a tree ... K I S S I N G. First comes love, then comes—"

"Shut up before I knock your teeth out with my fist and you go crying to your mommy like a baby in a baby carriage." Morgan spat on the kids below us as they marched toward the lake, fishing poles in one hand, tackle boxes in the other, dodging saliva bombs.

I ignored their snickers and smooching sounds. Morgan didn't ignore anything. Her parents called her Little

Firecracker, but not me—I called her Daisy because her middle name was Daisy and she hated it when I called her that.

"Have you ever hit anyone?" I asked as we continued our game of Go Fish, perched high in the old oak tree on the abandoned property a mile from our neighborhood.

I like this story. He's starting it from childhood with Morgan—the girl whose name his daughter bears. A firecracker … like his daughter. And they were ten … Morgan's and Gabe's age.

I flip through page after page. I can't read it fast enough. When my phone rings, I reach for it without taking my eyes off the words. "Hello?"

"Where are you?"

"Gabe?" I glance at my watch. "Shoot! Oh my gosh, I'm so sorry. I'm leaving right now."

I fly out the door to pick him up. He doesn't seem too bothered by my mistake. And just to make things right, I suggest we pick up pizza on the way home—my intentions not entirely selfless. As soon as we get home, I grab a slice of pizza, a can of lemon lime sparkling water from the fridge, and leave Gabe and Mr. Hans to eat the rest of the pizza and finish their chess game.

I read *Transcend,* only taking two bites of pizza. At some point, Gabe knocks on my bedroom door and tells me goodnight. By three a.m., I drift off to sleep with the final page pressed to my chest.

Spoiler alert: it ends with Morgan taking flowers to Jenna's grave, kissing the top of her headstone, and whispering, "I'm home, Mom."

Nate chronicles his time with Morgan Daisy, including her

death. How he met and fell in love with Jenna, the pivotal year after her death with baby Morgan and Swayze—the young nanny who knew everything about him. Part Two of the book is like a travel journal with dates and destinations—things that impacted them the most, the people they met along the way, and what he calls his *Unknown Journey to Elvis.* The chapter where we meet is titled *Fortuity.*

Transcend is everything. I laughed. I cried … actually sobbed. The words are real; the emotions are raw. The ending … is perfect.

This realization leads me to reply to him with a simple note on a piece of cream stationary. With a green marker, I write:

Thank you.

It's an honor to be loved by you.

Always,
G

I fold the note in half and slide it into an envelope.

Over the next couple of weeks leading to Christmas, I hear Gabe and Morgan chatting a lot, but I don't ask to say hi or see Nate.

When he left, I thought fate might bring us back together. It seemed like the right thing. After reading his manuscript, I don't know. The ending was bittersweet, beautiful, and … perfect.

Maybe not everything in life dies with a final breath.

Maybe some things just … end.

Maybe it's not forever.

Maybe it's for *now.*

Letting go doesn't hurt as much as the *fear* of letting go. I wore a bracelet around my wrist for over twenty years because I feared letting go. It ruined every relationship after Brandon.

When I was ready to let it go … I let the fear go too. And now I don't feel the pain. I feel free. The love is still there; it's just not the kind of love that hurts anymore.

If I hold on to Nate, the pain will cripple me. Hope shouldn't shackle the heart; it should free it. Right now, I want him so badly, the fear of never seeing him again feels like I'm starting the Brandon grieving for a second time.

We go to Montana for Christmas. I pour my heart into my family.

"You look good," my mom says. "I don't know if it's the longer hair … or you going back to your natural auburn color …" She twists her lips. "No, it's something else. You just have a glow to you."

I grin.

Her gaze falls to my wrist. "You let Brandon go." A sad smile graces her face.

Months ago, my hand would have gone to my wrist, needing that security of the bracelet. Not now. I slide my hands into my back pockets. "I let go of false hope."

Her eyes narrow a bit. After a few seconds, she nods. "You let go of Nathaniel too?"

I nod, blowing out a long breath. The pain is still there. It's like ripping off a Band-Aid; the sting lingers for a few seconds. "Missing people hurts too fucking much."

Her eyebrows jump up her forehead. I don't usually use that kind of language in front of her, but it's exactly how I feel. I guess I want her to not simply understand me; I want her to *feel* me. To steal from Nate: *Then she'll know …*

OVER THE NEXT six months, Morgan sends me three letters. I respond to all of them. I continue to follow her on social media, but I don't focus on the pictures she posts with Nate. He sent me a letter right after New Year's. I didn't open it. I just … couldn't.

It's been six months since we've had written contact, seven months since I've talked to him, and almost eleven months since I've touched him.

We died without a last breath.

With no one to blame.

Just … life.

"I'M GOING TO miss you."

Gabe gives me a half grin. "Going to miss you too." He hugs me.

I don't know how much Kyle and Emily hugged Gabe. I want to believe it was often. Over the past year together, I've hugged him more and more each day. And every day he hugs me back a little more. Now, he squeezes me so hard I feel it in my bones.

"Have fun," Mom smiles.

She and Dad offered to take Gabe on a two-week vacation this summer—road trip up to Seattle. I couldn't get two weeks off, but I'm taking my one week of paid vacation and going to Chicago for a friend's wedding. I haven't seen her since high school, but we've kept in touch on social media. This is her first marriage. I guess I'm not the *only* person who didn't get hitched and pop out two kids before thirty.

"It's my first time in Chicago. I'll definitely have fun."

"Don't get mugged."

"Thanks, Mom. Good tip."

"Ready?" Dad comes inside after loading Gabe's stuff into the SUV they rented.

"Bye." I give my parents hugs.

"Have a safe trip." Mr. Hans ruffles Gabe's hair.

I put on a brave face. He's with my parents. He couldn't be in better hands, except mine. Yes, I've gone from the hormonal mess who thought I had no business raising a child, to a mama bear. Still hormonal.

"What time is your flight?" Mr. Hans asks when I close the door.

"Four hours. I'd better finish packing." I grin.

"That looks nice on you."

I stop halfway up the stairs. "What does?"

"Excitement. I haven't seen that in your eyes in many months."

"I need this trip. It feels good."

CHAPTER THIRTY-NINE

THE WEDDING SCENE is nothing new to me. By forty-two, I've been to countless weddings. I'd say "always a bridesmaid," but that's not true. I've worn the big white gown once. Overrated?

Sadly … no.

It was the most exhilarating, special day of my life—until it wasn't.

One day.

For one day I felt like a princess. I had no idea feeling like a princess was a secret desire of mine until I had my hair and makeup done, legs shaved, girl parts waxed, manicure, pedicure, and a big white dress fitted perfectly to my body.

Veil.

The pendant from Michael.

A church full of family and friends looking on adoringly. A man waiting at the front of the church with so much love in his eyes, like he had never seen anything so beautiful.

It was a dream.

Surreal.

The wedding is tomorrow in Grant Park. The reception is at the hotel where I'm staying. Today … I'm shopping for a new dress to wear. Nothing flashy. It's Danni's and Aaron's day. I just want to find something that makes me feel like I'm twenty-five with endless possibilities, not forty-two with seven more years before I file for official cat lady status.

After checking into my hotel, I scour The Magnificent Mile, popping in and out of boutiques, waiting for something to catch my eye. Finally, a blushing pink off-the-shoulder, tea-length chiffon lace dress jumps out at me.

I try it on. It not only fits, it makes me feel a little more beautiful, which says a lot since I'm without makeup and my now longer hair is pulled into a high ponytail. I brush my fingertips over the beaded sequin bodice and sweetheart neckline. I pair it with three-inch silver caged heels, a mani-pedi, and an iced coffee as I stroll through the bustling streets back to my hotel.

After dropping off my dress and shoes at my room, I go down to one of the hotel's three bars and order a glass of red wine.

"Let me get that. And I'll have a whisky neat."

I glance over at the familiar face taking a seat on the barstool next to me. I point my finger at him and grin.

"Steve."

"Steve!" I slap my hand on the bar. "It was on the tip of my tongue."

Dark-haired, dimply smiled Steve eases his tall body onto the stool next to me. "Well, it's only been twenty-four years."

I laugh. "True. Marks … Steve Marks."

"Aw … you do remember."

"Some days I remember better than other days." I take a sip of my wine as soon as the bartender finishes pouring it.

"Danni's and Aaron's wedding?"

"Yes. I married Danni's younger sister. We're divorced now, but we remained friends. Our daughter, Kelsey, is the flower girl, so I got a pity invite to watch her walk down the aisle and throw petals."

"That's ..."

"Weird?"

"No." I grin. "Refreshing. Most divorces don't end so well."

"How about you? Are you married? I don't recall seeing you at any of the class reunions."

"I went to the first one. Me and three other people. So I passed on all the other ones."

"Makes sense now. I missed the first one but made it to the others. So ... are you married?"

Swallowing. I shake my head. "Sorry. I wasn't trying to dodge that question. No. Not married."

"Children?"

I start to shake my head but stop myself. "Yes. A boy. He's eleven."

"Is he with his dad?"

I drum my French manicured nails on the bar and stare at them. "No. It's complicated."

"Sorry. Not prying. Just making conversation."

"It's fine." I glance up and smile.

Steve was the popular kid in school, who didn't realize that *all* the girls liked him. He played and excelled at every sport.

"Do you live in Chicago?"

"Nah ... I'm still in Montana. You?"

"San Diego."

"Nice. What do you do there?"

Why is that always the follow-up question?

I shrug and grin just before taking another sip of wine. "I *live* there."

He chuckles. "Fair enough. What should we talk about

next?"

For the next hour we talk about high school, since that's all that's left. He never brings up Brandon's name. I'm not sure if he doesn't remember I dated him or if he just doesn't remember him at all. That's fine. It's more than fine.

We drink way too much, but it's a Friday night. What else do we have to do?

He nods to the waiter and points to my empty glass.

"No!" I pin his hand to the counter. "Three glasses is two glasses past my limit. I can't even see straight."

Numb.

Sleepy.

Carefree.

It's a fantastic feeling.

"I'd better get to my room before I don't remember where it's at."

"Sounds responsible." He grabs my elbow to steady me as I attempt to stand.

"Whoa …" I give my legs a few seconds to get the memo that we're moving now.

He pushes the button when we get to the elevators. Then he rests his hand on my lower back to keep me steady. "What floor?" he asks when the doors open.

"Twenty-seven." I shake my head as we step into the elevator. "No. Twenty-nine. No, twenty-seven. No. Twenty-nine. Definitely twenty-nine."

Steve chuckles. "We can try both. I'm on thirty."

We turn just as the doors start to shut. Just as they jerk to a stop and open again as a few more people crowd onto it. I look down at my feet, shuffling them until my back hits Steve's chest. His hand goes to my hips, which isn't necessary, but it's crowded, and I'm a little unstable. So I don't say anything. When I glance up, the man in front of me makes a quick glance back and even more quickly does a double take.

Nate.

He tries to angle his body to face mine, but he stops. My heavy gaze follows the path of his, and he's looking at Steve's hands on my hips.

Just as my thick tongue starts to say something, the elevator doors open, and Nate shoulders his way out. Not a single glance at me.

"Wait!" I don't even recognize the sound that comes out of my mouth. It's something so desperate that it cuts past my throat like a jagged piece of metal. With no manners, no excuse-me's or I'm-sorry's, I shove everyone out of my way and throw my arm between the doors to stop them, my body following close behind.

"Gracelyn?" Steve calls just before the doors completely shut.

I turn left then spin right. Where did he go?

I run to one hallway and look right and left. No Nate. My clumsy feet take me to the other hallway in a zigzag motion. I look right then left.

There.

"Nate!"

He keeps walking down the impossibly long hallway. It's like … a mile long.

"Stop … please …" I say feeling dizzy as I use the wall to help me down the hallway.

He turns right and swipes his card.

"You're here … Why are you here?" My mouth goes rogue since my brain exploded on the elevator.

As soon as I reach him, the door opens, and he steps inside.

"Stop!" I lunge for the door before it closes.

I hate this. I feel like someone drugged me, but I know I did this to myself. In my defense, I was just having a fun conversation over drinks with an old classmate. Not once did my thoughts go to Nate. And they most certainly would not have told me to stay sober in case I ran into him in the elevator … in a hotel in *Chicago*.

The chances are not one in a million. They are one in a trillion.

"Can we talk?"

With his back to me, he sighs. "Speak."

He's angry.

Fucking alcohol.

If I weren't intoxicated, I'd have all the right words. Lord knows I've recited them a million times on the off chance that I'd ever come face-to-face with him in this life.

"I've had too much to drink. I'm … I'm afraid I won't say it right."

He turns.

How can I be numb yet feel everything? It makes no sense.

"Ten," he says. "Six months ago, you sent me a note with ten words and a G—like you were fading away one word at a time." He tips his chin up and rolls his eyes to the ceiling as he draws in a slow breath. "I gave you ninety-seven thousand, four hundred and eighty-two words. And you replied with ten. And then … nothing. Did you read my last letter?"

I shake my head.

"Why?" he asks with an edge to his voice.

"I let go," I whisper, leaning my back against the door to hold it open, letting my tired eyes stare at the ugly multicolored swirl carpet.

"You gave up."

"On what?" My voice booms, and I flinch because my head is so damn dizzy. I force my gaze to stick to his. "On what?" I say in a softer, defeated tone. "Eight years?" My voice cracks. "You wanted me to what? Write you letters for eight years? Call you to tell you how fucking wonderful it was to not know if I'd ever see you again? Text you photos of my tears? Stalk Morgan on social media in hopes of catching small glimpses of you? Suffocate on my heart in my throat every time I hear Morgan and Gabe on FaceTime because hearing your voice just …" I pull the neck of my T-shirt up and wipe my eyes. "It h-hurts." Releasing my T-shirt, I rub my aching temples. Turning my head away from him, I roll my quivering lips together as more emotions blur my vision. "Missing you … it hurts too much." I grab the doorframe to steady myself. Then I force one foot in front of the other, making my way toward the elevators with a little more coordination.

I never wanted this. Blame. Why does it have to be anyone's fault? He did the right thing for the right reason. I did the right thing for the right reason. Our reasons are just two thousand miles apart.

CHAPTER FORTY

Nathaniel

I HAVE CONFERENCES at the hotel. After the university gave me the position, I knew I'd have a lot to do to be ready for fall classes. Of all the conferences … of all the hotels … how does she end up here?

Why was she drunk in an elevator with another man's hands on her?

The rest? I know.

I know why she didn't respond, why she let us go. I felt the same pain. I still do. I feel the impossibility of it all. Sometimes, you just want the impossible.

It takes everything I have in me to not chase her. Fuck the "hot" guy next door. Fuck the guy in the elevator with his hands on her. My hands shake as I fist them. They want to touch her so badly.

As I relax them, I remind myself that I have nothing new to offer her. So what if I catch her?

So what if I make up for nearly a year of not getting to touch her. Then what?

More letters?

Total disruption of two kids who have roots, friends, and lives they're navigating with one parent? Who makes the sacrifice? The boy who lost *both* of his parents? Or the girl who kissed her mother's gravestone, three blocks from our house, and whispered, "I'm home, Mom."

I could have called.

I could have texted.

When you have nothing to offer … it's best to just *let go.*

The next day I make it to the conference downstairs early so I don't miss out on the coffee and bagels. Yesterday, I made the mistake of assuming there would be enough to go around. Wrong.

When we break at eleven thirty for a ninety-minute lunch, I head back to my room to call Morgan and my parents. She's staying with them while I'm here.

The elevator doors open, and fate lands a hard punch in my gut. All reason and common sense that took place last night, during the little pep talk with myself, vanishes.

Poof!

Gracelyn looks up at me through thick mascara-covered eyelashes. Sexy as fuck red lips, glossed to perfection, rub together. My gaze can't decide where to stay.

Long, auburn hair curled in flawless waves.

Dangly diamond drop earrings.

A pink flowing dress that exposes all of her shoulders.

Gray heels that are just …

Fuck me …

I step on to the elevator. She gives me a shy smile and tries to move past me. I don't let her pass.

"Um …"

The doors close behind us.

"I need to get off." A nervous laugh escapes her as she nods toward the door.

I press the button to my floor before taking a step closer. She retreats, her hands grabbing the rail to steady her. Her gaze falls to my lanyard. "Conference?" she asks before swallowing hard.

"You're making it really hard to pretend you're not here."

Whisky eyes flit up to meet mine. "I need to get off. I have a wedding to attend."

I bend down bringing my lips a breath away from the skin along her neck. Without touching her, I make an invisible path from her shoulder to her ear with my lips.

She gasps and holds that breath.

"In case you were too drunk last night," I whisper. "I'm in room 923. And I'd be happy to help you *get off* later." The elevator stops on my floor.

Her lips part, and she blinks slowly at me as I stand straight and exit the elevator. I have no clue what my plan is or if she'll find me later. My forty-seven-year-old brain should have the maturity, education, and life experience to think of something logical and brilliant. In the meantime, my dick is thinking of how badly it wanted to fuck her right there in the elevator.

"You're a total bastard," I whisper to myself as I walk down the long hallway with a slight grin on my face.

When I get in my room, I bring up Morgan's name to video chat.

"Hey, Dad. Guess what?"

"What?"

"Gabe just messaged me. He said Gracelyn is in Chicago for a wedding. You should call her."

"I don't have her number."

"I'll send it to you."

I grin. All this time … and I've never asked for her number and she's never asked for mine. It's insane. Probably as insane as me thinking my daughter would grow up without the influence of cellphones and social media.

We could have talked every day, but I think we both knew that wouldn't make things better. It's why she said that night in her bathroom was the last time. She knew we needed to distance ourselves because every touch only made it harder.

"How are you doing?"

"Fine. Are you going to call her? I'm going to message her and give her your number too."

"You do that." I grin. "How are Grandma and Grandpa?"

"Fine. Can you get me cell service when you get home? Grandma said it might be a smart idea … for emergencies."

"How's Joby?"

"Daaad!"

"Listen. I just called to check in. I need to grab lunch before the afternoon session starts."

"Ugh! Fine. But call Gracelyn. Take her to dinner. She's there for a full week."

"Take her to dinner, huh? Why? She lives in San Diego. I can't actually date her."

"But she *loves* you. And someday you will be together. I just know it."

"Are you going to leave your new house, your grandparents, your friends, and move to San Diego with me?"

"I don't want to move. I'm going to tell Gabe he needs to move here. He would love it here! I think …"

"And why would he leave his friends if you don't want to leave yours?"

"Because it's California and there are earthquakes and wildfires. Hello!"

"I love you, smarty pants. I'm going to eat now. Tell Grandma and Grandpa hi."

"Love you too. Call me tomorrow. Okay?" She blows me a kiss.

I catch it and blow one back.

THE AFTERNOON SESSION drags on forever. I go out to dinner with a couple of colleagues. Then we grab beers at the sports bar in the hotel and watch the baseball game. Around nine, my phone vibrates with a text. I don't recognize the number. I open the screen to read it.

Who's the guy on your right? He's kinda cute.

I glance up, over my right shoulder, then my left shoulder before replying.

He's married.

"I'm going to call it a night. Thanks for the company. See you guys in the morning." I stand.

My phone vibrates again.

What about the guy on your left?

I grin, weaving my way through the crowd and out to the lobby.

Long auburn hair and the backside of a pink dress get onto an elevator. I take off running, but the doors close too soon. I push the up button a dozen times.

What's your room number?

It's unlikely she gets my text in the elevator. So I wait. My phone screen lights up just as another elevator's doors opens.

923

I grin, pressing the button for the ninth floor. 923 is my room. When I turn down the hallway, all I can see are two gray heeled shoes and legs. She's leaning against my door. As I get closer, bringing her whole body into view, she lifts a small bouquet to her nose.

"Guess who caught the bouquet?" She grins behind the flowers.

I slide my room key out of my pocket. "Three hundred and thirty-three."

She narrows her eyes a little.

I scan the keycard and push down on the door handle, bending close to her face. Her gaze goes straight to my lips. I pause for a few seconds to absorb the warmth of her body, memorize the rise and fall of her chest as her breaths deepen … for me. I do this to her. She, on the other hand, has no fucking clue what she does to me, but she's about to be enlightened.

"It's how many days it's been since I've touched you."

Her lips part, those breaths now audible. "You've been counting …" she whispers.

I grin. "The days … the hours … the heartbeats … yeah, I've been counting."

The bouquet falls to the floor, and her hand reaches for my face, pausing just shy of touching it. "Three hundred and thirty-three." A tiny smile bends her lips.

My eyes close for a few seconds when she finally touches me. Her palm on my cheek. Her thumb tracing my bottom lip like it's done so many times before.

When my eyes open, they find hers unblinking and searching. She's scared.

So am I.

"You. Are. Stunning."

Her smile swells as her thumb continues to trace my mouth. "It's the dress."

My head inches side to side. "It's the woman."

Her other hand finds my face, framing it, pulling me the last inch until our lips are nearly touching. "You have to make this right."

Us.

I have to make *us* right.

"Chase the girl ..." she whispers.

I grin. "Chase the girl."

Our lips meet and it feels like the air she ripped from my lungs, that day in the rain, is back. I push the door the rest of the way open, backing her into the room as we continue to kiss.

Gracelyn pulls back, leaving me breathless. She's really good at it. "I like this," she whispers, her fingers stroking my beard along my jaw.

"It's summer. I'm going to shave it."

"Not yet. Not until I know."

My fingers find the zipper to her dress and ease it down her back. "Know what?"

Her cheeks flush as her strapless dress pools at her feet, leaving her in nothing but pink panties and high heels. "How it feels."

My lips press to her shoulder, working their way to her ear as the tips of my fingers feather along her inner thigh. "How it feels *here*?"

Drawing in a shaky breath, she nods. "Yes."

How did I ever walk away?

She unbuttons my white shirt and slides it off my shoulders, kissing along my chest. With it half off, she takes her time unbuttoning my jeans. The need is almost painful, but the desire for this to last as long as possible wins over. Nothing gets rushed.

Not her lips pressing kisses along my abs.

Not my fingers threading through her long hair.

Not the ease of her panties down her legs.

Not the brush of my beard along her inner thighs.

"Nate …" Her fingers curl into my hair as her heavy eyelids drift shut.

She gives me the best fucking smile as I continue to kiss my way up her body, relearning every subtle peak and valley. The three elephants and stemmed cherry. I grin against her skin as she wiggles beneath me, her pelvis reaching, her need growing.

"God … Nate …" Her back bows as I suck and tease her hard nipple, tugging until her lips part, a deep gasp filling her chest. I'm not sure what brings me the most pleasure—tasting her or watching her.

The slow descent of her fingernails down my back draws a long moan from me as I devour the skin along her neck. She slowly pulls her knees up while curling her fingers into my glutes, guiding me … tempting me.

I pull back and we exchange a look. It's in her eyes, and I know it's in mine. It's a silent nod to cross a line that can't be uncrossed.

Her forehead tenses as I push into her, the heel of her foot sliding up the back of my leg to my backside, digging into me as she pushes hard to rock her pelvis against mine. My mouth crashes to hers, our tongues reaching for something deeper. We move together with purpose. It's *us.* For the first time in too long, it's not about Morgan and Gabe. It's about *us.*

It's about the lovers we've lost, the grief we've endured, and every lonely night that felt like a slow loss of the deepest part that makes us ... *human.*

The guilt.

For years, I've felt guilty for wanting this, for having everything *but* this. In the recesses of my conscience, I buried the desire, but it never died.

Now ... I can't stop it.

Gracelyn wraps herself around me like a vine around a tree, searching for new heights—for the light.

We roll as one body. She cages me in with her body over mine, her hair brushing my face, her fingers clawing at the pillow, every breath a whisper of longing.

"You're so fucking beautiful ..." I whisper.

She stops.

Tired eyes open as sweat beads on her brow. Her tongue slides along her lower lip, red and swollen from the bruising demand of my mouth, her cheeks flushed with heat, black mascara smeared below her eyes. We've let it build and fade so many times, trying to make this indescribable feeling last; we're nothing but flesh, sweat, and heat.

My hand snakes around her waist, and I sit up. Her arms encircle my neck, her legs gripping my waist.

"No regrets," she breathes just before her head dips to the side. The warmth of her tongue on my skin, the graze of her teeth ... I've never felt so wanted ... so needed in this way.

"No regrets," I say, gripping her ass and moving her over me, faster ... harder ... until I can't breathe.

Until my heart escapes my chest.

Until my body moves involuntarily.

Until her nails break the skin on my back and her cries

crack through the air.

After the final waves subside and all that's left is the pounding rhythms between our chests pressed flush, like every other inch of our bodies, I lie back with her. She slides to my side, tucked under my arm, her leg draped over me.

The euphoria settles into the most numbing exhaustion, and we sleep.

MY EYES PEEL open around six the next morning as a sliver of light cuts through the tiny gap in the curtains. It illuminates Gracelyn's back to me—the soft curve of her hip partially covered by the mess of sheets. The tattoo on her neck is visible with her hair fanned out on the pillow above her. I lean forward and press my lips to her inked hockey sticks. She stirs, but just slightly, before releasing a tiny sigh and falling still again.

Easing my legs over the side of the bed, I sit and run my fingers through my hair. I jump at her touch. Gracelyn's fingers feathering along my back.

"I did this ..." she says, softly outlining the cuts on my back.

"Is it bad?"

"Not if you don't look at it."

I chuckle.

She kneels behind me, pressing her naked body to my back as her fingers thread through my hair and her teeth tease my ear. "No regrets."

"None?" I reach behind with one hand and grab her ass, giving it a squeeze. I know she means the cuts on my back. I don't. There's something much bigger than that. A bigger elephant in the room.

She kisses the back of my neck. "None."

I twist my torso to see her face. She sits back on her heels and pulls the sheet up to cover her chest.

"I have to shower and get ready for my conference."

She frowns. "You should skip."

"I can't. I accepted the job at the university. They expect me to return with new knowledge."

"You took the job?" Her brow wrinkles as she chews on her bottom lip.

"Playtime was over. It's time to work again."

On a slow nod, she lifts her gaze to me. "That feels permanent."

"I'm going to talk to Gabe. Man to man. I think he'd love Madison."

"So … we're moving. Uprooting. My job doesn't matter. His friends. His soccer team. You left San Diego with no job and no home when you could have stayed. Morgan could have gone to school with Gabe and made friends. You could have applied to one of the colleges in San Diego."

I sigh. "I promised Morgan I'd take her home."

"I promised Gabe I wouldn't take him away from his."

Scrubbing my hands over my face, I shake my head. "We'll figure it out. I have to get going."

She gives me a slight nod and a sad smile. I lean in and kiss her frown before heading to the bathroom.

I turn, inspecting my back. "Damn … Gracelyn …" I whisper, cringing at the smeared blood that must be on the sheets as well. It gives me a weird sense of pride.

By the time I get out of the shower, she's gone. Sitting on the bed, I rub my towel over my head. This won't be easy, but I won't give up. I won't ever give up.

CHAPTER FORTY-ONE

Gracelyn

I SHOWER. STARE out the window for an hour. And convince myself to take a walk. By the time I return to the hotel, I'm hungry. The restaurants are busy, which makes me regret not grabbing something while I was exploring.

"Hey, stranger."

My head turns behind me to the sports bar. Steve waves at me from a high-top table.

I grin and squeeze through the crowd waiting to be seated. "That looks amazing." I eye his sandwich and fries.

He pops a fry into his mouth. "It is. I tried to find you at the reception after the hoopla of toasts and cake cutting."

"I—"

"Do you need a menu?" the waiter interrupts.

"Oh. I haven't put my name in. I'm just—"

"She's with me. Yes, a menu would be great." Steve nods to the other stool at the small table.

The waiter sets a menu on it.

I wrinkle my nose, not sure about this.

"I hear it's an hour wait. But maybe you're not hungry."

I hop onto the stool and rest my purse on my lap. "Starving actually."

"I didn't see you out on the dance floor. A lot of people were dancing into the wee hours, burning off all the food and cake."

I grin. I burned *plenty* of calories last night. "I ran into a friend. We … hung out."

"Would this be the friend you chased when we were in the elevator?"

The waiter sets a water on the table for me. "Have you decided?"

"Um …" I nod to Steve's plate. "Same thing he's having."

"Extra blue cheese too?"

"Oh," I wrinkle my nose. "No cheese."

The waiter nods and takes my menu.

I fold my hands on the table. "Yes. Same friend. We met last summer. I haven't seen him in months."

"Seemed like an…" he takes a swig of his soda "…odd exchange."

I shrug. "Just a misunderstanding. Your daughter did a great job yesterday. She's adorable."

"Thanks. She was upset that you caught the bouquet. Then you just … vanished. I was going to ask you for a dance. It felt like it was the least I could do after getting you drunk Friday."

"Dancing is your form of an apology? Wow … you must be quite the dancer."

He smirks. "You'll never know now."

"Where's your daughter today?"

"She flew home with her mom this morning."

"When are you going home?"

"Not sure. I ran into this woman Friday night. We went to high school together. She said she's here for a week. I thought maybe I'd see if she wants to check out the city with me."

My eyes nearly pop out of their sockets. "Oh … me?"

He grins. "Yes. You. Brilliant guess."

Mr. Popular Guy from high school skipped his flight—I think—to hang out with me.

"I could use the company, a little carefree time in Chicago to drink too much and hang out with a beautiful woman. What do you think?"

"Uh ..."

"She'll have to pass." Nate's voice startles me along with his hands sliding around my waist. His face nuzzles into my neck. I rest my hands over his, releasing a nervous laugh.

Steve's eyebrows lift into peaks. "I didn't realize you were ..."

"Uh ..." I can't seem to find a better word than uh. "Steve this is Nathaniel Hunt. Nate this is ..." My brain trips.

"Steve Marks," Steve fills in for my slow brain.

"Yeah ..." I whisper with an awkward smile.

"You didn't mention you had a lunch date," Nate says.

"I just was looking for someplace to eat, and there was a line and Steve was here so ..."

"I have a ninety-minute break. We can grab something together."

"She just ordered." Steve takes a bite of his sandwich.

Nate releases me and situates himself so he's leaning his arm on the top of the table with his back to Steve. We have a little stare off.

I lose. He has ninety minutes, and he wants to spend them with me. It's a disaster in the making, but who doesn't like a good disaster once in a while?

"I haven't eaten today," I give him a toothy grin.

"I'll have the waiter send your lunch to the room," Nate counters.

"I haven't paid for it yet."

Nate slides his hand into his front pocket, pulls out several folded bills, and tosses a fifty onto the table. "I'll go tell the waiter." Nate turns to Steve. "Nice meeting you."

Steve nods as I slide off the stool. "Seems like he's more than a friend."

I slide my purse strap onto my shoulder. "I hope so. It was nice catching up with you. Thanks for the drinks Friday, even if it was a couple glasses too many. Have a safe trip home."

Nate comes back over to the table and holds out his hand. I stare at it for a couple of seconds before placing mine in it.

"Did you just mark your territory back there?" I ask as he leads me to the elevators.

"If you're implying I pissed on something, then no. I'm too old for that."

He pushes the button and the doors open. Several people follow us onto the elevator. We stay silent on the way to the ninth floor. He leads me to the hallway, staying a few steps ahead of me, squeezing my hand.

"If you're implying I let a man who was hitting on you know that you weren't going to be sightseeing with him this week, then yes … I was marking my territory. You good with that?" He unlocks the door to the room and glances over his shoulder at me.

"Caveman." I try to hide my grin.

He doesn't. He just laughs. "I don't even know what that means. I'm old-school, not Homo neanderthalensis." Releasing my hand, he pushes open the door and holds it for me. "I settle property disputes with my fists, not urine."

I roll my eyes and walk into the room.

"Honestly, Neanderthals were not only intelligent but quite accomplished with much larger brains than men today. So I highly doubt they claimed women by pissing on things," he says.

"Wow … here I thought you were just a pretty face. You're actually kind of smart."

Nate starts to unbutton his shirt. "Eleven years of college. I just wanted to prove myself."

"Are you done proving yourself?"

"Not even close." His grin insinuates all kinds of naughty things.

I hug my stomach as it growls. "This morning, before you got in the shower …"

He shakes his head. "Don't worry about it. I'll figure something out."

"Gabe won't want to move."

He shrugs off his shirt, letting it fall to the floor. "Have you asked him? Or did you make the guilty assumption and then felt too afraid to ask, the way I was too afraid to ask Morgan. Are we guarding them too much? Military families don't pussyfoot around reality. When it's time to move, it's time to move. That's life." He sits on the bed and grabs my waist, pulling me to stand between his legs.

"Where was this tough love talk a year ago?" I rest my hands on his shoulders.

"I don't know if Morgan would have been receptive then. She was dealing with some pretty big life changes."

"It's not just about Morgan. It's about Gabe too. Jenna died over eleven years ago. Gabe's parents … *both* parents have only been gone a year. He still sees a psychologist. He still wants to spend every moment he can either playing with friends or playing soccer."

He lifts my shirt just enough to kiss along my belly, dipping his tongue into my navel. "Madison has soccer. He plays with his friends online … playing games most of the time. We have internet at our house. I know some very good psychiatrists. And the schools are good. He'll make plenty of new friends."

My stomach growls again, and he jumps back.

"Told you, I'm hungry." I step away and grab a granola bar from the food basket above the mini bar.

"That's extra. They'll charge my room for that."

I roll my eyes. "You paid fifty dollars for a ten-dollar sandwich and fries, but I'll pay you back."

He reaches forward, hooks his finger through the belt loop of my ripped denim shorts and pulls me between his legs again. "Want to go somewhere with me?" He lifts his gaze to mine.

"After my sandwich?" I mumble over my bite of granola bar. "Don't you have to be back in…" I glance at my watch "…less than ninety minutes?"

"It's my last day. We'll leave at five."

"Where are we going? I haven't really seen much of Chicago yet."

He unbuttons my shorts and pulls down the zipper. "It's a surprise." His hands slide up my bare legs until his thumb finds the crotch of my panties and slips underneath it.

My chewing slows to accommodate the surge in my pulse and the heavy breathing that comes with it. He teases me, all the while kissing along my hip bone and running his tongue to just below my navel.

Two knocks at the door ruin the moment. But … food!

Nate stands, looming over me for a few seconds as I start to zip and button my shorts.

"Leave it." He instructs with a stern look and challenging

lift of his eyebrow before answering the door. "Thanks." He slips the guy a tip and delivers my food. "Steve ... do we need to talk about him? Or did we cover everything? There was the elevator scene with his hands on your hips, not sure where you two were headed, but I have to wonder if it was to the same room, given your *state* that night. Then I find you cozied up to him in the sports bar today with him making a suggestive proposition for the week."

I take a bite of the sandwich, searching his face for signs of true jealousy. There are none. He sits back down on the bed with such a nonchalant expression and posture, like he doesn't really give a shit but it's just something to check off a list.

Instead of answering right away, I take another bite and study the fries. I shouldn't have them. They're not good for me. The ultimate comfort food. However, I don't need comfort food with Nathaniel Hunt shirtless on the bed.

Dropping the sandwich on the plate, I open one of the bottled waters, that's *not* free, and drink part of it. "Steve went to my high school. He married the sister of the bride." I screw the cap back onto the water. "They're divorced now, but he was still invited to the wedding because their daughter was the flower girl. He spotted me at the bar Friday. Bought me too many glasses of wine. Felt the need to steady my wobbly gait as he walked me to the elevators and again when a crowd, including yourself, packed into it just after us. Then I saw you, chased you, obsessed about you, nearly orgasmed just from your proximity when you cornered me in the elevator yesterday, went to the wedding, thought about you the whole time, and the rest is history. Except today he saw me waiting in a long line for lunch and offered me a seat to join him and get some food in my belly a little sooner. You showed up, pissed all over me like your property, and here we are. I think that about covers everything."

The sexiest grin slides up his face. I shrug off my T-shirt and shimmy out of my shorts that are already unfastened. Then I climb onto his lap, straddling him.

"You have less than an hour, Professor Hunt. What can you do with me in less than an hour?"

His hands slide up my back, easily unhooking my bra. "A lot."

CHAPTER FORTY-TWO

NATE TEXTS ME around four o'clock. I like that we're texting now. It's not as romantic as handwritten letters, but this is the age of instant gratification, and although I didn't grow up with it like Gabe's and Morgan's generation, I still have a fond appreciation for it.

Have your suitcase packed by 5.

I respond.

I'm booked through the week. Non-refundable.

I'll pay for your lost days.

It's my first time in Chicago. I haven't seen much of it.

His response is instant.

You have an hour. Get to seeing shit and be ready by 5.

I send him three more texts, but he doesn't respond … to the first two.

Why so bossy?

Where are we going?

I contemplate sending the last text. What if someone can see his phone?

You're the only man who has given me more than one

orgasm during sex. Is it your vast knowledge ... your eleven years of studying anatomy?

He responds right away.

You're welcome.

"So damn sure of yourself." I laugh, tossing my phone on the bed then packing my stuff for destination unknown.

By five, I'm in the lobby with my suitcase, butterflies in my tummy, and a ridiculous grin on my face. He steps off the elevator in cargo shorts, a white tee, and sunglasses on top of his head as he pulls his small suitcase behind him.

"Where are we going?" I ask as he jerks his head in the direction of the revolving door.

He says something to the valet before turning toward me.

"Where are we going?" I try again.

"You're glowing today. Have you recently been well fucked by an anatomy professor?"

I cough on my laugh as my head swivels in both directions to see if anyone heard him because he didn't use his library voice at all.

When I focus on him again, he bends down and presses his lips to mine, giving me a little peck and then another little peck. I like playful, flirty Nate. Well, I actually love him.

He stands erect again and slides his sunglasses onto his face as a gust of wind catches his wavy hair and blows mine in my face.

"This is us." He takes my suitcase and his and rolls them toward the gray Mercedes-Benz SUV. The valet loads them into the back. Nate tips him then opens my door. Once he's in the driver's seat, seat belt fastened, and vehicle in drive, I glance at him and try it one more time.

"Where are we going?"

He grins, eyes on the road. "Home."

During the two-and-a-half-hour drive to Madison, we don't say much. We listen to music. During part of the way, we have the windows rolled down. And occasionally Nate tells me random things that have happened since I last saw him … like Morgan freaking out when she got a puppy for Christmas. A shelter dog named Joby. They think she's a German shepherd mix.

I listen to him even though Morgan has told me most everything in her letters. The surreal feeling of him saying we're going *home* has left me in a daze.

"This is it." He pulls onto a cul-de-sac shrouded in trees.

I can barely see the houses tucked behind long drives. It's not the kind of cul-de-sac I'm used to seeing. When his house comes into view, a slow smile creeps up my face. It looks like a chalet. A wood cabin that has more windows than wood. He pulls around to the side of the house to enter from the garage.

After he kills the engine and presses the button to shut the garage door, I ease out of the vehicle and allow my squirrel brain to imagine—just for a second—that this is my home. Nate unloads our suitcases, and I follow him into the house.

I slip off my shoes as he carries our suitcases to the opposite end of the house and disappears around the corner. Two-story ceilings in the great room with an enormous floor-to-ceiling stonewall fireplace separating the kitchen from the living space.

"Where's Morgan?" I ask as Nate makes his way toward me.

"My parents' house."

"Oh. You said they were watching her and Joby. I assumed you meant they were watching her here."

"Nope." He slides his arms around my waist, pulling me flush to him.

I lift onto my toes and bury my face into his neck. "Are you saying it's just us?"

He kisses my forehead. "It's just us."

"For how long?"

"Until tomorrow night." He takes my hand and leads me to the sofa, plopping down and pulling me onto his lap so I'm straddling him, face-to-face.

"Twenty-four hours, huh?" I tickle the nape of his neck with my fingers, running them through his partial curls. "Then what?"

"I don't know. When do you fly back to California?" He slides his hands under my shirt and feathers his fingertips along my lower back.

"Thursday afternoon. I need to be to the airport by eleven."

"It's Sunday." He grins.

"Yes …" I lean into him, giving his bottom lip a tug with my teeth. "Your point?"

He gathers my hair into a ponytail and pulls it until I tip my chin up. "My point is I get you until Thursday." He kisses my neck.

"You get me until tomorrow. Then I'll be hanging out with my BFF Morgan in her awesome tree house I see out back. And playing fetch with Joby."

"And at night, you'll be riding my cock." He sits back, twisting his lips. "Huh … did I say that out loud?"

"Cute. You'd better clean that mouth up before your *eleven-year-old* daughter returns."

"I'll return to my best behavior when they pull in the driveway … *tomorrow.*"

"And today?"

"Today I'm going to pop a few Viagra and see what I can do with an eight-hour erection and naked Elvis."

I fall into a fit of giggles. "Sounds painful ... and really disturbing."

He returns to my neck where I love him the most. His chuckling tickles my skin. "How about a tour of the house?"

"With or without the eight-hour erection?"

He sucks my earlobe into his mouth and directs my hand between us to his erection. "I'd give it about twenty minutes."

"Then make the tour quick," I whisper, rubbing my thumb over the head of it, eliciting a moan from him.

"God ... I love you." He grabs my ass and rocks to standing with me hugged to him like a monkey. "Great room. Kitchen," he says, without taking his gaze off me.

"It's nice." I grin without looking at the kitchen or the great room.

He walks us down the wide hallway. "Office."

I hold on with one hand on his shoulder while running my other hand through his hair. "It's amazing." My gaze doesn't leave his face. I'm sure it's a fantastic office. I'll see it later. "Guest room. Morgan's room."

I tease my fingers along his scruffy jaw, brushing my thumb along his lips because his full lips are my addiction. "Uh-huh ..." I suck in my lower lip. I've already seen Morgan's room on video chat. The guest room can't look that much different.

"Bathroom." He nips at my thumb.

I feel it between my legs—that might be his erection.

"Master bedroom." He takes us into the bedroom and kicks the door shut. The first thing I get a good look at is the ceiling when my back hits the mattress.

Skylights. Nice.

"I REALIZE THIS is a little after-the-fact, but is this the bed you had with Jenna?" I walk my naked self from the bed to his walk-in closet. The light goes on automatically. "I'm going to snoop." I glance over my shoulder.

He's rolled on his side, head propped up on his bent arm, sheet barely covering the goods. "Snoop away. And no. It's a new bed."

I pull open several drawers and pluck out a soft tee of his, bringing it to my nose and then slipping it on. Nosing through a few more drawers, just because, I exit the closet. "Wisconsin guy with a Bears T-shirt." I tip my chin down at the blue and orange football tee. "Interesting."

"Is it strange that I want to fuck you in it and never wash it again?"

"No." I saunter to the door and open it. "It's strange that you think I'm not taking it back to California with me … because I totally am." Now that I'm thoroughly satisfied, I re-check out the other bedrooms, bathrooms, his office, and finally the kitchen.

His fridge could use some more food, but his gorgeous walk-in pantry has quite a bit of food. Grabbing whatever looks like it has potential, I lay out ingredients for dinner. A granola bar and two bites of a sandwich do not begin to replenish calories after having sex twice.

"Can I help?" Nate makes his way to the kitchen in jeans … only jeans. His hair looks nearly as fucked as I feel.

"I doubt it." I open and close drawers and doors until I find what I need. "Do you like pasta with marinara?"

"If you make it, I'll like it."

"Good." I glance up from the cutting board and onion.

His face turns serious as he sits on the stool at the island. "It's time."

"Time?" I chop the onion.

"I thought … the other night there was a look exchanged. It felt clear at the time. At least to me. Now … I'm not so sure."

"Sure of what?"

He runs his hands through his hair. "Gracelyn … don't do this."

I stop cutting and set the knife on the board. "I'm not on the pill," I whisper, keeping my gaze trained to him, looking for the slightest cringe, the tiniest flinch of regret or concern. "Tell me you didn't assume I was."

He remains neutral as he shakes his head. "I didn't assume it."

Curling my hair behind my ears, I lift my shoulder into a shrug. "So … what did you assume?"

He glances away, somewhere over my shoulder. And I hate it because for the first time since that night, I feel like we didn't just take a chance; we made a mistake. What if it can't be unmade?

After too many seconds of silence that open the door to all my repressed insecurities, I laugh.

It's a crazy laugh.

A nervous laugh.

A really fucking scared laugh.

"Say something! Say ANYTHING!" My voice booms out

of control as my breaths speed into total hyperventilation, riddled with panic. I grab my head, curling my fingers into my hair, taking a few wobbly steps backward. "I could be pregnant. PLEASE tell me this isn't news to you. Please tell me—"

"You're pregnant?" Morgan steps around the corner from the back door to the garage.

I heard nothing. When did she walk in? How much did she hear? Why is she here?

"Morgan …" Nate flies off the stool and rushes to her, pulling her into a hug. "What are you doing here, baby?"

I tug on the tee shirt, trying to pull it down. I'm not wearing anything beneath it. This is the second time she's caught me in nothing but her dad's shirt … in a kitchen. Only this time I'm not giving him head. Honestly, I think I'd prefer that to the pregnancy conversation. Maybe …

It might be a tie.

"What are *you* doing here?" She pulls away. "Is Gracelyn pregnant? Am I going to be a big sister? Please say yes. Please. Please. *Please* say yes!" She runs around the island and gives me a hug. "Oh my gosh … I'm so excited! Does Gabe know? Can I be the one to tell him? I hope it's a girl or a boy … I don't really care." Letting go of me, she jumps up and down clapping her hands in front of her.

"Mor-gan!" Nate says her name in a very stern voice.

Her excitement plummets like a dead bird falling out of the sky.

"Why. Are. You. Here?" He rests his hands loosely on his hips.

"Oh …" Her forehead wrinkles. "I forgot my swimsuit and Grandma and Grandpa are going to take me to the pool. They're waiting out in the car."

"Go to your room. Wait for me." He points toward her room.

She frowns, shuffling her flip-flop clad feet down the hall.

He sighs. "I need to tell them it's going to be a few minutes."

Pressing my lips together, feeling completely out of place, I nod, hugging my arms to my stomach.

Nate's eyebrows knit together, and he makes his way to me, cupping the back of my head and giving me a hard kiss. He pulls back just an inch, staying at my eye level. "I want a baby with you. A home. A *life* with you. Okay?"

I swallow back my emotions. "K …" I whisper.

He goes out the front door. I pick back up the knife and steady my shaky hand before continuing my chopping. A few minutes later, he comes back inside and heads straight to Morgan's room.

CHAPTER FORTY-THREE

Nathaniel

"WHY ARE YOU mad?" Morgan pouts, sitting on the edge of her bed without looking up at me after I shut her bedroom door.

"I'm not mad. I just thought you needed a timeout. You were losing it, and honestly I think you were scaring Gracelyn."

"Did you..." she glances up at me "...have sex with her? You promised you would never lie to me about sex. You said I could ask you *anything* and you'd tell me the truth."

I've hidden very little from her over the years, but it was easier when she was younger and didn't ask so many questions that nudged me to the edge of my comfort zone. Yes, I told her I would never lie to her about sex, but I also thought when I explained sex to her, she'd brush it off and not ask about it again for ... maybe ever. And the realistic part of my brain that knew she would ask something just assumed it would be about her own sex life—asking to be put on birth control. I will of course say hell no.

This ... I never thought we'd be discussing my sex life because I never thought I'd have one again.

"Yes."

Keep it simple.

"Did you use a condom?"

Fuck ...

"Because responsible people use condoms. And you are responsible. So if you didn't use one, then that means you want to have a baby with Gracelyn, right?"

When Morgan was five, she asked me how her mom died. I told her. Then she asked if she killed her mom. I assured her she didn't. Years later, she asked about it again. Again, I told her the truth, but in that moment, she had her own opinion. And that opinion was that she was the reason her mom died. It wasn't the truth. It also wasn't a lie.

That led to a conversation about risks and what is considered an acceptable risk. The other night, I wasn't thinking I wanted Gracelyn to get pregnant. I also wasn't thinking I *didn't* want her to get pregnant.

It's complicated.

I kneel down in front of her, resting my hands on her legs. "I love Gracelyn, but you already know that. And ..." I weigh my words for a few seconds. "She might be pregnant, but she might not be either. When people don't know, they don't tell anyone until they do know for sure. It's starting a rumor that doesn't need to be started."

"You don't want me to tell Gabe."

I nod. "Not just Gabe. I don't want you to tell anyone. Not your friends. Not Grandma and Grandpa. No one. Can you do that? Can you just pretend you never heard that? Because we *really* don't know."

"If she is pregnant, are they moving here?" A hopeful smile blooms along her face.

I shake my head. "I don't know. We have a lot to discuss."

"Can I name it?"

I chuckle. "Name what?"

"The baby?"

I lift an eyebrow. "What baby?"

She rolls her eyes and sighs. "Fine." Her fingers move across her lips like a zipper. "What baby?"

I wink. "Exactly."

"Did you get Joby out of the backseat? Did Grandma and Grandpa go home? My stuff is still at their house."

"They're outside. You're going back there for the night."

"But you're home."

I stand. "Yes. But I need some more time to talk about things with Gracelyn. Tomorrow afternoon, after you go swimming, I'll come get you and Joby, and we'll show Gracelyn our favorite things here in Madison."

"Fine." She jumps off her bed and grabs her swimsuit from her closet.

"Hey ..." I stop her before she opens her bedroom door. Cupping her face, I smile. "I love you to infinity. And no matter what happens, I will be honest with you. Okay?"

She wraps her arms around my waist. "Love you too, Daddy."

Daddy ...

I follow her out to the kitchen. Gracelyn still has on my shirt, but she's put her shorts on too.

Morgan runs to her and gives her another hug. She doesn't say anything. She just hugs her. Gracelyn's lips part and her eyes lift to meet my gaze. I don't miss the tears in them.

For a second, maybe two, I let my mind go there. I imagine going from two to five. And I like it.

"Goodnight!" Morgan calls as she runs to the door.

"Night, baby."

Gracelyn quickly wipes her eyes and adds the pasta to the boiling water. When she turns, I pull her into my embrace.

"Why did she leave?"

"Because we have more to say." My hands slide down to her ass. "We have more to do."

She presses her lips to my sternum. "What are we doing?" she whispers.

"Living. We're living." I kiss her head.

WOW! GRACELYN CAN cook. *Really* cook.

I devour two plates of pasta with her homemade sauce that she threw together without following a recipe. We clean the kitchen, take a walk, and end up in my big soaker tub a little before midnight.

"*Transcend ...*" she says, leaning her head back against my shoulder as I feather my fingers over her sternum that's just above the thin layer of suds. "Was it hard to really believe? To wrap your head around the idea that the young friend you lost at such a young age was ... at least in part ... inside the body of the woman you hired to be Morgan's nanny?"

"Yes and no. Reincarnation wasn't a stretch for my mind. It was the fact that it was someone I knew."

She nods, rubbing her lips together. "Brandon spoke to me. I heard his voice. I only told a few people, and when I did, I always made sure they knew that I knew it wasn't really him ... like a ghost. Just his voice in my head. But it wasn't. I believe it was him. It was too real. Do you think that's crazy?"

I slide my hand down her breast to her stomach. "No."

"Did you think you loved Swayze? Not the part of her that was Daisy, but the young college graduate. The woman who spent so much time taking care of Morgan. Did you start to think you were falling in love with her? Did the lines blur?"

"Yes, but it was a toxic combination of missing my wife, seeing Morgan in the arms of a nurturing woman, and all the elements of her that *did* feel like my friend."

"I cried so many times. Not just the loss you experienced. I cried when you let Swayze go. When you said, 'I think a part of you will be mine to love in every life.' God … I just bawled. I also cried when you were so candid with Morgan about life and death. When you let her feel emotional pain—when you didn't try to take it away because you said she will never know true happiness if she doesn't let the pain into her heart. You told her the most beautiful rainbows come from the harshest storms."

"Yeah …" I chuckle. "That's not scientifically true. She went through a big rainbow and unicorn phase, so I worked with what I had at the time."

She eases her body the other way, careful to not splash water out of the tub. I take her foot and rub it as she settles at the opposite end.

"You're a beautiful man. But … I don't have the words to describe how you are as a dad. I'm not sure the words exist. Watching you with her … reading your words … I'm speechless. And the idea of having a baby with you, it, too, leaves me speechless."

I smile. *She* leaves me speechless … breathless. "More …" I sit up and run my hands along the outside of her legs. "You have to wonder. I know I would. I *did* wonder, until that day in the rain when you let the bracelet drop to the ground … when you let it disappear without giving it a single glance because you were too busy *seeing* me. So the answer is more. I love you more than I loved Daisy."

Tears fill her eyes.

"I love you more than I loved Jenna. Not because I didn't love them with my whole heart. I did. It's just that my time away with Morgan has taught me one thing. Our capacity to love grows with time. It grows with every new person who touches our lives. So I love you more because my heart is bigger."

She blinks, setting the tears free.

TRUTH?

I don't know how this chapter of our story will end. A doctor's first rule is to do no harm. As Morgan and I drive Gracelyn back to the airport in Chicago, I think of the fun we've had. I took a million pictures of them in the tree house. The three of us, hand-in-hand, taking Joby for walks. Eating at Morgan's favorite restaurants. Game night where Morgan bankrupted Gracelyn and me in Monopoly.

Gracelyn teaching Morgan how to make perfect mashed potatoes and the chewiest chocolate chip cookies.

Morgan practicing her braiding technique on Gracelyn.

Gracelyn painting Morgan's fingernails and toenails in a bright shade of pink.

The girly giggles.

The endearing smiles.

Just everything.

But … Gracelyn is headed back to San Diego to her job and to wait for her next period and Gabe, when he returns in a week. We agreed that she would ask him how he feels about moving, and I would call him if she needed reinforcement. We agreed we would do no harm to him and his still fragile state, knowing that it will be years before he stops feeling the emptiness of his loss.

I unload her luggage as she and Morgan get out at the terminal drop-off.

"Hug Gabe and Mr. Hans for me." Morgan hugs her.

"I will. Take care of you and maybe keep an eye on your dad too. I'm going to miss you like crazy."

Morgan keeps her arms around Gracelyn's waist while looking up at her. "We'll see each other soon. Right?"

Gracelyn kisses Morgan's head. "I hope so. There's always video chat and TikTok dancing."

My daughter nods. "Okay. Bye. I'll get in the car in case my dad wants to kiss you goodbye."

We grin as she hops into the backseat.

I see the pain and dread on her face, in spite of the brave smile she's giving me. "What if I'm not …"

I shake my head and cradle her face in my hands. "It changes nothing."

She nods. "No more letters. I want … I *need* your voice and this face." Her hands press to my cheeks, mimicking mine on hers.

Her thumb rubs along my lips, making me grin even more.

"Lots of phone calls. Video chat. And dirty texts."

A bigger smile chases away her wavering fear. "Definitely."

"I'm a plane ride away. I'll grab a flight and be there if you need me."

"I know."

We stare at each other, neither one wanting to let go of the other.

"I have a flight to catch. If you're going to steal a kiss … now's the time."

I grab her wrist and move her hand over my mouth, kissing it … kissing down to where she used to be shackled to her past. Then I kiss her lips, knowing young eyes are too snoopy to not be on us. I don't care.

I promised Morgan honesty. This is it. This is what it looks like to love someone deeply … madly … to the depths of your soul. So much it rips your fucking heart out of your chest to let go. My daughter should never settle for less *if* I deem some guy worthy of her … twenty years from now.

Gracelyn pulls away, breathless, keeping her eyes closed. "Bye, my love." She turns, grabs her suitcase, and takes off to the terminal entrance.

I slide my hands in my front pockets and wait.

Give it to me …

At the last second, she glances over her shoulder.

"There it is," I whisper to myself.

CHAPTER FORTY-FOUR

Gracelyn

I GO HOME.

I don't know who I'm missing more—Nate and Morgan or Gabe.

Probably Gabe. I've been away from him longer.

We don't video chat because they're always where the connection is terrible. So other than a few texts, I get a phone call with him and my parents each night. I haven't told them I went to Nate's house, and since Gabe hasn't mentioned it, I know Morgan's managed to keep it a secret too.

Mr. Hans spends a lot of time eyeing me with an odd look and asking about Chicago. I dodge questions with vague answers and swift subject changes. I fear he's onto me.

Nate and Morgan video chat with me every day. Then after Morgan goes to bed, Nate calls me. I snuggle under my covers and fall asleep to his soothing voice every night. The next morning, he texts me and asks what's the last thing I remember him saying. I never remember what he said. I just remember how his voice in my ear made me feel.

"They're here!" Mr. Hans calls late the following Friday. I start the washer with my work clothes in it and run downstairs and out the door.

My heart bursts with sparkles and glitter because Gabe takes off running this way when he sees me. "Gah! I missed you."

"Missed you too," he says, hugging me tightly.

My parents smile as they make their way to us with Gabe's bag and pillow.

We settle in for dinner and all the stories from their trip. Again, like I've done with Mr. Hans, I turn all the questions they have about my trip into short answers and more questions about their trip.

The following day, my parents leave for home. And since I have the day off, I take the opportunity to have a heart-to-heart with Gabe.

"Hey, buddy. Can we talk?" I sit in the recliner adjacent to the sofa where he's perched watching TV.

"Sure." He keeps his attention on the TV.

"Can we talk without the TV on?"

He raises his eyebrows at me like it's the craziest request ever.

"Please."

With his customary sigh, he shuts off the TV.

"I want to talk to you about Nate and Morgan."

"O-kay," he says slowly.

"We never talk about relationships, well, at least not that much. You're a bit young. But ..."

This isn't going well. It's hard explaining grown-up love to an eleven-year-old boy. I have no clue what emotions he has had or can even begin to understand. So ... I go in a different direction.

"When Morgan and Nate were here last summer, Nate and I fell in love." Boom! There it is.

"O-kay." The same word again in slow motion.

"When grown-ups are in love, they want to be together.

Last summer didn't feel like the right time for us to try to be together because Morgan was so excited about going home to the rest of her family again, and she wanted to be close to her mom's grave. And … well … there were just a lot of things and a lot of uncertainty.

"But most important at the time, for me anyway, was you. I couldn't imagine asking you to change your life any more than it had already been changed. So I didn't say anything. I didn't even want you to have the stress of making a decision or feeling like you were letting anyone down if you didn't make 'the right' decision. And I don't know if there was a right decision. So we made the decision without discussing it with you or Morgan. We chose to not be together—not disrupt your lives by asking for you to give up anything or move away from your home."

Confusion camps out on his face and in the permanent squint of his eyes.

I wait for questions that never come. I wait for him to read into where this is going, but he doesn't.

Leaning forward, I rest my arms on my legs and fold my hands, squeezing them several times. "I ran into Nate at the hotel where I stayed in Chicago. The feelings we had last summer … the love … it's still there. Maybe even stronger. So instead of staying in Chicago the whole time, I went to his house in Wisconsin and stayed a few days with him and Morgan."

"You did?"

I nod.

"Morgan didn't tell me that."

"We asked her not to tell you."

"Why?"

"Because …"

Because I might be pregnant?

But mostly because I might not be pregnant?

I don't know how to answer that. He's eleven. I can't see him really understanding. Still, I have to try. How is he supposed to learn and understand new things if he's not given the chance?

"Do you know how babies are made?"

His face turns red. I take that as a yes.

"Why?"

That's not a yes.

"Because I assume in the next year or two they will talk about it at school, if they haven't already. And I don't know what your dad and mom discussed with you, but since it's you and me now … I think I should know what you know and what you don't know." I give myself an internal high five.

"I saw a video."

I nod. "At school?"

"No. At a friend's house."

Oh Jesus …

"Not really a video. A gif. Several gifs."

I clear my throat. I am so out of my league, my comfort zone, my mind! "Gifs about babies?" My face cringes a little.

"Well, supposedly how they are made."

Fuck. Fuck. Fuck.

"It's weird, but I get it."

"You do?"

He nods.

"So … first, I have to say whatever you saw is something you should not have seen. There is *a lot* on the internet that you should not see—that most adults should not see."

"It was at Jacob's house, but it was last year right after ..."

His mom and dad died. Yeah, I still pause before I say the actual words too. I nod to let him know I get it, and he doesn't have to say them.

"Jacob's mom found out and told TJ's and Cole's parents, but ..."

I nod again. "She didn't know who to go to about you seeing it too."

"Yeah."

"Listen, I'm a little worried that what you saw might not be exactly right, but it could be. I want you to have a healthy knowledge of sex. Do you know—"

"I know what it's called." He rolls his eyes and shakes his head.

"Okay. Do you think we should talk about it?"

"No."

"Okay." I chuckle. "We don't have to right now, but to return to what we were talking about ... I might be pregnant."

Gabe's eyes grow into saucers.

"Nate and I had ... sex. And there is *so* much to discuss about that and babies and *not* getting pregnant from sex, but we don't have to discuss that now if you don't want to. However, it will need to be discussed when you get older and start showing more interest in girls. Okay?"

He doesn't move. "You're going to have a baby?"

I shake my head. "I don't know yet. But maybe. That's why I want to talk with you about Nate and Morgan. How would you feel about living with them?"

"You mean they're moving next door again?"

"No ... I mean how would you feel about moving to Wisconsin?"

He shakes his head. "I don't want to move."

I blow out a slow breath. "I know. But *if* I'm pregnant, then Nate and I need to be together. This would be his baby too."

"So what's going to happen to me?"

Tension settles in my face. He's breaking my heart. I scoot over to the sofa and rest my hand on his. "Gabe, nothing is going to happen to you. We are a family now. You and I. So if I'm pregnant, it doesn't change us, it just adds to our family. Technically, it will be your cousin, but you'll grow up with him or her like a big brother."

"You want me to move?"

"Yeah. I want you to move."

"Do I have to?"

He's not making this easy at all.

"I mean … what if you're not pregnant. Then we don't have to move, right? I mean … I have friends here. My soccer team. This is my home."

"I know, but things change in life. I think you would like Wisconsin. And while you would miss your friends, you would make new ones. Find a new soccer team. You're young and you have lots of school years left and plenty of time to make new friends."

He stands, shaking his head over and over. "I don't want to go if I don't have to go."

"And what if I'm pregnant?"

He stops, halfway to his room. "Then I'll go. But if you're not, then we stay." The door slams shut.

"Shit …" I whisper.

I make my way downstairs. Mr. Hans hands me a glass of lemonade and nods to the porch.

"You were eavesdropping?" I follow him.

He smirks and sits on the swing. "Just had my hearing aid turned way up."

I grin and take a seat next to him.

"Let it settle a few days. Give him time to think about it. He'll come around."

I stare out at the water. "And if he doesn't?"

"You'll figure something out. He's not going to break."

"But he's lost a lot."

"We all suffer losses. Yes, his was a big loss at an early age, but he's surrounded by love and that's what's going to make him a strong young man. He will be resilient, more so than other young men his age who didn't have to suffer such a loss."

"What if I'm not pregnant?" I whisper my greatest fear. It's crazy. I'm forty-two. *Being* pregnant should be my greatest fear.

"Cross one bridge at a time. It's all Gabe can do right now too."

I nod. "Thank you."

CHAPTER FORTY-FIVE

I GET MY period.

The tears come instantly with plenty of help from my hormones. I knew it was coming. I've had night sweats for days, and they always happen before my period. Of course, I'm not pregnant. My unused uterus probably shriveled up years ago. Now it just hemorrhages bloody tears once a month to remind me what an epic fuckup my life has been.

Yeah … the hormones are strong.

After I told Nate about my talk with Gabe, he said if I wasn't pregnant, he'd fly out here and talk to Gabe man to man. He shouldn't have to do that.

Running on high octane estrogen, I march out to the living room and stand in front of Gabe's Saturday morning TV.

"Move, please." He cranes his head to see around me.

I snatch the remote and shut off the TV. "Listen, I want to be your friend. I don't like it when I have to act like an adult with you. It's much more fun to go Rollerblading and play games together. But you leave me with no choice. We are moving to Wisconsin. End of discussion."

"I know." He grabs the remote from the table and tries to angle it around me to turn back on the TV.

"Wait … what? How can you know? I just found out I'm not pregnant, but that doesn't change anything because I love Nate and Morgan, *and* Nate adores you and we will all be very happy together and …" I stop my rambling as my brain echoes his words again. "Wait … *how* did you know that we're moving? And why aren't you making an argument for staying?"

"No reason." He manages to get the TV turned back on. "Can you please move?"

"Did Nate call you?"

He huffs. "No. We're moving. Aren't you happy?"

Yes. No. Dammit! What is going on? I'm emotionally drowning in devastation that I'm not pregnant. And at the same time, Gabe has surrendered to moving, which is exactly what I wanted. The extreme swing of the pendulum leaves me dizzy, but the forty-something hormones win, and I just need a good cry. So I lock myself in my room, flop onto the bed, bury my face in a pillow, and cry.

When the tears stop, and I let my thoughts move past the fact that I'm not pregnant—since two weeks ago, I didn't know I wanted to be pregnant—I splash water on my face and call Nate.

He doesn't answer. I'm not sure a text is the way to tell him, but I *have* to tell him.

Hi.

Gabe has agreed to move, but it will just be the two of us.

I'm forty-two. He's forty-seven. Is it a good idea to start an eighteen-year process at this stage in our lives?

Still …

I let my heart go there. I let it dive off the cliff to the deepest depths of my imagination, reawakening old dreams with a bright new light.

And now …

I feel the loss of something I never had. I feel the loss of a dream all over again and … it hurts.

When I leave my room, Gabe pokes his head out of his bedroom. “Want to go Rollerblading?”

Gabe … Gabe … Gabe …

The men in my life are pretty damn spectacular—my dad, Mr. Hans, Nate, and Gabe. When one can’t be here for me, another one steps in.

“Yeah.” I smile. “I’d love to go Rollerblading.”

We drive to Mission Bay and hop on the trail.

“Will I be in Morgan’s class … in school?”

I glance over at him. Where did this come from? “I don’t know. I’m sure it depends on the size of the school. You’ll probably have different teachers and different groups of kids for each class. So there’s a chance you might have at least one class with her. Is that … okay?”

“Yeah. Whatever.”

After a few miles, we find a bench and grab a drink, watching the beachgoers covering nearly every inch of sand.

My phone vibrates and I pluck it from the pocket of my shorts. It’s Nate. I send it to voicemail. If I hear his voice, I’ll cry.

A few seconds later, my screen lights up with a text from him.

Morgan told me he said yes to coming. I assumed that meant yes to the other question. Call me.

I slip my phone back into my pocket before my emotions take a bad turn again.

“Feels like an ice cream day. Don’t you think?”

Gabe grins. “Definitely.”

We get ice cream, grab some fish to grill for dinner tonight, and head home. Mr. Hans does a great job of acting surprised when Gabe tells him we're moving. However, my surprise to Gabe's slight enthusiasm is very real.

After we finish the dinner dishes, I grab a shower, tell Gabe goodnight, and snuggle in my bed with my phone to call Nate before it gets any later. It's already eleven there. He's probably asleep.

"Hey," he answers on the third ring.

"Am I waking you?"

"No. I'm just reading. How … are you?"

"Fine," I say immediately.

"Are you sure?"

"Yes." I wipe a few tears he can't see.

"I guess we never discussed this. Really discussed this. I'm forty-seven. You're—"

"I know. I'm forty-two. It was probably a little insane, something that felt like a good idea in a time of passion. It doesn't matter now. For some unexplainable reason, Gabe is okay with moving, so the rest doesn't matter."

He doesn't say anything for a few seconds. "Unless it does."

I laugh while wiping more tears. "My uterus probably doesn't work. I'm not sure why I felt like I could get pregnant."

"Did you really want to be?"

Yes.

"Doesn't matter."

"Gracelyn, quit saying that. It matters to me."

"Well, it shouldn't."

"But it does. We should have talked about it. *Really* talked about it. And now I'm worried you're not telling me how you feel. You can—"

"Yes!" I cover my mouth, hoping Gabe didn't hear me. My

lips quiver, holding in the sobs.

"You wanted a baby," he whispers.

I nod several times before I can speak without completely losing it. "Yes."

He says nothing. I have to believe he's dealing with his own feelings about this. I just don't know exactly what they are.

"Nate …"

"Then come home. And let's make a baby."

I swallow all the doubt, the what-ifs, the hard reality that I might not be able to get pregnant. For now, I let hope back into my life.

"Okay."

I GIVE NOTICE at work.

Instead of fireworks on the beach for the Fourth, we start the packing process—where I throw away the silk nightie that I never wore because Brandon didn't make it out of the hospital—and Nate arranges everything else.

He doesn't want us driving that far, so he arranges a moving company to take our stuff, not that we have a lot. I sell Kyle's Land Rover. And Mr. Hans doesn't charge us extra for breaking our second-year lease six weeks into it.

However, he does get a little emotional when we say goodbye at the airport.

"You're family now. Just let me know when you need a place to hang out at the beach. The upstairs is yours."

I hug him and steal Nate's line. "If you're ever in Wisconsin …"

He chuckles.

Gabe hugs him too, and we set off on our new adventure. Never … not in a million years, did I imagine my life would go in this direction.

It takes us six hours and one connecting flight to get to Madison. A huge, glittery sign with our names on it greets us just outside of security. Morgan hands the sign to her dad and runs toward us. I think she's going to tackle-hug Gabe, but she doesn't. She hugs me, sending me back a few steps.

When she releases me, she shrugs at Gabe. "Sorry. I have to do it." Before he can protest, she throws her arms around his neck. He tolerates it for three seconds before wriggling out of her hold.

It's only been a month, but as Nate saunters toward me with his freshly shaven face and that smile … my heart sprints like it's been a year. He drops the sign and lifts me off the floor in a big hug.

"Tell me we're done leaving each other," I whisper in his ear.

"So done." He releases me to my feet, frames my face, and kisses me. It's hungry, but not inappropriate.

On the way home, Morgan talks Gabe's ear off in the backseat while Nate and I stick to flirty glances and gentle squeezes of our fingers interlaced on my lap.

"Okay. First you can see your room. Then you have to see the tree house, then …" Morgan jumps out of the vehicle as soon as it's parked.

Gabe follows her just as quickly.

"What do you think changed his mind?" Nate asks before we get out.

I shrug. "I really don't know. It was so weird. Did you ask Morgan?"

"Yes. She shrugged and said she had no idea."

"Huh ..." I open the door, and Nate gets our bags out of the back.

He sets the bags inside and holds open the door for me. "Welcome home."

I grin, taking his proffered hand.

Home ...

I haven't truly felt at home since Kyle and Emily died and I left my apartment in Boise.

"Pantry. Fridge. We went to the store yesterday, so it's fully stocked." Morgan finishes her indoor tour. "Now ... time for the tree house." She grabs Gabe's arm and pulls him toward the deck door.

Before the door closes, I hear Gabe say, "Wow! It's bigger than what it looked on the video."

It's the tone of his voice, the exuberant grin on his face, that tells me he will be fine. This is where we're meant to be.

"Do you regret not trying this last year?" Nate asks, hugging me from behind as we stand at the window and watch the kids climb into the tree house.

"No regrets." I lean my head back against him. "Timing in life is everything. It wasn't just him last summer. It was me too. I wasn't ready to ask him for something this big. It didn't feel right in my gut." I turn in his arms. "I was worth the wait. Right?"

His hands slide down to my ass as he ducks to kiss a trail from my shoulder to my ear. "We'll find out later after the kids are in bed."

CHAPTER FORTY-SIX

Nathaniel

IT ONLY TAKES a few weeks for everyone to get settled, the kids registered for school, Gabe a new soccer team, and Morgan starting up her figure skating lessons again with dreams of the Olympics.

Gracelyn's been looking for a job, but she doesn't know what she wants to do. I want to devote all of our free time before school starts getting her pregnant. She doesn't think sex twice a day and baking cookies is contributing enough to our new family.

I disagree.

The kids love her cookies. And I love … well … I think that's pretty clear.

"I have a flat tire. The car started to shimmy as I pulled into the neighborhood." She frowns, carrying groceries with the kids. "My car is weeks old and it already has a flat."

I set my empty glass on the counter and wipe my sweaty brow. We have a huge yard that took me two hours to mow. I might have to get a riding lawn mower.

"I'll change it and take it tomorrow to get it fixed."

"You're going to change a tire?" Gabe asks, setting the bag of groceries on the floor by the pantry.

"Yes. You want to help me?"

"Yeah." He grins.

"Cool. Let's go check it out." I nod toward the door. "Morgan, help put the groceries away, please."

"I will. I just need to pee." She wrinkles her nose before heading toward the bathroom.

As I take a step toward the garage to follow Gabe, Gracelyn hooks a finger into the waistband of my exercise shorts.

I turn, giving her the once-over as she stares at my bare chest for a few seconds before lifting her gaze to mine. "Can I help you?" I smirk. "The kids are awake, but I could make them take the dog for a long walk. And I'm sweaty, but I know you kind of like that."

She wets her lips. "Mmm … I do, but that's not it. I just want to say thank you."

"For what?"

"For showing Gabe how to change a tire. Kyle was going to show him how to do that … and change the oil … and stuff like that. But …"

I nod. "I've got this." Dropping a kiss on her lips, I grin. "*We've* got this."

When I get to the garage, Gabe's standing by the flat tire with his hands on his hips and his head cocked to the side. "I think we need a wrench."

"We do." I rest my arm around his shoulders and inspect the tire with him. "And a jack. And a spare tire."

Together, we change the tire. It reminds me of my dad teaching me. By the time we finish, I make sure we have some dirt and grease on our hands and face to make it official. Gabe snaps a picture of us and posts it for his friends to see.

"Thanks, buddy. Good job." I give him a fist bump. "Let's get washed up and see if Gracelyn needs help with dinner." I start toward the door to the house.

"Nate?"

I turn. "Yeah?"

Gabe's face scrunches and he stares at his feet. "I have to tell you something." He wrings his hands together. It feels serious, so I take a seat on the steps by the door.

"What's up?"

"I like it here. I … didn't think I would. But I do. I like my room. I like that you let me decorate it however I wanted to. The tree house is awesome. And my first day of soccer went well. The coach said I'm a really good player. And the other kids were nice. And Joby likes to sleep with me instead of Morgan. I know that makes her mad, but I like it because we never had a dog. Then today…" he glances up "…you let me help you with the tire."

I nod. "I'm glad you like it here. I like you being here. I like the family we have now. And maybe we'll have to get another pet, so Morgan stops whining about Joby choosing you." I wink at him.

Still … he has a painful look on his face.

"I did something I don't think I should have done."

"Hey." I pat the spot beside me on the step. "Come here. You can tell me anything."

Gabe drags his feet to me and plops down beside me with his head bowed. "Morgan really wanted me to move here. She begged me. But I didn't want to move. It didn't seem fair that I had to be the one to leave my friends when I've had my friends longer than she's had her friends. So … she paid me."

"Paid you? What do you mean?"

He glances over at me. "She said she had three thousand dollars that was hers, just hers from all of her birthdays and Christmases away from her grandparents."

"Yeah …" I say slowly. My parents and Jenna's dad and siblings put aside money for her since they couldn't give her presents when we were traveling. My mom has it in a fire safe at her house.

"She gave it to me. It's under my mattress."

"Okay. Can I ask how much she paid you?"

He shrugs. "All of it."

What the fuck?

I'm not mad. I'm … I don't even know.

"She told me I could buy so much stuff with it like a new bike, new Rollerblades, tons of soccer stuff, games, and more ice cream than I could ever eat. But I had to promise to never tell a single soul or I'd have to give all the money back. She said with … something that meant more money."

I grunt a laugh because he's trying to tell me that she planned on charging him interest. That's funny and I wouldn't expect less of my smarty pants little girl. However, the whole situation doesn't feel so funny. I liked it when I thought he came on his own free will. And I know Gracelyn found it quite amazing.

"Well … now you've told someone. Why?"

"It doesn't feel right to keep the money. I'm going to give it all back."

I wrap my arm around him and kiss the side of his head. "You're a good kid. Morgan is going to expect that interest on the money, but I'll pay it for you if you give me the money and let me be the one to return it to her. Deal?"

"Is she going to be in trouble?"

"I doubt it." I stand. "Go wash up. It's under your mattress?"

He nods.

"I'll get it."

"Thanks for not being mad."

I turn. "We're good. Us guys have to stick together."

The pain vanishes from his face, and he smiles.

Sure enough, there are thirty-one hundred dollar bills under his mattress bound with a rubber band. I take them and sneak down the hall to Morgan's room as Gabe talks to Gracelyn about what we should have for dinner.

I knock on her door.

"Come in."

"Hey. Whatcha doing?"

She shows me her folders. "Going through some stuff from last school year. Did you show Gabe how to change a tire?"

"I did. And he gave me something to give you."

"What?" She swivels in her desk chair.

"This." I toss the money on her bed.

Her eyes open to double their capacity as her jaw drops.

I wait for her. She stares at the money for a good ten seconds. "Don't be mad," she whispers.

"Why, Morgan? Why would you give him every penny you own? Eight years of money your grandparents saved for you. Help me understand."

She lifts her shoulders as her gaze sweeps across my face briefly before fixing to something out her window. "I wanted them to move here. I wanted to be a big sister."

I sit on the end of her bed. "That must have been a big disappointment when I told you she wasn't pregnant."

"Yeah, but …"

"You wanted the money back, didn't you?"

She shakes her head and looks at me with slightly narrowed eyes like my question is crazy. "No. I wanted the baby, but …"

"But?"

She sighs and looks at me with a soft smile. "I read a story about love. The character in the book said you can't buy a happily ever after … you can't buy love. But I could. For three thousand dollars I bought you and Gracelyn a happily-ever-after."

Oh … my … fucking … heart …

This girl.

I open my mouth to respond, but I choke and close it. She stands and steps between my legs, pressing her hands to my cheeks. "Are you going to cry? You don't cry."

I blink to keep my emotions in check. "Sometimes I cry." Covering her hands with mine, I smile. "It's complicated."

EPILOGUE

Eighteen months later.

"DAAAD! YES! WOOT! Woot!" Morgan jumps up and down. "That's two! He's scored two times!"

We cheer Nate on as he plays a game in his men's hockey league. I'm concerned … he's not a young guy anymore. But damn … I sure like to watch him play because he's so good.

For an old guy.

Gabe shoves his face with popcorn and watches half the time while playing a game on his phone the other half.

"Hey! Foul!" I stand when an asshole from the other team checks my husband into the boards.

Nate shoves him back. Then two other guys join in as the ref and a few sensible teammates try to break it up. Once it's broken up, Nate looks up at me. I blow him a kiss.

After the game, we grab pizza and head home because it's late and it's already past their bedtime.

"No dillydallying. School tomorrow," I say after we eat.

"Fine." Gabe and Morgan grumble in unison as they take Joby and Fritzy (Morgan's cat) to their rooms.

Nate starts to help me clean up.

"I've got it. You need a shower."

"I stink?"

I hold up my fingers an inch apart.

"Fine." He mimics the kids and skulks toward our bedroom.

A few minutes later, I pick up pet toys, fold a few blankets, and stare at the photos on the walls. The photos from our backyard wedding always bring joy to my heart—Morgan in a pink dress as my maid of honor and Gabe in a gray suit and pink tie as Nate's best man. We were surrounded by family and close friends, including Mr. Hans. The kids devoured cake as music serenaded us under strings of outdoor lights stretched like a spiderweb over the celebration.

"XO" by Keywest played when Nate took my hand and pulled me into his arms for our first dance.

"Elvis ..."

I grinned.

"Lover ..."

He grinned, pressing his lips to my bare shoulder. "My beautiful wife."

A world of emotions washed over me. I had everything and so much more.

"How did we get here?" I pulled back, shaking my head as my hand pressed to his cheek, my thumb brushing his bottom lip that I would kiss very soon.

He nipped at the pad of my thumb. "It's complicated."

I grin at the photos—the memories of yesterday, the dreams of tomorrow—as I shut off the lights and kiss Gabe then Morgan goodnight. Life is pretty damn good.

The kids love school. Gabe has more friends now than he had in San Diego. He's the star player on his soccer team. Morgan takes after Nate and is a natural at hockey—yes, she switched from figure skating to hockey. Her initial crush on Gabe is gone. She has a boyfriend at school that Nate doesn't know about yet, and she fights with Gabe like the brother he's become to her.

Me? Well, I bake and clean. Shop with Morgan. Help Gabe with homework. Walk the dog. Yeah … that's about it. I've done the odd job thing for years. I don't miss working forty-plus hours a week to make ends meet. Besides … I have some plans coming up.

"Not hogging all the hot water, are you?" I ask Nate as I remove my clothes.

"I'm trying. Feels good on my sore muscles."

"Your muscles wouldn't be sore if you didn't engage in bad behavior. You're too old to fight."

"Please stop prefacing everything with I'm too old."

I grin, opening the glass door to the shower filled with lots of body jets and a rainfall head from the ceiling. "Sorry. You're too mature." I take my loofa and scrub his back. "But…" I kiss along his shoulder blades "…I love watching you play. And the part of my brain that didn't worry about you getting hurt, thought you fighting back was kind of hot."

He turns, wearing a sexy grin. Wearing a sexy everything. All joking aside, my husband has kept his body in tip-top shape.

Me? Not so much, but you wouldn't know it from the way he looks at me.

"How hot?"

I grin, sliding my hands down his chest. "Really hot."

He watches my fingers trace his abs as they flex beneath my touch.

My gaze lifts to his. "Do you ever think about the people who had to die for us to meet? For us to be together? Do you ever wonder why? Like … is it a grand plan or is it just …" I shrug.

He smiles like for him it doesn't matter. Nate is the most optimistic person I have ever known. "Or just what?" He brushes his wet lips over mine, teasing me as his fingers glide up my inner thighs. "Fortuity?"

"Yes," I breathe into his mouth as he kisses me … as his fingers skip the part of my body I want him to touch. I know why he does it. He's itching to spread his large hands over my belly to hold our daughter.

The End

If you enjoyed *Fortuity*, please consider leaving a review and check out Chapter One of *Look the Part.*

PROLOGUE

HEIDI GAVE ME a son and then I killed her. Lucky were the bastards who learned life lessons from close calls. I envied those lucky bastards.

"DON'T DRINK TONIGHT. I want you to put another baby inside of me," my wife whispered as her hand slid up my leg under the table surrounded by twelve of our closest family and friends. Heidi picked my favorite steak house in Omaha and reserved the party room for my special day. I had no idea until everyone yelled surprise.

I loved her beyond words.

"And for the birthday boy?" The brunette waitress winked at me, readying her pen against the pad of paper in her hand.

"Whisky neat."

Heidi frowned.

I grabbed her hand and pressed it to my erection. "I'm not going to have any issues granting your request."

"We'll see." Her curt response held little confidence.

My parents drove in from Denver to surprise me, but my two-year-old son, Harrison, stole the show. They took turns gushing over him with Heidi's mom. I didn't anticipate being a father before I graduated college; I also didn't anticipate meeting the woman I couldn't live without at the exact moment I needed her the most.

She was a nursing student at the hospital they sent me to the day an ACL injury shattered my football career. I called her an angel. Heidi insisted it was the drugs they gave me for the pain.

"Monaghan said you're going to be his agent when he goes Pro." My dad gave me a curious look.

"Monaghan is full of shit. No team in their right mind will draft Pretty Boy. He's going to be a teacher. That right there shows you he's too much of a pussy to have a serious chance in the NFL."

The Cornhusker's young quarterback shot me a smirk from the other end of the table. We both knew he'd go Pro, but I wasn't going to inflate his ego on my birthday.

"Language, Hopkins," Heidi warned.

When she called me by my last name, I squirmed in my chair. It always meant a punishment would follow—and all of her punishments were doled out in the bedroom.

I loved her beyond words.

The night marched on without missing one perfect beat.

Dinner. Friends. Family. Food. Drinks.

My wife outdid herself. She excelled in making every day perfect. She also excelled in making me feel irresponsible for drinking. Every time the waitress placed another drink in front of me, Heidi's lips pursed into a disapproving frown.

I let it slide without argument. Before he died, her father drank a lot of alcohol and was abusive. When we met, she thought I didn't drink. At the time, it was true. Football was my life. I treated my body like a temple. But after my injury, I settled into a life where my body was no longer a temple and the occasional drink was exactly what I needed to ease the pain of lost dreams.

Heidi thought every guy who drank was an abusive alcoholic. I made it my mission to prove her wrong so maybe someday she, too, would relax a little and have a drink on special occasions.

"Happy birthday, Flint. Take care of my babies." My mother-in-law, Sandy, hugged me as everyone said their final birthday wishes and goodnights.

"That's code for hand the keys to your wife." Heidi nudged me with a playful smile that I knew was not at all meant to be playful.

Sandy squeezed my cheeks and looked into my eyes. "I think he's fine, sweetie. Nothing like your father was so give him some slack."

I shot Heidi an I-told-you-so look. Her mother loved me. I was everything her father hadn't been. Heidi hated that I could do no wrong in Sandy's eyes, but I loved it. A dangerous pride came with so much confidence.

After she fastened Harrison into his car seat, Heidi held out her hand.

"I'm fine." I opened the driver's door.

"You're not. You drank a lot tonight."

"I weigh a lot."

"Flint."

I slipped into the driver's seat. "Call me Hopkins, baby. I like where that leads."

"Flint, I'm serious. Our child is in the backseat." She stood between me and the door so I couldn't shut it.

"I want to be in my birthday suit with you. Get in so we can get Harrison to bed."

She crossed her arms over her chest, raven hair flowing in all directions, blue eyes piercing mine.

"I'm. Fine."

Heidi shrugged. "Great. Then don't be a chauvinistic pig. Just let me drive."

Thunder rumbled in the distance as a few drops of rain fell from the night sky.

"You're going to get wet."

She huffed and stomped to the other side of the car. "Stubborn ass," she mumbled as she buckled up.

"Language, Mommy." I chuckled as I started the car.

"There will be a special place in Hell for you, Flint Hopkins, if you kill us or anyone else with your drunk driving."

I put the car in drive and cupped the back of her head, pulling her forehead to mine before letting up on the brake. "You're my world. I would never hurt you. I love you beyond words."

"Jesus, Flint …" she whispered. "Your breath reeks of whisky. I'm begging you. Let me drive."

I released her and let up on the brake. As much as I loved my wife, I also loved being a man. And a strong man knew his limits and didn't have to be told when he was or wasn't capable of doing something.

THREE DAYS LATER I buried my wife in a cemetery two blocks from our house.

Acknowledgments

Why is it so hard to say thank you? At this point, I worry about forgetting someone. My stories come to life from more than a handful of people who make them sparkle. It's the inspiration and encouragement from readers who reach out via social media and email. I wish I could individually thank every single one of you by name.

I see you.

I appreciate you.

Of course, this story would not have seen the light of day without my readers asking for "more." It's an unreal sense of accomplishment to write something and have people want more. Thank you for asking for more Nate.

Thank you to my "guys" for letting me hide to get the words written. You are always my happily-ever-after.

My alpha and beta readers—Leslie (Mom), Kambra (Sis), Sian, and Shauna—you deserve a special thank-you for experiencing my stories at their absolute worst. Thank you to Max (The Polished Pen), Monique, Amy, and Bethany—a fantastic editing team—for making my shit shine.

Jenn Beach always deserves a huge thank-you, or at least a ride on a unicorn, for making me look so damn good in my newsletters. Let's be honest, you do *all* the things that make me look organized and functional.

Sarah Hansen with Okay Creations—another beautiful

cover. Thank you.

Ashlee O'Brien with Ashes & Vellichor, thank you for the beautiful trailer.

Social Butterfly PR, bloggers, Instagrammers, and Jonesies, and author buddies, thank you for your love and enthusiastic promotion of this story.

Paul with BB eBooks—you make the last step so seamless. Thank you.

Also by Jewel E. Ann

The Life Series

The Life That Mattered

The Life You Stole

Jack & Jill Series

End of Day

Middle of Knight

Dawn of Forever

Holding You Series

Holding You

Releasing Me

Transcend Series

Transcend

Epoch

Standalone Novels

Idle Bloom

Only Trick

Undeniably You

One

Scarlet Stone

When Life Happened

Look the Part

A Place Without You

Naked Love

Jersey Six

Perfectly Adequate

jeweleann.com

Receive a FREE book and stay informed of new releases, sales, and exclusive stories:

Monthly Mailing List

jeweleann.com/free-booksubscribe

About the Author

Jewel is a free-spirited romance junkie with a quirky sense of humor.

With 10 years of flossing lectures under her belt, she took early retirement from her dental hygiene career to stay home with her three awesome boys and manage the family business.

After her best friend of nearly 30 years suggested a few books from the Contemporary Romance genre, Jewel was hooked. Devouring two and three books a week but still craving more, she decided to practice sustainable reading, AKA writing.

When she's not donning her cape and saving the planet one tree at a time, she enjoys yoga with friends, good food with family, rock climbing with her kids, watching How I Met Your Mother reruns, and of course...heart-wrenching, tear-jerking, panty-scorching novels.

Made in the USA
Middletown, DE
18 July 2020

13169821R00229